D0105445

Late Night Dancing

By Diana Silber

Confessions
Late Night Dancing

Late Night Dancing

Diana Silber

BANTAM BOOKS
NEW YORK · TORONTO · LONDON · SYDNEY · AUCKLAND

LATE NIGHT DANCING
A Bantam Book / March 1991

All rights reserved.

Copyright © 1991 by Diana Henstell.

Book design by Susan Hood

*Grateful acknowledgment is made for permission to reprint
In The Air Tonight by Phil Collins. Used with the permission
of Effectsound Ltd./Hit & Run Music (Publishing) Ltd. (Both PRS).
Administered in USA & Canada by Hit & Run Music Publishing, Inc.
(ASCAP). All Rights Reserved.*

No part of this book may be reproduced or transmitted in any form or by any means, electronic or mechanical, including photocopying, recording, or by any information storage and retrieval system, without permission in writing from the publisher. For information address: Bantam Books.

Library of Congress Cataloging-in-Publication Data

Silber, Diana.
Late night dancing / Diana Silber.
p.   cm.
ISBN 0-553-07264-1
I. Title.
PS3569.I413L38   1991
813'.54—dc20   90-49867
CIP

Published simultaneously in the United States and Canada

Bantam Books are published by Bantam Books, a division of Bantam Doubleday Dell Publishing Group, Inc. Its trademark, consisting of the words "Bantam Books" and the portrayal of a rooster, is Registered in U.S. Patent and Trademark Office and in other countries. Marca Registrada. Bantam Books, 666 Fifth Avenue, New York, New York 10103.

PRINTED IN THE UNITED STATES OF AMERICA

BOMC offers recordings and compact discs, cassettes and records. For information and catalog write to BOMR, Camp Hill, PA 17012.

To Walt
who taught me about loving

1

Cassie fights for sleep, but like a defeated, war-weary survivor she retreats, dragging back to wakefulness. Her eyes reluctantly open. She lies on her back staring up at continents on the ceiling designed by the sun in a gauzy shimmer through the thin curtains.

Seven-thirty! God! Who's mowing the lawn at seven-thirty in the morning?

A tall stranger in a Raiders T-shirt and well-worn jeans pushes the mower across her grass, winnowing neat rows. From the window Cassie charts the perfectly aligned patterns as she shouts down to the unknown titan, but the roar of the machine swallows her voice. Finally, cranking the window closed in disgust, she pulls on a robe and goes downstairs.

"Hey, who are you?" She has stormed out to the back porch and waved him to a stop.

After so much racket the quiet is stunning, and all of a sudden Cassie feels uncomfortable. She is crinkled from sleep, her short blond hair uncombed, her face without the least touch of makeup. She shifts her bare feet on the cool wood. "Who are you?" she repeats. "What happened to Yang?"

"I'm working for him now. The name's Jake."

Cassie tugs the robe tighter and folds her arms across her breasts. His blue eyes are flinty, chips of lazulite, and his gaze is unwavering. He doesn't look at her as Yang does, off to the side and unfocused.

"Do you have to start so early? You woke me up." The accusation, sleep-riddled, comes out too harshly. Foolishly she almost apologizes. The anger, grainy and directed at the mower as much as the man—

can't they invent quiet machines?—begins to slip away from her. Faced with this Jake, she is somehow at fault. It must be the lost half hour of sleep. Every minute matters. Cassie loves sleep as a fat woman does ice cream. She envies insomniacs their endless nights of interrupted time.

She blames Mandy's going to college a month before for this weariness, but it had been the same when Doug left, three years ago last July. Whenever, in fact, life produces insoluble problems, sleep is the prescription. A stupid antidote; sleep is no solution at all, but an invisible weight will press her shoulders, bend her spine like a straw, as the air clots and she sinks down in her bed, grateful as a lover.

All this, she thinks, for a missed half hour!

Yang's Jake starts the mower again. She turns abruptly and leaves the cut grass blowing behind her.

By the time Cassie comes out again the gardener has gone. His truck no longer nudges its bumper to the curb. A collection of camellias in a tin can sits by the steps. Cassie almost trips over them. A penciled note sticks up between the leaves.

Sorry.

A nice gesture, Cassie thinks, carrying the can back into the house. She leaves it on the sink but brings the image of this Jake with her outside and down the steps. She sees the darkness of his eyes and the sweat shining on his upper lip and admonishes herself. Forget him! But he stubbornly clings in her memory.

Eve would tell her why. *Biology, pure and simple*, she hears Eve saying. But who was Eve to tell Cassie about biology? Cassie is the doctor; yet, *ha*, she hears Eve laugh in imaginary conversation, *you treat only women at the clinic and I'm the one who knows about men*. Did she? Did any woman?

Cassie hadn't known about Doug. Just as in magazine stories he came home every night for dinner. He never smelled of musky perfume. No long red or brown or any color but her own blond hair graced his jacket. He made love generously and on cue. Doug even brought her flowers when there was no occasion for gifts, except maybe to mark the stolen lunch hours shared with his lover. But there weren't all that many roses, not enough for him to pack up and leave, saying, with the pretended grace of a man swept by poetry, *I'm in love with another woman*. Are there any words so brutal? Cassie would banish them, tries to with sleep, but they scar her in hard ridges and

2

wait to greet her on awakening, the first bars of unharmonious dawn.
If Cassie isn't careful, Doug's lips repeatedly form the impossible:
another woman.

On principle she hates Tracy—Doug's lover and new wife—living
in glassy sun-splashed splendor in Marina del Rey. Mandy, returning
from twice-monthly visits, tells Cassie they aren't happy. Tracy drinks
Diet Pepsi for breakfast and listens to Julio Iglesias. Tracy isn't neat.
She ignores dishes in the sink and towels on the floor; she trails sand
in from the beach. But Cassie recognizes Mandy's reports for the
loving messages they are. Tracy is just a woman, if *another*.

Youngish and with a colt's awkwardness the one time she and Cassie
met, Tracy is sullen. If she hadn't stolen Cassie's husband she would
have captured someone else's. Tracy is a poacher. She displays the
heavy-lidded drowsiness of a female too lazy to do her own legitimate
hunting.

Cassie thinks too often of Doug. Not only in the first flush of shock
and bereavement when, wounded, she stumbled, wept, invented
heresies to believe in, but afterward. She recuperates because that is
what women do when their men betray them; otherwise they are
pitiful creatures, victims of those stubborn infections that won't
respond to treatment. Cassie agrees with her well-wishers that Doug
is a shit, better off forgotten, not worth a tear, a moment's unsound
sleep. Not that her sleep is interrupted by Doug, by any marauder.
Her sleep is medicinal. She should have given up the excess hours
long since—oh, yes, she knows she is, in a manner of speaking,
narcoleptic—and the dark dirges of unconsciousness. But she wants
him back, not for himself but to eradicate the bludgeon of rejection,
to be vindicated. A returning husband removes the stain of abandon-
ment.

The Magdalene Clinic is south of National, a jigsaw-puzzle area of
middle class and blue collar. A gynecologist-obstetrician, a woman's
doctor, Cassie lives a life given to secrets. The words *breasts, uterus,
cervix, ovaries, Fallopian tubes, vulva, vagina,* have everyday value
for her, as do, among others, *dysmenorrhea, conception, pregnancy,
abortion, hysterectomy*. There are so many diseases and conditions
women endure that are foreign to men, so many malfunctions of their
peculiar organs. The design of the female, though miraculous, is
imperfect. She knows herself the pain of childbirth, PMS, the breathless waiting for the late stain on her panties. Faced with fluttering

eyelids and sweaty hands, she explains the intricacies of birth control and wonders if the propagation of the species couldn't have been achieved in a more humane fashion. Why are women the bearers of the entire burden?

Despite Doug and the reality of her work, Cassie doesn't hate men. That would have been as foolish as loathing dogs because one bit her and others barked and leaped up with muddy paws. Men are only the opposite, the left to right, anodes to cathodes. They are just of a simpler construction.

Occasionally Cassie's patients consult her about colds, clogged sinuses, ailments other than gynecological, but unless they can be treated with aspirin or a prescription for nothing complicated, she sends them elsewhere. The human being goes wrong in so many ways that at moments she wishes she had taken up a different profession. The flawed bodies overwhelm her and she envies civilians their ignorance.

Today's appointments are mostly routine: Pap smears, diaphragms fitted, a twenty-year-old who has yet to menstruate, two cases of endometriosis, the usual complaints of yeast infections.

"I have Ms. Calman in four and Ms. Rodriquez in three, Cassie. Barbara has one and two right now, Karen's over at Cedars, and Jena phoned to say she'll be an hour late," the nurse on duty at the desk says, handing Cassie two charts.

Magdalene Clinic is functional, no-frills. Plain black-and-white squares of linoleum cover the floors; the chairs are Salvation Army and in need of paint. Fluorescent tubes spread a harsh unflattering light. On the walls, however, hang children's finger-paintings, wildly colorful and innocent as sunflowers, along with museum posters—Chagall's fantasies, Monet's waterlilies.

"Will you be able to work Wednesday afternoon if Karen takes off?" the nurse calls after Cassie as she heads for her tiny office in the doctors' crowded rabbit warren.

"Sure. No problem." Cassie fills as many hours with medicine as possible.

All the physicians and nurses in the clinic are women, perhaps not deliberately—they know too much about sexual discrimination to practice it themselves, they promise one another—but they haven't sought out males either. There are Harry Bryan in administration and Chris Tomlan, the staff accountant, and some of the cleaning crew are male; but basically Magdalene is a woman's domain. Cassie spends her days in the world of females.

How do you think you'll ever find a man? Eve demands, brushing away Cassie's I'm-not-looking.

Eve, Cassie's best friend, is in real estate, a much more male-oriented field, as she puts it, which is lucky for someone married three times and constantly auditioning future husbands. Eve's hunger for mates borders on the ridiculous, but she shrugs off Cassie's criticism by saying *Such is nature*. Men aren't necessary for every female at all times, Cassie counters in their running argument. She has had hers, plus marriage, a child. So what if there will be no long glide into twilight, days of gray hair and rocking chairs, the retirement porch of shuffling memories. She is certainly better off than her other close friend Nona, six months shy of forty and panicking, her biological clock ticking as loudly as a timer on dynamite.

The phone rings as Cassie buttons her white coat. It is Eve to remind her of dinner at seven. "You're driving. Okay? But tell me, before I hang up—met any good men?"

"Since I talked to you yesterday?"

"Well, miracles are known to occur. You could have bumped fenders with Sylvester Stallone. He's single, at least momentarily."

She has no time for Eve's teasing. "I have patients waiting."

"And I have a house weeping to be sold."

Men. She is getting as bad as Eve, catching herself as she goes through the day wondering whom she might meet. What is this, a sea change, a strange scent on the wind? Like Mandy, is she tricking herself into forgetting?

Cassie's stupidity could be crippling. She mourns for a husband who, even when in residence, was—in Eve's estimation—more silver plate than sterling. Oh, he isn't bad-looking, but he has a soft, cream center. Eve had never trusted Doug Morgan, and how time proved her right. Running off with his secretary—or was it the office receptionist?—was cheap, tacky melodrama. Who'd believe it? Cassie deserves more substance in a mate, a man of higher caliber. Though she denies it, she refuses to let go, and has cold eyes for any likely candidate, of which there are precious few these days. A drought has fallen over Los Angeles.

Most men are married—not that that bothered Tracy, Mrs. Morgan the second—and repulsive, just like the fat, balding husband, button-nosed and scowling at closets in the estate house Eve is selling. What does he think, that for a million eight he won't have enough room to hang his polyester jackets? The wife, however, coos over the kitchen, spun into song by Eve's lavish descriptions, her "No expense spared on renovation. And with a view of the pool too!" Eve waxes lyrical as the little brown wren gazes out the window.

Eve likes houses, the bigger the better, and empty, with aching rooms spread wide and begging for furniture. She cherishes most houses that need redoing, the "fixers," ones with shag carpeting and mirrors so ugly you immediately defend yourself, walls mapped by fingerprints and twenty-year-old bathrooms, houses with rusty shower doors and butchered moldings, homes crying for the loving touch. Possibilities make her heart beat faster. She imagines the gleam of bright paint, new sinks and bidets, imported tile and the absolutely essential Jacuzzi tub, skylights, new decking about the pool. Kitchens especially excite Eve and she coaxes prospective buyers with visions of Italian cabinets and granite counters.

She trawls skillfully. "They're expecting an offer momentarily. So you'll have to move quickly if this is for you." Her eyes reflect the solemnity of a corporate executive at the end of the third quarter, and she plays deftly to the wife's blossoming fright. Clients trust Eve, in linen and discreet pearl earrings, brows neatly plucked and lipstick between pink and blood-red. Her hair, expertly streaked, suggests Beverly Hills. The image she projects is of a woman who knows her business, an agent of distinction, one who never condescends to sell tidy little boxes or offers dross for gold. Eve's houses live up to expectations even if, in the end, they aren't all the happy castles she seems to promise when first opening the front door.

"What's the offer going to be?" the puffed-up husband demands in his office voice, rocking on the balls of little baby feet while his wife stares dreamily at the living room's flagstone fireplace.

"The asking price is a million eight, so my guess is two hundred thousand less."

"A guess! A guess!" He reddens with indignation. "I can't do business on a guess!"

Fuck you! Eve thinks, and reviews the loose Xeroxed sheet—known as a setup—describing the house. "It's been on the market a month and has had quite a lot of activity—which is to be expected even in a down market, given the location and the quality of construction. I doubt that they'll lower the price substantially." "They" means the owners and other agent, the opposition, the enemy against whom she works and has to outmaneuver. "If you're serious"—she underlines the word, meaning *don't waste my time*—"I'd suggest an immediate offer in the neighborhood of"—Eve taps her cheek with a Mark Cross pen—"a million six five. That is within your range, isn't it?" If it isn't, Eve intends dumping chubby and wife into the deep end of the pool.

"Harold, please!" The wife squeezes her ring-encrusted hands together.

"I'll think about it," the husband grunts, aware of his power, and stalks off for another look at the two-car garage. Eve and the wife exchange sympathetic glances, both thinking, *men*, but Eve senses the line tightening as the woman, determined, flees, calling "Harold!"

Eve glances upward. Disgraceful, not stripping the beams. She often broods about how people live with Formica and mustard walls. If taste isn't an attribute one acquires at birth, there are surely enough experts available to supply it. But so many people cling stubbornly to their imitations, odd colors, artifacts that bruise the eye and numb the heart's call for beauty.

Eve hears the husband and wife clattering through the laundry room and goes to meet a man subdued, a woman with her wrinkles smoothed out. Caught them, she gloats happily, automatically figuring the commission. She can coast right home with these two, and glances boldly at her watch to see if she has time for a manicure before she guides another yearning couple through a colonial in Westwood.

Nona's stomach is gassy. Heat plumes up into her chest. She slips into the shop's tiny bathroom and pops a Maalox, worrying if later she should ask Cassie what's wrong. Cassie probably won't mind, but Nona hates asking for free medical advice. Maybe she'd better make an appointment with Dr. Rubin. When she saw him three weeks ago her stomach was fine. Then it was her arm that mysteriously ached, but the X-rays revealed nothing beyond healthy tissue and bone. Nerves, Dr. Rubin decided when they reviewed the results, sitting so comfortably in his office with its shelves of books and framed pictures of children on the walls. Dr. Rubin's office is nothing like her father's was. Smaller, not on a corner and flagrant with light, and the desk isn't as large as an aircraft carrier; the chairs and meager couch are shopworn. Her father's office always looked to her like an airport first-class waiting lounge, a way station in which nameless travelers set themselves down between flights. She sat so precisely on her father's chairs, poised to run, an employee being seen for orders or repri-mands. Her father displayed no family photographs and not one object identifiable as his own. Dr. Rubin, however, fits his office like a hand in a glove, and huddles all the way back in a vinyl chair. Nona is an invited guest even when she hears him say *Nerves, Nona, nerves*.

Nerves. Oh, nerves. Everybody has nerves. Nobody dies of nerves, though, which had buoyed her up as she glided swanlike through Dr. Rubin's waiting room.

But stomach pains, a fire in spirals rising up between her breasts—that can be serious.

Lorraine is dancing attendance on a broad-bottomed waddling duck tugging at the skirt of an Anne Klein she models before the three-way mirror. If the woman holds her breath the fabric doesn't pucker. Nona smiles and passes her own fleeting reflection.

In the rear of the store she looks in another mirror. She thinks there are glints of silver in her hair. It seems impossible; at thirty-nine her hair is fading, the tarnished river of age so unstoppable and alarming. Soon she won't be able to wash the dullness away herself and, admitting defeat, will sneak off embarrassed to the beauty parlor. How guilty she will feel, whispering *Color the gray, please*. Like all those older women, like the one in mauve—absolutely the wrong color for her!—with Lorraine. Time is a sharp-toothed invader; time is cancer-ous. (Oh, no, the pain in her stomach can't be *that*—the dreaded nightmare, the disease that freezes the blood into ice floes.) The gilded clock ticks on the wall behind the counter, minutes and hours tickling the nape of Nona's neck.

Think positive thoughts! she admonishes herself and, scuttling the gray ghost of age, looks around the dress shop where she is the assistant manager. Flora's never fails to soothe her. Very upscale, muted, with coffee carpeting and an island of plump chairs surround-ing a glass table, it is peaceful even when busy. Flora's sells nothing cheap, but nothing extravagant either—no clothes so unsettling that customers are moved through corridors of guilt. Taste with reason is Flora's advertising slogan and the trade consists mostly of women over twenty-five. Girls seldom shop in Flora's unless for West Side weddings requiring dresses more prudent than usual.

Nona has worked at Flora's for two years now, the shop on the floating first tier of the Crystal Mall, a home away from home, an enclosed antiseptic environment superior to the department store up whose ladder she climbed rung by rung. *Smaller* improves Nona's easily ruffled disposition. She satisfies herself—again—that she has made the right choice, smoothing down her silk blouse and pushing aside the unhappy truth that she left Paxton's by request rather than design. Personnel had been so unreasonable about sick days. Nona is not at all to blame for her illnesses. Yet in memory Dr. Rubin sighs again, *Nerves, Nona, nerves. You imagine the worst when really you're incredibly healthy*. But delicate, Nona states firmly, as though Lorraine or Lorraine's customer has asked.

The woman, accepting her suit in a white box imprinted with yellow ribbons and *Flora's* in elegant script, frowns on leaving the store for the fishbowl light outside. A return, Nona guesses, imagining the woman before her full-length bedroom mirror, alone and no longer the recipient of Lorraine's murmurs, the deceitful adjectives. How much better clothes look in the store, how magically the right dress or suit and blouse transfigure, bequeathing in their newness so much hope. From Flora's, women carry home dreams cherished and folded, wrapped in tissue.

There is a pattern to the store's traffic. Mornings move slowly; hours have dead sinkholes in them. Then, just before noon and again around two, there is a flurry. Another after five. Flora's doors won't shut until nine, when all the mall shops close for the night, leaving only restaurants and movies open. The days stretch as long as freeways and wear Nona out, but she never complains to Lorraine and certainly not to the owners, businessmen from Laguna who acquired the store in impersonal bankruptcy proceedings.

The mall is a second home; Flora's, her private corner of it. Some days she thinks she could stay here forever, wandering the tile walkways with their strategically placed leatherette benches and grouped planters, watching the light's intensity falter, the pools shift, night darken the glass ceiling. She browses, seldom buying, comparing merchandise in better dress shops and boutiques, admiring housewares, stereo equipment, Erté art deco drawings in the gallery, reading the jacket copy on books in Walden and B. Dalton. Pets in

The Emporium push their wet noses out to her and Nona reluctantly obeys DON'T KNOCK ON THE GLASS!

The music in Flora's issues from hidden speakers, the sound at a reasonable level, songs with interesting words to them. Dan Fogelberg, Neil Diamond, Linda Ronstadt. Lorraine argues with the Laguna owners for Sting, U2, Peter Gabriel. Nona disagrees, quite content with Carly Simon. Women who buy Albert Nipon dresses might even, she believes, be more receptive to Mozart.

There is a sudden lull in which the clock's ticking accelerates, rushing Nona toward her fortieth birthday. Desires, safely filed in the counter drawer with credit card receipts, escape now, and Nona's hands worry each other over a faceless husband at the breakfast table and a baby in a highchair.

"Will this day last forever?" Lorraine groans. Lorraine, eager for work to be over, has the fearlessness of a woman committed. Engaged to an insurance salesman from Torrance who religiously drives in each night to worship by Lorraine's side at the altar of their future, she feels superior. "I want an hour at the health club before George shows up," she sniffs, tucking a strand of bottled ash-gold behind an ear. "There's this very dishy guy who does bench presses that are to die. And the last time I was there we had definite eye contact."

"What about George?"

"What do you mean, what about George? He's George."

"So why the eye contact?"

"Honestly, Nona." Lorraine gives her the pitying glance of an abbess skilled with feminine secrets, stopping Nona from reminding her that George expects a wedding ceremony in the summer, that a minister is already booked, a restaurant. Lorraine, threatening to cut down on next season's orders, has blackmailed a wholesaler into giving her a silk shantung with seed pearls studding the bodice like moonbeams.

Nona supposes she is naïve. Eve would understand the dishy health-club guy and Lorraine's motives immediately.

Nona suspects that Lorraine, with the freedom of enough exercise hours, will snag this second man, then have two males to choose from. Before George she dated Ralph, and before him Stanley, who soured into poor Stanley. What is it she knows that I don't? Nona often wonders.

The edge of her anxiety spreads the gassiness. She tries to count up her assets, to think brash sunrise thoughts rather than the gloomies of a rainy late afternoon as she returns to the counter fantasizing how tonight, when she's out with Cassie and Eve, there will be some man, alone or having dinner with a male friend from the office who, gazing across the room, holds his breath at the sight of her. He is a captive, a prisoner in solitary until he learns her name, where to find her. He sends over a round of drinks (no, champagne!) and when the waiter pours, he nods, smiling for Nona alone. Afterward he comes to the table and shyly excuses his boldness, asking Nona if he might call. He has tickets to a concert at the Bowl (which he doesn't of course—the tickets are a romantic ruse) and begs her to join him. Eve kicks Nona's leg under the table—Nona even feels the tip of Eve's shoe connecting with her shin—and Cassie, smiling, urges Nona to accept. It is obvious to her friends that Nona and this man have possibilities.

"Nona, are you listening to me?"

"What?"

Lorraine holds up a Liz Claiborne Collection jacket. "See if we can order this in a twelve."

"Yes." She ducks her head, hiding the blush the stranger's longing for her, his devotion, arouses. It can happen, after all. Life is filled with mysterious events. Maybe he'll have blond hair and blue eyes and will love children, animals, be ready to settle down and—

"Nona!"

2

The women crowd the small table, legs touching. Eve's foot nudges Nona's just as in her earlier fantasy, but there is no lovely man enjoying a steak and red wine nearby, bridging the distance with soulful longing and champagne. Mostly women fill the restaurant, or couples fighting for conversation over the congealed elevator music—which in Caesar's pours from amplifiers painted pink to match the decor. But the horseshoe bar on the opposite side of the large room from where Nona and Eve and Cassie eat pasta looks promising.

"See anything interesting?" Eve asks.

"A stray floret of broccoli in the primavera," Cassie replies. "Really, for eighteen ninety-five these portions are skimpy. Besides, the carrots and zucchini should be julienned. And look at these mushrooms." She spikes a mushroom and holds it aloft. "A clump. I always slice them paper thin. You can see the light through one of mine." Cassie is about to go on and criticize the chef's indelicate use of pepper, but Eve grins at her and Nona is giggling.

"Our own James Beard," Eve kids Cassie affectionately.

"Okay," Cassie admits, pink with embarrassment, "this place isn't known for its cuisine."

Nona, who barely eats, pokes at a plateful of angel hair. "I don't think the food is that bad."

Neither Nona nor Eve, however, is at Caesar's for the meal; they are more attentive to the bar thronged with hunting singles. But Cassie is haunted by all those former dinners she cooked for Doug.

She puts down her fork on tangled strands of tepid fettuccine. These days she rarely cooks, no meals lovingly designed and seasoned. Mandy when at home lives on pizza, takeout Chinese, Weight Watchers' frozen cannelloni. An ordinary teenager, she prefers junk food to *haute cuisine* and Cassie never urges her to the table with *canard à l'orange*.

"There's one in a beige sports jacket at the end of the bar. See, that one, drinking beer out of a bottle." Nona resists pointing.

Eve cranes her neck. "I think you can do better. He looks wilted around the edges, like week-old lettuce."

Nona rolls her eyes. "Eve, you're terrible."

"What's so terrible? It's a meat market, right? And who would pick a lamb chop indiscriminately? You consider the bones and the fat or whatever it is in a chop that makes it prime."

"With lamb chops—" Cassie starts to clarify but Eve waves a napkin at her.

"Stop! No Julia Child, pl-ease!" Eve strings out the request, only half-kidding Cassie. She hates talk of food. Food is for eating. Even in her very married days to Abramson she rarely cooked. Her bear thrived on macaroni and cheese, the kind they ate when children, the cheese orange and powdery, the short noodles greased by globs of butter. Now Eve can't stand to see a box of macaroni in the supermarket. She skirts that aisle, imagining the blue-and-white boxes leaping off the shelf into her cart, attacking with old grief. When she was with William, they toured restaurants and hired a caterer for at-home dinners. Cassie's skill in the kitchen alarms Eve. Has she missed or forgotten to learn a ritual necessary for women when married? Is her ineptitude in mingling ingredients a metaphor?

"Let's talk about the stock market, the deficit, maybe Picasso. Anything else. The books we're reading, a new movie. Is there anything we want to see?" Cassie, pried loose from a lecture on cooking, forages for a compelling subject to suck them in and sustain their interest. Any subject but men. She is made jittery by comments on those males draped as casually as loose jackets along the bar. Glass in hand, they are nonchalant, the species destined to move first. She pretends whenever she and Eve and Nona go out that they aren't women on the town looking.

"That's dangerous," Cassie counsels Nona, who has said wistfully about a man two tables over: "I'd go home with him." Fortunately or not, his companion, sleekly dark, an otter with makeup thick as surgical bandages, engrosses him.

"Oh, Cass, it's not fair!" Disappointment pools in Nona's eyes.

"AIDS has nothing to do with fairness. It's a disease. It kills with the savagery of Auschwitz." Usually anything medical relaxes the shy stiffness that tenses Cassie's shoulders and draws her full lips up at the corners. The life-and-death issues, where she has a hands-on possibility of doing good, of changing the seemingly inevitable, comfort her. But the fact that much lies out of her control, beyond a chasm no medical knowledge can yet breach, freezes her in painful helplessness.

Gazing ardently at Nona, as though she whispers romance, she says, "You know the statistics."

"I hate being frightened," Nona reminds them, in case they've forgotten. Cassie appears so stern when she's being the disciplinarian, the mother of *Stand up straight! Wash your hands! Don't mumble!*

"You should be scared out of your wits. Everyone in this restaurant has to realize—"

"—there's a plague on the land," Eve interrupts, tapping a water glass. She, too, has heard Cassie's refrain before, and like Nona sees no reason to listen to it again and again. Not when they're out to have a good time, to relax, and in the best of all possible evenings meet up with some interesting men. It puts a damper on, as they're looking over the various possibilities, to have Cassie repeat that sex can kill.

"I know I'm lecturing," Cassie says, wringing her napkin. Sometimes she doesn't know when to shut up.

"Our Cassandra."

Nona touches Cassie's arm. "You can say anything you want to us, and we'll listen."

Eve laughs, "Hey, wait a minute!"

Cassie turns away, thinking that at the clinic she is forever warning sexually active women how death trails so easily in the wake of pleasure. In her white coat she is an authority figure, though with her dire threats she sometimes hears herself sounding pompous. But how to soften what she feels compelled to counsel? Be vigilant! Disease and death hold them hostage, and the sexual revolution of their mothers has evolved too quickly into tyranny. Yet loneliness still drives the intrepid, the foolhardy, the needy, out into the night, to Caesar's or other watering holes on the Strip, in the marina, off Venice beach, downtown, in the airport hotels. Too often unhappiness strands them with risk.

"I would never crawl in bed with someone just because," Nona defends herself. "I need love."

Cassie thinks about love with a man, the sweaty feel of it, the musky perfumes and high-pitched bird sounds. Her memories are transparent and the three years since she slept with Doug intrude; not even her body remembers.

Eve elbows them. "Look at that woman's hair!"

Nona groans. "Not somebody, as my mother used to say, to ask to a dinner party."

"Don't stare," Cassie says, sneaking a glance sideways at the heavily painted female with her pink hair spun into lace.

The woman, perched on a bar stool, wears a tight red leather skirt shucked high on bony legs, a sweater of sequins and pearls and puffs of tiny feathers worked in a wavy design over little gooseberry breasts. One hand clings to the denim sleeve of a boy half her age, a slitty-eyed predator.

"She's the one who needs your bulletins from the tomb, Cassie," Eve says. "Silly trollop."

Sometimes, out late, banding together, warmed by their friendship, they poke fun at other women, avoiding their own reflections in distant mirrors. Poor fool with her wet smile, Cassie thinks. Poor fool, poor fool, Eve and Nona echo as if psychically linked, and the three of them yearn to catch hold of one another, link hands in a magic circle around the table. They are a troika and there is such comfort in being friends, none of them solitary like the woman at the bar swinging her foot, the gold bracelet on her ankle scattering the light into fragments.

Nona shuffles around and expresses an urgent need for water; Cassie decides on cappuccino; Eve lights one of her rare cigarettes. In their rearranging they all manage to touch. They are different. Grateful for one another's presence they relax and Nona asks, "Does anyone want to see that Neil Simon play at the Pasadena Playhouse? Howard gave me tickets for next Thursday."

"Who's Howard?" Eve asks.

"You know, one of the owners."

Cassie can't keep straight the two men who surge up now and again in Nona's conversation. "The fat one or the skinny one?"

"I am so sorry I told you that," Nona groans. "It's just that Howard is a little heavier, more muscular than Leonard. And taller. You could say the tall one and the short one."

Eve, teasing, puffs out her cheeks. "Does Howard look inflated?"

A second cappuccino Cassie doesn't remember ordering replaces the empty cup, and, distracted, she rotates a spoon around and around in it, depressed by noisy Caesar's, the meaningless pastel-colored paintings in harmony with the tablecloths, men and women who have diligently tended themselves like prize begonias before a public viewing. In such a world she is weightless, an alien. She thinks back to her marriage, a foreign planet with mysterious moons. She banked—supposedly—happiness, or was that happiness merely mindless comfort bred by years of familiarity? Still, marriage, Cassie primly believes, stubborn in the face of change, is intended to last forever, till the grave. No signs ever warned her that she walked the edge of a cliff, earth crumbling, until a whole slope of her life broke loose.

It is unjust that Doug, by his lust or greed for youth, maybe even out of love, has banished her to a bar late at night, and her anger surges at a husband she once protested meant the world. Her head stuffs up; her fingers tingle.

"Men have everything," Nona is saying. They have all, at one time or another, made the same statement, but is it true? Do they, Cassie thinks, appreciate the kind of friendship, the bonding, she has with Eve and Nona?

How odd that the three of them are so close, metaphorically sisters, for their differences are pronounced, all the more so when they come together. As a trio they seem unbalanced. Yet they do love one another, if not equally—for both Eve and Nona love Cassie best—then with enough parity to cement their tricornered relationship.

Eve instigated the friendship. She and Cassie met when she sold the Morgans their house. After escrow closed she stayed friends with them, or with Cassie, since Eve put Doug's back up. Too ballsy, he called her. Scared, Cassie thinks now, noticing that Eve's long red nails walk the table to the bud vase with its perfect white rose, then back, only to return again, and wonders if Doug saw such nails bared like a cat's to scratch his eyes out. She certainly threatened to when Doug left, and Cassie half wished Eve had gunned down to the marina and wreaked damage on a man who not only packed his bags but dyed his gray hair brown.

Nona asks, "Are we getting the check?"

As Eve found Cassie, she found Nona too. She simply bought a dress in Paxton's, and afterward the two women had mimosas in a nearby restaurant. Eventually Eve brought Nona around, as she might a stray pup, for Cassie to inspect. Nona enchanted Cassie that first night, kicking off her shoes and, bare feet up on the rung of a kitchen ladder-back, singing Beatles songs in a lisping whisper. She had instant recall of almost every song the group recorded, though Mandy tried to catch her up, and after the women killed four bottles of wine and ate a gallon of ice cream she sang them all again. It was two in the morning before the impromptu party broke up. Doug had been off on a business trip (or was he in a warm bed ensnared by Tracy's long limbs?) and when they finally met he called Nona a wet dream.

Of course the friends lasted and Doug didn't, and of all the women Cassie knew, they were the ones who faithfully shepherded her through the early days. She was shameless in displaying grief and anger before them. Eve denounced Doug, her endless litany punctuated by curses and the repeat "Screw all men!" Nona was the quiet one, brewing pots of tea. Such a homey grandmother's remedy often stopped Cassie's tears with its incongruity. Nona offered camomile in a cup and saucer of the best china, adding two heaping spoons of sugar and saying, "Here, drink this. You'll feel better." It brought Cassie up from the depths as much as anything.

The check arrives on a silver salver and Eve hustles them from the table to the bar, where the music thickens, hangs in a cloud. Cassie travels by instrument.

After their drinks arrive, Nona, leaning forward, the faint lines scored under her eyes darker, describes to Cassie her latest symptom. "What do you think it is? Is it serious?"

Cassie sympathizes with unknown Dr. Rubin, Nona's priest, to whose office she faithfully brings her aches and pains hoping for absolution. How forbearing he must be not to dismiss the hypochondriacal Nona, not to send her off clutching placebos, or, annoyed, chastise her for wasting his valuable time. Like Cassie he obviously recognizes that Nona craves periodic stays in her kingdom of imaginary illnesses. Or maybe he worries that just once her sickness will flower into something real. Cassie, also circumspect, suggests loudly enough to be heard over the throbbing beat, "It's probably indigestion. Try bland foods for a couple of days, and then, if the discomfort persists, see Dr. Rubin."

"But is it serious?" Nona asks, half in fright, half with longing.

Cassie, holding Nona's hand, automatically takes her pulse, which is normal. "No, I don't think so."

"Not an ulcer?" How hopeful she sounds. If Nona doesn't find a husband, will she marry sickness, her complaints children to be nurtured?

"That's always possible, but really it's much too early to worry. A bland diet," Cassie repeats, knowing Nona prefers a diagnosis that promises not death but a condition she can watch, water, and shift into sunlit windows like a plant.

Eve begins telling them about a new apartment complex, her fingers playing with a necklace of silver leaves about her neck, and since the noise swallows every second word, she makes little sense. At the middle of the war zone they sip syrupy liquors, feigning uninterest in the men around them.

In the crush a man with wispy threads of hair, slicked wetly to his scalp, crowds Eve. "I think we've met before," he says, tossing out a standard opening line. His practiced smile is shopworn.

Eve replies, her eyeteeth like fangs, "I don't like chains." His hand flies to the gold anchoring his throat, linked strands burnished against the loose folds of tanned skin.

"That was lethal," Cassie says as the stranger backpedals.

Eve isn't contrite. "Why waste my time?"

The man's overpowering cologne having offended her, Nona grimaces. "He is pretty gruesome."

"I don't see climbing a stairway to heaven with any of them, but let's give it another half an hour before moving on," Eve says. On their evenings out together she acts as scoutmaster. From gossipy clients and agents she picks up news about all the in-spots and leads Nona and Cassie like the Pied Piper. Tonight, however, Cassie groans that one singles bar is more than she can take, and no, she doesn't want to try Sid's on Melrose or the Blue Parrot, where there is dancing.

Eve, standing, elbows between the two women on barstools and asks Cassie—rather desperately, for she thinks her a malingerer when it comes to *looking*—"How do you expect to find a man if you don't make an effort?"

"Not by traipsing from one bar to another, that's for sure. And anyway, who says I'm interested in another husband?"

Eve replies, "I never said 'husband.' You did. I said 'man.' There are lots of things you can do with a man, Cassie, besides marry him."

"Okay, a lover then?" She is sour, convinced a man in her house, or even a steady date, would be an impediment. At noisy moments like this one, a quiet, thoughtful life is most compelling.

"You haven't had sex at all since your *late* husband," Eve whispers, but the truth out loud embarrasses Cassie. She wishes she had kept still about some things and that the women knew less.

Nona twists a curl about her finger. "Doug's not dead." Though Nona has taken Eve into her confidence, Cassie hasn't any idea that Doug once made a pass at Nona in the kitchen during a party, brushing up against her by the refrigerator, trapping her between the door and his erection. She kept a determined gaze on Cassie's pots of basil on a window ledge above the sink and asked him to please move, which he did eventually but not before fondling both her breasts. Nona still feels disloyal for the unwanted encounter.

"Medicine's more important than love," Cassie protests, pushed by Eve into uttering nonsense. This obsession with men, with finding a mate or at least a reliable escort with a decent car and credit cards, makes her drowsy.

Cassie recalls a braver time, when women spoke more passionately of careers, of having loud political voices, of throwing off shackles, than they did of love and sex. They held up clenched fists and marched along wide streets waving banners. They were replete with heady revolt and it seemed that taking a man home to bed was incidental, an aside, a riff. But she was married to Doug then, really a know-nothing.

A tanned sixty-year-old trying to look forty asks Nona a question that brings her listing to port. She crosses her legs, her body language announcing at least temporary interest. Eve, after a quick appraisal, decides, "An accountant."

"How can you tell?"

"A guess." But Eve's guesses are usually right on the mark. She has an uncanny intuition for what people do.

Nona's conversation has wandered into nowhere and she turns back to the women. "He's in town from Dallas for a meeting." Out-of-towners are useless. "He's a CPA."

"ESP." Eve grins, knowing Cassie has no belief in the paranormal.

An ex-football player melting to fat, a once-firm chin draped in jowls, offers to buy Cassie a drink. She hasn't finished the crème de menthe before her on the bar and declines.

"It's beside the point whether you're ready for another drink or not," Eve counsels. But Cassie doesn't want to meet anyone, not even for the moment. "Cassie, you have an attitude problem."

"What I have is a headache. I'm getting hearing loss from this music, and starving after that bird meal we just ate. Also, I feel like a cantaloupe in the produce section. Let's go. This is true pain."

Nona says, "I guess we should call it a night." Her mascara is smudged under her bottom lids. Cassie, taking Nona's hand in a clinic gesture, a human move when the Pap smear comes back positive, wishes she could write away to Sears and order Nona a husband.

"I surrender. Defeat." Eve's shoulders droop. "Going home alone isn't my favorite pastime. I like men. I like their arms around me, hard bodies, being in bed next to someone warm." She smiles wryly. "You both think I'm orgasm-crazy, admit it."

"Eve, you know we don't judge one another," Cassie reminds her.

"Oh, don't bother with me," Eve says, swiftly hugging Cassie. "I'm just weary of yet another wasted night of solo dance steps and going home to a cold, empty bed." One spectered by former husbands, Cassie thinks, as she hugs her back.

"Next week?" Nona asks, aligning her spine, walking tall, on display, merchandise unsold today but maybe tomorrow.

Cassie, tired though she is, smiles and—meaning it—says, "I wouldn't miss it."

3

Eve pretends to make light of her marriages: with a raised eyebrow disparaging the time spent as Mrs. Weber, Mrs. Abramson, Mrs. Sloan. Negotiating in the present and arranging escrows, watchful of the future—for both real estate and male contenders—she passes over the husbands far below, tiny tin soldiers paint-chipped and scarred, on the flat, unlovely plains of history. *What a bore. That was then; this is now. I used up my energy.* She acts as though the memories are tarnished, the married years verdigris. When Eve takes center stage, reading the script she both wrote and remembers, she sounds angry, and as weary as a marathon runner. In fact, bitterness and regret do close around her throat, for not one of the marriages—each husband unique—was as Eve pretended.

She met Jordan at a dinner table. He was sitting while Eve, twenty that summer, apple-cheeked, virginally innocent, crisp in her white uniform, served the food he had ordered. "Your breast touched my shoulder," he whispered later in the rustic room of rag carpets, milk-glass lamps, eiderdown, and a pine bed riding like an Arabian fantasy high off the floor. Across the hall his mother slept, plumply dreaming, content on her annual month's holiday in the mountains.

Jordan waited for Eve outside the kitchen and walked her down to the lake. Holding hands they splashed up lace in the cold water. The moon was a white dinner plate; the air smelled of green promise and newly spaded earth.

Eve fell in love with Jordan as he pointed out the sky's hunter, the bear, the North Star like one tiny rhinestone earring; as he organized drama from the starry confusion. On a lake shore in New Hampshire, Jordan navigated Eve with the skill of Columbus to a new world.

Their marriage was impractical. Eve dropped out of college and, love struck, followed a vagabond Jordan. Some weeks they lived in a van, some in cramped apartments tenanted by strangers, in sagging houses whose windows were always dirty and in which only miserly drafts of heat rose from antique furnaces. Periodically they camped in Philadelphia, spooned in Jordan's childhood bed under the baseball banners. During those stays his mother kept her silence with Eve and nested as always on that Weber money Jordan returned for. A carnival barker, a rabbit-from-a-hat magician, a three-card-monte player, he pried small payments out of the old woman's jeweled fingers, though she wasn't totally spineless, a jellyfish finding shape from love of her son. Jordan worked his charm and mined his mother's adoration. But sometimes, slyly, she was obstinate.

One night he lounged opposite her—as darkly romantic in his beauty as a young Byron—at the long dining room table, the ornate crystal chandelier overhead stirring in agitation from the tension between mother and son.

"You don't believe I'll do it," Jordan said with a smile, holding on to his steak knife.

"Don't be a silly child. You can't have another cent, and I mean it, unless you return to law school." Her marble eyes bulged; her bottom lip hung loose.

"I need five thousand dollars, Mother. It's simple." Jordan resembled Rock Hudson, Eve thought, but smaller.

His mother's fingers scrambled against the crumbs of her roll. "You won't tell me what you have to have it for," she said, but without a note of weakening in her voice. Eve understood the difficulty of holding out against Jordan. Hadn't he plucked her out of the resort easily as an apple from a low branch, said come with me, and like one of the Pied Piper's children she ran? Much later Eve would think she had been as witless as a kitten, dewy and stupid.

What Jordan did, why so many meetings—often in cars, fastfood restaurants, back rooms lit by guttering candles in wine bottles—how he made the little money they existed on, were mysteries. He shared information grudgingly and then told wildly varying stories. His dreams, though, he promised, were of utopias, where people acted out of the purest motives.

Eve, blindly infatuated with Jordan, his smooth skin, firm chin, flashing eyes, believed him. His sexiness set off drum rolls of excitement in her. He made love like a professional.

"I will slit my wrist and bleed on your damask tablecloth if you don't give me the money." Jordan also had a sense of the theatrical.

"Don't be silly," Eve broke in, but Jordan ignored her as he would his shadow.

Her own parents had stopped speaking to Eve when she simply quit the summer hotel job, then college, not bothering to go home even for a visit to introduce the man she so impetuously married. To Jordan's mother Eve was just as much an outcast, a whim, like a new bike or a sports jacket. They traveled for more than two years and Eve was tired. She asked Jordan about settling down. Couldn't they get a place of their own, jobs? The wizard of lies, he calmed her with kisses that delivered Eve from moment to moment. She couldn't leave him, though she hated the vans, the farmhouse they recently left in Minnesota, the blubbery girls with mean eyes and lank hair, the lumber-jacketed men growling slogans. She also detested his mother, so piggy fat and prosperous.

Eve thought Jordan stole. For a while she suspected he was Clyde, as in Bonnie and Clyde, and grew terrified of policemen, troopers, any authority. She wanted to go home but the sex was ecstasy, the grass highs secure as wool blankets.

"No." His mother stayed stubborn, putting her hands flat on the table.

"If that's your answer." Jordan effortlessly drew the knife over his upturned wrist. Blood spumed, poured red onto the tablecloth. His mother screamed; so did Eve. Jordan grimaced, for he was determined, not crazy, and no acolyte of pain.

Eve should have gone then, just fled, through the back door by which she'd actually entered Jordan's life. But she didn't. She bandaged his wrist, gave his mother a Valium, and cleaned up the mess, soaking the tablecloth and Jordan's shirt, scrubbing out the fading red-brown stains with a solution of Clorox.

Only one act could unmoor a lovesick, blinded, besotted, foolish girl pleading for valentines and breathless with orgasms.

They stopped in sleepy Tucson, and were staying with a professor friend of Jordan's when Eve walked from a hot, dusty street into the cold darkness of the air-conditioned bedroom and found all three of them—Jordan, the philosopher, and his red-haired wife— in *Kamasutra* copulation. Jordan insisted she join them. Whatever Eve had lost during the two-year marriage, traditional ideas of lovemaking remained. She packed the memory—of Jordan impaled in the wife, the husband attached at the rear to Jordan—with her clothes and took a Greyhound for California. First, though, she vomited on the bathroom floor and left the stinking puddle for the daisy chain to mop up.

Such was Eve's stint as Mrs. Weber.

She held out one picture however, of Jordan on the raft in the lake, and buried it with sachet under her lingerie. She trashed everything else, but the resurrecting memories sometimes nagged her unaware. Every woman married a shit at least once, she reasoned, some women forever. Look at Cassie with her Doug. Yet moments as magical as soap bubbles floated back in reminders. Jordan's laugh could swim from the past and trip her up. From time to time a toughened Eve weakened and wished he had been different.

She had no idea what had become of him. Was he still sponging off Mommy? Or had he plunged into the communes, grown a beard, fought off the rest of the world until now, or is he transformed, rested, a clean-shaven stockbroker? She supposed he had married again, lived an ordinary life, fathered children, and slam-danced in just the sort of life she had wanted with him. If he wasn't in jail or dead or blown loose into spaceland from drugs.

Whatever had happened to Jordan, Eve always felt she had gotten even.

At the end of another night alone, faced with empty sleep, Eve takes out the snapshot with guilt and remorse to stare at the time-stopped face, half shadow and light. For a pause he had been her lovely boy, the dazzling lover who had her dancing in heaven. His hand smoothed her hair, his lips kissed her eyelids, and she listened again to slow music drifting through the branches from the lounge in the main building. The lake's surface was an etching in silver.

"Oh damn, damn, damn," Eve swears and replaces Jordan

beneath her slips. Then she makes a scotch and soda while she watches David Letterman.

The note, trimmed with smily little cooks in chef's hats and aprons, had been slipped under Cassie's door. *I have somebody mucho interesting for you to meet. Call me in the morning. Beth.*

Beth and Al live on the other side of the fence in harmonious—and lengthy—matrimony. Doug's duplicity scandalized Beth, and then, after the requisite wake for a dead marriage, she worried about Cassie remaining single. The divorce statistics alarm Beth more than the threat of nuclear war or the destruction of the ozone layer. She needs fantasies of loving couples and happy families, so labors, as other women do for charities, at finding Cassie a husband.

Cassie groans and throws the note on the kitchen table, where the camellias have wilted in their tall glass. The petals are brown-edged and less lovely. Cassie thinks it makes no sense, is vaguely treacherous, to cut growing things, shorten already short lives, and not let flowers die as nature intended. Still, it was nice of Yang's new man, Jake.

She recalls him in the yard, his muscular arms, the T-shirt tight across his chest.

A man. Would he fit into any of Eve's categories? Nona's?

She thinks of men, even as she ministers to women, especially as she examines April DeVito. April has been raped, though she denies it. Her soft membranes are abused; dark-purple bruises stain her thighs. Married, with two children, she sweats unhappiness, her dark eyes bewildered and sunken.

"You leave a man who does this to you," Cassie angrily counsels her.

"Nobody did anything," April swears stubbornly. Twenty-five, twenty-six—Cassie can't quite remember, but older than the testimony of the child's pinched face she wears—April has the maimed look of a war zone survivor.

Cassie steals extra minutes from a busy afternoon to sit in the cubicle as April dresses and to argue against her low-voiced denials. Denials out of shame or fear or, God forbid, love? Cassie wonders, distressed at how little she understands of people, the women she treats, the ones she has pledged herself to help and with whom—as with April—she is in many essential ways impotent.

"April, don't bullshit me. He forced you. He was awful. He hurt you when having sex, which is a loving act, a beautiful sharing between people who care about each other." Cassie tries once more, staring at the milk-white part in the dark hair when April bends her head. "There are laws, and places you can go for help. I'll help you if you'll let me." Hearing her words reverberate against the green walls, the paper-covered examining table, she thinks that she sounds naïve, schoolmistressish. "April"—she touches the girl's arm—"why do you let him?"

"Let him? Let who? We made love and we got carried away. No big deal. It happens to everyone sooner or later. Jesus!" She is shrill, and her fingers pick up speed, threatening to rip off the buttons.

"A man who loves a woman is kind, gentle. No loving man tore you up, April."

April goes, with shoulders straightened momentarily. Has she lost her? Will the young woman come again, share her pain and allow Cassie to reach out for her? Some did. The stories whispered in examining rooms and offices pull the doctors like rudderless boats to sorrow.

Doctors and women, the clinic physicians exchange case histories at staff meetings while they drink coffee and watch the late sun climb up the windows.

"I have a Latino woman, thirty-five, with twelve children and worn to the marrow," says Jena. "Her skin is as loose as stretched-out sweats. When I saw her after the last delivery she had a BUN of thirty-five. I *strongly* suggested she had enough kids and another pregnancy was a no-no. Well, you guessed it." Jena is the oldest of the doctors, the one most responsible for the clinic, and Cassie's role model if she has one. Short, stocky, a woman in perpetual motion, she scorns makeup, twists her frizzed gray hair into a braid, and ignoring the Surgeon General, smokes three packs of Kools a day.

"Won't be able to carry to term," Barbara says from the end of the table. She has the long-necked beauty of a Modigliani and an indulgent husband rich as Croesus. Barbara bites her nails and inclines toward an impossible Marxism. When her husband isn't vigilant she pledges large donations to the clinic. "Abort her, Jena."

"I know she should be aborted. In the first trimester, but . . . ."

Cassie finishes for her: "But she's way beyond that and would rather die than abort. Right?"

"You got it. Her macho husband won't hear of it. Reflects on his manhood or some such nonsense. I told her let him have the baby. Let him die in labor."

Later, when Cassie touches the camellias less than delicately she thinks the petals will be wounded with fingerprints. She sits at the table, the single long light above the sink barely kissing the shadows. Working up energy to take herself to bed, to sleep, liable to zonk out right there on the chair in an awkward position, she wonders about the patients, so many of them moved by tides not their own. Is she any different, carried along with Nona and Eve to restaurants and bars trafficked by hunters? Why does she perch so solemnly, a doll on a shelf, waiting, hushed, for selection? Nothing seems to have changed in all the years since high school when, in a starched blouse and pleated skirt, she hovered with other girls at Friday night dances, stalled, shuffling, snapping her fingers, victim to some boy deciding whether or not he'd set her in motion. How can she understand her patients if she behaves so mysteriously herself? Cassie asks the camellias.

"Because I'm sick of being alone, like every other single dumped female," she says aloud. "I want to hear another voice asking, 'Hey, honey, what about a last glass of wine.' " Or ice cream, a dish of strawberries, an orgasm.

Feeling foolish talking to the flowers, an aging woman stranded in mothball loneliness, Cassie stands up in a hurry just as the phone rings.

"Hi, Mom."

"Hello, sweetheart."

To every mother her child is beautiful, a five-carat diamond plucked from drab rock. Cassie is no exception. Mandy—freckled, shy, twenty pounds overweight, with large breasts, a hunching adolescent—shears her mother's heart with love.

"I met this guy, Mom. At a DU dance. He's fantastic. His name's Ted and he's a math major. Would you believe that—me interested in somebody who gets a kick out of numbers?"

"There's always a first time," Cassie laughs, worrying. Will he call her? Ask her for a date? Treat Mandy's fragile feelings too harshly? She admonishes this unknown Ted: Don't pick some girl prettier, a girl more self-possessed and jaunty, with witty college talk. See Mandy's good qualities and be appreciative.

"And I know he takes economics the same time I do art history which means if I come out of McLaren on the south side I'll run into him."

Expectation whistled in the reedy slicing of wind through marsh grass. Cassie hunkered down, quiet as a rabbit frozen from the smell of humans, straining to please Doug—who had let her come only grudgingly—as she waited, as Doug and his hunter uncles waited. Her reward was the fireball sun scattering the night's last fringes, while theirs was the brace of ducks in miraculous flight.

Listening to Mandy girlishly plotting, the bell tone of hope in her voice, Cassie wants to tell her daughter how the victory of so much planning is too often the fall of dead birds. But such advice startles no vibrations in the air and Mandy won't have heard her; neither would Doug and his uncles, drinking coffee laced with bourbon.

There's a balance; things happen, Cassie says silently, and don't allow this Ted any power. Yet her frightened offerings, if spoken, would have as little effect as warning the ducks not to rise and fly. All Cassie cares about is saving Mandy from hurt, to secure her in separation from the longings of other women. She's younger than Nona and Eve, but not quintessentially different, Cassie acknowledges achingly.

Why doesn't Mandy secrete her infatuations? Cassie imagines the next phone call and the one after. He walked right by me. He didn't phone. He made a date, then broke it. All his love words dropped like pennies into water and sank.

Doug's example seems wasted on their daughter. She ignores his perfidy in order to keep loving him. Can Cassie blame her? Yet there must be some way to draw parallels between Doug's leaving and this Ted—or Gary, who talked about taking Mandy to a movie but didn't, and Evan at registration, making promises over late-night beer. Men with their power to pick and choose are cruel, their desires chancy. Would the ducks fly into the light or pick instead the dark safety of the marsh, where nature's camouflage saves them?

Cassie hangs up, headachy and defeated in a skirmish Mandy never realizes has taken place. She fights to protect her daughter from disappointment, from heartbreak, all the wet-pillow nights and Sahara mornings, but Mandy needs her own mistakes.

Sleep hangs chains on Cassie's back, but before she climbs up to her bed she throws the dying camellias into the trash.

Magic always waits by the door. He senses her light step along the carpeted outer hall or psychically picks up Nona's presence as she moves toward him. Whichever, she never enters the apartment to catch the cat unprepared. If he lies asleep on the bed, his white fur blending perfectly with the eyelet coverlet, he comes instantly awake and steps lightly on velvet pads across the hardwood.

He is a private creature and silent, voiceless except at night, when, cradled against her flank, he purrs. Magic's lulling sonata often ushers Nona into sleep. But at the door he never meows a greeting, just sits still as china and imperially allows her to stroke his neck.

What possessed her to pick him up from under a majestic maple four houses beyond the Tudor where she had gone to a Sunday brunch? The street, a leafy tunnel, slumbered peacefully, and Magic sat in an angle of raised roots beside Nona's car. She assumed he had escaped from one of the overpowering castles crowded as close as rush-hour Mercedes along the block. She meant to return him but he wore no collar. Once she picked him up, however, she acted ridiculously. Maybe it was his jeweled eyes or the luxury of his fur that caused her like a thief to spirit the tiny, wobbly-legged kitten home.

Nona knows nothing of animals. Her mother disliked dogs, cats, birds, fish, any living creature. Disease carriers, she groaned, lifting her brows, and so dirty.

If prayers were miraculously answered and a pet materialized, where would she have installed him? The house in Boston contained enough rooms, but it shone, windows so gleaming they were invisible, floors waxed until, when flooded by light, they seemed sheets of glass. In such a house a pet, even imagined, subtracted from rather than added to its perfection.

Later, alone, Nona never debates buying an animal. She pets friends' dogs or cats if a wet nose pushes under her hand or a ball of fur leaps into her lap. She has no prejudices, but it is children, babies to cradle, that dominate her fantasies, not kittens and puppies. Love suggests the smooth, downy feel of silk against her cheek, the smell of slightly off milk. Even Nona's vision of a happy family—a Christmas card photo of Daddy, Mommy, Baby—never contains, stretched out in front, a poodle or a golden retriever.

She hadn't stolen Magic. Whoever owned him had been derelict—a door left ajar, a window without a screen. Nona feels disengaged from those people, rather marvelously like Magic's savior. Still, early on, guilt disturbed her. She anticipated some retribution. She worried about allergies, fretting that her head would fill up, her eyes redden and water, but Magic never harms her.

Now he is her own. He displays the imperious confidence of an emperor, a sultan with boundless territory, and rules Nona's one-bedroom apartment.

He is a benevolent tyrant, however, and if not granting his attentions whenever Nona desires them, he also never treats her with feline disdain. Watching him as he performs his cat rituals, licking pink-pad paws, washing his face with its long, spidery whiskers, curling around her ankles as she confronts the angular woman of bleached ribs and tight skin in the mirror, he is the only male she loves.

The sensation of his fur rubbing her leg has Nona shivering until he glides off, leaving her alone with the other in the mirror, whose breasts jut firm and lovely, just full enough to defy gravity, peach-colored nipples as artful as a painter's fantasy. Compliments and the glow in men's eyes establish Nona's beauty, certify her loveliness, yet she whispers, *I'm too fat. My nose is ugly. Why are my ears so large?*

She owns emerald eyes and feathered brows, cheekbones elegantly shadowed. Her mouth is too broad, giving her face more sensuality than would geometric perfection. Her unblemished skin has the texture of satin. Yet Nona's beauty gives her no satisfaction, for she disbelieves it, and again and again she offers herself up to men as a sacrificial victim.

Before Nona's mother died she complained, *I don't understand* why you're not married, looking as you do. The backhanded praise fell on Nona like acid.

After her father's trial she asked him if he thought her beautiful. Before they shut him away she wanted some validation to carry out of his world of locked doors and barred windows. Her question really was: Do you still love me, Daddy? But she lacked the courage to ask that. His answer to her beauty was, *it no longer matters, Nona*.

Magic slips between her legs, oblivious to his appearance in the mirror. She bends to stroke him as his back rises; then she straightens. Naked, she brushes her hair and watches the unkind eyes mercilessly scrutinizing her. The crosshatched pain in her stomach has eased into soreness since she vomited. Once she separates herself from food so mindlessly and greedily eaten, her body always lightens.

Her throat is raw but a flattened stomach is safer. Once more she's escaped, rising, loosened, almost transparent, but the battle is constant. Fat is dangerous. It will smother Nona if she isn't vigilant.

She turns and criticizes the buttocks in a low slope below her spine. Is she bigger down there? She squints but can't decide. The scale swears Nona's weight is the same, but the scale often lies. Tomorrow she will buy a new one, an expensive version made in Japan.

Nona rotates and stares at her abdomen, wondering what damage pregnancy will do. How distended and bloated will she become? Can a baby add fat to her arms and legs? Nona sees the soft draping of flesh, puckered thighs, and drooping, old woman's dugs. In imagination she loses her ribs.

She splays a hand like a starfish over her face. An eye hangs in an angle like an unset jewel. Why is she worrying about pregnancy's destruction? To have a baby she needs a husband.

Eve suggests if Nona wants a baby so much she should just find the genetically proper stud and use him for breeding purposes. A marriage certificate isn't obligatory for motherhood. Eve cites statistics and swears having a baby—if Nona can't live without one—is almost glamorous. Nona is horrified. She isn't a feminist, or not in that way, and hates the thought of a crib in this winter-white apartment, bottled formula in the refrigerator, being condemned to worrying in solitude about rashes and fevers. A woman and a baby without a father to complete the triangle is unnatural, an affliction. Nona becomes angry with Eve for even talking about it. Eve says she is teasing, but still, if you long for something so much, you'd better reach out and take it. No one, Eve says, is ever given a thing in life.

Finding a man to impregnate her wouldn't be difficult. Lots of men lust to sleep with Nona, tear her clothes off, and work as vigorously as miners between her legs. But that is sex, and the issue is love and commitment.

Nona has gone on long trips, to Hawaii, Jamaica, carnival in Rio, to Paris, London, and Rome, all with eager men paying the airfare, springing for expensive suites and ordering prize meals she only picked at in terror. But they never escort her home for Christmas, introduce her to their parents (more often now their children), plan that these interludes be extended into the future. Stephen, a six-month affair, claimed Nona was too beautiful, that she made him feel deficient, that beauty is superficial while he requires more substance for the long haul. Warren, another lover, brooded about all the ways he could lose her, the men tempting this beauty with gold apples, promising furs and Ferraris. All Nona's lovers have had their excuses, one even lamenting it would be too painful to witness her aging. Each withdrew, from her looks, her worries, the neediness that turned them sweaty, each man swimming off with the tide, drawn away inexplicably by a force greater than the pull of the sea.

Her fright is pervasive, touching the men with icy caresses. Her need is a net she casts, only to watch the threads unravel, and one after another the boys and men leave without her. Beauty isn't enough, an inner voice cautions. Her looks are transient, movie images.

Lacking peace, she frightens men. But what peace is there for Nona nearing forty unanchored, even though she was always the prettiest girl in school? Later there were boys who might have married her—at least Nona looking back thinks so—but that was too soon and she enjoyed dancing more than settling. Time had neither gates nor bars on the windows, she foolishly supposed.

Of course there had been Simon. . . .

How sad the woman opposite makes Nona, overburdened with

flesh, graying beneath the Clairol, how angry. Nona shuns her and tugging loose sees by the clock that they've watched each other for over an hour. Her dead father is annoyed at the waste of unproductive minutes. He shakes a manicured finger. She hears his ghostly disapproval and swallows a Halcion because sleep will be sparse and difficult. Asleep she dreams of her parents' dinner parties when she was brought for approval, dressed in white and blue organdy with bows in her hair and a timid smile.

Nona climbs into bed, Magic already settled and purring. She curves a black-eyed teddy bear under her arm and flies off to the whispered *pretty girl, pretty.*

4

No diamonds glisten on the grass. The impatiens, camellias, petunias falter, birds of paradise stall in flight, their stiletto leaves pointing earthward. It is Yang's—now Jake's—day, though he hasn't shown up by the time Cassie is ready to leave for the clinic.

She lingers on the back steps thinking again of the flowers in the tin can with their *sorry*, and the morning seems dislocated. Thin sunlight transparent as gauze trails through an early haze.

He said he started here in the Palisades with her house, but it's nearly nine. What went wrong? And why is she bothering with this gardener, his hair needing a cut, the shaggy curls speckled by gray, a man eroded and not just by age? There is more than time in the stitched lines of his face.

Embarrassed, as if she isn't alone on her own property, Cassie rushes, thinking, I'm late.

He surprises her. Coming home Cassie turns the corner and sees the truck, then Jake with fronds from the palm cradled in his arms. He disappears around to the garbage cans behind the garage, and Cassie almost collides with him after she's locked the overhead door.

"I figured you'd be happier if I finished here rather than putting you first for the day," he says. He wears a denim shirt rolled up over the elbows and Cassie notices a faded blue eagle on the inside of his right arm.

"Thank you," she replies, hearing, to her disgust, a distance in

34

her voice she doesn't mean. He stares her down and she starts to circle around him before he walks off, back to his truck.

The moment shatters as if someone has thrown a rock through it. She calls to his back: "And thanks for the camellias." Why does he seem to saunter in slow motion? Cassie hurries on: "It's awfully hot. Would you like a soda, or a beer?"

"A beer's okay." He follows her to the kitchen steps, where he stops, waiting.

She watches him through the screen, a vagrant, a wanderer such as the men her mother fed with thick sandwiches and tall glasses of milk. They lived in Ohio, not that far from the main highway. Men were always hitching, traveling from one end of the country to the other, directionless, tossed by the wind, knapsacks creating Quasimodo humps between their shoulders. Not hippies, not kids, but older men (old to a child but maybe the same age as, maybe younger than, Cassie is now), out of work, edgy, poor, and dream-wrecked, unable to stay put, brush fires burning in their eyes. They hopped off the big rigs, pickups, whatever car carried them a few miles more. Some raked leaves, washed out trash cans, took down the summer screens and hung storm windows for their handouts. Not that Cassie's mother asked, but these tramps (her father's term) packed a certain pride amid their belongings. They were less beggars than itinerant workers paid in chicken or meat-loaf sandwiches. Unfailingly polite, they called Cassie's mother "Missus" and her "Little Miss," and were careful men on frozen ponds of despair. So many towns ran them off, those who had unfamiliar bristly faces and didn't belong, taking the men to the town line with a warning to keep moving, but Landry was more lackadaisical, or maybe no one knew that the tramps stopped at Cassie's house like vacationers taking a break for gas and hamburgers at a roadside diner.

There is, however, nothing that obsequious in Jake's stance. Unlike her mother's vagrants he doesn't shuffle or rock on the balls of his feet. Nor does his gaze flutter on moth wings afraid to rest, certainly not on a soft female face.

"Here." She hands out the beer and Jake advances two steps to take it. The shadow he throws, separated from her only by thin mesh, alarms Cassie, and angling away from him she slams the heavier door. Even as she does she thinks how foolish this is, a scared housewife's response, the fear of a woman alone in a house.

Moments later she hears the truck drive off.

Cassie doesn't read the *Los Angeles Times* until the end of the day, when the news is antique, all the stories having grown cold as corpses. Only bad news is ever written up—wars, terrorist attacks, murders, robberies, abuses of women and children and animals, corporate chicanery, governmental philandering with the public trust. The list stretches on depressingly, plundering whatever good humor the clinic has left her. The crimes and outrages humans perform assault Cassie and if she doesn't take care she feels the suffering of strangers as if it were her own.

To confront the paper she needs a drink, and she fails to comprehend how people read of the world's agonies with breakfast, nestled in ordinary sunlight as they sip orange juice. How do you digest "Indian Ferry Sinks, 300 Lost" with an English muffin? She supposes—metaphorically speaking—one side of the brain shuts down, the synapses between neurons frozen for twenty minutes or so. Of course after the clinic, after bad mornings or afternoons of neoplasms, ectopic pregnancies, emergency hysterectomies in the O.R. of St. John's, deformed infants born to silence, or dead babies, the distant cruelties throbbed even more intensely.

Weariness along with wine strengthens Cassie, lounging in a chair at the kitchen table, against "Three Drive-by Killings," "Father Shoots Family," "Mass Starvation in the Sudan." She skims warily with half-shuttered eyes until, relieved, she finds Snoopy on his doghouse. She has a smile for overweight Garfield and then stumbles, before she can retreat, onto a peculiar story in Santa Monica. Old bones uncovered by workers digging for a new foundation. The house torn down, a Victorian from the twenties, had nested on skeletons through seventy years. The bones were—on preliminary evidence—young women's, and jumbled with shreds of colored cloth, a pink ribbon, leather slippers. A police spokesman was quoted: "We're investigating but right now we don't even know if these were homicides." The bodies, decomposed, had been hidden a long, long time.

The forgotten women sour Cassie's wine. There are ashes on her tongue, and she folds up the paper to throw it in the trash.

At the sink she splashes cold water on her cheeks, and peers beyond her softened reflection painted on the window, into the dark. She can't help asking how had they gotten under the house, to lie there forgotten while the living went on day after day over their heads. The dead are dead and gone, no matter how she imagines them stirring in the dirt, protesting their unorthodox burial. She laughs at herself. "Come on, stop being melodramatic. Movie time."

She holds up her hands as if the dead might be coming over the sill toward her, and the doorbell rings.

Nona arrives at Cassie's unannounced, as she does often, suddenly just there in the puddle of tepid light. Cassie, despite Nona's beauty, is reminded of a scabby-kneed Brownie selling cookies, or a gangly girl in cheap print, a wearer of thick stockings and sensible black laced shoes, talking of salvation and handing out pamphlets. There is that same tentativeness in Nona, poised on one foot, which causes in Cassie the scratch of tears. Nona sports her expensive Flora clothes like a model, soft sweaters and beautifully tailored skirts, French jeans, artless little dresses in linen or the best cotton, when with people; but when she is alone the designers' masterful creations hang limply, as though on the rack. She so lacks confidence that Cassie struggles not to shake her. Once inside, however, after a glass of wine, her hair if pinned up now loosened and curling, her laughter finds a passage into the open. She is, at thirty-nine, in many ways as much a teenager as Mandy.

Long before, Cassie gave up asking Nona to phone. The request stopped the visits cold. Nona needs a safe harbor into which she can carefully sail as if by chance, always to be allowed anchorage with a smile and a hug. She possesses scores of friends, but in the five or six years they have known each other, Cassie realizes these friends are merely window dressing. The sort Eve humorlessly calls the "hello, darling!" people. Only a few have any ballast in Nona's life and Cassie wonders why she has been chosen to be one of them.

Cassie displays the watched-for smile. She kisses Nona's cheek and smells jasmine. "Did you eat?"

"Oh, sure."

"Well, I'm making myself a salad if you want some." Nona stirs

Cassie's motherly feelings, and now that Mandy has gone off to college Cassie welcomes these sporadic visits more than she admits.

"Here," she says, pouring another glass of wine as Nona settles by the table. "It's a pretty decent Beaujolais." Clinking glasses they drink, the wine not staining Cassie's mouth, as before, with sorrow for the mysterious old bones, those unfinished lives once belonging to girls. Warmed by having Nona in the empty house, she tastes instead clear days, green tangled fields, schooner clouds in cobalt skies.

She won't discuss those women with Nona, for Nona shies, frightened of the unpleasant. She wants only pretties, as Eve criticizes her, and Cassie obliges, instinctively allowing silence on the dead to clot in her throat.

"I just had to run out to the store so I thought I'd drop over." Nona invariably offers reasons for finding herself at Cassie's front door. Since she lives in Westwood and Cassie miles west, nearer the ocean, her explanations are transparent but necessary to her. Amused, Cassie supposes if Nona had a dog she'd pretend she was taking the animal on a ten-mile walk. She considers several times saying this game they play has tattered edges to it, but like asking Nona to phone, such honesty will catch painfully in that soft vulnerable part of her.

Pretense distresses Cassie, though she finds it endemic, especially to women. Women cling to make-believe like rock climbers on sheer stone.

This afternoon Cassie examined a fifteen-year-old, five months pregnant, who chewed bubble gum as she lay naked under a sheet. She crossed her heart, swearing to virginity with the lopsided tilt of a guileless child. *I never did it, not once, never.*

"We're having a sale next week," Nona is saying. "There's a really luscious Donna Karan knit, that vivid green which is positively your color, Cassie. If you come in I'll hold it so you can get the sale price. That, plus my twenty percent, makes it only two hundred and seventy-five." Nona brings discounts to these nighttime visits, bestowing her bargains on Cassie rather than candy or wine. "Not tight. Loose. The top comes to here." She stands up to demonstrate.

"Nona, sit down. Here, have some salad." While Nona talks

about gored skirts and wide sleeves, Cassie sets another plate on the table. She longs to feed the too-thin Nona, who she fears has an eating disorder—not that Nona plays the usual little tricks with her meals, cutting up food into microscopic pieces and moving it around the plate in complicated patterns, leaving uneaten as much as she orders, or tempting others with tastes, protesting she consumed a banquet only two hours earlier.

"Honestly, Cassie, you'll adore it."

"Even if I had two hundred and seventy-five dollars to spend on a dress, I wouldn't. My miserly soul balks at the frivolous."

"A Donna Karan is an investment."

"I'll stick to CDs, and for right now I plan to eat my supper. And I want you to eat with me," she says as though they are off on a ballroom duet. Nona, sighing, returns to her chair, momentarily a child forced into orderly compromise. This, too, is a game between the two women.

Cassie starts to command Nona to eat as Nona prods a tomato, but swallows the word with a sliver of cheese. Nona is an adult, a woman at midlife, though she looks in her twenties with few intimations of age furrowing her face.

"How's Mandy?" Nona asks.

"Learning to adjust. She likes her English class and Greek history and she doesn't outright hate her roommate, which helps."

"She'll do fine, Cassie. Don't you worry." Nona pats Cassie's hand as if she needs consoling. Ignoring the food she drinks another glass of wine, which sparks diamonds in her eyes.

Cassie finishes clearing the table and they go into the living room, where Nona curls in a corner of the gaily flowered couch, which Cassie, in an act of irrationality, had recovered from its homey gray stripes two months after Doug left. She intended to do the whole place, to strip the Cape Cod from top to bottom, rip out memories in a fury of change, but got no further than the couch. Even before the upholsterer returned the unfamiliar sofa Cassie realized a new outside wouldn't alter a single feeling. She was the one needing renovation, her mind liposuctioned, her heart transplanted. Still she keeps swatches of material, rug samples, brochures for French doors and windows, pictures cut from *HG* and *House Beautiful,* and here sits the couch, a visitor on the Berber rug, antagonistic to the charcoal armchairs with their pink throw pillows. She should reaffirm the room around it, or at least buy a slipcover more friendly to the other furniture. Sometimes she thinks she will leave the couch alone, a garden party female misplaced at more somber Sunday morning services, as a reminder of her foolishness. The colorful couch smirks at her for believing Doug, and trusting a man twenty years her husband.

"I met a man today," Nona says when Cassie finally settles in the rocker where once she nursed Mandy in another smaller house, the two of them alone during reassured late nights while Doug slept, perhaps already swimming in unfaithful dreams.

"Meeting men isn't your problem."

"Then what is?" she asks, half-expecting Cassie to diagnose, hoping. It is no secret that she posits wisdom in Cassie, though Cassie often finds her belief burdensome.

Now Cassie rocks, refusing to suggest there's no one problem locked in a little black box, only the jumbled feelings, thorns of shaken memories, earlier experiences, history, and rough fears with suckers, all fitting in complex patterns like Escher drawings.

"Tell me about this man," Cassie says, waiting.

He appeared beside Nona in the mall. Proper, in a business suit, carrying an expensive briefcase, he eased through the crystal prisms of light on the top floor as if on his way from one important meeting to another. Hurrying, he consulted his watch, then asked as Nona passed, "Excuse me, but do you have the time?"

"Two-fifteen," Nona replied as they somehow began walking together, as if they had been with each other all along.

"That certainly doesn't give me more than a few minutes to buy the present," he said, annoyed. "For my secretary. It's her birthday. Can you suggest which store I should try?"

He was so unexceptional, a walking nonentity at five nine or ten, clean-shaven, grayish, and understated. He presented an instantly forgettable face and the blandness of a bank teller. Only his voice, with the snap of an army colonel in it, made him stand out in the midday mall.

"Do you have anything special in mind?" Nona asked politely as they descended on the escalator to the second tier.

The man was vague. "I'm sure all my choices would be wrong.

Women are so particular. But something that displays feeling; an item she can't possibly ignore."

"A scarf? A piece of costume jewelry? Cologne?"

The man had the confident air of one of her father's old associates and shook his head, severe and disdainful at each suggestion. "All too mundane." He lifted a hand of manicured nails to tame a lazy tic by his right eye.

Nona imagined him at a conference table, jotting notes on a yellow pad. She imagined him, as she once did her father, sitting straight back in his chair.

"What about lingerie?" the man wondered.

They continued walking, not quite a pair, as the man leaned conspiratorially toward Nona, who rejected intimate apparel.

"A sheer . . . what do you call them? Teddies? With lace? A gauzy garment through which you can see her nipples hardening? Or a pair of those little bikini panties cut so narrow the hair curls around the edges? Silky, I think, and clinging to the crack in her ass."

Nona stumbled to a stop in front of a bookstore wide open for browsers, the man so near her shoulder she smelled oranges on his breath. "Or a garter belt that leaves her pussy bare," he said seriously, not smiling.

"I thought it was a joke, that somebody put him up to it. Maybe he was an actor and the deadpan way he mouthed his garbage was supposed to be funny. But it was just too scary."

Nona wishes Cassie on the couch instead of the rocker so she can creep close for comfort, lowering her head in Cassie's lap. Right from the moment she washed her face and hands in Flora's tiny bathroom—as if the graphic words splattered her skin like mud and she could scrub them off—she'd heard her frightened replay of the scene to Cassie. In fact Nona struggled not to run immediately from the shop to the Magdalene Clinic.

Now, her mouth working like a wound, Cassie explodes. "Why didn't you just leave him heavy-breathing over the best-sellers?"

"Cement legs," Nona explains, dabbing at slow tears. "Did you ever have something happen where you had to move but couldn't? It was so eerie, like a dream, this corporate vice-president talking about tits and ass with as much emotion as ball bearings. No spit dribbling off his lips, and he never tried to jump me."

"When you did finally get away from him, did he follow you?"

Nona shakes her head. "On the escalator going down I looked back and saw him standing like a flagpole where I left him." Waiting, Cassie thinks, for some other poor fool, and suggests that Nona would have been more than justified to call mall security.

Nona, little girl lost, begging to be allowed out alone, warned about wolves and unshaven men leering, about men in trench coats exposing themselves, cries, "And have to tell them what he said? Repeat all those words?"

The grown-ups are right after all. Nowhere is safe for the innocent, women being helpful, the unsuspecting minding their own business. Deliberate acts of emotional vandalism swirl in webs around girls, women, if they forget to be vigilant. Why is life for women so often a Beirut, an Afghanistan? Cassie wonders, changing from the rocker to the couch, holding Nona's icy hand.

I met a man, Nona had begun.

"He wasn't a man; he was a male sicko!" Cassie says. But indignation isn't good enough. It shatters only chips out of rock.

"Why pick me?" Nona's cheeks are blotchy.

"Why pick any of us?" Cassie asks, weary and angry with men who should be locked up, have their minds drained of sexual desire gone toxic. The scientist in Cassie, the levelheaded, balanced, non-gendered person, dips and the purely female rises, fists shaking, ready to yell *castrate them!*—all the abusers, rapists, perverts, fiends preying on children.

She feels outrage and shame in equal portions.

Nona, having confessed, leaves lightened, but for the first night in a very long while Cassie sleeps uneasily, drifting to bob up in splintered moments of sweaty wakefulness. Each time she stares in the dark at Nona's wretched face reflected in shop windows and hears, *do you have the time . . .*

Saturdays without Mandy are barren. The last few years they seldom ran together, two girls hanging out as they had before Mandy got her driver's license, but there was the stray afternoon for shopping at Santa Monica Place or the Crystal Mall, and if

Cassie asked, Mandy, groaning, accompanied her to the supermarket. At least she was here, in the house.

It is the sounds most of all that Cassie misses, the shower running, the thunk of the refrigerator door, a deafening blast of U2 or Michael Jackson when Mandy pulled into the driveway. Her leaving has sucked all human noises from the house except for those Cassie creates herself.

With Mandy gone Cassie feels impotent, the loser of magic. A powerful intimacy existing only between mother and child (particularly between mother and daughter) was dissolving. Their separating is compulsory, already decided when Mandy slipped from the womb. Yet daily life without her daughter affects Cassie like a chronic disease. In this process of detaching she also confronts age, her own march forward into an older generation, and as she seldom did before, reads the mirror for omens.

If I could have another child . . .

A sublime and unthinkable craziness bubbles under her heart, throbs mid-month in her ovaries, for her womb to swell and to fulfill itself once again. Finally liberated (excluding holidays and summer vacations), she wishes once more for motherhood and further grounding. Primal mother love, which in the waning of the twentieth century seems bred out of some women, leaving them indifferent, is making more complex claims than the practice of medicine on Cassie.

Even love of Doug and marriage never sunk such shafts into Cassie as Mandy does. If before Doug's *another woman* declaration a choice had been demanded, she saw herself without question, in a split-second explosion, leaping from her husband to save her child. Though time and space intervene she still sometimes dreams they weave together, she and Mandy, revolving shadows, spinning one into the other, interlocking molecules, as when Mandy curled in her womb.

At her age, and in her profession, these mystical, these *romantic* feelings embarrass Cassie. Of course it is arrogant to think only barren women, Nona for example, hunger for a child and hold out trembling arms to receive a baby into them, but Cassie can't help herself. Alone in the house she too often suffers from what Eve calls Nona's disease—babies on the brain.

When Cassie closes her eyes and fantasizes making love, all she creates is a patchwork quilt of wavery lines on the inside of her lids. No tingles. No electrical sparks at the tail of her spine. Physically she is in working order, though her breasts and vagina feel cast in brass, but being naked in her bed with a man is even more unthinkable than having another child suckling.

There is neither a man lusting before sex nor lolling afterward and not even a ghost child in a crib in the guest bedroom, and just wanting—as her mother always said—never makes things happen. So Cassie, rejecting the two-piece linen, takes the silk wraparound off the hanger. She intended after her last blind date to refuse any man she hadn't seen firsthand. *No* was a decent, necessary word but it turned to sand on Cassie's tongue when her friend and neighbor Beth trapped her.

Girls Mandy's age sally out on blind dates, not grown women, not self-supporting professionals who handle their lives in an organized fashion. How awkward it is to dress up and smile for a nervous stranger, both of you palmed off on each other like unmatched mittens.

It was bad enough in college waiting for the doorbell to ring, closing her eyes and fervently praying: Don't let him be hideous, disfigured, fat, homely, with blubbery lips! Please God no pimples! Or else the alternative: If he's a hunk, football material, sophisticated, with sharp creases in his chinos—let him like me! The mating game produced the same nausea as pregnancy.

Why isn't Doug here to save her from the humiliating charade, keeping her safe in marriage, on home base, delivered! Of all the horrors, being a commodity, ordered to mingle, offered up for cold-eyed inspection is among the worst.

I will stay unmarried to death, be a good doctor, work at the clinic, diagnose and treat, save, be happy with Mandy growing. I'll shepherd Mandy for the last stretch of childhood, enjoy her successes (and hopefully her children). I'll be content and not watch my weight. There are so many books I've never read, Cassie reminds herself as she attaches pearl clips to her earlobes.

In Landry there were just such solitary females, Miss Mac-Namara, the algebra teacher, for example, prim in starched blouses and pleated skirts, hats—a small tan flower pot for spring and fall, an angora tam for winter with a heavy scarf tied over it in the worst storms—straight, tailored coats, the faintest dab of flesh-colored powder on her nose, and lipstick pale as wilting carnations. During the long summer hiatus Miss Mac, as they called her, took tours with solitary Landryites, elderly couples and widows, bus trips to the Grand Canyon, Florida, Montreal. Old maid, spinster, her own equations mysterious, Miss Mac was ridiculed by all of them when she turned and wrote on the blackboard. Unloved, she walked alone to church, to the movie, or to the women's club suppers with her marshmallow and sweet-potato casserole, worrying if she had made enough. Warmed only by mathematics, she prepared solitary meals at home and gave the wives, mothers, teenagers (men ignored Miss Mac the invisible) nothing to gossip over.

Miss Mac, Cassie thinks, spraying eau de cologne on her neck. Miss Mac seemed happy, complete. Why? Because she never burst into tears on Main Street?

They pitied Miss Mac. Poor Mac, Cassie's mother called her. None of the kids believed she had once been pretty, went to dances as they did, paired off with a boy on spring hayrides, that she had ever received a valentine, a corsage, held hands, kissed. She couldn't actually have *done it,* Miss Mac with her wool skirts and artificial flowers pinned above a plump left breast.

Cassie shaded her upper lids and remembered Miss Mac, single from birth to the grave.

I'm not like that. No woman is now. The world changed with plastics and computers, the pill, trips to the moon, graphic sex on the screen.

Besides, Cassie argues, I know what love is. I knew. I have a child.

Beth Levinson's cheese puffs are love, her tiny hot dogs wrapped in bacon, her pâté gritty with peppercorns.

A generous woman, Beth possesses a large imagination, wider than her spreading middle-aged hips, and already dreams love for Cassie and marriage with "a new guy in Al's office." "A prince, isn't he, hon?" Beth asks her comfortable husband as she brings in a Lucite basket in which chunks of ice glitter like a sheik's diamonds. Before Al can interject an opinion Beth rushes on, "He's very nice. Just what you need, Cassie. A steady, reliable guy, the sort who understands about responsibilities and has no pipe dreams of boogeying off with a teeny-bopper."

The two couples had a friendship across the hedges, and Beth doesn't forgive Doug his desertion. He left Cassie, split up a homey foursome, and the only time she has seen Doug in the last three years was at a distance. Looking up once at the Levinsons' bedroom window as Doug arrived for Mandy, Cassie saw Beth glaring down, her fingers forming a cross as though Doug were a vampire to be warded off.

"How do you know he's so nice?" Al teases Beth. "You never met the man."

Beth shakes her permed curls. "I know what you told me. He sounds like a winner or I wouldn't have suggested you introduce him to Cassie. After all, Cassie deserves the best, not a fly-by-night, a just Mr. Anybody. He's terrific. I can feel it in my bones, so don't make Cassie nervous or she'll sweat. It's not a piece of cake being single, in case you've forgotten."

"Was I ever single? Seems to me we got married in nursery school."

"Ha! You're cute, Levinson. Now fix Cassie a drink," Beth says, returning to the kitchen.

"A drink, Cassie. You heard her. What will it be?" Al asks, pretending resignation as he lumbers over to the bar. He is a big man, over six feet, gently softening like a melon. His pink scalp shines in jigsaw patches through fading russet hair.

"Wine, I guess. White if you have it."

"Do we have white wine! Does the Pope have holy water?"

"No Catholic jokes!" Beth yells.

Al's bushy eyebrows climb. He has the bemused look of a clown without makeup. "How does she do it? My hearing's dimming, the batteries or whatever's in there weakening. But my wife! She hears a pin drop in Australia."

Cassie likes Al Levinson. He has the leftover good looks from his younger days, a wry sense of humor, and a placid, easygoing nature that curves companionably with Beth's fussiness and enthusiasms. He is the image of a man lucky in life, a journeyer on unrutted freeways, swerving unerringly from the wrong choices. But Cassie knows, for Beth shamelessly confides, that they passed through jungles, the worst of bad times, and nothing, not their modest house in the Palisades or their son, Tony, has been earned without problems. Married right out of high school, sneaking away in the night from Pennsylvania and across the Maryland border, they were outcasts to parents who emphatically did not believe in mixed marriages. A justice of the peace joined Beth, a Catholic, and Al, a Jew, and the renegades renewed their vows thirty years later, in an act of whimsy as much as devotion, with the aid of a Unitarian minister. Together they put Al through Penn State and tried, first lovingly and then with grim determination, to have a child. Beth tells a horror story of thermometers and meticulously kept ovulation charts, of doctors and fertility specialists, of sex in designated positions, of lovemaking not for pleasure after a while. An unconceived fetus accompanied every orgasm.

When Beth heard about Doug she screamed, disparaged men having midlife crises, younger women lacking morals. One weepy Sunday out on the patio she even cried with Cassie as if the loss was hers, cried of love lost and the end to romance.

Al, on the other hand, dove-gray eyes storming darker, patted Cassie's arm and said he was sorry—for her, because divorce wasn't what she ordered; for Doug, misguided, a fool who'd find hell, not paradise. His quiet commiseration touched her more than Beth's loud outbursts.

"Try one of these," Beth insists, bringing out a plate of cheese puffs.

"Delicious!" Cassie compliments her.

"Okay, babe."

"Okay? What do you know? Did you tell her about Jim?"

"I presume you gave her the poor man's dossier. What's left for me to say? That he wears a four-carat diamond on his pinkie finger?"

"He doesn't!"

"Beth!" Cassie laughs.

"Wouldn't you think she'd know when I'm putting her on?" Al sounds offended, but he receives a certain pleasure from teasing his wife, sending her around on her heels and having her suck her lips until they all but disappear.

"I'm not talking to you," Beth says, piqued. Al's literal-mindedness, his placidity, his ebullience, wear her down. On occasions worry drives ditches across his brow and clenches his jaw. Every so often he grinds his teeth in his sleep, attributing nocturnal mastication to bad dreams or something he ate, while Beth, alerted to perfidy by Doug Morgan, searches his pockets and sniffs his jacket for incriminating evidence.

"Okay," Al says with a sigh, putting his feet up on the coffee table to have them shooed down by Beth. "Jim Harvetti is an engineer for the firm." The firm is Arco Construction, where Al works as the head accountant. "Divorced, forty-three—"

"So don't tell him your age," Beth cautions. She sits in an overstuffed chair opposite Al, with Cassie on the couch between them.

"Beth, I'm only forty-four."

"Doesn't matter. Something to do with dominance. That's what I read in a magazine. Unless, of course, there's a world of difference—I mean decades, like fifteen or twenty years. Then it's very chic, a kind of Hollywood thing. Like Cher."

"Maybe Cassie should start dating Tony," Al suggests.

"Funny!"

"You just said older women, younger men are the in thing. So why shouldn't Cassie be stylish? Tony's twenty-four, so *voila!* There's your generation gap."

The joking about their only child, a boy/man slipping and sliding, ejected from college, from several colleges, sometimes a movie extra, more often a waiter, finding himself, talented but searching, in Beth's description, isn't acceptable.

Beth had decided, if not in the delivery room then soon after, that Tony was destined to be a doctor. She boasted a doctor uncle whom she looked up to, and wanted Tony to follow in his footsteps for the prestige, the secure niche in any community, and the good karma. (In the sixties Beth took a brief swing through Eastern religions.) In second place was law, and after that becoming a CPA like his father. Tony cares for none of the above. Still, there is time. Kids start later now. One day, over the hedges, Beth acknowledged with a flush of embarrassment, "Tony has to get his shit together."

"Jim better be cute, or else," Beth says now, pushing the noxious idea of her son and any older woman firmly aside and bringing Al back to this evening's date.

"Cute. What do I know from cute? He's a guy, two arms, two legs, a head—"

"Hair?"

"He's got so much hair you could hide birds in it," Al says.

"Stop, you two. You're making it worse. I want to crawl under the rug."

"Cassie, honey, I'm sorry." Beth flies over to the couch and grabs Cassie's hand, her long silver earrings swinging, tinkling with compassion.

"It's okay. I will survive. We all will."

Cassie knows it isn't Harrison Ford about to turn up on the front stoop. A sixth sense, too much recent experience, Beth's eagerness and lack of discrimination, Al's bottomless love for his wife, which has him endlessly trying to please her, tell Cassie that the Levinsons' Jim is not awful but not for her either.

Is there any man for her out there, another Doug (no, not that!), a man kind and understanding, a friend, a lover? And why is she doing this, gussied up, waiting for a man she doesn't care to meet? She is a rogue planet off its orbit and free-floating in her single state. Yet five days a week she is an authority figure, a rock by which other women take their sightings.

Loneliness, the untreatable female disease.

In earlier centuries, Cassie thinks, sitting on the middle cushion of the Levinsons' striped couch with which her dress clashes, pioneer women snowed in for grueling winters, whited out in their houses, went mad by spring. Others, those in cities, took to attics. Women alone, historically, were forever unhappy.

"After two drinks, if Jim looks stalled, I'll just say 'I suppose you people want to get along to dinner.' " Beth is scripting as the doorbell rings. "There he is!" It is Beth who pats her hair, straightens her skirt, and adjusts the smile on her lips as if she were one of the starring players.

Of course he is a nice man, they all are. Pleasant, with the sort of face that Cassie, if forced to describe it from memory, would say leaves the impression of sand. His voice is low, unaccented, and he emphasizes no words as he talks about his job, his ex-wife, the marriage that dissolved much like sodden tissue, his children. He lives in Manhattan Beach but hasn't a view of the water. This bothers him more than anything else and they talk as if Cassie is a coconspirator in his various plans to move.

Over margaritas, chips, and salsa in the Mexican restaurant he has chosen, they are as two-dimensional as the awkward figures drawn on the back wall's clumsy mural.

Jim asks about doctoring but with little interest. She replies that she treats women only and Cassie thinks as he cramps on his chair that her profession embarrasses him. Women's secrets are frightening, she supposes, but he slowly unfreezes as she speaks of Mandy. Everyone, or almost everyone their age, possesses children. Children act as ballast in conversations between strangers.

"Try the chicken fajitas," he suggests when it comes time to order.

Cassie agrees because it seems important to him, but she wishes for home, leftover lentil soup, and sourdough toast. She regrets the dead space between them.

The air as they eat is cold, though he tries to warm it with a joke that she forgets as soon as their laughter trickles into silence.

Later, when he drops her at her door Cassie looks up at Beth and Al's window, where the curtain might be whispering. Jim says he had a great time; he says he'll call. Cassie knows he won't and is grateful.

His lips leave a chilly impression on her cheek and she hopes, going in the door, he doesn't resent the lost night, the fifty or sixty dollars he spent taking a woman he won't recognize tomorrow out for dinner.

5

A wavery aquatic creature in blurred motion hoses down the borders. Cassie had heard the water splattering the kitchen window and had come quickly downstairs to watch Jake until he glanced up and saw her through the streaking rivulets.

Later, when he finishes, she goes outside and asks, "A beer?"

He pushes the silent mower across the lawn and, lifting it easily onto the bed of the pickup, answers over his shoulder: "Sure."

Walking toward her, he rolls down the sleeves of his bleached work shirt as if the offer of a beer is formal and they understand that this time she will invite him into the kitchen. Still, when she holds the screen door open he hesitates, much like one of Doug's uncle's retrievers, stiffening, scenting the wind, before he follows. He has a dancer's loose-limbed grace, stepping lightly on the balls of his feet, and Cassie wonders if the blades of grass behind him bend down from his weight.

She has the Coors out—two, one for her also—and considers their sitting at the table. But he lounges against the counter and she leans next to the refrigerator feeling slightly unstable, as though the kitchen floor were water.

Cassie knows she imagines the air changing, the static and the charged particles flying around them. Still, her kitchen feels different with Jake in it. He rearranges the familiar.

Needing to shatter the quiet, so much more ponderous than that she shared with the blind date Jim, Cassie seizes the first words she thinks of. "The garden looks wonderful."

"There's nothing to taking care of it." He drinks, then holds the cold can next to his cheek just as Doug would on a hot day, though this afternoon carries chilled drafts in it.

"I know—it's not your biggest piece of property."

"Grass, hedges, a palm tree, flowers. What more do you need?"

"Oh, I'm not complaining. This is just fine for me. Not too much, not too little. But Mandy always wanted a pool." She explains: "Mandy's my daughter."

"Where is she? I never see her."

"In school, college. It's her first year. And I miss her something awful. It's so lonely in the house without her, especially on weekends. I ricochet around here like a loose marble." Cassie is about to go on and say sometimes she could weep just wanting the sound of a human voice, but she's afraid all of a sudden that he'll misunderstand. She doesn't want him to think she's slyly hinting, that she's coming on to him.

He drains the Coors and she expects him to crumple it in his fist, but instead he carefully puts the empty can by the sink.

"Another one?" Cassie asks, reaching for the refrigerator handle, wondering *why am I doing this?* Because last week I treated him so coolly, like one of Mama's tramps?

"No, thanks. I've got to be going."

"Of course," she agrees hastily, worrying that he does think she's a bored housewife, another sex-starved female. Only what does she care? Maybe she's not screeching on a back-alley fence for sex, but she knows she can't stand the dull throbbing emptiness that covers her life like lichen these days.

She hears the bell tone of Eve's *biology,* as if someone stretches out the syllables and plucks them in crystal notes. And she scoffs: Oh, no, not me, not with the gardener! The idea of Lady Chatterley keels her almost to laughter.

"By the way," he is saying, "I think next week I better trim the hedges. And over by the driveway you really ought to cut them back."

"If you say so."

She likes this Jake's face, inhospitable at some angles, a face used too much. As they talk she wants to ask him how he broke his straight nose and what accident carved the crescent-shaped scar on his left cheekbone. And because she does, she hurries: "You do whatever you think should be done around the yard. I can barely tell a marigold from a tulip. No, you decide on flowers, hedges, grass. In fact I'm usually not around all that much. This afternoon is an exception." Cassie goes on, hoping to distance herself from any unflattering, demeaning image. "I had an emergency over at the hospital and it was too late to go back to the clinic. A placenta previa. Normally I would have done a Caesarian but she was already dilating."

Now that is too much explaining. Can't she ever find some balance?

"I know," he says, "you're an M.D. *Dr*. Morgan, not Mrs. Yang told me."

"Yes. Well." Cassie shoves her hands into the pockets of her white tailored slacks.

Jake has one foot in the kitchen, the other on the porch. He'll just keep going now, wave good-bye, and say thanks for the beer. Cassie's cheeks burn for having him in the house in the first place. But he stops and asks, "Do you like music?"

"Sure. Who doesn't?"

"What kind?"

"Oh, anything, I guess, but hard rock. That heavy-metal stuff sounds like a symphony of car crashes. Why?"

"I play some, guitar. Nothing special. And Saturday I'm sitting in on a couple of sets at Malone's on Seventh, south of Arizona. Maybe you'll want to come over."

"Maybe," she says. Is he asking her for a *date*?

He seems undecided. "We start at nine and play to midnight. In between sets I could buy you a beer. Return the favor."

He expects some answer and Cassie moves around the table, centering the bowl of fruit, aligning the folded *Times* precisely with the edge. Should she go or stay away? What does she want? she asks herself, as if wanting matters. A little music, a beer in a bar, a man she likes well enough to invite into the kitchen . . .

Cassie doesn't know who unsettles her more, her own self or this Jake. *This Jake*, she thinks of him as, using the modifier to create space between them.

She has to look at him, *this Jake*, still waiting for his answer, *this Jake* gripping the screen, and suddenly angry with the jittery feeling she can neither define nor diagnose as anything medical, she says, "I don't know. I'll see." Then, the screen hushing behind him, she softens her words with another "maybe."

The Geoffrey Booker Real Estate Agency employs 125 agents in offices throughout the Southland. There are housewives with empty-nest syndrome, young divorcées supplementing alimony and thinking, oh, anybody can sell real estate, along with flighty men nervous about property over half a million, polyester old uncles primly dressed as if for funerals. The core of the Booker team, however, is a hard-driving group, stylish and up-to-the-minute, hellbent on turning over properties like an Iowa farmer's spring soil. It isn't gender but temperament and flaming ambition that define the movers and shakers of the volatile market, those who work contacts, group together to buy condos, hungry agents stretching for the next big sale. These diviners, clairvoyants of real estate, are wired in to the moment, keen to equivocating offers and counters, quick dealers of points and mortgages.

In the Booker Beverly Hills office—the agency's flagship—these agents never sit like pool stenographers in the center of the floor. They have won desks to the back, and the real pontiffs among them occupy private offices safely away from the tall front windows through which strollers wandering along Rexford can look in. They belong not to the lowly Million Dollar Club but to the Gold Circle, which alerts those in the know that these agents earn incomes in the mid-six figures.

Eve, on the office's inner rim, twenty steps from a paneled sanctuary, gazes hungrily at Titus Reynolds's domain, its door ajar and the pearly light within reflecting warmly on the wood. Titus, a vice-president, deals with old money and the sort of people living in the Beverly Hills flats for thirty years or more, widows, men forced into lucrative retirement, thinking of Palm Springs or a simpler apartment life in the Wilshire corridor. He also has his coterie of Hancock Park cronies who call him if they decide against deeding the family home to middle-aged children. At seventy, Titus, a pixie with tufts of white hair haloing a freckled tonsure, is the essence of old Los Angeles rather than brash show-biz Hollywood. He never works with immigrants, the fabled wealthy from Iran—calling themselves Persians in California—the Koreans, the unfailingly polite Japanese. These newcomers with money to burn, to bury beside the swimming pools, so much money that figures become meaningless, confuse Titus, a seventh-generation Angeleno. His talent is for underplaying, and he never nudges a client, whispering a house's good points while closing his narrow lips until they disappear over the bad.

It is more an honor to the client than the reverse for Titus to handle a sale, to help prospective buyers find the one suitable property. But it is six months since Titus was the number one producer for Beverly Hills, and during the last three he has slipped from his comfortable niche of being among the top 10 percent companywide.

It is his office Eve hungers to take title to.

Somebody should turn his light off, Eve thinks, knowing Titus isn't at his desk. The old man works five days a week, ten to six, and a pop-up jack-in-the-box schedule on Saturdays and Sundays.

The crazy, unpredictable market this last year and a half scorches and burns even major agents in its heat. Some houses never get listed in the multiples but are snatched up instantly, while others languish for a year. Unrealistic or stubborn owners, thinking their little ranches or split-levels on handkerchief-size lots should go for somewhere in the million range because of location— location is dogma in the religion of Los Angeles real estate—are more and more finding no takers. On caravan—the weekly tour by agents through the newest listings—there is often disagreement as to whether or not a property's tagged with the right price. It is difficult these days to pinpoint a house's value, which means the absolute most a buyer will pay. A seller with expectations inflated beyond the outer reaches of possibility, or one who finds his house yanked out from under him because it's a bargain, always blames the agent. Such an unlucky agent eventually receives a dressing-down from Tom Holloway, the Beverly Hills manager, for he has become an enemy of the seller. A client, therefore, is lost for the future.

In rootless Southern California, where the ground quivers in constant seismic twitches, a transient population plays real estate musical chairs. Moving up—or, God forbid, slipping—people returning home at day's end often forget where they live. Children in school have to think before announcing their addresses. Real estate is a Los Angeles board game and homes are pawns that players pursue in deadly earnest, so that wives and husbands constantly find themselves uprooted, their furniture on moving vans with each roll of the dice. A change in the interest rate is headline news even on a day when a five-point quake sets downtown buildings swaying like stalks of asparagus. That a sizable portion of the state might splinter from the mainland and drift westward to Catalina worries some of the natives less than a fluctuation in land values.

Eve's phone rings. She answers, expecting reception to announce her client, but a male voice says, "Eve, this is Johnny."

Eve needs to thumb through her mental index file to bring up Johnny Who? as she trills, "Hello, darling! How are you? Long time no see."

"I've been meaning to call but time passes."

Finally the voice clicks. It is Johnny Lerner, commodities trader, married, divorced, married again for fifteen minutes, a million-five Santa Fe in Malibu, and as gossip has it, a stint in the Betty Ford Clinic to get his head freshly laundered. Johnny, a fat man perpetually off center, sports a waxy complexion in sunny California, a strawberry birthmark under his chin, and a shy grin like a Norman Rockwell waif.

"Yesterday, on the plane coming in from Heathrow, I saw a woman who reminded me of you. Good old Eve, I thought. I haven't seen her since the last ice age."

"Foggy London, how much fun!" Eve says, playing, smiling as if the phone were equipped with television.

"Foggy! They had a heat wave. Sixty-five for a week!" He laughs. "A woman fainted at the wedding, it was so bad!"

"I didn't know you took the plunge again," she says, unbending a paper clip, her mind drifting. All the men in the world are married or gay.

"Not me, my sister."

"Then London wasn't business." Eve glances at her watch. The client should have materialized by now.

"God, no! I'm out of that business. Haven't you heard?"

Were the rumors true then? "It seems we have to play catch-up, darling."

"Tonight's the perfect occasion then."

Johnny has remembered a party he promised to drop in on.

Would she be a good sport and forgive him this last minute? He hates big bashes. "Hold my hand, okay?"

"Only for you." The fool probably wants to get laid, but why her? They have never had so much as a casual grope and feel. Still . . . he isn't so bad, and it has been too long since she spent the night with a man.

"Pick you up at eight."

She should have said no, feigned remorse over a previous engagement, warned Johnny to give her sufficient notice next time. Wise women play that way, never available on short notice, but Eve convinces herself that it is the party, not Johnny. Parties are sources of possible buyers and sellers. One works whatever living room or pool area, tosses in "a fantastic buy north of the hotel!" "a real steal for the money!" at the buffet table. Bargains, particularly that jewel in a prime location, charm those only romanticizing about moving. No, it certainly isn't Johnny, but business. Johnny is fat and a bore, she decides.

Johnny Lerner has changed. He is lean and slope-shouldered, without the bulk Eve remembers, and standing in her doorway he looks like a silhouette, easily picked up and hung on a hanger. Time—though she saw him last when? six? eight months? a year?—has crushed his face. Back-country roads wind under his eyelids. The weight loss also bares his cheekbones so that they jut out dramatically. His color is better, too, no longer the off-white of dough; and unpuffed by fifty excess pounds, he is handsomer, though older. Only his strawberry mark remains the same, Australia shaped, reddish-thick as jelly.

"You look fabulous!" she cries. "What happened?"

"I sobered up, went straight, stopped stuffing myself like the Christmas goose. No more booze, greasy foods, mammoth meals in Chinoise and Trumps. And I am off all foreign substances. I'm probably the only case in recorded history that didn't turn into a skeleton from too much blow." He smiles, and his smile sits on his lips differently too.

As they wait by the elevator in her Wilshire high-rise, this Johnny of hard angles disturbs her.

Johnny sanitized is quiet and careful. A wary man beneath the sunny exterior, he has lost, besides poundage, the Malibu beachfront, money market accounts, stocks, bonds, and the lucrative job that provided all the luxuries. Gone, too, is his reputation as a smart trader.

"I sucked my nerve up my nostrils and blew several fortunes." He snaps his fingers, seemingly accommodated to the lost, bygone days. "No way could I go back and remake it. No way would I want to. Amen to pork bellies and living on the high wire. The only future I want to deal with is the one happening today," he pronounces with the intensity of a TV evangelist.

For a man with a few thousand in the bank, a rental below Olympic, and an easy job doing research for a Fortune 500, he is, Eve thinks, remarkably well adjusted.

On a deck in upper Bel Air hanging out over nowhere, he drinks designer water slowly, as if savoring its tastelessness, and explains, "I know now what counts. I have priorities. Dope is death, Eve." He leans toward her, and in the shadowy light his stain is invisible.

"Don't we all," she replies, sipping a Chardonnay of undistinguished vintage and gazing back through glass doors at Johnny's new friends, the previously driven and now righteously sobered, off one hook or another. No clients in this crowd, no men climbing or women ready to relocate on a whim for something more spacious. These people, out of their bomb shelters, are all too shaky.

"I have," Johnny continues, his smile now flowing onto Eve like milk, "a program for living."

She feels obligated to inquire: "What is it?"

"Day by day," he announces and lights a Marlboro.

How about cigarettes? she almost asks him, but shrugs and says, "Go for it."

Johnny has dropped the gold ring, thumped off the merry-go-round, and sits hugging his bones on the sidelines. But he is still male, and gender makes him acceptable. Some women Eve knows, several in fact, would want to take him home for the winter and keep him, which is why Eve, needing a man, asks him to Allie's bash for singles. The party has a very simple idea. Single women bring unattached males in whom they have no proprietary interest, and generously offer them up to friends.

"One woman's slow pulse is another's cardiac arrest," Eve says to Cassie over the phone in their daily conversation. For years now they have gotten into the habit of checking in, usually with nothing serious, only data.

Eve, the receiver tucked against her shoulder, draws vines around her name on her note pad and explains the party's purpose.

"It sounds like a garage sale."

Eve sketches hummocks, a wall, anchors the lettering as though her scripted name needs pruning. "You're missing an opportunity, Cassie. The most likable men turn up in the most *un*likely places. It's all a matter of sifting out the crazies and the uglies." She starts a house below the wall, but the roof pitches at an impossible angle and she scratches over it.

"It's just like a singles party."

"It *is* a singles party, but in Allie's living room, all white and ocher. Quite pretty actually, even if it's not my taste." Eve prefers the scramble of paisleys and prints, the wild, lush, jungly look. She has two Orientals and Ralph Lauren sheets. "Nona's going," she adds.

"You told me. But I have plans."

"What plans?" Eve asks, suspicious. It isn't like Cassie to have plans, or to be doing the sort of thing she calls *a plan*.

"Listen, can't talk. They're paging me."

Eve hears nothing in the background, no tinny voice on the P.A. intoning *Dr. Morgan! Dr. Morgan!* Is Cassie lying? And to her? Eve whistles down the line, I don't believe you! a violation of trust; but it doesn't matter. Cassie has hung up.

Eve and Cassie are cautious about honesty; even flighty Nona never lies, though she might carve an inch or two off the truth. Without ever discussing it, the three of them provide a safe place for one another. No judgments. Nobody yanking anyone around, yelling *'fess up!*

Of course Cassie isn't juggling lies. But what plans?

Eve phones Nona, who says, "It's a clinic, Eve. Sick people. Some of them bleeding. Oh, my God, can't you just imagine it? Miscarriages. Hemorrhages. I have a customer whose sister almost bled to death before the doctors could do a thing. Not in Magdalene—in a hospital in Chicago. Anyway, that's why Cassie couldn't stay on the phone and explain. I'm just sorry she's not going with us. It will be fun."

Why is Nona so sure she's going to have a good time? Allie is Eve's friend, an acerbic, pinch-faced, narrow blonde who slithers, hungry as a wolf in a fairy tale. Eve almost tells Nona that she won't like Allie; almost, feeling bitchy, starts an argument.

Cassie is right. The party will be a garage sale, women cleaning their closets and tossing out the faded, unwanted relics from a hundred years ago. Why should she pick up any castoff, another woman's reject?

"An investment banker," Nona is promising. "Just too stuffy for me, but nice. Really nice, Eve. I swear on a *Bible*." Nona thinks swearing or crossing her heart will make people believe any words that spill from her mouth.

"Does *nice* mean he has acne scars?" Eve is skeptical of *nice* altogether. *Nice* is what her mother calls someone that even a dead person wouldn't want to spend time with.

"Don't be silly. His complexion is fine."

"Bald then?"

"You said once you liked bald men, that no hair is a sign of virility."

"That's crazy! I never said any such thing!"

"Cross my heart and hope to die, you did. Ask Cassie if you think I'm making it up."

The other line is flashing. "Well, I'm not going to argue with you about it now. I'll see you and Mr. Wall Street Saturday night," Eve says, hanging up. But she doesn't, after all, meet Nona's banker. At the last minute he had to rush out to Tarzana on a prior wife's urgency, leaving Nona without a male as her potluck offering. Can she come alone? she phones Eve to ask. She is plaintive, and Eve, annoyed, finds herself compelled into saying all right, she will square it with Allie.

"The whole purpose of this party is to meet men, not women." Allie breathes fire over the wires. Her anger singes Eve's eyelashes. "We all know too many females as it is."

"The sisters' confederacy," Eve says. "The underground."

"Oh, for Christ's sake, Eve, don't talk gibberish. Women being good to women! As if solidarity is a holy mission. As if any of us really believes in it. You know as well as I do we'd spit and roast one another for a man, money, a promotion."

Eve has never realized how vulgar Allie is, despite her careful lacquering by Elizabeth Arden, her expensive streaking at José Eber's. Chanel suits do not necessarily dress ladies, Eve thinks, recalling that her mother shops at J. C. Penney.

"I agree entirely," Eve says, playing her own softened form of hardball. Silence, she learned during negotiations, is often the most effective weapon. As Eve expects, Allie sputters for another minute but eventually capitulates, though with little grace.

"I'll see you at eight and don't forget the two bottles of champagne I have you down for."

"Of course, darling, whatever you say." But she will have to get a better brand than she originally intended, Eve decides, hoping Nona appreciates what an effort she makes on her behalf.

But Nona doesn't. Her gratitude is lacy; air blows through it. Then, at the party in the hills, above the lights of the city strung out in streamers, Nona, neat in black and pearls, is just too pretty. Allie gushes over Nona's loveliness, Nona a dark angel, breathless, winged with youth.

"She's thirty-nine," Eve counters, for Allie is seething, eager to knife Eve as well as Nona. Nona, less provisional than the other women, draws attention. She tips the party out of kilter.

Eve, who loves Nona, who sees below the surface and isn't daunted by her looks, listens to Allie's mendacious compliments without flinching, just wishing for one man whose eyes are lanterns. She escapes at last to the patio, to be followed by Johnny. Conversation and modulated Gershwin swim behind them. All the shadows are tucked in drawers and folded.

"You're supposed to be back there attracting a female. Maybe two or three. It's why I brought you, remember?"

Johnny is amused. "Don't be mad at me. I didn't do anything."

"I'm not mad at you, just at Allie for being furious with Nona, and Nona because she's beautiful. After this, Allie won't ask me to a funeral. Which shatters my heart, of course."

"She is striking, isn't she?" Johnny says, watching Nona with equanimity, neither drawn nor frightened.

"Go talk to her," Eve orders, hoping suddenly that he won't leave her. Not that she cares if Nona snags Johnny out of this sad group. A covey of insurance brokers, she thinks.

"I want to talk to you."

"We're not supposed to be together. Our lofty purpose is to

meet strangers, to get acquainted with members of the opposite sex whom we don't know."

"So I should find a woman to romance." Johnny laughs. "Even when I was rich and fat I was a disastrous single. Not that I improved with marriages. Then I was just an errant male bedding some female temporarily. In season, you might say."

"What did fat have to do with it?"

"All that weight insulated my feelings. There were miles of subcutaneous tissue between any emotion and the cause or effect. Spongy, greasy walls. Very effective. Even love sank in and got drowned."

"That sounds disgusting," Eve says, but she doesn't back away; she takes the cigarette Johnny offers her. "And too easy." Eve distrusts the less than difficult. "An analyst's drivel." She is try-ing—for no good reason she can immediately think of—to wound Johnny, but he relaxes against the stone railing, keeping his smile, smoking. A goddam movie actor, she thinks, wondering if Johnny would change his stripes, look different in New Hampshire.

"What are you two chattering about out here? Circulate!" Allie, unforgiving, is upon them. Like a drill sergeant she takes Johnny's arm and marches him back inside the house, tugging him onstage as Eve stays behind. At times like this, when she finds all men unappealing, the husbands send out strong signals of memory.

Johnny, retreating, still walks like a fat man, rolling, reminding her of Abramson, so heavy, loose, unconscious of his physical being. Abramson regularly bumped into furniture. He entered the wrong room, forgot why he rose and put himself in motion. Absent-minded and a professor, he was a joke, Eve teased him. And so much younger then, she loved him hopelessly, she remembers. . . .

Her father's steel-edged voice sliced out orders, for her to return home, pick up her education where she had dropped it like a sweater, a glove, a book only partially read, and continue. On his ladder, painting, transforming drab walls, he dreamed dreams for all his daughters and refused, when he had even a partial hold on Eve, to let her go. But Eve, in California, lacked energy those first weeks after Jordan to do more than sit at the edge of the ocean and watch the waves. She was scared. On the sand she sat clutching her knees and imagined that the Pacific spilled on forever because she felt so liquidy herself, without a solid center, dislocated, an orphan washed up on the shore and ready to set sail for nowhere.

Her own body evolving had become the enemy.

Where could she go? Not back east across the continent to the bedroom she once shared with her youngest sister, counting rosebuds on the wallpaper, wishing on a trickle of moonlight through an open summer window.

Once she'd left Jordan, her father insisted Eve was the same girl, though tarnished. She needed polishing, a fresh coat of glossy enamel. He yelled, "It's over! I forgive you! Come home. Forget the whole business." As if she could. Her father never understood that the past was a commitment. Even before Abramson, before the books he assigned, Eve knew there was no returning. If time is a river she was too poor a swimmer to struggle her way back upstream.

When Eve tried to explain, her father interrupted: "I'll send you a ticket."

"That's not what I mean."

Time, whether endless or stoppable, wasn't—however else it might be defined—reversible.

Eve's mother, listening in on the extension to protracted negotiations that would breed no profitable deal, interjecting her *oh, my dears* and questions about what Eve was eating, finally, in secret and despair, sent five hundred dollars to General Delivery. It arrived just at the last minute, with Eve a week behind on the rent for her one-room-no-cooking. After that she cadged a job in a Greek restaurant, where the owner, a Minoan bull, wore the help out with his complaints and ill will.

Those were the worst months, fragments of her life that needed burying like dead bones, as Eve, learning obstinacy, shied from regret. After her three days in the hospital she quit by phone and found another job in a different restaurant, this one farther east and with a tonier clientele.

For a long while—a year, two, even three—she couldn't decide whom she hated more, herself or Jordan.

In one way her father's determination wore her down, however. She enrolled in college to finish her degree at night. There she met Abramson teaching American literature.

If Southwest College had a star it was the bear, with his slouch and ruffled gray hair, puffy cheeks, nose like a squash blossom. He dripped ashes on his vest from the cigarette welded between his lips, had a stomach that strained buttons. The writer when in his twenties of a well-received novel, author of slender, elegantly designed short stories that seemed to have come out of a leaner man, a geometric mind (not his mind at all), Abramson groped along the halls. His head, some student said of him, was full of images. Later Eve learned it was words like fireballs that kept Abramson occupied. He loved the sounds they made, alone or bumping into each other.

Eve took every course Abramson taught, until even he admitted she looked familiar. "Where do I know you from? Twentieth Century? The Naturalists? Pound and Eliot?" he asked one day when they were in line at the cafeteria.

"Do you remember me?" she teased him later when he appeared at the breakfast table after his shower, a book already open in his hand.

"Of course I do. You're Isabel Archer, aren't you?" Abramson also possessed a sense of humor. Besides, he'd say, "I'm not so vacant."

"Oh, not vacant, only in another world—worlds. With your words, stories, those people you create."

But he wondered himself if it was creation. Was he a minor god in California, lost years ago from the Bronx, spinning tales of lives with a magician's skill? "Maybe," he said, "it's only remembering . . . ."

"Not you, who can't get the groceries straight!" She loved him so much her heart threatened to jolt off its moorings.

". . . and it's all there, everything, just waiting. What I put down might be revealed rather than made up, thought up, worried over like a father and his unborn children. It feels like that sometimes."

"Maybe you're a conduit."

"Maybe."

All this was when they finally married. Beauty and the beast, Eve heard it was whispered of them, though she was no real beauty and Abramson, shaggy and ill-kempt as a child's pony, was no beast.

"Why did you notice me?" Eve asked him once.

Abramson, awkward with deceit, replied honestly: "I don't know. You were just there and so persistent." Then even he realized this was no answer to give a wife. "You're lovely to look at. I liked your face. I picked up magic in your nearness," he said, paraphrasing Pound.

And of course Eve pursued him. Shamelessly. Thirty years her senior—not even twenty, which would at least have been reasonable—he reminded her not at all of her father. And certainly Abramson bore no resemblance to Jordan, but symbolized instead—shambling, loose, overweight—a solidness. A Stonehenge monolith, something that couldn't be battered either by time or the exigencies of life. Abramson was no fool. He considered.

"But I never considered you," he said with some surprise the first time they were together in bed. "You simply are and so am I. Wanting, lust, attraction, need, desire." He tasted the last as he looked in her eyes. "I swim in you," he said, with more than a little apprehension.

Earlier, Abramson struggled against Eve's efforts. "I'm married. I don't have affairs. Lustful romping with students is *de rigueur* for professors, I know. But not for me. Truthfully, Eve, I seldom find younger women attractive. They're too dewy. They lack weight."

"What about me?" she said, knowing already but worrying she didn't.

"You're different," he groaned and she exulted, realizing she had netted him. Still her pursuit was urgent. Chasing him, she walked barefoot over hot coals. She waited after class, strolled innocently beside him to his car, or sometimes slyly drew him along the parking lot to hers. She bombarded him with questions about Faulkner, Lowell, Bellow, Dreiser, Hart Crane riding subways. She worked his knowledge like a miner a mother lode. Some nights, when she was bone weary in her bed, alone, counting the dollars she had in the bank, charting up her memories as if for an autobiography, her flesh felt cold. She wanted Abramson for—among other things—his warmth, and supposed she would be safe with the bear through a lifetime of winters.

During an unprecedented May rainstorm, when the drains flooded and the streets about Southwest were rivery, she cajoled Abramson into taking her out for dinner. They drove warily to a nearby restaurant, a small Italian café in a mini-mall. The lights were low and upon checkered tablecloths empty Chianti bottles sprouted dripping candles. It was just the sort of clichéd romantic place Eve might have dreamed up and took the luck as an omen. "Fate," she pointed out to Abramson, who dried his face with a paper napkin.

"My dear, what do you want?" He cleaned rain spots off his glasses with a corner of the tablecloth. His eyes were owlish, soft brown and remarkably lacking in the knowing glaze of experience. His eyes were a young boy's, prettier even than Jordan's.

"To love you," Eve said simply.

"I don't understand." He returned his glasses to the bridge of his nose, but no longer seemed so professorial. A young lover slept buried in Abramson's bulk. "There are more appropriate men all over campus, all over Los Angeles. And if you don't want a student, if you must have an academician, well, what about Ed Furst? He's single and in his thirties. A good catch, Ed. Or the new man in history, what's his name? Stenson, I think. He can't be forty. And isn't one of the philosophy people divorced? But Furst is my recommendation. My wife and I had him to dinner last week. He's looking for a woman; he told us so."

"Abramson, you're a fool." Eve laughed, watching him wiggle. Where had she gotten this strength with a man? Surely nothing in her experience with Jordan trained her to be so determined. It had to be love, she was certain, a new love, love in a different dimension. "Abramson," she said, taking his hand, "it's you."

"How do you know?" In spite of his uneasiness curiosity gripped him.

"Gut instinct. My bones tell me Lady Brett and Jake Barnes."

Abramson roared. "My God! I hope not!"

After that the seduction was easier, though she still needed to tug him, cajole him, make him outrageous romantic promises. "I'll love you forever."

Primly he lectured: "Love is always forever in the beginning. And I don't want forever, Eve. I have a wife, a home. Grown children. I have a leather chair in my study and worn, comfortable slippers. The only imaginary journeying I indulge myself with is on paper." Yet in his car, kissing her, he gasped, "You'll drive me mad, you know."

She hadn't thought she could claim him for the ordinary Sunday afternoons, holiday dinners, the quiet moments that compound normal living. He wouldn't go that far; he said so.

"We married at twenty-one and what would life be like without her? I can't conjure that reality, not even for you, my dear."

Another time he confessed, "So much is habit. We bend toward and away from each other like dancers. She needs me too, of course, and that's habit also."

Eve took Abramson off one day, up the coast to a solitary beach scalloped by rocks, cliffs straining behind them high as skyscrapers. She called in sick; he canceled his one afternoon class.

He hummed with courage over playing hooky. "I feel like a kidnap victim," he joked.

She knew him well enough by then to say, "Well you're a participating victim. So don't protest so much."

"Like the lady? Role reversal?" he asked, but his hand was on her leg.

Abramson was loosening up, enjoying sex, love, her, romance. For a second on the coast road Eve wondered what she was doing to this man. *Her* courage flagged.

When starting school she had vowed to have goals, as her father loudly shouted from New Hampshire. Keep an end in view! Know how things will turn out, how you want them to! Don't make foolish choices and let yourself be buffeted around! Which translated to: Literature is fine but get a degree in business. For once, Eve listened.

In the cove she chose for her middle-aged lover, they picnicked in the company of nervous gulls and spindly sandpipers. The sea crashed farther out, on a sharp promontory of rock, but reached shore tamed, and Abramson, his pant legs rolled, waded.

"I was hopeless in sports, as you might suspect," he confided. "I sank, tripped, stumbled, fell over my dangling shoelaces, dropped every ball anyone unwisely threw me. For years I pretended such physical ineptitude was related to being an intellectual. Or to being a Jew, for that matter. Who ever heard of a famous Jewish athlete besides Max Baer or Hank Greenberg? And they were aberrations, the examples to prove the rule."

Eve could tell Abramson of Sandy Koufax, like Abramson dragging five thousand years of history, and still on the pitcher's mound a knight in shining armor, but she loved her professor's confusion. His sadness quickened her. She laughed at his mournful look and told him instead: "You're a champ in the only sport that counts with women." And she pulled him down into the surf, feebly protesting, the foamy edge of water lapping them. She rucked up her dress. "Love me, Abramson, right here." He discovered her bare, waiting, and moaned like the sea in the wind.

"We're getting wet," he whispered over the pounding, but did love her, vigorously. The sand created fretwork on their bare skin and as the sky clouded up, the magnesium-colored sea washed them clean.

Even after such love they mightn't have married but for Abramson's wife. He knew her so little. Her quietness worked between them like a wedge of wood, leaving splinters. "I despise myself," Abramson cried after her death.

So did Eve, or herself seeing the woman in flickering shades, blurry, transparent, the light passing through her. In the house where Eve and Abramson lived after their marriage, the wife was still a tenant. She presented to Eve the face of a woman betrayed and with her chilled ubiquity caused unwanted tears.

"It's cold out here," Nona says.

Eve, wrenched away from memories, flails and comes around, striking against Nona's shoulder. "Don't sneak up on me like that!"

"I'm sorry, but I walked straight toward you, out the door. See, it's still open. Eve?"

"Let's go. This party is terrible. Drones and salesmen. Boring people. Even the women. Smiling. Ghosts. It's incredible. I don't know why we came in the first place."

Eve talks too quickly, the words unstoppable, while all the while she is remembering Abramson, how soft his mouth was. She wants desperately, just once more, to kiss him.

"Eve?"

Eve brushes by Nona. She has the urgency of a woman in flight, but gets no farther than the dining room when a man halts her. "Have you tried the duck pâté? Here, you must." And he hands her a cracker with a sample.

6

Lorraine surprises Nona.

In Flora's, Lorraine, as reed-thin as Nona but of harder construction, her bones as prominent as copper tubing, cuts with the sharp edge of polished metal. Her professional demeanor has no froth in it. Deadpan and humorless, she never enthuses or bubbles when selling. She often intimidates customers just as she does Nona, so that when she praises, the women feel absurdly privileged. Reliable with inventory, with placing precise orders, her taste, though severe, is exemplary. If she lacks imagination and won't, for instance, think to mate silk with denim, she has style and an unerring eye for accessories.

Nona wonders about her private life and, looking at her, often supposes that making love she bruises her George rather than pleases him. But there is no question that Lorraine satisfies herself, whatever else she does. The universe rotates about Lorraine, the epicenter, and weather changes she hasn't mandated infuriate her.

The crash was therefore bound to have Lorraine thinking she had been deliberately inconvenienced. That reaction Nona expected, but Lorraine shocks her when, with a red flush of embarrassment highlighting the small acne scars not completely submerged under her makeup, she asks almost angrily, "Will you come with me? Of course I'm not afraid to go myself. Why should I be? I didn't hit anybody. It wasn't my fault. But it's smart to be careful with lawyers."

Nona never accepts lawyers so calmly herself, not after all those months of lawyers coming and going almost on the hour, passing grim-faced under the foyer's crystal chandelier. At first saviors, dark, double-breasted heroes, dour defenders with clipped protests and complicated legalities, in time they came to seem to Nona nothing more than paper people, apologizers. Their efforts had the weight of mist. Even so, they claimed great amounts of money, more in fact than anyone possessed, certainly not her father, who had amassed much less than his enemies maintained and had spent most of that.

The lawyers disappointed because Nona put such faith in their arrogant declarations. They had the authority of Episcopalian ministers, school principals, men who, like her father, held patents on the truth. Nona believed they would keep their promises, but as the trial dragged on, their voices grew faint until they mouthed only whispers. In the end, destabilized, they slunk off into the shadows, washing their hands of her ruined father, gray and anonymous, behind bars.

"Sure I'll go with you," Nona agreed.

"George would come but driving from the Valley in his condition is *not* easy." Lorraine reminds Nona she is only a stand-in.

"Won't he have to give a deposition?"

Lorraine's eyes crinkle with suspicion. "What do you know about depositions?"

Nona hangs a necklace of gold coins on the window mannequin. "Six-thirty?" Nona asks.

"As soon as we can get downtown from here."

"The traffic on the freeway will be awful."

"I've had enough of freeways for the moment, thank you." The accident occurred on the San Diego, and Lorraine spreads blame to everyone except herself behind the wheel. "We'll take surface streets." And take forever, Nona thinks, but doesn't argue, Lorraine saying, "At least we'll get some money out of this mess. We better." She sounds dangerous and Nona feels a shaft of pity for the unknown lawyer. "The inconvenience alone is worth a few hundred thousand, never mind the medical bills. George's leg snapped like a dead branch on impact. He is out of work for months, and what about the wedding?" Lorraine asks, as if Nona has an answer.

Nona dislikes the mauve wool skirt with the striped Vittadini blouse on the mannequin and wonders how Lorraine will take her changing it for a pink-toned sweater. Now, however, isn't the time to ask. "Even with his leg in a cast George can get married," she says soothingly.

Lorraine inflates like a puff adder. "Do you think I want to traipse down the aisle with a man *riding*!"

"Riding? Oh, you mean in a wheelchair."

"Or hobbling along on crutches! God!" The thought obviously brings Lorraine pain. She leaves Nona in the window, tossing back, "Fix those earrings. They're lying around like chunks of glass." The earrings *are* chunks of glass, rhinestone and too heavy for the rest of a tailored display.

Lorraine leans against the counter smoking a cigarette, which she shouldn't be doing in the store. "If I change the date, then we're into fall or, damn, winter."

Nona, forming a half-circle with the three pairs of earrings, calls, "What's wrong with fall? Lots of people get married in the fall and especially around Christmas."

"Chiffon will be all wrong. That's what. I'll need something heavier. Maybe a moiré." Lorraine has opted for the nontraditional, rejecting as ordinary the usual white, tulle, seed pearls, train, and veil. "Ricardo has nothing just right in his fall line, which means I'll have to tap another house. Ratty Ricardo will grab the chiffon back, too, if I don't wear it—never mind that I've given him orders season after season when he wasn't selling a button."

From inside Flora's the earrings look fine. Before Nona goes out to check the window browser's view she says, "Give it back then. You won't need it."

Lorraine screeches, "Honestly, Nona!"

Honestly what? Honesty has nothing to do with this as far as Nona can see, since Lorraine is pressuring Ricardo into handing her a dress for free. The Laguna owners will be very displeased if they ever find out. Honesty? Lorraine's wedding deal is simple extortion.

"I am just so mad I could scream!" Lorraine cries, actually clutching fistfuls of her straight hair, which never holds a curl without being permed. She has been threatening to howl her head off since the day after the three-car smack-up—from which she emerged unscathed—and in the smooth informality of the lawyer's beige office voices her displeasure. Nona thinks she should be grateful that she drove in and out of disaster without smudging her makeup, but Lorraine doesn't see it that way. The accident ruined her timetable, she explains to the lawyer, who takes notes on a yellow legal pad.

"And you were a passenger, Miss—?"

"No, she wasn't. Nona's just here because we're going out afterward," Lorraine lies, easily too, stylishly offhand with the truth. She determines to hide her apprehension. "A dinner party," she adds, elaborating. With her legs uncrossed, jammed together, and white-knuckled hands tightly clasped in her lap, Lorraine shrinks to a delinquent student in the school office.

"Lorraine and I work together," Nona volunteers, solemn, not venturing a smile, though under other circumstances she would light up for this man across the desk from her. He is handsome, resembling an actor in a computer commercial she's seen on every network the last few weeks.

The lawyer's heavy-lidded brown eyes stare at her, not as if she is on the stand but not as if she's off it either. Nona—whose legs *are* crossed—nervously swings a foot, and the strap on her Ferragamo sling-back slips off. Before they leave she will have to lean down and ungracefully fix it.

"Not together exactly. I mentioned, didn't I, that I'm the manager of Flora's in the Crystal Mall? Nona works for me. She's my assistant." Even self-absorbed, Lorraine notices the attorney's interest and resents it.

Not amused at Lorraine's belittling her, particularly since she is doing her a favor, Nona counters, "Assistant manager."

The eye contact dissolves rather than snapping off abruptly, and Alan Stevens returns to his note taking. Nona follows his hand moving across the pad.

The lawyer hasn't done anything untoward, only looked at her as men have been doing all her life, but the square chin with a dimple in it, the way his hair fits his skull like a cap, the downward slant to his eyes, distract her. Without saying a word he sets her to imagining a beach at dawn, the pearly abalone pink of sunrise.

After he extracts from Lorraine everything she is going to tell him, he stands, shakes hands with both women, but keeps Nona's two beats longer. He repeats her name as if to avoid forgetting it.

Descending in the elevator, Nona, the firm pressure of his fingers lingering, and the tiding of attraction like wings in her chest, says, "He was very nice."

Lorraine rolls her eyes. "Oh, you think everybody's nice! You'd probably coo at Herman the handyman if he was in here with us!" She is angry at Nona, and Nona can't think why. Maybe she should listen to Eve, who says *Don't always be so helpful.*

———

But Nona was brought up to be nice, sweet as spun sugar. She was so often ornamental, her parents' little jewel.

What a darling! How precious! their friends would exclaim as she moved in careful princess steps down one side of the refectory dining table. Hands floated out to touch her curls. Lips soft as crushed velvet brushed her cheeks. Warm, moist breath whispered like the frailest cobwebs. The women smelled musky. Mysterious aromas drifted up from between their breasts. The men laughed and joked as she passed their chairs. Some—usually the ones who laughed the loudest—had funny eyes.

All those nights when she was kept up past her bedtime, dressed as elaborately as any of her parents' guests, curtsying first, then sent in a lonely walk along the table, she glanced from the florid faces to her father. Her mother sat at the opposite end, near the sliding doors, and after she gave permission with a slight nod of her lacquered curls, Nona started for *him*. He sat, commanding the head of the table, a large man in white and black. When Nona reached his chair, one terrible moment lasted forever while, her heart pounding, he decided whether to accept her. Had she done well enough with the smiling women and the men whose hands avoided her, but whose touch she later took into dreaming? Only her father could pass judgment.

Each time she was afraid she failed him, and as she waited, solemn as a painted infanta, she struggled with tears, sure he planned to withhold his pleasure. But just when she expected banishment, or words of censure, he relented with a roar of laughter and kissed her.

The frightening smell of whiskey clouded his breath, yet her father's kiss was the sweetest she remembered.

Nona's return trip on dinner party nights went swiftly. She skipped in triumph even as the women closed in on her. Inevitably one caught Nona, holding her too close and squeezing. Nona, hurrying, wanting to be back upstairs, felt suffocated.

She remembers those parties so vividly, even on days when her entire childhood eddies away in a maelstrom of forgetfulness, as if those years lie shipwrecked on the sea's sandy bottom. She remembers the light splintering from the tinkly chandeliers high overhead like crystal stars, and the women, creatures under glass, exotic aquarium beings, glittery with jewels, sequins, ornaments crested in their hair. Their wet lips shone and they had her mother's identical mandarin nails. When Nona was at her littlest—before she knew how they meant to smother her, to draw out something from her to themselves—she wanted to climb onto the taffeta laps, to push against the crisp bosoms and bone ridges of what they wore under the shimmery dresses to the flesh beneath. Under their clothes they smelled of cinnamon.

She remembered the men, black as night rivers, with white snowy shirtfronts. How big they loomed, though still not as huge as her father. If those giants leaned near they exuded wintry odors, minty, cucumber scents, but they warmed her skin rather than chilled it. Even when she was very little their glances stroked her with fire.

Nona must have been two or three when they first started showing her off at their dinners, her pale cameo face, ebony ringlets, offered as entertainment before the soup.

Her mother kept a silver bell beside her plate which when shaken tinkled like a wind chime. Outside the closed dining room doors Nona waited with her nurse, Nanny fussing with the lace collar of the black velvet dress, licking a finger and smoothing it over Nona's brows, checking her one last time. And then they heard the importunate bell, straightened up quickly for Nanny to slide the doors aside as the lingering ping set off reverberations in Nona's tummy. The same tone unexpectedly heard years afterward froze Nona mid-step and set the memories cascading like an earth slide.

Eventually Nona was granted her own place at that table, and a child's ghost, the sound of Mary Janes tapping faintly on parquet, iced the air as her mother rang for the maid. Once she had a plate, silverware, glasses for wine and water, the table shrank, no longer the length of a Boston block. No jewels lay scattered amid the candlesticks and bowls of flowers. The women lost their silvery sheen; the men blew up like balloons, stuffed geese pouched and wrinkled. But what never changed was how her father watched her. He had the unremitting eyes of an eagle, eyes that reminded her of their secrets and how she loved him.

Adam's girl, they all called her. She was Adam's girl.

The memories, as always, catch her unprepared, slip a chain about her heart and trip her up. Effortlessly she revolves into the past, crossing the foyer from the dining room on rainy Sundays to her father calling from his study as her mother napped upstairs. Dusty voices, thirty-five-year-old laughter, stilted motions of the dead soft as leaves breaking loose and falling, unknown hands raising wine to mouths never seen again, carry the cargo of the past on a flood into the present.

Nothing seems to happen in her life. All her romances start off on a high note and then quickly descend into nowhere. When she has a romance at all, for most of the men she wishes for are either disappointingly gay, or like Lorraine's lawyer, married. So she is both surprised and pleased when Alan Stevens calls to invite her out for lunch at a dimly lit and very elegant restaurant owned by a graduate of Ma Maison. Guiltily her heart pounds, and though she knows she shouldn't say yes, she agrees with a dry mouth and a husky voice.

Of course she must pretend to Lorraine that she has a medical appointment, some tests suggested by Dr. Rubin. Lorraine, who is forever accusing Nona of being a hypochondriac, holds her tongue, however, for she owes Nona. Now the delicate balance in Flora's teeters back into equilibrium. Debts paid. After this Nona will have to be sick on her own time, but driving over to meet the lawyer on whose desk sit wife and children in silver frames, she feels light-headed, free as a girl.

Shafts of muted light from the wall sconces strike the pale-gold Pouilly Fuissé Alan has ordered. In a high-backed chair, sequestering himself as if sitting for the defense in court, he sips, eyes nearly closed. Satisfied, he nods at the waiter to pour. Then, lightly clicking his glass to hers, he says, "To a very attractive woman. No, not attractive. *Beautiful* is the word. That face . . ." His manner is precise, as trim and neat as his well-tailored suit. He is a man who, with judicious skill, promises clarification of the complicated. Across the table, Nona relaxes, despite Alan's being an attorney.

In his continued contemplation of her he thrusts his dimpled chin forward. She likes his eyes, sleepier than they appeared in his office. She likes his mouth, too, plump lips almost womanish, and his ears, high up on his skull and small. She decides he doesn't look like the actor in the commercial but more like Kurt Russell, only not as soft.

Slowly he draws her downward in the eddy of his compliments, and Nona offers no resistance. She floats as though an inch or two off the velvet cushioned chair. In the hush of the expensive French restaurant he might as well have already taken her to bed.

Often enough men praise her. Men are verbal jugglers; they toss words into the air like oranges. They might say anything—and not only, as she had been warned when younger, to entice a girl into sexual submission. They create worlds that never existed—hadn't her father?—and live lives that appear intentional but are as tenuous as kites lofting on the wind. Nona's knowledge of men, if she should ever join the separate experiences into one continuous whole, is considerable. But between not listening, and hearing only what she wants to, she misses entirely Alan's bewilderment. How can she do this to him! *This* means attract him so. She seduces him by doing nothing more than just being Nona, but still he blames her. His back up, his shoulders squared, he judges her delinquent.

Naturally Nona falls in love with him before the pear Hélène. Her penchant for loving is as instinctual as the sexy pelvic thrust when she walks.

That night she equivocates to the disapproving woman in the mirror: "I won't do anything. I'll be quiet about it. I have no intention of going out with him again if he calls." The reflection spins worry lines deep as rivers. They both know, Nona and her other, that Alan is married, has children. They remember Cassie and unfaithful Doug. "I am totally different from that awful Tracy!" she swears into eyes darkened by such lying, and two nights later goes to dinner with Alan when his wife supposes him at a Bar Association meeting.

After the wine—Château Margaux '68—is poured, he reaches across the irises and with a manicured nail traces her cheekbones. "So beautiful," he murmurs. And, "I'll never get divorced. Divorce isn't expedient." To a Nona barely breathing, he continues: "I have a good life. My boys are terrific. There's talk, too, of my running for the State Assembly in the next election. California's a community property state," he says, as if she demands these reasons he recites like rosary beads.

His summation of the situation is flawless, but Nona slumbers, a princess dreaming, always in suspended animation until a man—now this Alan—kisses her. Besides, she reads his eyes, which tell a different story. In his eyes she sees waking at three in the morning for love, beaches and palm trees, sunset and the two of them walking side by side.

Nona knits a lacy weave of romance and ignores that Alan speaks not of love but of pleasure.

She made vows to the mirror and refused over candlelight to

remember them. Having sworn she won't, Nona, a little while later, allows Alan to go home with her.

Subsequently Nona holds Lorraine responsible, smiling warmly at her manager, who is the most unlikely of cupids. Not that Nona so much as whispers a word of this new love to Lorraine, who would slit her wrists. And Lorraine is such a snake, capable of phoning Alan's wife or complaining to the owners that Nona engages in unbecoming conduct. Of course even a word of reproach to either Leonard Simpson or Howard Tully will be useless, since Leonard once put his hand on Nona's arm and suggested they might have dinner one night, and Howard gazes at her from piglet eyes with the hunger of a starving adolescent. It doesn't matter to either owner that they have wives and children down in Laguna.

Adultery as sin. Ridiculous in the twentieth century. Eve says so to Cassie on the phone one night. "It's not as though she's taken up bank robbing or shoplifting. Married men might be stupid but not illegal."

"That's probably how Tracy excused swooping down on Doug."

Eve, trapped into defending Nona, whom personally she considers an empty-headed fool in dangerous waters and no more in love than a concrete pillar, says, "It's a whim, a three-day wonder. Romantic glances, a dozen roses, the usual shit. You know."

"I don't. The only married man I was ever involved with was my husband."

"Don't drag in your own garbage, Cass. This is Nona, not Tracy, and some lawyer named Alan who will probably be old news in a couple of weeks. Besides, maybe his marriage is a bombed-out waste, one step from the drawing up of papers. Or she might be an invalid, unable to perform and feeling guilty."

"What hot air! And even if there are any of your *valid* reasons, I'll be drawn and quartered before I'll excuse some man of cheating. Besides, think of Nona. She always gets clobbered. He'll make elaborate promises, give her a few off hours, let her sit home on New Year's Eve, and then eventually fling himself back into Mrs. Alan's warm arms. Profoundly regretful, of course. What will Nona have then? Maybe a silver necklace—gold if he's generous."

Cassie switches back and forth between anger and worry. Nona will be damned if she gets her man and equally damned if she doesn't.

Eve has her own guilt to contend with, an adultery she passed off as love because that's what it was. Things change; people change, she could tell Cassie. Men lose their step, walk off cliffs, stumble in the explosion of passion. Just like Doug Morgan, whom Eve loathes and whom she understands.

Cassie, however, has a black-and-white view of the world. She knows right from wrong and makes no exceptions. What, Eve wonders, listening, would she have said about Abramson, so unlikely a sinner, a man trapped out of his house and in a forest?

"You're a cynic," Eve says when Cassie pauses.

"It's about time, wouldn't you say?"

They breathe at each other, Eve trying to think how to talk normally even-tempered Cassie to safe ground from her indignation. "Well, this Alan's better than Nona's friendly afternoon pervert, a real cut above that sort of freak, even if he comes with wedding ring and children."

Eve turns a bracelet of gold links around and around on her wrist—the circle complete, neither beginning nor ending—annoyed with Cassie, annoyed more with Nona for not being properly secretive. Why did she have to babble about her infatuation? But Eve knows why. Men can keep love quiet, but for women, feelings need articulation or they aren't real.

"That's not funny," Cassie is saying. Does she sound a little mollified?

"Just let her do her thing, Cass, and don't get involved. Next week, next month, it will be somebody else."

"Who? Another married man? Oh, Eve, why? She's so beautiful and sweet."

"And sometimes she acts like Edith Bunker—forget being needy as a one-year-old. Looks! I'm so tired of looks! What do you think, that beauty entitles Nona to life as Cinderella?"

"She's got a good job, Eve, so stop acting as though she's Miss America."

"I never said she was a femme fatale unable to earn a living, but all this whining about how terrific Nona looks, the exquisite Miss Dixon, sets my teeth on edge." She thinks Cassie will accuse her of being envious, and she isn't, for Nona's beauty comes with too much fragility. She is a Ming vase vulnerable to shattering.

But if Eve isn't jealous, Cassie occasionally catches herself wishing for Nona's beauty, some feature of it anyway—the large, luminous eyes, the generous mouth. Though she has accommodated to her own square face with its imperfections, her eyes of forgettable color, ever since medical school, when the interior landscape of anybody took precedence over the outer, Cassie, given the choice, enjoys gazing at Nona more than at herself. She's learned to accept that, at first glance, she never startles anyone. Cassie takes getting used to. But since Doug—who swore her face entranced him—exited so jarringly from her life, Cassie would prefer, if only marginally, to be exceptional. For protection, she supposes, as if beauty provides insulation against the cold drafts of rejection, as if Nona's beauty hasn't undermined and trapped her. Beauty never guarantees freedom and Cassie knows this but wants to believe that it does.

She's the opposite side of town from Tracy, a woman, not a girl, and I have no right to identify with this lawyer's wife, Cassie whispers to herself. Lying back on the bed she monitors her breathing, in, out, in, out, chasing off thoughts of Nona's newest infatuation, her perfidy, and stares up at a map of cracks in the ceiling.

This house is old, or old for California, and needs painting. When was the furniture last gathered together in the middle of the rooms, huddled under dropcloths like hiding children? In that frenzy of redecorating, which struck like a storm, she had meant to paint then. But the weather tempered. She hadn't the energy. Grief was weakening and she managed nothing beyond the lonely living room couch.

Looking up, Cassie wonders how many millions of women have spent how many millions of hours staring at ceilings as if they were television screens and important scenes from their lives were being drawn in a confluence of lines and cracks.

She follows the cracks to an embryo, then to a chambered heart with veins and arteries leading nowhere. She traces roads out of Southern California to foreign territory, but disappointingly the longest meandering line travels around on itself.

Soon she will have to commission a paint job and maybe new plaster. The earth so near the coast shifts constantly, gentle shudders, like the final tremors of lovemaking, unsettling it. The house's foundation is just microscopically off. Cassie fantasizes a tilt to her bones, medically impossible.

Oh, why isn't she simply an M.D., the perfect scientific machine, more like Jena with her total devotion to the uteruses and ovaries of other women rather than her own! Why does she have an imagination, needs, the desires of a lonely woman aging, withering! Why is she becoming an old house herself, cracking, peeling!

An old house . . . Old bones . . .

On Saturday night in Santa Monica, on the way to Malone's, she drives by the Victorian. It is already dark, the streetlamps throw shallow puddles of light, and all she sees is the large, dilapidated building. Where had the workmen found the dead bodies? Reading the article, Cassie thought the house had been leveled, the concrete torn up, and there in the earth a treasure trove of brittle femurs and tibias, ulnas, clavicles, bare skulls, and naked phalanges without their fleshy gloves. But the front of the house stands upright like a movie flat, with the sides clawed in jagged slates.

She doesn't go out of her way to see the house, but it isn't necessary to take this street either. She hadn't planned to drive by and gawk with ghoulish interest at the unlikely burial ground, imagining the crowds pressing against the wooden sawhorses, and black zipper bags being loaded into an ambulance. Of course now the girls are long gone, over to the morgue, and no curious throngs mill on the sidewalk. Nothing remains, not even the flickering red lights. The girls' retrieval seems a second death.

How perishable they all are, every living soul of them, even the ones she labors over, even her friends, Mandy, herself. In the clinic, try hard as she can, she only stalls time. The years granted, in the history of the universe, are brief as seconds.

I'm forty-four and lonely. . . .

Night thickens and Cassie starts off again, driving at a steady twenty-five—the speed limit in residential neighborhoods—to hear Jake the gardener play his music.

She doesn't come to music naturally but rather in a side shuffle. During high school when the phonograph played nonstop, songs slid off the charts and evaporated from her memory except for the bone-shattering, foot-stomping, heartbeat-synchronized rhythms like the Twist. Listening in her car, or alone at night while doing up reports, she enjoys, for example, Handel's *Concerto Grosso*, but the next time she hears the Handel it is unrecognizable. She possesses no aural recall, has less hold on music than on water. But she likes it, that much is true. She isn't sunk in a sealed cavern, deaf by choice. She deplores, however, loud, clamorous noise, the disharmonious sounds, the clashing, clanging fury of angry, sweaty boys boiling from the radio like molten lava before she quickly switches stations, or the kind that thunders across the hedges from the Levinsons' when Tony is at home. That music drives iron prongs into her brain.

It is all a matter of generations, Mandy tells Cassie. Cassie wonders and asks April, who though a mother is still a child with braids, tank tops, popsicle-colored stretch pants, how she feels about hard rock. April scrunches up her face and reels off her particular choices, all popular love songs. The groups whose renditions touch her include, surprisingly, some Cassie relates to, like the Beach Boys.

Jake's music comes from a different angle altogether. It is an eclectic mix with echoes of Hank Williams, Woody Guthrie, Muddy Waters. The songs shimmer, with a sad, antique feel to them. A few Jake plays alone, crouched over the guitar that lies across his legs like the recumbent body of a lover. For others he is smoothly joined by the elderly black piano player, or the fat, rowdy-looking youth on the cornet at his elbow, and the clarinetist slim and silvery as his instrument.

The scattering of couples, the women white- or gray-haired and rouged, the men chicken-necked and balding, a few younger romantics holding hands, the dancers cheek-to-cheek on the tiny scuffed floor, are appreciative. A collection of late teenagers, dressed as conservatively as fundamentalist Baptists on Sunday morning, are especially intent, seldom even raising their glasses while Jake plays, and then with subtle, silent gestures. But the loners by the bar hunch their backs to the music, undaunted by a melodic accompaniment to their drinking. In seedy Malone's, years of long nights and just as long afternoons paint the walls with layers of grime and ancient cigarette smoke. The dim photographs of forgotten men draping their arms around one another's shoulders are muddy, and clouded eyes stare blindly at the musicians.

In the old Irish pub, with a tattered green banner strung from the ceiling, the music is incidental, the misplaced sadness of another world entirely.

Cassie, neither of the drinkers nor the couples at their tables, sits at the bar, discomfited by being unaccompanied, the recipient of sidelong glances. She arrives just as Jake begins something called "Will The Circle Be Unbroken?" and is so nervous she misses the words along with whatever artistry details his playing. After the applause, however, he hushes the crowd with a heartbreaker. "This world is not my home," he sings in a gravelly baritone that makes Cassie think he sings directly to her. The lighting in Malone's is even. No spots illuminate the slightly raised platform. So it is possible that he sees her, but though she hopes, she can't tell, for there is too much distance between them.

The set ends abruptly, the piano player leaning to the mike to say, "We're taking ourselves some drinking time now, but we'll be back." They break apart then, no longer the group that captured individual notes and wove them into a whole.

Cassie's shoulders tense. What if he doesn't come over? Surely he has friends here. He'll stop at a table, sit down, have a beer. He never said she should expect attention. But laying the guitar down carefully, he jumps off the stage and makes his way straight through the room to her. Cassie turns around so that he won't think she's expecting him.

"How's it going?" He slips between Cassie and the rumpled jacket of an old man on the next stool. "A Corona," he calls out to the bartender.

The metallic taste of nervousness in her mouth, Cassie says, "I like your music."

Under the artificial lights his darkness deepens. He reminds Cassie of boys back home, the ones over by the mill, the ones always more knowing, older somehow than she could ever be, strutting in tight jeans, wise with secrets. "It's okay." He shrugs, finally looking directly at her when he has the bottle to his mouth.

"I never expected you to sing, for some reason. The songs are wonderful. Are they yours?"

He laughs. "No, I didn't write them. Other people did—better musicians than I'll ever be." He is matter-of-fact, but pleased by her compliment.

It is suddenly important to convince Jake that his music didn't wash over her, accidental sounds, but she fumbles her praise until the words dry up on her tongue. "Well, I like the way you play and sing." She lamely repeats herself.

He smiles and for the first time his eyes are involved. "Thanks," he says, and Cassie hears Nona lilting about some guy, *so gorgeous he was to die!* and feels that way now as their glances lock. Heat brews between them while strange voices ebb and flow, hitting high peaks of laughter, isolated words. "Another." "Wouldn't you—" "But, Sal!" "Oh, how could he!" "Damn it all!" "Sal, don't!" "Three Feathers—" "Over here." Cassie listens intently, trying to escape the hold Jake has on her. How did other women, the Eves and Nonas of the world, do this so effortlessly, at night and with men they barely know? Next to them, and beside this Jake, she is such a girl. Her heart's dislocation is making her sweat.

"Another beer?" he asks, signaling for the bartender.

The faded eagle flies out from under his sleeve. "Where did you get the tattoo?" She resists the impulse to trace the surprisingly delicate blue wings.

"In Vietnam."

Of course. The war, the stain of their generation, the cancer that consumed their youth. The war was why she and Doug rushed into marriage, why he went off to law school. *I love you*, he said, wanting to stay out of Southeast Asia. But they both behaved honorably, signing petitions, marching on hot afternoons. Cassie rushed from the freezing anatomy lab, from dismembered bodies, lifeless flesh clamped open, to the sweaty euphoria of protest. From the quiet rite of dissecting the dead, she threw herself into the turmoil of saving the living. Once she walked for miles holding up a photograph of a bayoneted baby until the pain in her arms squeezed out a scream with the slogans, and then she stopped feeling her arms altogether.

They're dopes, fools, too stupid to tie their shoelaces—Doug and his friends criticized those who went rather than struggling not to. All it takes is planning, some smarts, swearing to homosexuality, starving down a skeleton too frail to fight, going for a physical so stoned you slid along the wall to the floor. Only idiots marched off to die, saluting, singing "The Star-Spangled Banner," babbling about God and country, saving the world from communism.

And one day the war ended. "They" came home, the ones she and Doug screamed about, with wounds for a lifetime no doctors were ever able to fix. And all this time Cassie never faced one of those she'd once considered as much an enemy as the politicians.

Jake's saying *Vietnam* brings up new pangs. He must have been a boy then. "Twenty," he tells her when she asks.

"I started off in college, but there was air space in my head. I never had any idea what to do there except play a little football, which I didn't do well enough to keep from getting cut from the team. That, plus the partying . . ." The old man on the next stool slips off and stumbles around the bar to a doorway. Jake sits, farther from her now. The eagle turns sideways, hiding except for one yellow claw. "Then, Merry Christmas, I'm out in the cold, no exemption. The draft was waiting like Count Dracula."

Cassie remembers Doug saying to his brother Mark, when Mark talked about dropping out of Ohio U., going west, maybe hanging out on the beaches for a while, *Don't be an asshole! The only beaches you'll see will be in Vietnam.*

The war was a quagmire that threatened to swallow all of them once, but unbelievably she hasn't thought of it in years. Long gone My Lai, the Tet offensive, the unlawful plundering into Cambodia. The war lies muffled in memory, like her first kiss. Now, thinking back, what had she ever done in that great swirl of protesting except have a good time? All the rallies and cheering, the singing, hugging one another, making peace signs, getting high. In those days loving the victims was a course requirement, and being against the war a rite of passage.

His feet on a rung of the stool, knees up, guarding his soft underbelly, Jake says, "In Saigon on R and R during my first tour. Got so drunk I barely remember doing it. Some buddies of mine figured having a tattoo was a hot idea, and I guess I said, what the hell, why not? So"—he lifts a shoulder—"we dragged around some back alleys until we found this little hole in the wall. A woman did it."

"Gave you the tattoo?"

"Yeah. Old, wrinkled like a walnut, and stripped to the waist. The damn room was hot as Hades, and when I saw her, concentrating over a grunt's arm, shiny with sweat, I remember laughing my head off. Then, I don't know, one of the guys passed me a Thai stick and the next thing"—he swings his arm around to look at the eagle—"I had old baldy. He wasn't what I had in mind."

"What did you want?"

"Oh, a star, I guess. Small. On my wrist."

"Why a star? Why not a heart? Or the name of your girlfriend?"

The old man returns from the men's room. He has the draggy-eyed look and red-veined nose of a practiced drinker. Bantam-small, with laps of skin in folds under his pointy chin, he pokes Jake belligerently. "You got my seat."

Jake tenses, and Cassie thinks he doesn't like to be touched. "Yeah," he says, standing up. The old man pushes in behind him, crowding Jake close to Cassie. He brushes her arm, her leg; a hand wings across her shoulder.

His nearness startles flutters of panic. Sweat prickles between her breasts. Cassie remembers the Levinsons' blind date—whose name she has forgotten forever—and his cold, surgical lips to her cheek. Such a kiss is what she expects, has trained herself to, not this dampness on her neck blossoming from no real touch at all.

"Jake, hey, Jake!" The piano player beckons him from the platform. "Enough boozing! Time to go to work."

"I'll see you after this set. It's the last."

"No. I can't stay. Really. I've got to get home. Tomorrow's a busy day," she says before realizing this is Saturday night.

Jake slips sideways. "Yeah. Well, okay then. Thanks for coming."

"It was wonderful, the music, hearing you play. . . ." Such a fool, such a dummy, a teenager, worse than Mandy on a first date. Infinitely worse, Cassie thinks, sorry now as Jake walks away.

7

Eve, waiting for Johnny, can't tune out the voices from the next booth. Inexorably they float over the top of the padded leather. Even shifting to the other side of the table, Eve fails to escape them, the slow, easy drone of older women—old women.

"Tuesday night I went to the Music Center with Sonya Berger. She had an extra ticket. After Jack died she kept their subscription."

"Nice."

"Pleasant. But it's not the same. Going alone is going alone."

"You weren't alone, you were with Sonya."

"True, but you know what I mean. Though Sonya drove and picked me up. I hate to drive at night. Jonah did most of the driving even in the daytime."

"So did Leo. Once he retired he wouldn't let me go anywhere by myself. He said I had an awful sense of direction. Now, I get in the car and I have to think, what are the best streets to take to Bullock's Wilshire? Or is half an hour enough to get to Century City?"

"Anyway, the concert was enjoyable. Bruckner. And there's a very nice man who sits in the seat next to Sonya."

"Who is he?"

"She has no idea. But he's always alone. They say hello, make a little small talk. That's it."

"How old?"

"Late seventies maybe. Nicely dressed. Presentable. Sonya

keeps thinking he'll suggest coffee afterwards. Why not? But so far he hasn't even asked her name."

"It's hard."

"Well, I don't know about hard, but it wouldn't be so bad to have someone to go out with for dinner now and then, or a movie. Just a man to be friendly with."

"There's this man in my Spanish class . . ."

"And?"

"Last Thursday we walked out together. He might be interested."

"So? That's good."

"Who can tell."

"What's he like?"

"A man. Very talky in class. He has a million questions—not like Leo, who went for days without saying a word. I'm not used to so much conversation."

"It's easier if you have someone who does the talking. For me anyway."

"Well, quiet is nice too."

"Will you go out with him if he asks?"

"Maybe. I'll see."

"Don't be so stuck up. Go. You'll have a good time."

"But what do I do when he takes me home?"

"What do you mean what do you do?"

"What if he wants to kiss me? Do I let him? On the first date?"

"Why not? A kiss isn't so terrible. You've been kissed before."

"Last week my sister-in-law Greta had a date. A fix-up. A retired coat manufacturer. His wife died two years ago from throat cancer. Greta said he said it was very ugly."

"Tell me about the date, not about his dead wife. I have enough dead of my own."

"They had dinner in Trader Vic's."

"And afterwards?"

". . . he got insistent. Trying to touch her, do things. She was so embarrassed. She had no idea how to handle it, what to do, say. *Don't*—that's what she told me she told him. How could he think she was that kind of woman, somebody cheap who has no standards."

"And?"

"Eventually she got him out the door. She explained that she liked him, but they didn't know one another well enough for— well, you know. Maybe next time. Not that she promised next time. Like she said, how could there be any time with her thighs and oh, dear, everything sagging. Greta is so overweight. Not that it matters, because he never called again."

"She should call him. It's not like when we were young. Now it's okay for a woman to invite a man to some event. To pay her share of the check even."

The waiter, a boy with dark hair and arrogant eyes, appears at the women's table. They fall discreetly silent as he clears away the plates. Eve hopes they will talk about something else, anything else: their grandchildren, which both surely possess, clothes, the high cost of food. . . .

"Sonya's very high on a cruise for meeting somebody. I was thinking we might go together."

"Sonya's all wet. Last year when I went on that Alaska trip, the one I took with Emily Gruber . . ."

"I remember."

"There was only one single man our age on board, and Emily heard a rumor the cruise line *paid* his way so the girls would have somebody to dance with."

"That's humiliating!"

"Tell me. So save your money."

"Maybe the Caribbean cruises are better. That's what Sonya suggested."

"Money thrown out if she thinks she'll find a single man under the stars."

"You're probably right."

Eve signals the waiter, ready to change tables, when she sees Johnny come in the door. She waves frantically, the sound of his voice, her own, necessary to drown the women's sadness, their faint hopes and fears. She has been sinking in the river of loneliness they drink with their dinners.

"You're late. I've been waiting twenty minutes at least," Eve accuses him when Johnny slides in opposite, his back to the women, his shoulders a barrier.

He rubs the strawberry mark that flushes over his chin. "Sorry. They're tearing up Sunset again."

"You should have taken Wilshire."

"Too much traffic this time of day."

"It's still better than Sunset," Eve can't stop herself from saying. Johnny nods toward her glass. "What are you drinking?"

"Whatever fancy water they serve in this place. In your honor." She takes one of his cigarettes when he lays the pack on the table. She smokes more than she ever had since seeing Johnny—whom she doesn't consider she is seeing. He's only a friend. *Someone to go out with, a dinner now and then, a movie. . . .*

What does he think they are doing?

"Want to tell me why you're so pissed off at me, Eve?" he asks easily, for he doesn't take her seriously. Johnny is disgustingly more mellow straight than stoned. She remembers the old Johnny Lerner as prickly, a high-strung tightrope walker, not at all insult-proof, with a voice of varying decibels.

"Who said I'm mad at you? It's just been a bad day." Eve lies, for the day has been ordinary, minus trials or joys, a more and more usual gray day of matted clouds and sallow light.

"Okay, then, let's eat."

"I'm sorry." His easy acceptance forces her to retreat. He is such a nice man. . . . *A very nice man . . . just a man to be friendly with. . . .*

The waiter brings Johnny's club soda and menus. Eve orders a steak, rare; Johnny considers the steamed vegetable platter. Johnny rejects meat now as he does chemicals, very fussy about what he eats, how the kitchen cooks his broccoli and carrots. No salt or additives of any sort. No butter. He peers over his reading glasses at the waiter, whom he might be auditioning. The boy is compliant, more eager to please Johnny than he has been the older women in the next booth. Who knows if Johnny, in his corduroy jacket with leather patches on the elbows, tie loosened, is in the industry, if he wields the authority to create fantastical careers like fairy kingdoms, or is only another ignorable nobody? Hollywood has no dress code of success, and the tattiest attire can mask the most significant power broker, so it is never safe to be insolent or lofty with customers, not for pretty boys eager to get before the cameras.

When Johnny feels satisfied the steamed vegetables are uncontaminated he hands the menus back to the boy and relaxes. Eve says, "You're becoming a real pain in the ass about what you put in your mouth, you know that? There's a limit to being health-conscious, Johnny. Besides . . ." She waves her lit cigarette in his face.

"Next week, Monday, I'm going cold turkey. I'm stable enough now and I've built up a resistance to the worst part of withdrawal."

"Keep one bad habit, Johnny, please!"

He glowers. "Eve, I want to live a long, long time. Once I got myself out of the trees I could see the future like an open highway through Kansas."

Eve laughs. "You and Judy Garland." She really likes Johnny, but he has grown so self-righteous about coming clean, as if hundreds, no thousands, of other people haven't done the same thing, put their blitzed-out days behind them like the war, and reconstructed. He isn't the only person who has a pitted, wasted terrain of a past.

Eve has her own bad deeds that aren't so easily wiped away. But she doesn't dwell on what was, not on Jordan and his packages wrapped in innocuous brown paper, his cheap suitcases left in bus-station lockers. Who knows what damage they caused? And there is Abramson's wife, the walking undead. Oh, Abramson's goddam wife, holding her damaged head and weeping.

To avoid seeing the wraith weaving around the tables, Eve returns to Johnny's pontificating.

"I handed myself a present, like a kid at Christmas. I'm the parent and I'm the child, both at the same time, and I'm being good to myself, giving myself the future, a healthy body, a mind that isn't a filthy fish tank." The dessert cart wheels by them, pushed by an older, plodding waiter. "Poison," Johnny says, pointing at a Black Forest cake. He holds up the salt shaker. "Poison."

Johnny is right, of course. No one would argue with him. But he is so ardent, a preacher thundering against everlasting damnation, that Eve can't help saying, "So's air."

"That's right. Los Angeles has terrible air. We might as well be breathing raw sewage, and all the controls in the world, all the damn laws passed for emission devices, doubling up in cars during rush hours, filtering industrial shit, fining toxic chemical dumpers, aren't worth a dime. This town has too many people in it, none of whom give a damn. Once we weren't all jammed up on the freeways, Sunset was a country road, and this"—he spreads his arms as if to sing the "Hallelujah Chorus"—"sweet-smelling grass-lands with honest-to-God vegetation and not florist-pretty plants arranged by gardeners."

She has forgotten Johnny is a native. "You weren't around then. It's all pictures to you, what you heard from your grandparents. That wasn't your world. This is. No living in yesterday, Johnny-o." She squeezes his hand, trying to jolly him out of his regrets for being in the wrong century, trapped by time. He sings an anguished complaint. For the past. Always for the past, Eve thinks, when there is as much life behind as what lies, even in Johnny's Kansas, before them both.

He avoids her hand and glances around the restaurant. "Where the hell's our food? I'm starving." His outburst embarrasses him. It is, she realizes, his first genuine display of emotion since he dropped back into her life, laundered and sanitized—and then about the environment, of all things. The women appear from the next booth. Both smartly dressed, one in a knit jacket and skirt, the other in a muted navy print, bridge party females with identical short haircuts, they arrange themselves to leave. In territory where each grain of time is cherished, they are preserved, the intaglios of lines hidden under makeup. The feeling of kinship with the departing women frightens Eve and she stops the passing waiter for something stronger than bottled water.

"Poison," Johnny reminds her automatically.

"Only one, for Christ's sake!"

"It starts with one."

Oh, the reformed are such sermonizers, magisterial in revenge. They clamor from the promised land, chastened sinners. "Everything starts with one," Eve says.

"Don't be smug. You never had the monkey. The gut-clenching pain, the shakes, nightmares. Days you can't get out of bed, and nights your eyelids are stapled open to your skull. Ever see spiders climbing down the wall, or snakes under the sheets?"

The food arrives and Johnny goes on, unstoppable, as if the waiter isn't by his elbow asking if everything is all right. Eve curtly nods him off as Johnny's eyes eat through her, to the hell he survived, she supposes. He has the red glare of a maniac. In a moment he can start shouting. But he drops into silence abruptly, slams a door, and whispers, "Thank God I made it. I'm really okay now. I'm good. I'm fine." His hands steeple over his plate and Eve wonders if he is praying.

Eve sips her scotch slowly, afraid of rattling the ice cubes. She is no longer hungry but Johnny tears into his vegetables as if the expiration of his rage leaves him famished.

"Of course I ruined my life," he says matter-of-factly, between bites. "Sniffed, smoked, drank, swallowed up a career, money, a house, cars, friends, family. My ex still refuses to let me see Terry except for the occasional visit."

Eve doesn't want to hear about his son either.

"He's fourteen now and out in New Mexico. I got a letter from him last week. He plays basketball and is into riding in a big way. His stepfather bought him a horse. A horse!" He rolls his eyes. "Before I became a first-class Malibu junkie I could have bought the kid a whole stable. Now I can't afford a cheap saddle. I'm broke! Dusted, busted!" He lays down his fork and tears glisten in his eyes.

Johnny's dark angels stir up the air with their wings, and Eve hunches to keep clear of them. But she can't help saying, "The worst is behind you. Try not to think about what happened. You're clean now and starting over." And a loser, she thinks, her emotions an embroidery of pity and anger. Why is she always hearing some poor man's story, forever a recipient of male sorrow? She owns enough sadnesses herself and keeps them quiet, packages her griefs in the tissues of memory and agitates no one else about them. Even Cassie and Nona know little of Eve's old lives. Eve swallows her secrets and pretends she hasn't any.

Johnny is apologizing. "You're right. I don't know what was dragging at me. It's solid Johnny Lerner these days. And I do have Terry. He's a fabulous kid. I love him. The only good thing I managed to do. Anyway, sorry, Eve. Usually I take my shit to group, where it belongs." His good humor restored, he smiles and lights a cigarette, staring at her through the smoke. "Something about you, Eve. You were always a good scout."

"Boy, girl, or Tonto?"

He laughs.

"Come on, Johnny, all I ever remember doing is driving you home a couple of times when you would have been a menace behind the wheel. We weren't even what you could call friends—

more party acquaintances, the usual Beverly Hills fancy dancers at galas."

"Yeah, well, I remember you. The lady with the eyes."

"What eyes? What are you talking about? Everybody has eyes."

"Yours are sad, that's all."

She pushes her plate away. "Oh, don't be annoying. What did you know anyway? In those days you couldn't have told my eyes from a pair of dominoes." But he retains his smile, satisfied. Eve prefers him tarnished, abused with self-pity.

"And still sad. Maybe more than before."

"Enough bull about my eyes! Are you ready for coffee?"

In the angles of the booth she can't get comfortable. An achy pain spreads below her stomach. She crosses her legs and immediately crosses them in the opposite direction. Her period is coming. The fullness throbs unpleasantly. She really doesn't want coffee, but just to go home, as if she were capable of outrunning her body as well as Johnny. But he lingers now, conversational about his son, whom he hopes to claim. "I can see the two of us living together, palling around, hanging out. What's wrong with that? He's my kid too. It's time I started being a father. And I'm hellbent on doing it. I never abandoned him, no way!"

Oh, shut up! Eve bites back the words. The glow of fatherhood illuminates Johnny until the shine of his halo all but throws his face into shadow.

Finally, to Eve's relief, the check arrives. As usual, Johnny's asking her out to dinner means they're going Dutch. He could at least offer to treat—not that she would let him, since her income is three times his or more.

"Let's see, you owe twenty-four fifty—no, twenty-five with the tip," he says, seriously calculating through his half-glasses. He computes her meal down to the penny and his cheapness offends her.

Her insides now blooming with pain, Eve snaps, "Oh, here's thirty. Keep the change!"

"That's settled then," he says, not insulted as she intended him to be. "Ready?"

When she stands, Eve isn't sure for a moment that she can walk. The pain scissors around to her back. Then she feels the warm release of blood between her legs like a deluge breaking and she moves through the pulsing, a buried fist opening, closing. The primitive femaleness overwhelms her. She might as well be stripped naked, squatting in the field. The gold bracelet clanks against her Cartier watch as she reaches for the door.

"Here, let me be the gent, Eve." Johnny holds it for her.

Out on the sidewalk the trees are webbed in mist, a translucent whiteness drifting up from the ocean. The mist dampens her cheeks. She feels a trickle of blood down her leg and, lightheaded, she rushes Johnny between wavering shadows.

In her own car, driving east, the streets are gossamer, scenes shot through cheesecloth, and the lights on Wilshire undulate like palm fronds. Chill air blows in the open windows without relieving the pain over which she crouches. A tide roars down, bursts, and thankfully surges away, only to gather force and come rushing through her again. Nails of a beastly deformed creature claw at the soft female parts.

She should have told Johnny she felt sick, beyond driving inland to Beverly Hills from Santa Monica, instead of acting jaunty, in full command. Such a trooper! But weakness humiliates her, that monthly bleeding women hide. Rather, in the parking lot she elaborated a pretense of having enjoyed dinner. *Let's get together again!*

She crosses under the San Diego Freeway, traffic in Westwood crowding her right and left. She is squeezed in a middle lane, imprisoned in metal. Scattered spots of color break like fireballs. She rides on a carpet of pain, sweaty and nauseous.

What is this cruel joke being played on her body? She has never suffered this kind of cramping, not even the first time. It feels more like childbirth, a part of her breaking loose and pushing down, too large, into a narrow channel, she thinks in panic, and irrationally wants to scream out loud.

As she comes past Westwood Village the spasms ebb. She monitors her pounding heart, breathing deeply, swallowing hungry mouthfuls of air warmer than in Santa Monica. Rivulets of moisture trickle off her eyebrows. Beneath her skirt she is drenched.

No reason to call Cassie. Just another monthly, maybe worse, but so what? Nothing wrong with me, nothing. Tired, overworked.

And perversely the cramps testify to her superiority over the women in the restaurant. She isn't old and dried up.

But okay, if there were only somebody home waiting for her!

An ambulance siren roars up behind her, demonically screeching. Traffic slams to a dead halt and Eve is grateful for the respite. Shaking, she loosens her hands from the wheel and wipes sticky palms on her jacket.

Less than a mile.

A century later, a millennium, she weaves into the underground garage. Getting out of the car she sees she has bled through her skirt. Blood smears the gray leather seat. She'll leave the mess until tomorrow.

Bent over and pleated with pain, hoping she won't meet one of the neighbors, she inches to the elevator, in whose glossy metallic walls she faces herself weeping like a girl.

Oh, it hurts so!

8

Like Nona on her nocturnal visits, Mandy arrives without warning. She never even bothers to call Cassie from the airport, but enters through the back door to say "Hi, Mom. I'm home for the week-end."

Cassie is frightened into responding "What's wrong? Why aren't you at school?"

"Because." *Because* is a standard Mandy answer.

Cassie kisses her, and Mandy lists softly in her mother's arms for a second before spinning off. "What are you doing home? And how did you get here?"

Mandy is halfway across the room, cheating Cassie of a chance to pat her all over, touch, stroke, caress, to check her like an anxious mother cat.

"Do we have anything to eat? All they had on the plane were plastic sandwiches. I'm starving." Already Mandy is half-buried in the refrigerator. "Gross, Mom. Only veggie stuff and yogurt."

"I'm on a diet."

Mandy reappears clutching a Coke. "Let's order in Chinese. Portland's idea of hot and sour soup is lukewarm dishwater. I'm in the provinces, Mom. You wouldn't believe it," she moans, reaching for the phone, dialing the King Dragon number from memory, and ordering what to Cassie sounds like a banquet.

She darts around the first floor, then upstairs, with Cassie following, asking again: "Mandy, I didn't expect you home until Thanksgiving, so why are you here now?"

"If you don't want me, just say so." She flops on her bed and scoops up all the stuffed animals that can fit in her arms, mounding herself in teddy bears, leggy cotton dolls, and plush amphibians.

Cassie sits on the ruffled spread. "Of course I want you, as you well know. I'm just surprised, okay? Okay?" Cassie explores a smile that doesn't feel quite right on her mouth and trails loving fingers along Mandy's downy arm.

Mandy has gained weight. A roll of flesh bulges through her Rolling Stones T-shirt. At times Cassie catches a future pretty woman twisting and turning in the teenager, a presence behind knit cotton and stone-washed denim, still incomplete and disordered.

Mandy had been a difficult baby, a fretter, irritated by loud noises, her stomach constantly churning. The world, or life itself, or a genetic schema from poorly matched parents—whatever, something disturbed her. She cried into the toddler stage before quieting down to become as pacific and good-humored as Al Levinson next door.

The change in her was a relief, but Cassie kept waiting for another shift, a leeward tilt of the usually even-tempered Mandy. However, except for minor squalls, she remained a pleasant child even through divorce, which—theoretically—should have unbalanced her. Experts warned of upheavals in all the books Cassie read, but Mandy, fifteen when Doug married Tracy—then a sulky twenty-five-year-old—remained amazingly levelheaded, more philosophical than her mother. Not that Mandy in her late teen years isn't mercurial. Days can begin with her "Leave me alone!" to Cassie's morning "Hello, chicken." Her essential sunniness is, on odd days, obscured by cloud cover. Saturnine at times, a roving storm threatening to break, she moves diagonally, but Cassie, carrying a discretionary umbrella, learns to weather Mandy's moods.

Obviously hormones play a part in this capriciousness. Cassie the physician understands her daughter's burgeoning sex drive, but as a mother she finds that this uneasy metamorphosis from child to woman often grates on her. She senses loss, Mandy slipping through foreign streams, and wants to retain her daughter, if only for a little while longer. *I want my baby back, the nights rocking her, so much love in my arms, dependent,* she thinks in lonely moments. For a scientist such longings are, if not shameful, unrealistic. She must be sensible.

"Mandy, why did you come home for the weekend without calling first?" She straightens Mandy's skewed T-shirt.

"Maybe it's not for the weekend. Maybe it's forever." Mandy's bottom lip puffs out in the jutting gesture she's had since babyhood. Cassie's heart flip-flops.

"Sweetheart, what's wrong?"

Pushing up against the headboard, Mandy scatters the plush animals like a moody giant. She ducks her head and her long uncurled blond hair splashes down her face. Between the strands brown eyes peek out like burrowed animals.

"Don't hyperventilate, Mom. I'll go back. I have a round-trip ticket," she says. The reversal is typical and she only brought a small weekend canvas bag, Cassie realizes, relaxing. "I just hate it, that's all. It's boring and pointless. You think I'm learning something, but I'm not. Nothing has relevance."

Cassie pushes back the hair so she can see Mandy's face. "You're adjusting, that's all. And the first year—Mandy, we discussed this—is filled with requirements, courses you might not enjoy but you need, to graduate."

Reason, however, isn't what Mandy wants to hear. "Why do I have to learn what I am mortally uninterested in? What is the purpose of earth science in my life? I mean, a rock is just a boring rock."

Is there any point in saying that knowledge of the earth's physical structure is necessary for oil production? Should Mandy know where iron, copper, diamonds come from, or is geology to be just another sinkhole over which Mandy blithely skips, oblivious and proud of it?

Mandy, Cassie discovered not so long ago, had glided through several years of school without being taught geography. America consisted of the State of California, dabs called New York and Boston, the speck of Chicago, and a southern somewhere known as Miami. She shudders, still reluctant to ask her eighteen-year-old such questions as where is Morocco? and what about Kenya? Nepal? Never mind the exotic, such as Tasmania. For a modern child who probably can't name the countries of Scandinavia, what use are mica and pitchblende?

Mandy curls her lip. "Mother, I have no intention *any time in my life* of dragging around chipping away at mountains!"

"What about your other classes? Modern European history, for instance? History was one of your favorite subjects in high school."

"You don't understand!" The charge is familiar, yet as withering as always.

Cassie, sliding to defeat, shifts gears. "How's the social life?" Under a fold of the pink cotton spread she crosses her fingers. Was this unscheduled appearance the result of a boy's cruelty?

"There's nobody worth bothering about. They're all dorks or sleaze types or druggies—" Tears spring up in Mandy's eyes. "Oh, Mommy, nobody loves me!" she explodes, crawling into Cassie's arms and throwing her off balance.

Cassie holds her sobbing child, whispers, "Hush, it's all right," over Mandy's hair, and feels as wretched and helpless as she does in the clinic when confronted by a terminal diagnosis.

Each weekend to come shimmers like an oasis, magical and full of promise. Golden Saturday nights are, in the distance, studded with hope and maybes. The women trail years of experience behind them like tattered evening cloaks and should know better, do, but by Thursday, yearning overtakes them. Something exciting might happen *this* weekend, something more than just dinner, a blind date that leads to nowhere, a party flat as day-old champagne.

But this particular weekend is no more exceptional than any Monday or Tuesday.

Cassie and Eve make tentative plans for a movie. Nona is on hold, undecided, since they all have such divergent ideas about movies. The last one they attended together Cassie hated for what she saw as gender condescension, women used as conveniences in a moth-eaten plot. Eve thought the comedy trashy, not as good as the reviews, while Nona found the film funny, though she couldn't actually defend the humor afterward when they stopped off for pizza.

Nona, however, has received no better offer—actually no certifiable invitation at all—and is caught between watching television at home alone or joining them. In her pillowy bed, a white sailing ship of lace and ruffles, she can sip—as she has on other lonely nights—enough Chardonnay or Merlot so the screen blurs and her flat stomach bloats. Eventually she will feel swallowed by the mattress, by her own flesh, which she will stroke and imagine a man is caressing, until around two A.M. all that's left on television are confusing old films no one has heard of, splintered by used-car commercials. The wine will tide in her throat and she won't need to stick her fingers behind her tongue and press. With enough wine she automatically throws up, gasping, her head over the toilet, dizzy but purged.

Nona decides on the movie, only the movie never materializes, for Eve is trawled in as a last-minute replacement for a rich client's husband, and Cassie insists on staying around the house in case Mandy is available, which seems unlikely. Mandy, on the phone, promises "later" to a girlfriend or two or three, at somebody's house, hanging out, by chance a party, maybe burgers at a restaurant in Westwood that shows music videos. Mandy, regurgitating her unhappiness, leaves it with her mother—for the weekend at least—who worries.

So Nona goes over to Cassie's.

Cassie, wooing her daughter, has spent the afternoon in the kitchen making lasagna and lemon meringue pie. But between Friday night and Saturday night Mandy has gone on a diet.

"And I never eat pie!" Has her mother in only a few weeks forgotten her likes and dislikes?

Cassie shouldn't be surprised but is, caught on one foot, and cries, "Lemon meringue pie is your absolutely all-time favorite thing in the world. At least it was before you went to school! And you adore lasagna."

"I hate lasagna!" Cassie has followed Mandy into the bathroom, where, her long hair in one thick braid down her back, she enters the shower. Thankfully, Mandy undressed looks thinner than in clothes.

Cassie struggles with the inevitable, which she ought to have been clear-sighted enough to see before she started cooking. Mandy has no intention of eating dinner at home.

Nona's coming over offers no satisfaction, though Cassie won't either have to eat alone or put the entire meal down the disposal. Whatever Nona's praise for Cassie's cooking, it is tarnished, because only Mandy across the table can appease her mother. Cassie measures out Mandy's time away from home with an eyedropper and tries to adjust. She paces her longing carefully across the calendar, but Mandy's surprise appearance has disarranged the schedule. Seeing Mandy when she hadn't expected to brings up the sadness inside in equal measure with the joy.

As the lasagna warms in the oven Mandy pours out a rush of details about the latest romantic hang-up to Nona. She had spared Cassie the "who said what to whom" and how badly "he" behaved, but she confides it all to Nona in a low voice. The two heads, one dark, the other light, bend close together, nodding like wind-kissed flowers.

When Mandy pauses, Nona advises, "Never care for any guy more than he cares for you," which is something she has heard from Eve. Cassie knows, because Eve has said it often enough. She would drill a channel in Nona's head and pour the words of sense right through the bone if it were possible. In no other way does Nona seem to "get" it. And now here she is, the guru of romance, spreading the gospel to Mandy.

Oh, give us all a break, Cassie wants to scream, and takes out the trash without either Mandy or Nona noticing.

Stars sequin the night sky. A wedge of moon pins itself against the velvet dark. Only a dog's barking plunders the silence, still as death in the yard.

Cassie leans against the side of the garage, clutches her elbows, and waits for revelation, as she did so long ago when young in Ohio, home on a Saturday night, an outsider while the rest of Landry laughed and danced, held hands in the movies. She felt caught out in a game of musical chairs and mooned (her mother's old-fashioned term). Silly girl! Her mother's light scolding to stop brooding and do something sent her, as tonight, out of the house. Usually she ended up at the back fence behind her father's vegetable garden and the patch of wild raspberries, at the last slope of their acre and a half. She'd haul herself up on the top rail and glance back at the house, up on its rise, silhouetted like a paper cutout on the scrim of moonlight.

There was so much more land around that house where she grew up, where she had her joys as well as heartbreaks, but on a night like tonight it is only the bone-crunching sorrows she remembers. How painful it was to be young and straddling an old wood fence at the other side of the garden on a Saturday night.

Her father planted corn, tomatoes, carrots, melons, and acorn squash in his garden, and by late October even the squash was finished, leaving tangled vines. The garden was fallow then, and those nights the air was brittle, so sharp it hurt her teeth when she inhaled.

Every year since moving west, Cassie missed the dying year's crackle, morning frost, perfumed bonfires. In California the seasons blurred; time shivered like cobwebs in motion. In Los Angeles there are no epiphanies of weather.

The whine of cars, large rigs speeding cross-country, the Cleveland bus, all sang harmonies out on the highway which, closing her eyes, she can bring back more acutely than any music. The guilty desire then to be somewhere else, anywhere other than Landry, set Cassie to rocking on the fence and searching for shooting stars plummeting to earth on which to make wishes.

Take me away! Anywhere . . . Casablanca, the South of France, a river boat floating down the Amazon.

At fifteen, sixteen, all foreign places were equally romantic.

Beware of getting what you ask for, Cassie thinks, having gone from the Midwest to Los Angeles, this plot of ground in the Palisades smaller than her parents' vegetable garden. For what? For more Saturday nights of staring up at the heavens.

Would Jupiter have been far enough away? Mars? A slow spaceship to Venus?

When does a woman stop being a silly girl?

Last Saturday night she had been in Malone's listening to Jake the gardener singing a wretched song about the lonely—with her wet palms and pounding heart, as if she were still in Ohio, life yet unmapped and to be explored.

Running off on Jake was juvenile, a thirteen-year-old's panic. She'd planned to apologize on Thursday but she'd had an emergency delivery and missed him. Yesterday she'd fantasized he would call, but of course he didn't.

Still, Cassie hopes—which, with her good common sense she would counsel Mandy, in the matter of men, not to do. Don't wait for *that* call. Phone wires are arteries leading to women's hearts, the beats synchronized to unanswered rings.

The Levinson house broods on the other side of the hedges, the amber glow of a downstairs lamp scuttling the shadows. Beth and

Al are out on married business, and it is unbelievable to Cassie that once her Saturday nights were also programmed with other couples, that she was one flank of a twosome that lacked social propulsion on its—her—own. When she and Doug entered a crowded restaurant she saw people, not simply men framed and hung up.

God forgive me, she prays, blaming herself for the bottomless loneliness, for yearning to re-enter the closed society where once she held a tenured position.

Yet marriage, though convenient, isn't such a garden. She knows this truth; she isn't a fool. And her own marriage to Doug was, so it developed, a thick jungle of weeds. Others are rutted terrains, bombed and dangerous Beiruts, like poor little April's.

With her anger undiminished, and a last glance at the light in the Levinsons' window, Cassie returns up the back steps.

Nona and Mandy break guiltily apart. A chair scrapes on the vinyl. "I've got to get over to Sherri's house," Mandy says, rising. Nona has wound Mandy's hair up, with loose tendrils wisping around her face. She seems much older, and Cassie's breath clots in her throat.

"What are you going to do? Are you staying at Sherri's?"

Mandy grabs her jacket and slips the straps of a denim bag over her shoulder.

"Wait, turn down the collar," Nona says, jumping up and fluttering about Mandy. She steps back. "I don't know. Those earrings. Here, try these." She unhooks her own hoops and fastens them into Mandy's lobes. "Now, what do you think?"

They hustle past Cassie to the mirror in the foyer. This is larceny! Cassie screams silently, her teeth clenched. Mandy's not Nona's child.

Cassie follows to the archway and asks again, "Where are you going?"

"To Sherri's," Mandy says, admiring herself. "They're perfect, Nona."

"Out where?"

"Mom, when I'm in Portland you never know if I'm out or in, with who—"

"Whom," Cassie blurts automatically.

Mandy continues, "—if it's late or early." She gives Nona a

swirling hug, then at the door, wings by Cassie's cheek. The breeze is thick with regret.

I have to let her go, now, later, Cassie despairs, sitting down by the table. She picks at the sunflower seeds from the opened package Mandy has left behind. Cashews, almonds, pistachios—Mandy nibbles at nuts like a chipmunk. Red pistachio shells litter her room. Cassie doesn't have to go upstairs to see them in a trail across the bed.

Nona hefts the warmed lasagna out of the oven, carrying it aloft in padded mitts like giant's paws, and places it before Cassie. But Cassie has no interest in eating her own food if it doesn't taste of love.

"What about a late movie?" Nona asks, nervous on her chair, hands fluttering, touching the silverware, the wineglasses, the salt and pepper shakers. "There's a revival in Santa Monica. I checked the paper. *Mrs. Miniver* goes on at ten o'clock."

Cassie is a sucker for old classics, but her mouth puckers up as she says, "*Mrs. Miniver*? Why would I want to see *Mrs. Miniver*?"

"Greer Garson is one of your favorites."

"Who says so?"

Cassie acts unreasonably, which is so rare that Nona, who needs people to behave as they always do, to be programmed, backs up hastily. "Maybe there's something else around you want to see."

"It's Saturday night, Nona. Why aren't you out on a date?" Cassie's anger chills the air.

"Cassie, don't be silly. Nobody asked me."

The lasagna, red and white and cream-colored, spread across the plate, reminds Nona of an Italian wool and angora sweater Flora's stocked last winter.

"Somebody could have. Some man should have asked you. They're swarming in hordes."

"Well, many of them are gay," Nona says earnestly, as if having to explain to Cassie.

Cassie preaches, just as she did when still married. She wrinkles her nose and sniffs, pretending for a moment not to be an unmarried woman, alone out in the world.

"You're just available to the wrong sort, the kind who do you no good. And there you are—I couldn't believe my ears—pontificating to Mandy about getting involved with a boy who's more interested in her than she is in him. As if I hadn't told you that, and Eve too." Going on to Mandy as if your advice is original, Cassie thinks, miffed. She slides slowly downhill, greased by a rising anger though unsure who annoys her—herself, Nona, Mandy. They are all such prisoners and so stupid. Entering their jail cells and slamming the doors.

Why do men have more balance? Or seem to? When men lose their grip it is in a big way. They take off to Tahiti like Gauguin or kill people.

"What's wrong with telling Mandy that?" Nona asks, worried. She knocks over a salt cellar and, embarrassed, takes a pinch from the tiny mound on the place mat and flings it recklessly over her shoulder.

"I didn't say it was *wrong*. It's good advice. Why should Mandy be hopelessly infatuated? Tied up like a roped calf? Let some boy come unglued over her and not vice-versa. Good God, Nona, I'm Mandy's mother." And not you. "I don't want her to be hurt. And don't think I couldn't kill this latest boy for his indifference." Or whatever he's done that Mandy's told Nona about, chapter and verse, and not her. "But Mandy allows these things to happen to her, the same way you do. In fact, you're a fine one to talk, twirling your heart around like a parasol. At least Mandy's a child. She doesn't know any better."

Cassie frightens Nona with her vehemence, but Nona still manages to say, "Mandy's eighteen."

"And you're almost forty—"

"Don't remind me!" Nona shrieks, her terror real.

"You've been taking a course in romance all your life, Nona, and you've still never managed to graduate."

The cruel prong of *forty* snares Nona and swings her wide, so she doesn't even hear Cassie criticizing. She trails her dark hair through her fingers and wonders how she arrived at "that age" without even noticing. Falling asleep in a Pullman car and being hauled across country.

Cassie continues: "And now what are you involved in? Oh, listen to you, so wise, counseling Mandy, while all this time what are you doing? Having an affair with a married man! I hope you weren't going to tell Mandy that."

They have arrived at the way station to which they have been heading ever since Mandy left and supper got served. Cassie's anger isn't perfunctory. Her mouth holds fire in it and has since Nona first blurted out—unthinkingly—that she is *seeing* Alan. Not *seeing* as just looking at, but entwined, tangled up together in passion's knots.

The uncurtained window squared above the sink is a patch of blackness blemished by shifting reflections. Out there in the night, beyond those phantom people, past that darkness, is a lighted world where happier people sit over meals eaten rather than barely touched, as do Nona and Cassie. There is Alan, for one. He and his wife attend a dinner party at a fair replica of Tara in lower Bel Air, a black-tie affair more elaborate even than the dinners Nona's parents once held.

Nona thinks the mush-faced woman only vaguely remembered in the frame on Alan's desk can't be much of an asset in that company.

"This is Saturday night and where is he?" Cassie asks. "Not with you. With the woman he's married to. Living their life together. Being happy."

Nona protests, waving the flag of her love and grappling for Alan's allegiance, "He's not."

"And how do you know that? Because he told you? Do you think you can believe anything a man says when he wants to get you in bed? When he wants to have his way with you?" Cassie yells, unaware that she sounds Victorian.

"Ah . . . ," Nona struggles, then rushes with "You think I've miscalculated."

"Miscalculated!" Cassie flings up her hands. "Just tell me, if Alan's so unhappy with his wife, then why doesn't he divorce her, make a decent quick end to what is supposedly an impossible situation? I'll tell you why." Cassie is relentless. "Because it's all bullshit. My God, you've had a thousand affairs—"

"Not anywhere near that number, Cassie, honestly!"

"—and still you seem newly hatched each time."

Nona should never have—stupidly—told Cassie a thing about Alan, or at least should have omitted the fact that he's married, knowing that Cassie reacts violently to adultery. Of all people, Nona understands about keeping secrets, holding her breath, still as a bough on a windless afternoon. She knows what it means to hold one foot off the ground, to be on guard, but this once she spoke without thinking. She leaks love, a container too full. Love sloughs off her tongue and she has no one to blame for the consequences of such indiscretion except her own ignorant self.

Nona whispers, "Don't be mad at me, Cass, please!"

"God damn it!" Cassie cries. She flings her glass, half full of wine, across the room. It shatters against the refrigerator door, startling them both, Cassie—for whom such drama is foreign—no less than Nona.

Cassie never loses her temper, not explosively in fireworks and fandangos, and this aberration propels her off the ladder-back chair and out of the kitchen.

Nona, stunned, hears her overhead, footsteps creaking on the bedroom floorboards. She sits frozen, waiting for Cassie's return, a statue but with a thundering in her chest. An ache that excites Nona to imagining the referred pain of a coronary sizzles down her left arm.

She should call for Cassie, tell her she hurts, that her heart is perfidious. But she is too shaken by the drama of Cassie's anger.

After a while she collects the shards of glass, mops up sticky smears of wine with a paper towel, and accepts that Cassie's gone for the night. Still, she listens to the ticking of the hall clock for another ten minutes before she lets herself out, making sure the front door locks behind her.

A damp, dreary Sunday morning, gray as old age, does nothing for Nona's mood. Metallic light coats the window. Depressed, she covets golden sunlight in a cloudless sky, and a hard three-mile jog. But rain threatens. She can see getting as far as the park on Veteran when the suety heavens will part. Instead she tunnels back under the ruffled quilt (with eyelet trim and ribbons that are a match for Mandy's) and with Magic sprawled at the hump of her feet, she sleeps.

When she wanders up from the gravelly dark where she is most often happiest, the weather is the same slate-colored dampness. The day is a prison sentence, leaving her with few choices.

She brews a pot of hot chocolate, arranges a circle of oatmeal cookies on a flowered dish, and carries it all back on a silver tray to the bedroom. As she inserts a cassette into the VCR her spirits lift. She has two and a half hours of her soap—*The McKenzies*—faithfully recorded each afternoon at three, to watch.

Nona's relationship with the McKenzie clan is of long standing. It began when, bedded by flu and fever, she lay rudderless, eddying in and out of the curve of sleep, too weak for any activity but television. The McKenzies with their internecine warfare—at the time (among many story lines) Brad and Helen were scheming to take over the firm from their sister Deirdre, married to Brad's wife's ex-husband Jed and in a coma from a car crash that Helen was inadvertently responsible for—transformed the logy week. All the other soaps were only tepidly interesting, but *The McKenzies* entranced her. Was it her awareness of the resemblance between the actress portraying Deirdre and the familiar face in the mirror? Or maybe Houston Bernard, the CEO of a rival firm, intent on a corporate takeover though still in love with Helen—his childhood crush—displayed some of her father's characteristics. But dreaming through her fever, down whatever corridor of sleep she drifted, Nona managed by Thursday and Friday to come aground in time to catch *The McKenzies'* half hour of daily anguish. Returning to the store, she taped Monday's segment to view that night, did the same on Tuesday, Wednesday, the rest of the week, and found by the end of the month she was hooked. Now she knows the McKenzies as intimately as her own family (better, since the only relatives Nona has, except for invisible cousins in Chicago, are buried underground or ashes in stone urns). She suffers, in fact, visceral reactions to each of the McKenzies, a family of two sisters, two brothers, various wives and husbands, in-laws, children, lovers, ex-spouses, a matriarchal despot shifting affection and considerable power from one sibling to another almost whimsically, and a cast that to any but the initiated seems to number in the thousands.

Depending on her social life, Nona either watches each day's episode that night or saves up for an orgy of viewing on the weekend.

Against plumped-up pillows she cautiously sips the hot chocolate so as not to spill even a drop on bedding as lovely and elegant as any in a *House Beautiful* display. And in her silk nightgown and peignoir she could be modeling for a Saks or Neiman-Marcus ad.

The only sounds—except for the TV—are Magic's melodic purr and the clink of the cup on the saucer. During the commercials she eats cookies and thinks about the previous night—as she hasn't meant to—and wants to change mental stations to make the painful scene dissolve, even as Deirdre McKenzie's stricken face has just done.

Cassie's eruption was a shocking disharmony, and in Nona's memory the glass shatters once again.

Of course she's in a better mood now and sorry, Nona thinks as Brad McKenzie slips his mother's will out of a desk drawer and pockets it. She'll call and say *I don't know what was wrong with me*. Mandy's coming home out of the blue, that could be it. Cassie needs structure and order. *I'm not one*, she always says, *for surprises*.

The phone, however, remains stubbornly silent. It is after five. The autumn light drenching the window softens into a fusion with dusk.

Nona's excuses for why she hasn't heard from Cassie are varied. Cassie has to take Mandy to the airport. They, mother and daughter, are out for a late lunch. Cassie has a headache, is sleeping, is waiting for dark and a glass of wine, for Mandy to be on the plane, to be alone, for the right words. Or she has been summoned to the hospital. A patient in labor. Nona imagines the slick, wet infant sliding into Cassie's hands, one of her palms under the buttocks, the other high up on the back supporting the too-heavy head.

Though Nona's stomach turns at the sight of blood and she dislikes the ugliness of distorted bodies, she envies Cassie ministering to birthing women. How lovely in fantasy that all seems, how much Nona aches to carry her own child, tucked up under her heart, and to deliver it (never mind the agony). To give birth. To be a mother, like Cassie, even like her own mother with her infrequent hugs and kisses cold as a lizard's. But better, of course.

The click of locks, keys turning, fills Nona's memory. She grew up in shadowy corridors, in a house so quiet that up on the second floor in midafternoon it was possible to hear the soft murmur of cook's radio down below in the kitchen.

When she went to school it was to a clamorous outside world, a sharp, color-struck landscape, strident with tangled melodies. First, from the stone steps she listened to the birds in the maples, hawking, mean-spirited fliers, and below their shrilling the muted notes of oboes and bassoons, the traffic distant on Commonwealth. As she went farther from the house the tempo increased, an allegro of noises, until on the playground other children's cries were brassy and hurt.

Again at home, when she brought friends, their voices sank to unnatural whispers.

Mostly Nona remembers playing dolls in her room with little girls, a blonde named Melissa, a pouty slim child called Norah. Afterwards cook would give them cookies and milk at the scrubbed pine table in the kitchen.

If her mother appeared at all she would be highly polished and lacquered, with the same sort of sheen the Cadillac had when newly buffed and waxed. Marian was never bedraggled coming up on Nona and a friend.

Marian lunched out every day and shopped. Her philosophy of life was a straightforward commitment to spending money, buy-ing—usually from elegant little shops (like Flora's)—and carrying home a trophy in triumph each afternoon. Her "lovelies" were wrapped in crushed tissue paper and occasionally were meant for Nona—a maroon velvet dress with a white crocheted collar, a pink angora sweater, a matching rabbit hat and muff when Nona turned seven.

After one of Marian's luncheons when she didn't work off her energy shopping but lounged with the "girls," playing bridge, talking of those low-voiced mysteries that had her pulling in her chin and ducking her head, she came home unrested and grace-less. When she stopped at the door of Nona's room her seams would be the least bit crooked, and she ruffled the air, set currents stirring in motion as she gave Nona a moth kiss. Alcohol soured the perfume of her mother's breath, and slouching against the jamb, she bared her teeth in a lipstick smile at Nona and a visiting classmate. She asked them about school and struck them dumb.

On those afternoons Marian lost her preciseness, and the whites of her eyes were reddish. But she seemed to Nona more accessible, not just a painted lady, and she shouldn't have frightened whichever friend was visiting. Perhaps it was that at those times she appeared to be imitating a mother, rather than the real mother Nona's friend was used to.

Every few months or so, Marian, however, became grimly maternal. She toned down her makeup and pulled back her dark curls in a chignon. Then would come the clothes from Bonwit's or Filene's. She'd drive Nona herself to dancing lessons, pick her up at Melissa's, and talk at dinner to Adam of *the things we did, oh, my God, busy! morning to night! So much fun, didn't we, darling?*

They went to the movies, a cartoon with towering orange cats, fanged and drooling, slobbering bulldogs, holes in the sky through which dead birds fell and immediately came alive. Marian slipped out for a cigarette and left Nona eating popcorn. She returned and disappeared again. Nona's hands were sticky. Her stomach hurt. *Mommy, don't go!*

One afternoon she took Nona to the zoo. Nobody bothered with the zoo in Boston, a shabby little place attached like an orphan to the Gardens, with dusty paths and moth-eaten ancient animals.

But Nona was excited. "Animals in big cages!" she cried, widening her hands, then narrowing them. "Little tiny ones too." Her voice growly as she said, "Snarly old tigers," and gazed out of the corners of her eyes to see if Marian reacted.

Marian's hand, with the square emerald set in a nest of diamonds, tightened on the steering wheel. "Don't jump around so!"

"Elephants, Mommy."

"Yes, elephants."

"Alligators?"

"Alligators."

"Nanny says if you fall in the alligator's house he'll eat you up."

"That woman is a fool. You won't fall in the pond or pool, or whatever it is. There's a tall fence. A very high fence with spikes on it to keep people out."

"Does the fence have a door in it?" Nona asked, smoothing the neat blue dress over her knees. She wore white socks with lace on the cuffs and new white Mary Janes. The zoo was a dress-up occasion.

Nanny warned her to be careful, and not just of the alligators. *Be sure you stay clean and don't get dirty. That dress is a monster to iron.* How could a dress be a monster? Monsters had big teeth and hairy ears and leaped out from behind bushes to snatch bad little girls. Nona had a healthy fear of beasts who lived at the bottom of the garden after dark. At night they climbed up the outside wall and scratched at her window while she lay awake in her bed and prayed *Please don't come in!*

Nanny said she was a foolish little girl making something out of nothing. The sounds she heard were only the wind and the branches of the tree by the side of the house. But Nona knew better than that. The monsters wanted to hurt her. When she sat on her father's lap and his heavy hand lay warm on her leg, she thought of asking him why. Why did the monsters want to eat her alive, to crunch her bones and drink her blood? Instinctively Nona knew these weren't proper questions for her mother.

When she finally asked her father, he brought his face so close to hers his eyes became puddles. He never denied there were monsters down by the crumbly stone wall, in the thick of brush and scratchy brambles; he wouldn't argue away their prowling. But no monster was going to get his love, his doll, his baby, not if she was good as gold, quiet as a mouse . . . if she listened to Daddy. If she behaved, his angel, he intended to save her from the beasts who walked at midnight.

Nona had no idea why her mother was afflicted with sudden impulses to take her out like a dog on a leash. Years later she realized that children made Marian uncomfortable; they were foreign creatures, as mysterious as the zoo animals behind bars.

Marian became a mother as a corollary. A woman married, then—as night followed day—produced a child with no more fuss, ideally, than she would a sit-down dinner for twelve. Maybe Nona's father expected a child, or maybe it had been an awful mistake, which forty years ago wasn't easy to rectify. But Marian did have Nona and the two of them were unhappily saddled with each other. So, from time to time, either sorrowing or play-acting, Nona's mother imitated the mothers of Nona's friends. She forwent her lunch or bridge game or shopping foray and the two of them got into the car. By the age of eight or nine Nona knew enough to regret the outing before it occurred and fantasized saying the magic words that would absolve her mother (and her) from the unwanted obligation.

The day of the zoo, though, Nona, so much younger and innocent, was excited. She was to have her mother all to herself and out of the house.

"Sit quietly," Marian scolded, and Nona settled, worried that her mother would turn back, until they parked.

It was late spring but hot as August, and the heat had Marian, crisp in yellow piqué, complaining and fanning her face with a lace-edged hanky before they advanced too far. Now that they had gotten to the zoo—over what might have been tortuous terrain and at hazardous cost, to judge by her displeasure—she hurried Nona.

"Don't dawdle," she criticized, when Nona lingered by the feisty black seals, smiling puckishly as they played.

As they passed by the big cats, a lion opened a mouth wide as a cave and roared an angry bellow that hurtled Nona against Marian's legs.

"Stop that! You're mussing my skirt!"

Nona remembers the day as a topographical map with a geometry of paths and animals set up in their cages, and puffs of dust discoloring her Mary Janes on the longish walk to the elephants' pen. She waited for Marian to notice, and when she didn't, Nona, emboldened, swung her arms and raced ahead to the monkeys.

There weren't just monkeys but gibbons, baboons, mandrills, orangutans, chimps. Marmosets swung with acrobatic grace from dangling ropes; spiders scampered on the bars. A ringtail bared its fierce yellow teeth. They all had small heads and saucer ears and snaky tails and were only intermittently interested in the world of pointing humans.

In the heat the smell of monkeys was rancid. "Stink-o," Nona said, wrinkling her nose. She expected at any moment to hear her mother's cut-glass disapproval as she swung on the railing. Firm hands would pluck her up in the air and set her on the ground.

"Stink-o," Nona repeated, glancing around.

The next few seconds fell one by one, into disbelief, then worry, then terror. Marian wasn't behind her.

Nona inched away from the cages, taking several steps out into the middle of the walk, and called, "Mommy?" The word was leaden.

She had never been on her own before. Even in the garden Nanny kept guard from the back terrace, perched calmly on a chair. If Nona glanced up she met the watchful eye. Never untethered except inside the house, she clenched small fists in her pockets. The prickly sensation of tears filled up her nose. Along the path, colors bruised and hard lines softened like strokes of charcoal. The world turned filmy.

A bigger boy sprinting from nowhere to nowhere knocked against her. The contact pushed Nona into action and she ran through darkly striped corridors, around grown-ups with their much longer legs.

Mommy went away, Mommy left, Mommy got lost, hit by a car, don't ever go out on the street, Nona! cars! bad! Mommy taken away, Mommeeee . . .

In frenzy she spun like a top. The terror of being thrown loose in this foreign zoo country, where wild beasts at night broke out of their cages, roamed free as the whiskers of wind to eat wandering, locked-in, unwanted children, brought on more tears. Her face was wet as a seal pup's. Damp circles splotched the new blue dress. Oh, Nanny would be so unhappy—if Nanny ever saw her again.

A frantic Nona ran in search of yellow piqué, but none of the giants about her, moving aside for the crying child, wore her mother's face.

The zoo, wonderfully soft in the pastels of picture books, became on the hot warped afternoon a menacing sinkhole of terror. The monkeys, when Nona came around on them again, screeched in monkey gibberish. She tripped, falling on the cement edge of the drainage ditch, and bloodied her knee. Her shriek sliced into the afternoon and stopped the monkeys' yammering for a moment of utter silence.

An old man shepherding his grandchildren bent to ask her: "Little girl, are you lost?"

"Nona, for heaven's sake, stop making a spectacle of yourself!" Her mother arrived as effortlessly as morning, appearing like the sun over the lip of the earth, and scooped Nona up. "Why did you wander off on me?" she chided. But she didn't push Nona away as the child clung to her, smearing the yellow dress with tears and dirty fingerprints.

"I turned around for a second and she was gone," Marian apologized to the unknown grandfather.

"Oh, they're all little devils!"

And Nona, contented, lolled against her, lolls back on the heaped-up pillows remembering, thinking that Deirdre McKenzie will get *her* daughter returned, too, unless little Virginia has been kidnapped, as Deirdre fears. Ginny is epileptic, the seizures held in check by daily doses of medicine, which the kidnappers of course won't have. Ginny, unsedated, can die in seventy-two hours. . . .

Nona sighs and rewinds the tape.

Night pushes blackly on the window. The room is dark except for the light of the television set. Having ingested a week of *The McKenzies,* Nona feels sedated herself, the strain in her back eased, the tightness gone from under her heart. Good feelings buoy her and she sits up at last.

"In a minute," she says to Magic meowing for his dinner. She pops out the cassette and switches the channel. A movie she vaguely remembers comes up on eleven.

The phone rings. Cassie at last. *I'm so sorry.* . . .

"Nona Engels, please."

"Who?"

"Is this Nona Engels?"

Nona folds up on the edge of the rumpled bed in a cloud of violet scent from the mist she sprays between the sheets. A wave of sweat breaks over her body. On the TV screen a man and woman walk along a rain-soaked street, shoulder to shoulder, their gazes interlocked, in ardent, silent discussion. A close-up of the woman makes her mouth look as huge as the lion's to a Nona now scaled down to child size, as the beat issuing through the receiver continues.

Nona Engels, Nona Engels.

"Wrong number!" she gasps, spittle on the white receiver.

She slams down the phone and Magic jumps up beside her, to circle about the folds of silk. Nona clutches at him.

"It's just a mistake, that's all. Nothing. A mistake."

Magic answers with a shrill mew, for Nona grips him too hard. He struggles but it takes her a moment before she lets him down.

"A mistake," she says, as if she expects the disappearing cat to return and argue with her.

Later, around nine, Cassie apologizes. "I should have called earlier. . . ."

9

"I don't know what came over me. . . ."

"Let me not be the one to play shrink, but . . ." Eve makes a *moue,* hesitant to criticize. She eases out of the wicker chair, careful not to bump her head on the hood. All the while she and Cassie have been eating lunch in the café she has felt imprisoned in a Venus flytrap, as if the silly chair were about to swallow her.

"But what?"

On the subject of children one treads in a mine field. The best of friends stiffen like pointers when their offspring are mentioned. Cassie is no less immune than other mothers.

"Jealousy? At least a little? Mandy and Nona are big chums."

Out on the sidewalk Cassie takes a half turn into the sunlight. A plumb line hangs on one corner of her mouth, pulling her smile off kilter. Eve wishes she hadn't said anything. What does she know? She is, after all, a tabula rasa when it comes to children. Little ones seem to her as insignificant as pets, talking versions of Nona's cat, and teenagers are experimental models of humans, not yet fully formed. She has probably spoken fewer than ten words to Mandy in any one year, passing around her as though she were an unreliable piece of furniture. Not that she has ever been negative. When Cassie takes a long tour in her mother mode Eve listens politely, as she will to a client with only half a million unrealistically dreaming of a high-tech kitchen in a three-bedroom on the West Side, north of Sunset. Children for Eve simply exist in another dimension. They are fantasies, pie in the sky, never mind their real-life problems—dramatically portrayed on television—or the way they shoulder worries onto their parents like sandbags.

In fact, Eve dislikes thinking of children at all, and switches the channel away from car crashes, drugs, alcoholism, peer pressure, bad grades, messy heartbreaks.

"I have no idea why you're implying that I'm jealous of Nona. Naturally she and Mandy are friendly. You're friendly with Mandy too," Cassie says, arching her back.

Is Cassie blind in both eyes? She never sits around dishing dirt with Mandy about rock groups and soap stars. When has Cassie seen Eve doing a makeup or hair routine on her daughter? Meeting haphazardly like apartment neighbors on a checkout line in Ralph's, the two seldom say more than *Hello, how are you?* Yet Eve agrees. "Sure, I get along with Mandy, but she and Nona are tighter. It's not Mandy. It's Nona. Ms. Teeny-Bopper. Flaming youth. Arrested development. You know how Nona is. It's part of her charm, right?"

Cassie ignores Nona's perpetual youth and says, "I'm just upset that Mandy popped up with no warning. She never asked if she could come home. Not that she has to, but to charge a plane ticket and fly to L.A., well . . ."

Is it Mandy's sudden independence that triggers Cassie's bad temper? And has she forgotten how earlier she worried Mandy wouldn't survive at college, that she was too timid and umbilically linked to her, Cassie?

Eve takes the middle ground, saying, "She couldn't have if you didn't give her a credit card." Logic is everything. "Up to now she's been on a strict allowance, plus whatever she earned babysitting."

While Eve and Mandy have no personal involvement, Eve knows a goodly amount about the girl. Mandy is Cassie's star player. Eve has learned over the years about her marks, friends, the emotional teenage sideshow, her plodding, noncommittal reaction to the divorce. At times Eve, bored, suppresses a yawn in the middle of Cassie's parental rhetoric. But she forgives such love, particularly in the last few years, for raising a child alone demands herculean strength and the endurance of a water buffalo. Cassie strides along in the ranks of heroines.

Why are women so eager to have babies? Just look at Nona,

salivating at the mention of layettes and nursery school. Surely the propagation of the species can't be worth so much trouble, Eve often thinks, investing her money in apartment buildings rather than giving it away to a college.

"What choice do I have? She can run out of money at school—"

"So she calls you."

"And what if I'm not home or at the clinic?"

"Then she calls What's-His-Name," Eve says, snide as always about Doug the Betrayer.

"Oh, Doug." Cassie sniffs at the memory of her ex-husband.

They walk along Main Street away from Eve's car. Eve picked up Cassie at the clinic and now will drive her back. They are going in the wrong direction but Cassie doesn't seem to care and Eve has the time. Her next appointment isn't until three in the Palisades. Cassie obviously needs to clear her conscience, still cloudy, though it has been days since she mistreated Nona, and Eve's heard about it from both of them at least twice. *Mistreated* is Cassie's word, not Eve's.

"You didn't take an ax to her psyche. You lost your cool. Blew up. Big deal and Happy New Year. Nona probably doesn't even remember it," Eve lies.

Light and shadow divide the street and they stroll the sun-washed side.

"Nona remembers every slight of the last thirty years," Cassie says, but nonjudgmentally. "She has no outer plating."

"Well, you did apologize."

"Of course, though probably not soon enough. But I was so appalled at my bad behavior. I mean yelling at Nona is like kicking the cat. And then I was involved with Mandy, mainly traipsing around her and asking what was wrong."

"What is wrong?" Eve asks because Cassie expects her to.

"Nothing—being eighteen, away at school freshman year, hormones probably—but don't let the feminists hear me say that. We all function fabulously despite our hormones or because of them; I forget what's the latest party line."

"I'm glad to hear Mandy has hormones," Eve says.

"Oh, shut up," Cassie says, reddening and swatting the air by Eve's arm. "Anyway, Nona always makes me feel clumsy, which is another reason it took me all day to telephone."

"You have the neatest stitch of any doctor in the group. That's what you told me once."

"Oh, I was bragging, and I mean psychologically clumsy anyway."

"I know that. I'm just trying to josh you out of your funk, which is unnecessary and ill-advised. We spend too much time worrying about Nona, about her *delicacy,* as if she's a paper doll, unfit for modern life."

"She is, in a way."

They hesitate in a pool of shade, before monsters glaring metallically at them through a gallery window, shiny creatures, a long-dead artist's mythical beings. Steel fingers point as if in nightmare sleep. Eve shivers and moves along.

They stop again before a window of sheer white gowns, antique, lacy, older than either of them and frail as smoke. In the mirrored wall at the rear of the small shop they stand shoulder to shoulder, two women pocked in the speckled glass, whispering across time. They appear conspiratorial to Cassie and she steps back for distance. Her heart is heavy. Meanness to Nona creates a knot of guilt below her breastbone, like indigestion, which hasn't been eased by talking with Eve and is absurdly worse now after the heavy sandwiches at lunch.

Cassie's weight is still up and she feels cumbersome. Ten pounds more than she is accustomed to make her sluggish. To her patients she advises simplicity, a multiple-vitamin, calcium-rich food, plenty of water, but is slipshod with her own diet.

Eve, having had enough of Nona and Cassie's *mea culpa*s, urges Cassie on across the street and back toward the parking lot. On the other side they pass a cluttered display of Mexican pottery, a window with artifacts of stained glass, a gallery decorated by fiery paintings of flaming color in oddly shaped frames. A few short blocks away to the west lies the ocean, hidden behind shops and condominiums, quietly lapping at the sand, oblivious. And odorless. The Pacific might as well be bath water for all the smells it emits, not like the Atlantic, fishy and salt-tasting when the wind blows.

They reach the car, and once they are riding up Main Street, Eve announces, "I've got news."

"Good, bad, or so-so?"

"Fabulous. Seven million on the hoof."

"What?"

"I have a listing for seven million."

Cassie stops Eve with a hand to her arm. "From whom? How?" Seven million is a stratosphere figure, a number from beyond the moon. Other people talk—and live—in millions but Cassie isn't sure she'd want to if she could.

"Would you believe a walk-in? Right out of the wild blue. A dimply little Iranian whose wife left him for a rock singer and who's overjoyed because now he can move to New York. Where the action is, he says."

"You should be pleased as an Oscar winner."

"Clam-happy, though I didn't do anything to get it. It would be even better if I made it happen instead of being under the tree when the apple fell."

"You're hairsplitting."

Eve turns up her nose and recites, "Good fortune gained without elbow grease doesn't feel as complete."

"What's that from, Sunday school?" Cassie asks, surprised. It's not like Eve to be so self-righteous.

Eve sniffs, annoyed. "I can't help it if that's how I feel."

"Don't huff at me. I'm not criticizing. In fact it's a *good* thing, not a *bad* thing, to feel you have to earn life's rewards."

"Well, I'm not tossing over my little château in Holmby Hills because of morality. My philosophy and bank account travel in separate crowds."

That sounds more like Eve. "We'll have a case of champagne at the closing."

"Tah-dah," Eve says, but she isn't mollified. Why does Cassie find it so difficult to see that she does have morals, a sound New England ethic? Is it because she's in real estate with its constant buying and selling, the millions that get tossed around like tiddly-winks? Real estate isn't a charlatan's trade, without rules and obligations, Eve feels like telling Cassie—but won't. She hates to fight with her. Cassie is her lodestar, her touchstone, and Eve has a scratchy need for Cassie's approval, a light nod of benediction at least. So of course she can't say that the seven-million listing should have been old Titus Reynolds's, but Titus, fey and peculiar, with sour ideas, would have turned up his nose at the Iranian—

the "Persian." Taking over the city. Look at that lovely house on Sunset, he moans still, though the house is long gone and the lot just sits there, a vacant piece of expensive property. Destroyed, utterly. *They* paint statues green! And fig leaves yet! The poor Hartman place! Titus moans, as though the vanished house still stands and is infected and had been—which it never was—owned by Iranians.

Titus is a stick. His nose jams up the behinds of the landed gentry, and good for him that he hasn't gotten Ahmer's house to put on the market.

Titus's values depress Eve. Hasn't he learned through all his decades that money has no color? Once he said to Eve, in his wood-paneled office with a Bokhara on the floor: *I'm too far advanced for trauma. Foreigners are difficult. They're different than we are.*

It's the rich who are different, Eve thought then to tell him, but she needed—needs—Titus's good will.

"Wait!" Cassie says urgently. "You should have turned right at that corner."

"This is the way I came," Eve snaps.

"I guess so. Maybe I wasn't paying attention—but if you drive by the hospital and then swing east rather than coming so far north, you won't have to backtrack."

"Cassie, who's driving, you or me?" Eve asks with a tight smile that is more a grimace and sets Cassie wondering at her sudden stubbornness.

"You, of course," Cassie replies and stares out the window, mystified.

But what can Eve say—that I never take that street, that I won't pass that hospital and haven't for so long it's automatic to drive blocks out of the way? No, this isn't a confession she will make to Cassie, though she wishes she could say:

Once upon a time, Cassie, when I was young and stupid . . .

To Eve's relief they finally pull up in front of the clinic. She stops the car and they lean toward each other, fanning the air with their kisses. All is forgiven, harsh words, spurts of temper. Affection, even love, floats along their bones and in a spontaneous moment that strikes both women at the same time, as if there were a witchery shared between them, they hug, whisper: Cassie's *Be good* to Eve's *Don't fret.*

122

Cassie walks away and only then does Eve want to cry after her: I'm still bleeding, too much, buckets of blood! Something's going wrong. Gone wrong. I'm scared!

But this flux is an aberration, nothing serious, because the idea that her body is behaving treacherously is out of the question. Eve refuses to allow such a betrayal. So she rolls down her car windows and turns up the stereo with the raw beat of something disharmonious and proceeds to forget.

By the time Eve arrives over a winding road at Temecula Canyon she's in a foul mood. Feverishly out of temper, she is bloated and waterlogged. Immediately on crossing the tile foyer she excuses herself to the widow whose split-level she will be showing and rushes to the powder room.

The small bath needs redoing, though only cosmetically, Eve thinks, steadying her attention on the upcoming low-keyed sales pitch she plans rather than the blood still flowing copiously.

She changes napkins and wishes she didn't have to deposit the bloody one in the widow's plastic wastebasket, which looks as though it's never had so much as a dirty Kleenex in it. Eve feels humiliated, even with another woman, to be so vulnerably female.

"Eve?" the widow calls timidly, her voice so close her lips might be pressed against the door.

But when Eve emerges the woman is trying to appear uninvolved, lounging in a studied pose on the patio with the newspaper. The client waits in the living room already checking her watch, counting minutes. "I don't have much time," she says, tapping a well-shod foot impatiently.

Anger tarnishes Eve's vision. Screw you, she thinks, and says in a dry, sandy tone, as detached as the business woman in her man-tailored navy suit and a shirt buttoned to the collar, "Let's not waste a moment then, shall we?"

The woman is another agent's client and the agent should be here, too, nipping at everyone's elbows, but she is a part-timer derailed by a sick child or a school meeting, some unprofessional reason.

Single, the woman is shopping both for a home and an investment. "I want a good buy," she informs Eve as they tour the split-level, implying that Eve might try to sell her something else.

They pass from room to room rather quickly, the client continually one step ahead. She isn't a poker, barely glancing at closets. Through the sliding glass doors and windows Eve sees the widow darting anxious peeks, her pale rabbit's eyes raised above the rims of her sunglasses.

The house has been on the market more than six months and the widow is sweaty to move to Phoenix, where she has a son and daughter-in-law. Now that she's alone the house presses on her neck like an ox-collar. It stands isolated from the neighbors at a bend in the canyon road, and though an elaborate configuration of wires and light beams guards all the doors and windows, the widow worries about intruders. She feasts on gory stories in the paper, on robberies and rapes. Alone, expecting victimization (though only in her imagination up to now), and against Eve's advice, she panics and lowers the price of the house by $50,000.

The client, stalking across the hardwood in her Bally pumps, is the antithesis of the widow. The house's location doesn't bother her. "It's a plus," she says, "not to see the neighbors."

"And the view," Eve prompts, motioning from the master bedroom to the hills knobby with other houses. "On a clear day you can see Catalina." The sight of the island—a speck in the ocean— is always a prime selling point.

The ocean captivates the woman for one breath, two; then she retreats to the laundry room and inspects the water heater. "This has no business here. If it breaks the house will be flooded," she says, disapproving of the widow and her dead husband for being remiss. "And," she continues, back in the kitchen after a forward advance as fast as the Wehrmacht, "this has got to be redone, top to bottom." She flings out the hand not encumbered by a briefcase, free with condemnation. "Old-fashioned and ugly as sin. Really, some people." The woman makes no attempt to modulate her disdain, though the owner is barely a few feet away. The patio drifts with afternoon shadows, and the widow, legs outstretched, lies under striations.

Eve turns to avoid her eyes and stares at a watercolor of purple flowers. The widow's first name is scratched in the right-hand corner.

"You have to expect to do some work, whatever you buy," Eve

says, unprofessionally hoping that the woman won't settle here and sweep away the widow's memories.

"The less the better."

She checks her watch again and Eve is relieved her client is the widow, overweight, leathered by the sun, with jiggly thighs and breasts cushy as sofa pillows. Eve feels protective of her, lost at sea (or, rather, in her canyon) without a man at the helm. Eve silently calls to the nervous owner: *Pay no attention!* The prospective buyer, after all, is in no superior position; she hasn't a man either and if she buys the house will sleep alone with the identical view of the ocean for company. In that, buyer and seller are, except for details, much the same.

Nothing concluded, the woman leaves. The widow comes inside and together she and Eve listen to the car reverse in the drive, as if the gravelly sound of the tires can tell them something explicit.

"The quiet is a strong feature," Eve says when they can no longer hear the car on the canyon road. But the widow isn't convinced, for it is the quiet most of all that works against her.

"Stay for coffee," she says to Eve, and Eve suspects she'd like to hold her into the evening, for dinner and after.

"Another time." Eve smiles, insinuating that pressing business needs attention, when in fact all she has on her desk is paperwork that can wait.

Before she goes she uses the powder room again, and again changes the bloody pad. This time she carries the basket out to the trash container in the back, over the widow's insistence that "You don't have to." But removing the evidence makes Eve feel at least marginally better.

Cassie realizes she is making far too much of her outburst. She is not such a saint that she's never lost her temper, or yelled, or been left high and dry on the far shore of anger, but Saturday night she went too far. And with Nona. Why?

Eve's insinuation—jealousy—rankles, though Cassie recalls *her* daughter's soul-searching with *her* friend and again feels left out. She was a wall, a chair, a thing, or at best an observer.

So much of the world passes through her. She screens symptoms, computes them against her knowledge and experience, diagnoses, decides, but it is always for someone else, another woman. Naturally she has no desire to sicken herself, lie down and gag, cough, ache or pain, have Jena or Barbara examine her, make "poor" Cassie the other, but she does weary of being continually outside. She wants to participate. In a world divided into those who watch and those who act, she belongs to the former. She ministers, hands almost like puppeteer's hands coming out of the dark through a curtain. At least once she'd give a lot to slip onstage.

Cassie has seen four patients in the hour she's been back from lunch and another appointment waits when the nurse on the desk calls through: "April DeVito is here, Cassie."

"Is she scheduled?" Cassie runs a squared unpolished nail down the list of the afternoon's appointments but doesn't see April's name.

"No, but you should squeeze her in."

Cassie's antennae quiver. Helen's tone is ominous and there's something she keeps from saying.

"Okay. Put her in three if it's vacant. And explain to Mrs. Cera that I'll be another few minutes."

Not waiting for April to get settled, Cassie is on the heels of the nurse, who shakes her taffy-colored curls as she holds the door ajar.

"What's the problem, April?" Cassie asks before April turns her bony back and faces her. Cassie cries, "Oh, my God!"

April is diminutive, a hair above five feet and with arms and legs as skinny as birch branches. She is the stick drawing a child does at a kindergarten table and, ironically in a world of overweight women struggling with suffocating flesh, unable to gain a pound.

A great purple-black bruise rings April's left eye socket and spills like runny ink over the rise of her cheekbone. The eye itself is bulging, shuttered except for a needle-thin slit between the lashes. The slangy term for April's lower lip is *fat*. Swollen to twice its normal size, the lip gives the bottom half of what is normally a tiny pixie face a lopsided distortion.

A jagged cut scars the corner of the lip and the wound must have bled profusely.

"I fell down the stairs," April says, speaking slowly around the misshapen lip, which she pushes out to protect from the rub of her teeth. It appears that April's teeth are all in place but one or two are probably loosened.

"Down the stairs?"

"Uh-huh."

A fall is possible but unlikely, Cassie thinks as she carefully turns April's head, viewing the damage. April winces, though the uninjured blue eye stares like the glassy eye of a doll.

Cassie doesn't dare part the swollen lids of the other. "Can you see out of that?" she asks softly.

"A little."

"Hurt?"

"Not as much as last night."

"When you fell down the stairs."

A painkiller isn't indicated if April has lasted this long without one, but Cassie calls over the intercom for atropine to dilate the pupil. "I want you to see an ophthalmologist, in case there's some real damage, like a detached retina, which isn't so unusual with a sock to the eye."

"Nobody hit me," April counters defensively.

"Or in the mouth." The slash in the lip has already closed unstitched, but will surely leave a scar. Gingerly Cassie probes April's mouth and the girl cries deep in her throat.

"Sorry," Cassie says automatically.

"My wrist hurts too."

For the first time Cassie notices that April is protectively cradling one hand with the other. A soft cuff swells around the bone, and when Cassie tries to bend April's wrist the faint cry wings upward.

"A bad sprain or maybe a ligament's torn, April. But I can't tell without an X-ray." When Helen brings the atropine Cassie tells her she wants pictures of April's wrist.

"Let's go, lady pirate," Helen says with a smile, seriously friendly, a first-grade teacher, helping her off the table once the drops have gone into the squash-blossom eye and a patch is cushioned over it.

When Cassie rotated to the emergency room of a large inner-city hospital during her residency, the battered combatants of street brawls appeared with stupefying regularity, as did the female victims of men's anger. With the grim humor of young doctors reeling in shift after shift of war zone casualties, these injured were called ring survivors or Ali's sparring partners. So, *down the stairs, my ass*, Cassie seethes as Helen returns the girl. Cassie's guess is confirmed. The wrist is merely sprained, not broken. She tapes it and writes down the name and phone number of an ophthalmologist for April to consult.

"What else did he do to you?" Cassie asks when they've finished. "Anything sexual?"

"I don't know what you're talking about." A pulse quivers in April's throat like a small bird trapped under the skin.

"Why did you come to see me, April? I'm your gynecologist. I treat female problems like your yeast infection and the cyst you had last year. And that very mysterious tearing of your vagina. Remember that?" Cassie raises one brow at April before consulting her chart. "Dr. Allerman is your internist. He's the one you'd see for a fall down the steps. Unless you've changed doctors."

"No. He's still the one."

Cassie waits, prepared to keep Mrs. Cera on hold for the remainder of the afternoon if need be, and the other appointments backed up behind her. She will take root in this chilly examining room until April satisfies her. But how can she? The truth will only stoke Cassie's anger, not dampen it.

"I don't have to ask who, because we both know who slams you around. You're your husband's favorite punching bag. You and the kids!"

"He never touches them." April bristles.

"Because you throw yourself in the middle and let him hit you rather than one of them. Right?"

April has nothing to say to that and Cassie visualizes this little rag doll flying into the raining blows in order to protect her children. Cassie understands in her gut how it would be to snatch Mandy from harm's way and take the impact of a speeding car, a train, a knife, a bullet. But not a husband's fists, a father's. Just as instinctively she'd pack up and move, but of course she is not April, and Doug, no matter what she can say of him, wasn't the least like April's husband.

Cassie asks, "Are you going to pretend that he didn't do this?" April, still sitting on the table, dangles her feet in their laced-up sneakers and stares at the floor—not the best position for her black eye.

Cassie wants April home on the bed with an ice pack resting

gently over the swollen eye. She tries again. "I think you came to Magdalene, to me, because you want to talk about this. You want me to help you, or to find somebody who will. And a woman doctor is more comfortable than a man. You sense that a woman will understand. Am I wrong?"

"Can I have something for the pain?" is all that April will say.

"Which pain? Your eye? Your lip? Your wrist? All of them? Or the hurt inside that nobody can bandage up?"

April folds into herself, defiantly silent.

"How long do you think you can survive this abuse, April? Before it was rape—"

"Nobody can get raped by their husband!"

Cassie wants to shake the girl, shake her and hug her simultaneously. Realistically, if she could, she'd pack up April's belongings and transport her and the two kids to a safe life, beyond the reach of a husband and father who swings murderously above their heads like a sharp-edged scimitar. Soon he will strike one blow too many, or the wrong one, and April will become another short paragraph in the newspapers, just the sort of story Cassie jerks away from when reading the *Times*. Maybe one set of the old bones in Santa Monica was originally a girl like April.

"Sometimes he has one too many," April says, surprising Cassie, who has given up any hope of her speaking today. "Then"—her bony bird shoulders twitch—"he loses it. Like a Dr. Jekyll or a Mr. Hyde, I always forget which, but you know. Somebody the kids and me are like strangers with." She talks to the floor, her head cast down and the pale skin of her neck exposed. Cassie's heart shudders in her chest at the whiteness and the knobby little bones. "After, like the next morning, he never remembers. He says it's a mistake, that he didn't mean nothing by it. Or sometimes he says I made it up, that he never."

Before she can stop, Cassie explodes: "Made *this* up?" She eases April's head up. The good eye swims with tears like a jewel in a filmy aquarium.

"He says he loves me."

"This isn't love!"

"And for days and days, weeks even, he's so good."

"April, you're a battered woman and you need help. Listen, there's a halfway house right near National where they'll take you and the kids in, help you find an apartment, a job. They'll get you a lawyer and if necessary a restraining order."

April's face hangs before Cassie like a picture on a wall, the only sign of life the tear winding in slow motion down her cheek. "April?"

"He'll kill me if I leave."

"He'll kill you if you don't." Cassie suddenly realizes they're whispering and the words are cold as frost.

April slides off the table, forcing Cassie to back up. She is losing her.

Tonight, tomorrow, next week, when April's bruises fade to yellow, her husband will hurt her again. It is inevitable as morning glories blooming in the sun. Cassie, the custodian of too many dire statistics, knows this.

What she can't calculate is how long April will survive before she snaps like a twig. But Cassie has no clear vision of how to save her. She has sworn to help but without April's acquiescence she is powerless.

Plead, warn, threaten?

"At least let me give you the name and address—"

Cassie leans into air, scattering April's *thank you*s. The girl goes, taking her shadow, and Cassie feels the shivers her mother used to call the graveyard dancers.

10

The witches twitter like blackbirds, their little faces delicious compositions of rubber and raisin eyes. They are wicked in their delight, skipping along, careening off one another. Conical cardboard hats slip sideways on their curly heads and would fall off if not anchored by elastic chin straps.

Ghosts collide in the sooty dusk. With a loud, spiraling cry a devil trips over his forked paper tail and is scooped up by a strongman in leopard cloth. On a patch of tidy lawn a cowboy whinnies and gallops in unfenced fantasy. A cumbersome tin man walks arm in arm with the Great Pumpkin.

The night, tasting of apples, is alive with miniature demons clutching UNICEF bags.

Nona walks home from the boulevard amid the frenzied children, a sack of groceries in her arms. The children are October's leaves and a windy exuberance blows in their wake.

A dwarfed Spider Man attacks Nona's leg and cries, "Treat!"

"Come on, Jeddie!" an impatient older ballerina orders and drags him away.

Nona laughs, wishing she, too, could run through the night, and remembers long-ago Halloweens, frost on her tongue and pumpkins in uncurtained windows. Candy corn and Tootsie Rolls—how old had she been? Eight, nine? Surely younger than ten, when they sent her off to Miss Pettet's in the mountains.

And—

"I don't want to go!"

"Growing up wild as a weed. I won't have it." Marian intended to get her way, and for once Nona's father had no reserves against her mother's anger.

Their arguments were sour, spoiling the atmosphere day after day until Adam finally gave in and Nona was flung into silence. She clung to him in the study when Marian went up to bed with one of her headaches—but only after Adam promised—and wept, "I hate her!"

Adam stroked her head with a heavy hand. Where would she be without him? She had been Adam's girl as long as she remembered. She needed her father, who whispered when no one could hear him *flesh of my flesh,* and who swore to protect her from the monsters in the garden.

But still Nona went.

Miss Pettet's was as drab as a reformatory, with stone walls and black iron grillwork over the front windows. Cold drafts whiffled up between the floorboards.

The girls all wore gray uniforms like petitioners and slept six to a room on miserly mattresses.

By Halloween the trees for as far as they could see from the upstairs windows were stripped bare and lay against the sky in slashes of charcoal. The land was yellow and brittle and the dry grass crunched when they walked on it.

Miss Pettet's Halloween was a sad little party of girls dunking for apples, careful not to get their starched white collars wet. They had jack-o'-lanterns but no costumes, just black half-masks, and for fun they played musical chairs. Then they listened to Miss Croydon, who taught English and geography, read ghost tales that scared the younger girls into nightmarish fits after lights out.

The girls were *never* allowed candy, and sighed with thanks on Halloween, for now October passed into November, ushering them closer to Thanksgiving vacation, ever nearer to three weeks at Christmas.

Nona dropped penny after penny from her meager allowance off the bridge over the stream behind the horse barn, in exchange for wishes. She wanted her own ruffled bed, rocking chair, the porcelain dolls untouched on the shelf, soft rugs, the warm kitchen. She wanted her father, his lap, the smell of whiskey and smuggled Cuban cigars, the smoothness of his cheek when he shaved, the rough bristles when he didn't. In his arms she felt safe and his hands were gentle.

"Stop crawling on top of your father! You're too old for that now," her mother ordered when Nona went home for vacation. But he was so warm; he hugged her.

I'll protect you is what he tickled Nona's ear with when Marian couldn't hear him. And had she forgotten the black-fanged beast, blood-red eyes and a nose like a corkscrew?

Nona passes a teenager, plumed as a peacock in orange hair, who walks with one hand in a leather boy's back pocket. The girl wears a T-shirt—TO HELL AND BACK—over her large, unfettered breasts. The nipples round as bottle caps swell against the thin cotton. She might as well be naked, at least from the waist up, Nona thinks, considering herself old-fashioned. She swam through an uncorseted generation always wearing a brassiere.

Cheap, tarts, whores, her father castigated the girls in rags and tatters, beaded Little Orphan Annies, his friends' children strumming guitars and shouting slogans. When she came home from Yardley—where she went after Miss Pettet's—Nona heard his denunciations to friends. *Those* children were locusts, termites undermining the foundations of nurturing homes and the businesses that supported them. His tirades sounded bleak with omens.

Adam hated the dirt, the lewdness of those lice-infested savages so unlike his lovely Nona, infidels gathering in packs on the Common, along Commonwealth, in the very precincts *God damn it!* of Harvard Square. Is nothing to be left standing? Nothing sacred anymore?

Nona met the cousin of a Yardley girl at a party and he explained: *We want our rights*.

He brought Nona home. A cousin from the wrong side of the tracks, the blanket, a half-breed, a poor younger brother's mistake, her father ranted. Just look at his ear with a ring in it! Why not his nose? And what rights? To dress like derelicts? To smell?

Nona liked the cousin's eyes but washed her hands in the downstairs bathroom after her father showed him the door.

After her last year at Yardley she was sent to a small college on the French Canadian border that had originally been a coal baron's estate. The nuns ran it and Marian exploded. It's for Catholics!

They'll turn her into a black crow! But a sister of charity, of mercy, of the poor, her father preferred—if it came to that—to a daughter with long, unwashed hair, granny glasses, mini-skirts, no undergarments, cursing, smoking dope. So he slyly made fun of the religious issue and stressed the college's small classes, varied curriculum, and students from upper-class families.

St. Celeste's was even colder than Miss Pettet's, as bleak as the grave, the sky continually gray, the land uncolored.

Nona wrote to her mother, suddenly an ally, *I hate it!* Yet at twenty she never thought to pack up and take to the road. Half the country was in transit but Nona waited.

Adam drove up alone to see her.

They had dinner at a country inn, near the fire. Adam ordered a fine Chablis and plied her with questions.

What was wrong with St. Celeste's?

Why didn't she like it?

Were they mean to her? Wasn't she learning?

Did she want to come back to Boston and be like the scum at B.U.?

"Do you know I have to take a course in Home Science *every* semester?"

"So?" He looked amused.

"Home Science is cooking and sewing. Oh, Daddy, it's embroidery in *college!*"

"What's wrong with that?"

Nona had taken her father's visit as a reprieve. He was going to relent and bring her in from the wilderness. Instead he brought a manila folder out of his briefcase. "Here, I've brought something to show you. I think you're old enough to understand where the loose living so many others indulge in can lead to." He spread the pictures on the table. They were in color, of men and women with boils, scabrous rashes, lesions, ugly distortions. Their pustules were tiny yellow-capped mountains.

"These are people suffering with sexual diseases. This is the kind of monster one can turn into if she's not careful." He touched her cheek lightly, just with a fingertip. "I can't bear to think of such beautiful skin becoming too hideous to look at, never mind touch."

Nona shivered. "I'd never."

"Last week my secretary's son OD'd. Died. Dead. He won't come back to life like an actor on television." Adam flung a picture onto her plate, of a young girl with raven hair trailing off a metal table. Her white body was naked. "That's a dead girl who took LSD. She walked out a window."

Nona swore she would never take drugs if he let her come back to Boston, but he countered, didn't she want to please him? Be good? Flow effortlessly downstream, lazy as a skiff on the Charles in another century? He thought the dangerous times they lived in would pass; a war undeclared had soon to be mediated. Things had to change, return to normal. In the meanwhile she could wait. Here. Safe. Let her miss a whole universe, the largest party, a better party than on Halloween in Los Angeles, a sixties into seventies bash, rebellion. And, her father said, they all smell foul while you smell like eau de cologne.

Violets on Nona's breath pleased Adam.

Nona sighs and puts away her memories as she does the few items she has bought in the market. She likes to shop in little dribs and drabs, likes the walking seven blocks. Besides, it's better to keep the cupboards mostly empty so she won't be tempted.

She heats water for a cup of soup.

She could go out. There's a party at the Urban Sports Club, replete with champagne punch, hors d'oeuvres, prizes for the best costumes. In the polished chrome bar, singles will circulate, but Nona needs to meet no one. Alan in her life frees her from *looking*.

At the glass table Nona sees her feet, bare toes, as if she's cleft in two, the top half of her body divorced from the bottom. Magic slides around her ankles, and taking careful spoons of soup, Nona watches him. But she can't watch a cat forever. After a while the apartment throbs with silence. Despite her resolve Nona leaves and drives over to Cassie's. Cassie will have candy and bubblegum, pennies, nickels, McIntosh apples for the wandering children. But Cassie isn't home. Only the porch light is lit.

Nona can't know that Cassie has gone with Jake on . . .

. . . Well, yes, it is a formal date, different from the Thursdays when they have a beer together in the kitchen.

Cassie rushes home on Thursdays not to miss Jake, holding her breath until she rounds the corner and sees the truck, until she can call airily *oh you must be thirsty* or *it's so hot,* any throwaway line for him to grab hold of and swim across the mown lawn, the felled flowers, and rise up into the kitchen, where she has dropped her bag on the counter and snatched two Coronas out of the fridge.

This Thursday she worries she's missed him, kept late by a lingering patient. But he waits, leaning against the truck as though he has all the time in the world. And maybe he does. What does she know about him?

"I didn't think you were coming," he says, as if this already is their date, when she eases up to the garage door and gets out of the car.

Tongue-tied, nervous laughter bubbling behind her teeth, she replies with the first stupid remark that flies into her head. "The world's sick. Too much of it." She stumbles on: "I mean I was ear-deep in patients."

He has disconcerted her by not having disappeared in Yang's truck when the yard was done—raked, watered, dead branches trimmed. *He waited*. And then he asks her. The words come out so simply. She has heard them before, after all.

Would you like to have dinner?

There is nothing so strange about a man inviting a woman out and a woman accepting. The mating dance. Eve's biology. But Cassie, embarrassed, blushes scarlet and is pleased to her toes. She says simply *yes*, breathing it out in a long sigh, and now here she is in Jake's Honda Civic that has seen better days.

The car is clean except for the ashtray with one lone cigarette butt in it. Cassie suspects Jake tidies the Honda as a woman does her house, with a fussiness that is uncharacteristic of men—except, in Cassie's experience, her father. Her father swept and vacuumed his Buick's interior. He whisk-broomed the seats, dusted the dash, spit-polished the chrome, and swabbed the windows inside and out with vinegar water. Each warm Saturday he hosed and soaped the sedan, lovingly rubbing down the fenders as broad as a fat woman's thighs, humming intently like a man wrapped in live electrical wires.

A man and his car, Cassie's mother would say, shaking her head as she kept an eye on him through the kitchen window, as if a mysterious male ritual was taking place out on the drive.

What will she talk about? Cassie fretted before Jake picked her up. She remembers Malone's and her throat closing, the soft tissues swelling from terror. Now she will be alone with him.

He has asked her out. Cassie is going on a boy-girl, man-woman date with the gardener who wears an eagle on his arm, whose last name she realizes guiltily she's never heard.

This Jake is much more a stranger—and totally unvalidated—than the Levinsons' engineer. Yet she sweeps her fears aside, for his nearness makes her feel airborne.

Jake doesn't share her nervousness, or if her presence unsettles him he hides it well, or again, he covers it over with music. He shoves a cassette of Bix Beiderbecke into the tape deck. Does she know Bix?

"Only by reputation."

Jake lays out facts for her, that Bix was the best, that he died at twenty-eight, and how he had been a man of too much talent, swallowed by his genius. "As a kid," Jake says, driving easily, in that one-handed way men have, "he played on the river boats until his father caught him. He was white and in love with black music."

If Cassie were Eve, Jake's statement about Bix would give her easy access to the coy question *And what are you in love with, Jake?* Then she could start him talking about himself instead of a musician dead over fifty years. But she lacks Eve's forthrightness and knows little of Jake beyond his having been in Vietnam.

In Malone's, with a drink in her hand, Cassie was able at least to string words together, but now, driving across the city, alone in the car, she wishes she had prepared a list of topics to discuss, for she can't think of anything more than to ask about Yang.

Talking over tinny music, old-fashioned as an accompaniment to a silent movie, Jake says, "I know Yang from the war. We did some stuff together."

Stuff? What does stuff mean? Cassie thinks to ask him but he has a question of his own.

"How long are you divorced, Cassie?"

He's never used her name before and the sound of it in his mouth excites her. If he would only say it again. She wants to anticipate it rather than let *Cassie* come and go quickly off his lips.

"Three years."

She resists explaining how Doug left for a younger Tracy in a string bikini down at the Marina. Cassie isn't conscious of her ex-husband sitting between her and Jake, as she has been with so many other men.

"Long time," Jake says.

"It seems like forever." And right then it does, though it didn't yesterday. It's like that with her ex-husband. Tomorrow Doug can as easily return to wander ghostlike up and down the steps, to roll over lightly in her bed and brush his cobwebby memory against her flank. But for now it really seems he's gone for good, that her anger is shelved and her regrets wiped away.

"A doctor?"

"No. A lawyer."

Doctor, lawyer, Indian chief, and what has Jake been doing all these years before he started mowing grass for a man he did stuff with back in the war? Cassie doesn't have to ask to know Jake will have a long story, as complicated as the old bones that came and went in the paper without any explanation. Have the authorities buried them yet and who would officiate? Priest, minister, rabbi? How can anybody decide?

To her surprise, Jake—for in the kitchen his talk is of the garden, baseball, will the long drought end soon with a decent rain— reveals he has had a marriage of his own. "On and off, mostly off, for twelve years."

The woman, whom he designates not by name but as *my ex*, lives down in Galveston, married again and then for a third time, and is the mother of his two daughters. Cassie is about to ask their names and ages when he says, "What do you think of Bix?"

Of all the brassy instruments on the tape Cassie can't tell which is the silvery cornet. There is no one cutting tone. To Cassie's untutored ear the horns go from blending their metallic notes to hurling combatively at one another's throats, until, all of a sudden, a pure crystal sound floats from the car's speakers with nothing fuzzy around it, only a high lone bird climbing. For the too-brief instant, it stops Cassie cold. When it fades finally, leaving nostalgia for the loss that is almost heartbreaking, Cassie looks over at Jake. He is smiling.

If honesty and sharing are two essential components of friendship, then Cassie is delinquent, for she hasn't even hinted to Eve and Nona of her interest in Jake the gardener. For all the women know, the same faceless anonymity who has forever done Cassie's yard work still appears weekly to mow the lawn and rake weeds. Gardeners aren't a pressing concern to apartment dwellers like Eve and Nona. Bushes and palm trees don't crowd the corners of their fantasies. Flowers come from the florist already cut. Of course, if Cassie ever said that a hunk in jeans and a T-shirt, with graying dark hair that falls like silk over cliffs of bones, waters my azaleas, if she described Jake's broad shoulders and narrow waist, blue eyes and the fine webbing of lines crisscrossing his tan, mentioned that his nose is memorable, his mouth full, the women would have tensed and arched their backs.

Cassie can't think of any reason she's forgotten to apprise her friends of the Thursdays, when her heart—despite medical evidence—beats a little faster, and how by three in the afternoon anticipation has her running back and forth to the bathroom to empty her bladder. Before she leaves the clinic she brushes her hair with a brush and not with her fingers, and strokes on extra mascara, rouges her cheeks, refreshes the half-chewed-off lipstick. Eve and Nona think Thursdays are the same as the four other days in the work week.

Why hasn't she told the women? Surely it can't be because of what Jake does, gardening (not landscape architecture!) as a hired hand instead of with his own truck and crew. Cassie hates to think she is class-conscious, chalking a line between blue and white collar. These men are acceptable; these aren't. After all, she lives in California, lotus land, the sunshine state of rags to riches where strivers rise to the social surface like oil on water, where no one possesses a history earlier than yesterday morning. What is she afraid of? That Eve in particular will scream that Jake's inappropriate? Not suitable for her to have a crush on?

Oh, a crush! Crushes are for Mandy and her friends, not for mothers. Mothers should have more sense and not be swept along in rampaging romantic currents. How can mothers advise their daughters if they allow their own feet to leave the ground, if they sprout wings and walk out of windows?

Would the women point out that Jake is fine for a roll in the hay, a toss and tumble between serious attachments (not one of which Cassie has enjoyed since her divorce), a diversion, a Gallo Red kind of adventure? That he lacks the accouterments for permanent bonding? That he simply, bottom line, doesn't have a profession, a real job, business, enough money?

It is money that Cassie calculates once they've finished dinner. The simple Japanese restaurant where they sit cross-legged on meager floor cushions in the back room is inexpensive but Cassie deliberates—should she offer to pay her share? What is the proper etiquette? Will Jake expect her to reach for her wallet? On other dates the man always picked up the check, but now Cassie's fingers itch. Will he be offended at the suggestion of going Dutch or more annoyed if she says nothing?

Until the courteous waiter, bowing, places the bill on the table slightly closer to Jake, Cassie is relaxed, even mellow. Her fears that she won't have words to carry them through the evening, and then that once the music is ended, a quiet pool of discomfort will rise up and drown her, turn out to have no more substance than mist. Starting out disconcerted by female stirrings (oh, surely not lust!), and a little afraid of Jake because of that, she settles easily, helped by two cups of sake.

At first they have the timely business of ordering, agreeing to share, and then, apropos, Jake's stories of Japan, where he had gone on leave. He found the Japanese busy, wasps building, reconstructing, reaching skyward through the clouds. They are taking over the world, he says, much amused and without any bigotry, as if he means *let them have it and good riddance*. Vietnam broke America's grip of world domination and thank God. "It's all right with me if we let everyone fight their own battles."

"Do you think we were wrong?" She remembers again that he is the first authentic veteran she's known; he's the true-blue real McCoy, the gun-toting monster (she blushes now in memory) in the flesh.

He shifts, easing his legs, and there's a hard light of winter in his eyes. "It's too late to be wrong or right," he replies and a coldness stirs around him that wasn't there before. Cassie instinctively draws back, though her desire is to put her hand over his.

"But I wouldn't go again."

If time reversed and he were given the choice he'd run, north to Canada, to Scandinavia, to an uninhabited atoll in the South Seas, anywhere. But the past forever unchangeable lies behind him and he carries it attached to his soul.

Cassie sees fire storms in his memory, hears the thundering of heavy artillery, the whirling *slat-slat* sound of helicopters churning the air overhead, the shrieks of the wounded, the dying, and her imagination is Technicolored by the bloody red of war movies.

Jake has his money out, and two twenties go next to the check. Cassie can't think of a fitting way to ask how much she owes, any more than she can question Jake—*what was it like?* Across from him she feels submissive, lacking authority. She is tissue paper, a female starting out in life and not a woman, a physician, midstream and stable. Is it simply his looks that cut her adrift and the heavy masculine weight of him? Surely it must be something else, more substantial qualities, that cause such awkwardness.

Her palms sweating, surreptitiously she wipes her hand down the side of her dress before letting Jake grip it to help her up. His strength doesn't surprise her, nor the quivery sensation that runs up her arm. Tiny hairs where the collar of the dress skims her neck rise in a ruff.

It all comes down to chemistry. *It's either there or it's not,* Nona has said with a blush, and Cassie has said *You read too many romances.* And Eve has said *Don't avoid the obvious advantages of chemistry.* And Cassie, walking out of the restaurant in front of Jake, tries to recall if she's felt this way before. Surely she must remember, but there is fog in her memory. She can barely bring up Doug and their courting, and the men before him were only boys. But she does know that in three long years of being alone, no wave of emotion stirred her as does the tidal turning in her stomach at this moment.

11

Nona remembers—the light for one, how it slats between the blinds, how it spills from a bedside lamp, insinuates itself through the gap in the curtains, appears in patches on a car's windows. She recalls the places in which she has been made love to—the motel rooms rented hurriedly after dances and parties, the hotels, apartments, houses, the cars parked in out-of-the-way spots, blankets in the woods, fields, on the beach—more sometimes than the men. When she's caught up, flushed with excitement, all the men come together in her memory.

In the beginning, the first few times, she felt as though she were being worked over, and then she timidly lay back thinking of oil wells pumping, of pistons, of steam engines, but mostly of her father's pictures.

Adam would have exploded with anger if he knew, if he ever saw her so helpless. Nona shut her eyes against Adam as she did against the man with whom she lay naked. But she couldn't keep from hearing her father whisper *Every act has its consequences!*

After a while Adam's voice went away, or entered into the river of voices, streams that twist, wind, until the words unravel and it is as impossible as sifting water to tell one from the other.

Oh, Nona, please let me . . .

No dries on Nona's lips like tears.

Love me, she thinks when they touch her breasts, squeeze, press her in tight desire. They dance her away, out of her clothes, into bed, under them, and with her eyes closed they are all dark moons, and as wondrously the same, never mind their differences,

142

as the first one, a boy named Joe with a mysterious smile and a growly voice. Joe bought Nona dinner in a restaurant he could ill afford, ordered a too-sweet Napa Valley wine, and said he once saw a painting in a museum that looked exactly like her. He said he needed her, that he'd die right there in the car if he couldn't stroke her breasts, between her legs, if she'd just let him for a little bit. Don't worry. Nothing will happen, nothing, but oh, please, let me! And she did, because he wanted it so. The pain was exciting, the penalty for his pleasure, for her own sensations, and his groaning *God, you're terrific, ohohohohoh* . . . Little girl, little, she would think as the fanged beast of the garden howled above her, not so scary even scattering shadows, screaming his *Good, Jesus, good, better than I, oh, Christ* . . .

"What the hell!" Alan yells, pulling off her. His sudden departure leaves Nona exposed and the wetness on her skin is transformed into ice. "Get out of here!" He tries to backhand Magic, but the cat, screeching angrily, is far too agile. He leaps acrobatically over the high hills of quilt and sheets.

Magic has been padding up the bed to curve beside Nona's arm in sleep. It is his house, his bed, his mistress, and he hisses from the dresser at the stranger yelling "That goddam cat! Jesus, I hate cats! Sneaky sons of bitches!"

"Alan, don't!" She lifts up her arms for him but he swings away and falls on his back. Nona rolls over and huddles against him as he lies satisfied but now indifferent. He shrinks from her, withdrawn, retreating along endless interior corridors while she pushes, eager to crawl inside the body just seconds before inside hers.

With a perfunctory gesture he pats the arm draped over his chest. "I never liked cats, even as a kid. Did I tell you that?" He did but doesn't wait for her reply. "Dogs are great. You know where a dog is. You can trust a dog. Brother, if a dog means to attack, you know it. But cats . . ." He bolts up. "Where is that fucker?" Where Magic is now is on the boudoir chair on Alan's shirt, washing an already too-clean white paw.

"Hey, get off my clothes!" Magic ignores him as Nona tugs Alan to embrace her. She needs his warmth. "Get rid of him, Nona," Alan says when he finally slides back down.

"What?"

"That cat. Get rid of him."

"Give Magic away?" She has ice on her breath from an arctic terror of impending loss. Alan can't be serious. In a moment she expects him to laugh, to grin, kiss her cheek, say *Sorry, just teasing*.

"Find somebody to take him. Or what about the pound?" Anger distorts his features. "I hate cats!"

"You can't hate Magic. There's nothing to hate. He's my cat." Like he's my child, my son, not my chair or lamp or table.

"Nona, I don't want him here when I come over." His voice is sharp and grates on her painfully. Alan never talks to her like this; Alan is sweet, loving, kind.

"I'll lock him up," she promises, a tapestry of fears weaving around her heart.

Nona tugs the sheet, but already Alan is getting out of bed, walking across the room to the chair as if he means to do Magic some damage. But the cat's sixth sense has him moving fast, high-wire flying back to the dresser and from there with another graceful arc to the floor. He is out the bedroom door before Alan grabs the shirt and curses, "Jesus, there are cat hairs all over it. How am I going to go home with cat hairs?" As if Magic's white hairs are blond or red, a woman's strands, clues to infidelity.

"I'll brush them off, that's all. Don't worry." She scurries from the bed naked, damp with his sweat and hers, to the hall closet and reappears with a whisk broom. But he is already half-dressed.

"Where are you going?"

"It's late. I should have been home half an hour ago."

"It's early."

"Nona, don't start."

He holds Magic against her, and barefooted, buttoning his shirt, he scowls. He is a man dressing after sex. Yes, that's what he is: a man who's been here to do his thing and, having accomplished it, is edgy about moving on. Getting his rocks off—an ugly expression, as if actual stones were thundered up into her, Nona thinks guiltily, for the expression is devoid of love. And having dropped his load— more ugliness (oh, how like Adam's pictures!)—is on his way out the door.

"Oh, no, Alan," she cries and flings herself at his chest.

"Don't—" He reacts with sharp-pronged annoyance and then

immediately relents. His arms find her after all, his hands kneading her buttocks. "I have to go, honey, you know that. Marjorie will be suspicious if I stay out any longer."

Let her, let her worry her eyeballs out, weep blood on the pillow. Haven't I done that? She should pace the floor and peek between the curtains and sit with her hand on the phone. And when Alan's key turns in the lock, the fear should pierce her heart in a poison arrow. *Where has he been?*

Alan is trying to protect his shirt from her tears and at the same time console her, as though he is more than a lover leaving a woman with whom he has no right to be. Perhaps he is a warrior off to battle, a diver ready for the deep, an adventurer at the foot of Mount Whitney, Rainier, Everest. Nona imagines him as any of these, as all of them, as any other man but the one who, having committed adultery, is now on his way home with a firm order as she holds the door: "Do something about that cat!"

As Nona curls up with a teddy bear under one wing and Magic once again in possession of his territory anchored by her legs, she employs various strategies for sleep. She walks in her imagination along an empty beach, a strand without limits, at the edge of a sea whose gunmetal water stretches to the horizon. While the air lies motionless and the sea furls and unfurls soundlessly and Nona calibrates how many steps she will need to take to reach a deadened, dreamless universe, Cassie and Jake are finishing a late dinner. This is their second *real* date. After the first, when he guided her to the front door with too light a touch at the small of her back for such a big man, she said it was fun, thank you, and almost surrendered the words *let's do it again,* but lacked courage. He leaned over to maybe kiss her cheek, only Cassie nervously turned (or deliberately?) and Jake's lips found hers. His mouth was softer than she thought it would be and she *has* thought how his lips would feel, but before she can take in that kiss and enjoy it the moment shifts, and in seconds Jake is gone.

He calls the next morning before she leaves for the clinic. He calls from a pay phone out on the street, and behind his voice she hears the incidental music of traffic. "I didn't want to wait till Thursday to tell you it was—" The screeching of brakes rips the word off the wires. Great? Good? Okay? "And I want to see you again." Even inexperienced Cassie realizes he means *see* as more than look at. *See* like to go out with. She is ridiculously pleased by his approval and, emboldened, asks him to dinner.

"Yes. Right. Sure. Why not?" His mouth seems pressed to her ear rather than the plastic receiver and she relives the too-short kiss even as she begins to plan what she will cook.

Cassie isn't about to fix Jake an ordinary meal, to put on his plate the sort of lackluster food he might buy in any routine restaurant. She takes down Julia Child, Craig Claiborne, an expensive glossy collection of French recipes Mandy gave her the previous Christmas, and wishes, flipping pages, she had more time to create a banquet so subtle and airy the tastes will commingle in Jake's mouth like love. Yes, love. She thinks the word as she prepares a *beurre blanc* for the fish *mousselines*, as she had when peeling the pears for *poires au gratin* and when braising the peas. Tenderness gentles the red-leaf lettuce she tears in making the salad.

It isn't enough simply to impress Jake with her skill in the kitchen. Feeling must be conveyed with the food and something of herself also, to guide Jake as he eats into an intimacy of the senses so that he will consume the quickening emotions she is unable to express, that edge inside her both frightening and delicious. She offers him on the wedding Rosenthal taken down for special occasions what she still has no voice for, not only the gift of herbs and spices and tenderly roasted lamb, but of her heart.

It is only when the table is laid, the candles lit, each dish at its apocalyptic moment, and Jake already ringing the front bell rather than knocking on the back door, that the hair on the back of her neck stands straight up with worry. What if he prefers meat and potatoes, a good steak grilled on the barbecue, heavily spiced spareribs, a meaty stew, a crisp roast chicken? But it's too late. Here he is with a sweet wine that Cassie will drink, though it coats the inside of her mouth. She doesn't really taste it, however, any more than the food she has crafted as carefully as Millay one of her sonnets.

All the time they eat Cassie watches Jake, charts each forkful of food he lifts to his lips, prays with the devotion of a novitiate that he means what he says. "This is wonderful!" He savors the fish. "I didn't know you were such a fantastic cook, better than the best restaurant chef."

"You're exaggerating. It's just dinner, nothing outrageous." She tucks a loose hair behind an ear and counters with a compliment on the wine. Nervousness deadens her palate and only a fear of appearing foolish motivates her to eat at all. She'd rather watch Jake and the way the flickering tongues of light travel along his cheekbones as he chews, and drape shadows in the hollows of his face. If she could taste what he does and (oh, how forward!) lick the salad oil off his mouth, she would, and blushes at a sensuality long dormant and now riotous. She is her mother's spring garden in bloom, the stem of desire bending her awkwardly.

How sharp with awareness she is of his hands, the blunt nails, the large scarred knuckles, of his arms, the wide shoulders in a freshly ironed shirt, and the clean smell she imagines as if he embraces her and she is pressed just above his heart.

Stop it, Cassie, stop it, she criticizes herself silently, standing off and observing the woman finishing the *poire au gratin* as Jake puts down his spoon in the empty dish. Nothing will happen after coffee. He'll lean back in his chair and sigh, as one does when replete. Maybe they'll have a second cup in the living room with only one of them on the couch. Then he'll thank her and go. On Thursday he'll mention the *mousselines* or the lamb, perhaps the braised peas and the pears, while they have their beer right here but in a different, a duskier light. Nothing will happen. . . .

Jake volunteers, "I'll do the dishes."

"No," she protests, "I'm going to leave them for the morning." But he is already up, carrying plates and cups to the sink.

"It's only fair," he says. "A division of labor. You cooked; I clean up."

Cassie really doesn't want the meal swept away so fast, the kitchen restored to order, everything washed and cleaned and neatened up so it will seem as if they have never shared this dinner. She prefers to have the table exactly as it is, with the empty wine bottle, the smudged glasses, the last traces of food adhering to the plates. How nice it will be in the morning to come downstairs to the memory of the night before vivid in the sunlight and sit where she does and conjure up Jake. She will hear him say, "I hung out in New Mexico for a while, mostly in Taos. . . ." Hung out. The bits and pieces of his life sound temporary to her, as if he were always starting out, tuning up, preparing to get on with the real thing, unlike her, unlike Doug clawing his way from case to bigger case, preening when his name got in the paper.

In minutes he has the dishes rinsed and in the dishwasher without wasting a motion. "I spent enough time working in hash joints," he laughs, "though never as a cook. I can throw together a basic meal that won't poison anybody, but nothing sensational like what we've just had. Where did you learn to cook like this?"

She shrugs. Is he making too much of her skills? Has she turned out too elaborate a meal for him?

"From books. If you can read you can cook. The truth." She raises a hand. "Also, my mother was a good cook and a marvelous baker. She made a lemon chiffon cake that just floated."

"Make it for me sometime," he says.

Make it for me some time, next time, another meal, the two of them. He implies a future as he extracts a promise from her.

Having righted the kitchen except for the pots soaking in the sink, he must mean to go, but asks instead, "Any more coffee left?"

"I think so." But when she tips the hammered pewter pot, barely a trickle falls into Jake's cup. "I'll make some more."

"No, forget it."

"Really, it's no bother."

They are standing by the table and Cassie moves, not looking at him as he says, "I can live without more coffee, but not without this." And before she can process what he means, the pot is back on its tray, she is turned around, and he holds her face sequestered between his callused palms. This time there's no mistake that the kiss is intentional. It goes on and on like a summer afternoon, until Cassie's knees weaken and she has to loop her arms around Jake's neck while they explore each other's mouths. Cassie flounders but Jake seems assured, practiced, confident that he is doing this exactly right, and of course he has had experience, more than Cassie, innocent divorcée. Ten women, twenty, hundreds? Who knows how many? She feels helplessly shy, inadequate, embarrassed that she knows no man but Doug and has already forgotten him.

The kiss comes to an end but there is the briefest intermission before the second act and Jake's reoccupation of her mouth, her tentative probes into his. Their tongues and lips are less strange this time and Cassie curves more naturally against the hard body, almost laughing as she thinks *hard body,* Eve's *hard bodies,* and she has the maddest of all desires to call her friends to watch her perform this most ordinary and most exhilarating of acts. *See, I'm not the ice queen, I can do it, too, I like it.* And she does, still surprised at how much, and how really lovely Jake of no last name feels, tastes, smells. In his masculinity he is a revelation and she knows as he cups her breast, stroking the nipple to dispatch electrical impulses unerringly to her groin, that Jake won't be leaving right away, or drinking a last cup of coffee and lavishing her with further compliments on the *mousselines* and lamb.

Eve's sister Louise has phoned from Indiana. Six months have gone by since Eve heard from her last and it is at least that, if not nearer to a year, since she has spoken with their oldest sister, JoAnne. Nothing keeps the sisters from communicating more often, no harsh words or bad memories, just time and distance. JoAnne remains in New Hampshire, three blocks from the house they all grew up in, where their mother still hunkers down in her plush velvet living room crocheting afghans for all her grandchildren.

The sisters are, if no closer than when girls, no further apart, but with little to say to one another except a recitation of details. Both Louise and JoAnne are married to their original husbands and have children, a battalion of them, it seems to Eve, who must count up all her nieces and nephews in order to remember them. Baby faces have thinned out and firmed up and these children have taken on their own personalities. The youngest, one of JoAnne's, must be ready for high school, Eve thinks, but won't ask Louise, who has ages and names, likes, goals, medals won, honors achieved, prizes snatched up, on the tip of her tongue, eager to recite every child's glories as well as losses and problems. Eve, armored against children, has no desire to hear about this younger generation to whom she is genetically but not emotionally linked.

Eve has expected Louise's call or JoAnne's, since each fall her sisters phone to see if they can airlift Eve from California to New Hampshire for Thanksgiving or Christmas. The family meets ritually in Laconia, filling up the old house, which must feel bloated with so many Standfords. The walls strain, the vines and tea roses on the living room wallpaper bruise, the wide plank floors groan, and the windows threaten to crack with the cacophony of voices. There is little space left for Eve to occupy, and since she is a stranger to her sisters, who will miss her? But Louise calls anyway.

Mother is getting older, she informs Eve, in case Eve has the erroneous idea that their mother of all humans on the planet slips backward in time rather than cartwheeling ahead. And since Louise seasons her conversation with clichés, she has to add she won't be around forever. Eve refuses to be goaded by her sister into retorting *Who will?* but can't escape thinking no one is immune from final oblivion. If Eve's bear, Abramson, can die, anyone can, though Eve, who has no complaint with her mother, wishes the older woman eternal life. But no amount of love keeps even one person from the grave and nothing can motivate Eve into flying east for the discomfort of a New Hampshire winter plus the claustrophobic warmth of family.

It has been years since Eve set foot in Laconia, and though Louise reminds her that their father is weakening, Eve doesn't intend going this December. Their father won't recognize Eve if she sits beside his bed in the nursing home where he lies as inert as a carrot, baby-talking and weeping, gone, long gone, from present time into an infancy that necessitates diapers and puréed vegetables. He has nothing to say to her, nor to anyone else in the world, his only conversation the cries and gurgles of a newborn at the breast. While Eve hasn't seen their father prostrate, curled fetuslike and whimpering, Louise's description is graphic enough to transport the poor man in his crib to Eve's Los Angeles living room.

Louise, not waiting for occasions, makes periodic runs to New Hampshire. She flies alone or with her husband, Dick, or with whichever child she can cajole, to hold a shrunken father's hand and croon in unrelieved mourning for a man once six feet tall and now sticks covered by tissue-paper skin. The disconnection of their father's brain is a crime to Louise, to Eve also, but still no justice will be served if Eve agrees to join a family Christmas. Both she and Louise on the other end of the phone are aware that Eve never bothers to send presents except for a check to their mother. The card will read, as it always does, "Buy yourself something special."

This call of Louise's is longer, if no more eloquent, than what Eve remembers of the last one. She has turned down the television sound and watches silent figures gesturing in a courtroom while her sister says, "Poor Daddy, he's terrible. I bet there's not eighty pounds left on his bones and Mama swears he's being starved to death. Last time I was home she baked him a spongecake and we trotted it out to St. Mary's but the damn nurses wouldn't let us give him any. They said he'd choke on it. Imagine! Mama just burst into tears, saying they thought she was trying to kill a man she lived with for fifty years, or fifty years minus the time they've had him out in St. Mary's. And kill him with his favorite sponge-cake yet. My blood runs cold to think of poor Daddy. You should just see him."

"I don't want to," says Eve.

Louise gasps, "That's heartless!"

"No, it isn't. I want to remember him as he was and not shriveled up with no mind left. I want Daddy standing in the backyard smoking his pipe and staring up at the sky and talking about how when we grow up we'll be traveling around the planets as easily as we go down to Concord or Boston."

"Oh, I remember that! And when they walked on the moon Daddy was just glued to the TV. He couldn't eat, he was so excited." A beat of silence falls between them, and if Eve's lucky, Louise will be off and running down memory lane as far away from St. Mary's Nursing Home as the moon is from Laconia, New Hampshire. But Louise is not to be diverted. "We won't have Daddy much longer, Eve." She is divining the future and taunting Eve to ignore her.

Eve, however, won't be budged. "He's not Daddy."

"Don't say such an awful thing! Of course he's Daddy, just different. He's been transformed, the way we all have."

"We're not out of our minds or lost in space or any other way you want to put it."

"Well, I for one am gray and twenty pounds overweight and going swaybacked, so help me. I'm not a teenage girl mooning along with Daddy after supper in the backyard." She means Eve, for Louise was the most practical of the sisters, planted in the ground as firmly as the maple by the fence.

"Like me."

"If the shoe fits . . ."

Oh, Louise is maddening and Eve doesn't want to talk to her after all. When she first heard Louise's voice she was pleased and even echoed Louise's *we don't talk often enough,* but half an hour of her sister reminds her that what links them is only the past. Time has acid in it and has etched different women out of the girls they once had been, though Louise chooses willfully to believe the girls still exist. Eve, on the other hand, sometimes wonders, if she chanced upon Louise or JoAnne in a neutral location, an airport, say, or a parking lot, how long it would take her to recognize her sisters. Maybe she'd just pass them by and think for one fleeting moment: Those women look familiar.

In order to get Louise off the phone Eve lies: "I'll try, that's the most I can promise. The real estate market is in flux out here and I'm just so busy."

"You're as bad as JoAnne, complaining she never has a second to take Mama to the mall or spend a Sunday hour with Daddy." JoAnne is a lawyer with an active practice, and as far as Louise is concerned, she puts on airs. "You'd think she's the only woman in the world who works and has a family. As if the magazines write about anything else. As if we're not all being told how to do it." Louise graduated in the top third of her class at the University of New Hampshire but never did a thing with her psychology degree except fret over her children's psyches. She resents JoAnne for making money with her education. "But she's got the time to sun herself for a week after New Year's in the Caribbean. Of course she won't think of asking Mama to go with her and Dave, and Mama needs a rest as much—more—than either of them. Mama troops out to St. Mary's whenever she can find anyone nice enough to offer her a ride. Some sunshine would be a blessing for her, she's that stressed out."

Is Louise hinting that Eve should invite their mother out to California for a visit?

Before her father's mind went for a hundred-mile walk, both Eve's parents flew west and stayed the longest ten days in human history. Eve and William were married at the time and the only good thing about that trip was that the house in the hills had enough bathrooms for the four of them. Maybe the guy lines in her father's mind were already loosening, since he billowed with dislike for William, constantly calling him Sonny. Eve's mother apologized to William in private, explaining that Sonny was a boyhood friend dead since 1950 who once wrecked a bicycle or broke a window or did something that got Eve's father into trouble. Not that William, as far as Eve's mother recalled, looked the least like Sonny Potter.

During that visit her mother was the easy one, the peacemaker, sweeping the first contentious words aside before they could build into arguments, as she would the invisible dust on the dining room credenza. The soother, a smiler until her teeth ached, a silent worrier, Eve's mother at seventy-three still is a secret romantic. All those years ago, when Eve was with Jordan, her mother—after Eve's father was off the extension—encouraged: *Love is everything*. To her Eve was a soap opera heroine and when Eve beached up in California, alone and parted from the handsome husband the family knew only through snapshots, her mother was heartbroken.

It takes ten minutes before Eve manages to get Louise off the phone and she hopes another six months will pass before they speak again. A digital clock sits on the end table beside the couch and all through the long conversation green numbers flicked by. That had been her life slipping away, second by second, Eve thinks, resenting her sister Louise as she hasn't since the tenth grade, when she overheard beside the lockers a boy refer to Louise as the pretty Standford. Once again Louise had stolen something from her. Forty-eight minutes.

The loss of time grates, though Eve had been doing nothing important when the phone rang and has no plans for the evening except to watch television, look through the latest *Vogue*, or read a novel by a South American whose picture reminds her of Abramson but whose prose is lush. She can straighten her drawers, usually geometrically neat but now disarrayed. She can give herself a pedicure, call Cassie or Nona or any of a dozen friends; she can, in effect, keep herself busy until bedtime. But the apartment seems oppressive. She still hears the endless family tattle and Louise's griping and the charges that Eve's not a good daughter bitten off unsaid but underlying the silences.

Eve makes herself a weak scotch and soda and, passing through the dining alcove, stares back at the forlorn woman in the mirrored wall whose hair is newly streaked with strands of pale gold. She doesn't want to drink alone. In Cicero, in Laconia, her sisters are bedding down with their husbands, content as hibernating bears, loved despite spreading hips and uncolored grayish hair.

She doesn't consider very long before she goes to the hall closet for her handbag and coat.

Angelenos eat early.

By ten o'clock the dining room has only a sprinkling of patrons but each rattan stool along the bar is occupied. Eve nurses her second Dewar's, concentrating on the webby feeling in her head, trying to enjoy it but not quite succeeding. Though there are bodies to the right and left, she drinks solo, as she would have if she'd stayed home. The mere congruity of flesh is not enough to raise her spirits. She has yet to trade even banalities with anyone except the bartender, who speaks his few supporting lines disinterestedly. For all the company she has she could be on her couch watching *L.A. Law* and toasting beaming housewives in coffee commercials.

She is readying herself to go when a boisterous trio of men arrives. High-spirited, they are all in tuxedos, collars undone, black bow ties hanging by one hook. A burly linebacker straining his jacket slips quarters into the jukebox and the Eurythmics explode with rowdy sound. Gesturing hands stop in midair and heads bend closer to each other to hear words lost against the music. A black-sleeved arm extends over Eve's shoulder and a glass is put into a hand pelted with fine dark hair. The arm retracts, then returns for a second, then a third glass.

The three men adjust themselves in the narrow space, move about in their formal clothes, and, though large, take up more room than they should. They stand behind Eve and to her side, shouting at one another. As the Eurythmics fade Eve hears so close to her ear that she jerks: "Grover was shit-faced."

"Like he is every year."

"For a guy who has ten thousand—"

And Phil Collins is singing *"I can feel it coming in the air . . ."*

Eve is jarred. The drink almost to her lips splashes and drops of liquor fall on her skirt.

"Oh, hey, sorry. Bartender, some napkins here." A round puffy face thatched by strawberry hair hangs over her. "Here, miss, let me do that." They collide reaching for the paper napkin together.

"Thanks. I can do it myself."

"It's all been a pack of lies . . ."

"At least let me buy you another, since I spilled most of that." He angles in by her side, squeezing against the woman on the next stool, who beams disgust at Eve.

Only a spoonful of scotch has been wasted, but the ice cubes are melting. "Why not," she agrees, turning her head to look past him at his grinning friends. *"Wipe that grin off your face,"* Phil Collins sings. Good advice, Eve thinks and gives her attention to the one ordering her another of the same.

He is almost attractive, with a flush like algae spread across his pitted cheeks. He focuses a watery gaze of interest on Eve and keeps talking as Steppenwolfe shatters whatever it is he says. She drinks and smiles and when his thigh presses hers she doesn't inch away. And before too long he buys her another drink, then one more, the liquor buzz now a roar as loud as the music.

Eve's muscles loosen, the stanchions in her neck go rubbery, and her nipples slide against the lace of her brassiere. In a minute she will say she really must go and he will say what for, it's early, and then one trite line or another will find its way across her tongue. Tomorrow's another day. . . . A girl needs her sleep. . . .

He'll knuckle her chin and laugh off—as she intends for him to do—all her excuses, and in a few short moments they will come to terms.

So they do, going off to Eve's in separate cars.

If there were a camera it would pan along the couch of beige linen, over the pale-orange striped armchairs, to the chrome *étagère* and the meticulous arrangement of a marbleized egg on a teak stand, a silver box, a white shell with milk veins, a pearl and pink conch in which the ocean roars at high tide, one fragile Chinese lady, an Acoma bowl, to the edge of a picture frame and half of a large, solemn Abramson face. The camera would freeze for a significant moment on a free-form ceramic ashtray in the middle of the glass coffee table with two cigarette butts (Marlboro) and two tall goblets, empty except for shrinking ice cubes. Then, hurrying, the camera would pan to the stereo, red "on" light, and continue around to the hall, along its beige carpet to a half-open doorway.

If there were a camera and a reel of film and an audience observing . . .

The scene isn't unusual, nor are mussed coverings and the tossed clothing. A man's tuxedo pants, jacket, white ruffled shirt, black socks balled, high-polished shoes, Eve's yellow dress, crumpled panty hose, wispy lace bra, and high heels lie on the carpet.

Eve, nesting on pillows, slurs, "What are you doing?"

"Looking for a rubber—I know I've got one here somewhere." His bare back turned to her so she sees it rippled by tiny whiteheads down the spine, he fumbles with his wallet. "Yeah, here it is, praise sweet Jesus. You can't be too careful these days."

His body is whale-belly white, hairless, pliant as the goose-down pillows. In Eve's dizzying state, lines waffle, shapes soften, and the man oozes around her.

"Now, little lady, where were we?"

He twitches her breasts, slaps at her stomach, and his mouth when it meets hers tastes rancid. Wait! she tries to call out, but his groans slip down her throat. Before she can halt the entry he is inside and moving, lifting himself up on shaky arms and cawing. He is a raven with a pinched twist to his lips, sucking in air, eating up passion over his teeth. Rising, he is astride the top of the tallest tree with a solemn death mask. For a nanosecond he freezes, then shrieks and swoops down, greedy, gulping raven descending, and collapses, as good as shot through the heart.

The scratchy pain between Eve's legs subsides into discomfort and as she shifts, burrowing into the pillow to escape the hot, sour breath, he retracts. No more than two, three minutes have slipped by, and already the man deflates, sighing. He strips off the condom and, before she can stop him, drops it in a china bowl of potpourri.

"Got to go," he groans, sliding to the edge of the bed, sitting up.

"That's silly." Eve leans up on an elbow.

He grabs for his clothes, covering himself as fast as he undressed. "Have to move, hon. It's late."

She is plaintive. "I thought you'd spend the night."

He laughs. "And risk World War Three with my wife? No can do."

Eve reaches out to touch him but he won't meet her eyes and her hand waves uselessly in the air. "I thought you were separated." Hadn't he said *breaking up . . . leaving . . . the bitch wants my balls*? Hadn't he?

"Working on separating. It's not easy. But we'll get to it sooner or later. Only now's not the time. Besides, why should I move out and pay for an apartment?" He pats his pockets. "Keys," he says, a man distracted. Satisfied, he leans over and rushes a perfunctory kiss across her hair. "It's been great, Evelyn—"

"Eve! My name's Eve!"

"Eve. I'll give you a call and we'll get together again. Okay? No, you stay in bed." He motions her back. "I'll let myself out." And presto, fast as Houdini, he is gone. Eve hears the apartment front door close quietly, as though he is a thief, a second-story man, furtive and light-footed in his haste not to leave evidence.

For one breath, then two, she expects him to return, though knowing he is already in the elevator going down. She sees him out the lobby, to the street, his car, driving off, and Eve screams, with a cry so loud the curtains dance at the darkened window: "You didn't even take my number!"

12

The quiet streets down which Nona slowly travels without a map, arbitrarily turning corners, are deserted. The first timid light of dawn creeps up the eastern sky, and in minutes the fiery morning sun will sluice away the last traces of night, and shades in blind windows will start to snap up. Even now a bathrobed early riser steps out on his porch for the newspaper.

The houses in this neighborhood of Santa Monica all have front lawns and backyards and, she hopes, people of principle in them. Many also shelter children, if one can judge by a basketball hoop on a garage door, a bicycle behind a fence, a cutout pumpkin left over from Halloween in a second-floor window.

Magic mews agitatedly from his carrying case on the backseat. The cat dislikes the car and has cried since they left Westwood. Maybe he thinks they are going to the vet's and a waiting room of dogs who sniff his cage and growl when he hisses behind the mesh. But this time Nona whispers no comfort, as she always does on the yearly trips, saying, hush, we'll be home in an hour.

Nona wanders, her vision swimming with tears, trying to tune out the high-pitched note of Magic's meow with Alan's *I love you*. He said it: *I love you*. Not *I like you* or *I think I love you* or *I'm stricken, falling*, or *shaken, confused*. There was nothing tentative about Alan's *I love you*, spoken midday at lunch, and she only regrets, crying hard now, that Alan's declaration was mired in that terribly painful conversation about Magic.

"I'm not being mean, Nona, just honest," Alan says. "Do you want me to pretend, to lie about how I feel?"

"Of course I don't," she replies, stung.

"Well, I can't lie to you anyway, Nona, because"—and then come the jeweled words—"I love you." His hand captures hers, and Nona could die right then, so happy she has to remember how to breathe. Shivering with excitement she almost misses what Alan says next. "And if you love me—"

"You know I do. I love you so much, like the stars, the heavens—"

Alan shushes her poetry. "I know, darling. But if it's true, then doing this little favor for me should be easy. Pleasing me ought to make you happy, like my pleasing you does me."

That first *I love you* time Nona actually laughs when Alan says, "I want you, for me, to get rid of the cat."

But Alan persists. He hates cats, though Nona could argue, if she were a fractious woman, that one white neutered male cat is no big deal, not at all equal to a wife and children and a house in Brentwood.

"Cats are sly, sneaky," Alan reminds her. "In myths and nursery stories they're evil. They steal your breath."

Nona counters, "That's silly. Magic's my friend."

Magic becomes an obsession with Alan, for the truth is that cats terrify Alan, six feet, a marathon runner and once upon a time rower for Princeton. He insists Nona lock Magic up whenever he is there and if he discovers hairs on the bed pillows he accuses her of tormenting him, of not loving him really.

"It's a small request," he says one night, dressing. "I don't ask much. I'm easy to get along with and I love you, remember?" He leans over and kisses her with dry after-sex lips. "Why are you starting trouble between us?"

"What about your wife?"

"My wife? What does she have to do with that damn cat?" Outside the bedroom Magic meows. He resents Alan as much as Alan does him.

Nona starts to cry, though Alan disapproves of tears. They are together to be happy, to enjoy, to have the best of good times with each other. Tears have no place in their affair.

"I'm tired of having an affair. I want to get married." There, she finally says what shouldn't be verbalized, what Marian cautioned her against. It's up to the man to ask, the woman to answer. *We don't push. We are demure, quiet.*

"Stop! I told you in the beginning marriage was impossible." Nona cries on as Alan knots his tie. "I know this is hard for you— don't think I don't. But what about me? I'm just as unhappy as you are with this deception. And God, the guilt! It's torture leaving you and going home to Marjorie." Now it is his eyes that grow cloudy with tears.

Nona weeps. Whenever he speaks his wife's name she gets sick to her stomach. Saying *Marjorie* for *wife* makes the woman a real live person.

Alan reaches for her, his arms suddenly flung wide, and a jagged cry breaks off his lips as they clutch each other. He trembles and whispers, "I don't know what to do! I can't lose you! The thought of you being with somebody else—! Oh, God, no! Never!"

Yes, Alan loves her. Like a Bedouin searching for an oasis, Nona behind the wheel prowls Santa Monica assured that Alan cares. He promises her that their relationship isn't an affair—meaning a tawdry, sly carrying-on, with one partner committed elsewhere. He doesn't do what he does with her lightly, for, he says, his heart is engaged. He loves her, which elevates the quality of their sex. There is an emotional element involved when their flesh comes together and a spiritual rending when they part. And Nona in return loves Alan with breathy wonder. It's as though there have been no men before him. She's virginal, unhandled, never crudely penetrated in sweaty flesh-slapping lust. She is the princess in the tower.

Only Magic comes between them on soft cat pads, moving silently. His whiskers twitch; his smile is Cheshire-like, for cat-wise he intuits that Alan dislikes him.

One night Magic escapes from the kitchen to leap onto the arm of a chair where Alan sits drinking brandy. Alan screams as the liquor slops darkly on his pants. "Get him out of here!"

Another night Nona lies on the couch with Alan leaning above her. As he reaches to unbutton her blouse Magic creeps in his low-belly crawl and scratches Alan's hand. A bloody track wanders at the base of the three middle fingers. Alan spins and falls in terror, clawing the air. He would kill Magic if he could get his hands around the cat's neck.

"Either that cat goes or I do!"

Alan, his face tight with no love inscribed on it, refuses to let

Nona wash off the scratch, and puts on the Band-Aid himself. He repeats, ice on his tongue, "The cat or me."

"That's the dumbest thing."

"I've said it before. It's not as though this is something new between us. You're just being stubborn, and silly too. Or maybe you do care about a cat more than about me." He seems to need her to choose, to show that he's important.

Nona's white shadow slips behind a closet door. "No, I won't give him up." Of course I won't, she signals silently.

"Then I have to go." She reads in his eyes how much he wants her to stop him, but tells him to go if that's how he feels. Then Nona waves at him, as if he were a cat himself, as if she warns him off. She thinks to frighten Alan with theatrical gestures but he surprises her.

Nona expects a call of apology, love words floating down the wires, promises hanging in ether. He will call and make amends, say he hadn't known what he was doing, that Magic means nothing, nor does his wife, that Nona is everything. He'll take her up the coast to Geoffrey's tomorrow night. They will watch the sun sinking into the Pacific and drink margaritas. He'll hold her hand, then whisper when night settles how much he loves her. More than yesterday, less than tomorrow.

But Alan is silent.

In Friday's paper she reads about the Bar Association gala at the Century Plaza, black tie. The theme was "Roman Holiday," and a raffle gave away Venetian glass and Italian vacations. Nona looks for Alan's name and finds his wife's on one of the committees. She smooths her finger over the type, rubs back and forth until a hole widens in the paper. Marjorie Stevens shreds, and for the rest of the day Nona wonders what she wore. Something long? street length? chiffon? crepe? silk? taffeta? black? Black is always safest; black hides a figure's imperfections.

Nona drives by Alan's house on Anita, crouched low over the wheel like a thief planning an intrusion, casing the colonial for a break-in.

She drives by his office, though what does she think, that she'll see him coming out of the large glass building?

Again on a Sunday she circles his home, up one street and down another, but there is nothing to see, only a green lawn, white columns, a red front door.

Nona says to Magic: "I'm a single woman with a cat. I'm lonely. Talk to me." Magic purrs and cleans himself. "A cat's not enough. You know that, don't you? Oh, Magic!"

In her arms Magic is warm, his green eyes riveting. Nona wonders if cats have souls.

When she calls Alan he is lyrical with devotion. "I love you. Oh, how I love you! And do you know how much I want to see you?" His voice trembles on the question and Nona chokes with longing. She hungers for his smiles, his touches. "But I have this thing about cats, and your Magic knows it. Whenever I go into your apartment my skin crawls. I'm sorry." Is he? Nona only knows she ends the conversation feeling lost and lonely.

She can't take Magic to the pound. Even for love some acts are beyond her, and certainly handing Magic over to a stranger uniformed in gray, inured to pain, is one of those. She can see thin smoke rising from the pound's chimney, twisting in the warm breeze like a dead man on a rope, and gets sick.

Nona takes Magic to Santa Monica instead, sure that because he is such a beautiful cat, a white sheik, imperial, independent, some family in one of the homes she passes will adopt him. They'll buy Magic a wicker basket identical to the one she bought him, and another rhinestone collar. He'll drowse into his old cat's age, fat and contented. He'll lap cream, day in and day out, from a crystal saucer.

Nona chooses one block, then another, unable to make up her mind where to stop. It's as though she's selecting the site for an accident, a particular corner to crash her car.

I am not about to do something wrong, she tells herself, not on the edge of what Cassie terms a *bad deed*. Though she can't be arrested, even ticketed, she experiences the cotton-mouthed anxiety of an intruder positioned at a window with one leg over the edge, a shoplifter gliding past counter displays. The smell of guilt permeates the car and no shower will be long enough or sleep so deep that she won't catch now and again a whiff of it seeping from her pores.

A rhythmic pain pulses in Nona's right temple, radiating down her jaw. She hasn't closed her eyes for a moment during the slow-moving night, though she stayed in bed until almost five listening to the clock's faint ticking as she would a baby's whiffling breath. Having come aground with the ugly decision, she stared blindly into the dark.

I don't have to, she thought, thinks, and of course nothing chains her to the promise except . . . Alan's claims of love.

Magic continues to mew as Nona struggles not to listen. He already condemns her, though still in his case and not yet free. What kind of freedom will it be for Magic out where sidewalks run in ribbons and metal lamp poles commandeer the street corners? At least she's brought him some distance from coyote country, from the canyons and neighborhoods haunted by predators. Not very far north the coyotes—light-footedly prancing and mistaken for dogs—trot bold as residents on morning jogs. They root for garbage in cans not tightly lidded and snare any small animals that play outside.

Here Magic is safe and can wander down the walk of the brick split-level or around the side of the Mediterranean.

Reaching behind the seat, Nona unlatches the lock and flips the lid. Magic rises like a pop-up, arching his silky back.

"Everything's going to be fine. Don't you worry, darling," she soothes the cat, who flows effortlessly into her arms and butts his head against her chin. "You'll have a bigger house to live in and children to play with. You can go outside instead of just looking through the window. Won't that be nice?" She cries as Magic settles in her lap. He has no knowledge of betrayal and thinks, if at all—nudging her hand to scratch behind his ears—that this strange ride on which he's been taken is for a human's peculiar reason that need not concern him. His person can be trusted. Though he shakes her tears from his whiskers, the touch is still familiar. What can a cat know of grief from the canticles Nona whispers at him?

But before Magic curls himself into languid cat sleep Nona has the door open. He is lifted. Suspended, not yet set down on the curb, he must suspect the unknown future about to rush up to meet him, for he meows sharply, corkscrews his sinewy cat body around, and glares, stunned, back at her.

The grass is unusual, the earth under his pads alien terrain, and he makes a motion as though to leap into the car, but the car isn't there.

Nona has driven away without one backward glance.

"That's just the weirdest thing I've ever heard. Not that I know diddly about cats, or if I ever did I forgot," Eve is saying. "To just jump out of your arms when you're carrying him back to the car. To run off? He's a house cat. And why didn't you have him in his case?"

"It doesn't matter." Cassie stops Eve. "The important thing is that Magic's gone and Nona feels awful."

Nona dabs her tears with a napkin. Such public anguish embarrasses Eve, but she can't seem to change the subject. "Why didn't you lock him in his case while you were inside the vet's office? Why were you waiting until you got to the car?"

Eve senses something off kilter about Nona's story but can't ferret out what it is. Nona is woolly-headed at times but her feelings for Magic are real enough. She should have been careful.

"I wasn't thinking, that's all." She coughs and Cassie hands her a glass of water.

Cassie asks, "Did you put signs up in the neighborhood in case somebody finds him?" Nona stares at her over the rim of the glass, eyes wide as an urchin child's in a painting. "And you told the vet, of course. What about the pound? Did you check there? You can also put an ad in the papers. Offer a reward."

Eve agrees. "Money motivates people."

Nona's grief is prodigious. Eve signals a waiter and orders her a stiff scotch and soda. Nona needs a bracer to get her through dinner—they all do—for the cat plans to haunt them.

"You'll get him back." Cassie encourages Nona in what Eve thinks is wrongheadedness. There's no guarantee that the cat will be found.

Nona whips her head from side to side. "No, no, he's gone forever. It's always been like this. When someone leaves me he vanishes. Poof! Up in smoke!" She flaps her hands. "He slides off the end of the world or he dies. You think they'll come back or change their minds but it's all over. Like Simon."

Cassie and Eve cast angled glances at one other. Simon? "Who's Simon?" Cassie asks. "I thought it was Alan."

Nona greedily works on her scotch, and this second drink might not have been the best idea, though not as destructive as the third or fourth that, it seems apparent, Nona means to order. She has the aura of a person preparing to slide into soddenness.

"Alan is now. Simon was before."

Eve sniffs. "Oh, before. There are so many of those. We could probably fill this room with our befores. Not you, of course, Cassie. Just Nona and me. But which one was Simon?"

"If I married Simon, Magic wouldn't be lost. I wouldn't have Magic and I wouldn't even be here—"

Eve interrupts, "If fishes had wings!"

"We planned to live in Newton—not immediately, of course, but after we had children. Simon thought we should have three. Two boys and a girl. He even had the design of the house he intended to build, with the children's rooms facing east, in his head. Simon was an architect."

"I never knew you were engaged," Cassie says.

The ice cubes in Nona's glass tinkle. She has finished off the scotch and holds the glass up in the air to attract a passing waiter's attention. "Another," she orders, her smile sliding.

"You're drinking too fast," Cassie admonishes. "Let's order something to eat."

"I don't want to eat." Nona's features harden into a stubborn mask. "I want another scotch."

"You've had two already."

"What's two drinks? A drop, two drops. I feel sick for Sim— No, not Simon. Magic. My poor kitten, out alone in the world." She grabs Cassie's hand. "Somebody will take him in and love him, won't they?"

"Of course they will. And they'll put an ad in the paper, or call around to the pounds, the vets. You'll see. Magic will come home."

"No, he won't. He's faded away like in the movies."

"I want to hear about Simon," Eve says, jiggling her own ice cubes.

"It's sad, me and Simon." In the ocher light of the restaurant Nona is luminescent.

"Okay. We'll cry," Eve decides.

The waiter brings Nona's drink and Cassie asks for menus. They'll order in a second. She suggests to the women, "The chicken looks interesting," but neither Nona nor Eve cares right now about food.

This is Nona's story . . .

. . . Of how her father never knew about Simon, knew that Anderson, with whom he did business, had a son who was Simon, or he might not have taken Nona along to that Christmas party. He probably didn't think over the possibilities, not of a Simon, even though he warned Nona all the time in words and with his medical pictures, *Be careful of boys*. Marian did, however, and had since Nona started wearing a brassiere, thought of marrying her off in the backyard with a tent and a band and fountains of champagne and a gown whose train would need to be carried down the white silk runner rivering across the grass like the Milky Way. So when Simon appeared on the scene Marian cried, cold-eyed and calculating, "He's divine! Don't pass him up. Men like Simon don't grow on trees." And Nona didn't, because Simon was (perhaps still is) divine, with lustrous blond curls and spidery lashes as long and fine as a girl's. He had a Botticelli face and he smelled like fresh bread. Nona never knew a man could smell like Simon, rather than too sweet from after-shave or sour with last night's drinks on his breath.

Simon treated her gently from the first, even reverentially. He trembled, afraid she would break, and was awed that he could circle her wrist with his fingers and still have room to park a truck.

Adam, however, was suspicious of him. He worried that Simon would be mean or unkind or faithless. He said, "After the wedding men become indifferent. They have their work. They compartmentalize, a little box for this, another for that. And when the orange blossoms are dried and pressed in books, how much will he please you then? He'll think of himself and won't make you happy." Not happy as he could make her was what Nona's father meant. "You'll be a doll," he complained, as if she weren't already a doll to him.

With steely tones her mother countered, "You never treated me like porcelain, so why criticize Simon for something that hasn't happened yet and might never? Not that your frets will stop this wedding, Adam." Eventually Adam shrugged and stood back.

It would have been the most beautiful wedding despite Adam's reluctance to give her away. Marian's knack, after all, was for

parties. Two hundred people responded yes to engraved invitations, but that was before July Fourth, when they all flew out to
Martha's Vineyard and the promontory off which the Anderson
house rose, gray and weathered, a wooden prong of the Atlantic.

The finger of land thrust out from the shoreline with steep rocky
banks and stiff grass. The house itself had pitched roofs—the
highest capped by a widow's walk—along with ells and abutments
connected to the original perfect square, and was seasoned by two
hundred years of wind and salt spray. Time had turned the
clapboard the gray-green color of lichen and the windows staring
out to the sea were misty from the spray flung at them by the
wind. Windows were cut everywhere, bringing as much of the
outside in as the house could hold, and Nona would remember
little of the interior that wasn't framed by mullions and sills and
draped with light.

The Andersons themselves were rock-bound, New England-
boned, their history and ethic making them impervious to the
capriciousness of nature. Both Simon and his father stood as tall as
Adam but weren't as fleshy. The old man had the shipwrecked
boniness of a colonial sailor, which was how, Nona's father promised, time would handle Simon. His golden good looks were
destined to fade, and age would change him year by year to
polished ivory.

But if the Andersons were more January people than not, that
July Fourth they bloomed with sunlit smiles and laughter. Marian
basked in the Anderson lineage, as though Nona's marriage to
Simon would transform her too. But Adam said *marrying you for
my money*, whispering poison into Nona's ear. Adam thought his
money magic dust and that the Andersons welcomed them because
Caleb knew what side his bread was buttered on. That weekend
they enjoyed a clambake down on the shore, brunch along the sea-
fronting porch. They sailed on Simon's ketch, sunned on the rocky
outcroppings, and even swam a little in the frigid ocean. Simon
ferried them in groups over to Edgartown in his new outboard. He
bought Nona a fisherman's sweater and a hand-carved penguin
while they strolled the narrow streets, their fathers talking stocks;
their mothers, color schemes.

Eric, Simon's Harvard suitemate, acted courtly, presenting
Nona with roses from a vendor and encouraging her smiles with

silly treats—popcorn and cotton candy and jelly doughnuts—even though moaning that she was kidnapping his best friend. No more good times, Eric said, his arm around Simon's shoulders, because marriage was serious business. Eric expected to remain a bachelor for years at least, if not forever.

Nona thought Eric sweet, Marian enjoyed his lean good looks, for he resembled Simon enough to be his brother, and Adam called him a viper.

"I'm just skeptical," Adam replied when his wife accused him of acting coolly toward well-meaning people.

And she added, "You're angry with Nona for being happy."

He answered, "Don't be a fool. I just refuse to judge Simon a prince among men."

Nona, wishing to float that weekend, was held taut by the guy wires of Adam's worry. How right could this marriage be if her father thought so little of it, whatever the advantages, and of her feelings for Simon—the only boy she courted with who hadn't taken her to bed? Not that Simon knew he could have had her before the ceremony just by needing her and asking nicely.

On the night of the Fourth itself the Andersons planned a party with a four-piece band and dancing. At ten, fireworks were to explode on the shore and from a boat anchored off the sea wall. The event was for introductions, to present Nona formally—a rite, a public statement. The Andersons invited everyone they knew at the Vineyard and guests from all over New England. They left no friend unasked and families were expected with all their small children.

Marian had taken Nona to the designers' salon at Jordan Marsh for exactly the right dress, not white, of course, but a sheer yellow cotton, tight at the waist and off the shoulder, a rather old-fashioned milkmaid's dress, though the skirt was short. Nona looked, with her slight tan, "pretty as ten thousand pictures," Simon sighed. "Oh, I love you so. I can't wait till we're married."

During the slow dances he secured her against the bulge of his desire. His gaze, as he stared down into her eyes, glinted hungrily. "I'll die," he moaned, and Nona, who had heard all this before, understood the seriousness of Simon's longing.

Nona was upstairs before a mirror when the band stopped

playing and the guests spilled out onto the porches and down onto the lawn. Voices fluted expectantly against the drumming of the ocean. Excitement shot shrill sparks into the night and suddenly in a great burst of colored fire, pinwheels spun in the dark sky. The screams of delighted children rose in puffballs, but still Nona heard someone calling, "Nona, Nona . . ."

She rushed in search of Simon, which was how she would tell her story to the women eighteen years later in the anomalous universe of Los Angeles, and she found him, them, with no distance between their bodies.

"I saw Simon with Eric," Nona explains to the women struck in stone, the food artfully arranged on their plates uneaten.

"Saw him how?" Cassie asks.

"After that we couldn't get married."

Eve kicks Cassie under the table. "God, after that I should hope not!"

"Were you sure?"

"Oh, Cassie, of course she was sure! There are some things you can't get confused about. Homosexual love . . . Oh, the *shit!*"

"He left me. There wasn't anything else he could do. That's what he said and I understood."

"You sweet little fool! Being understanding! My God, I can just hear you saying the whole business was your fault. And he just went along, blaming you for not satisfying him, right?" Eve hurried on, wiping a bad taste out of her mouth with her wine. "But they must have been doing it before that Fourth of July. They didn't start with the fireworks. Pop, here, suck my cock!"

"Eve, shut up!" Cassie pushes her arm.

"You have the mind and heart and soul of a perpetual virgin, Cassie. For a doctor you're the world's biggest innocent. Men suck cocks, at least men do who are into that sort of thing."

"Do you have to be so graphic? I know what homosexuals do together, so please stop acting as though I'm an idiot."

They argue, relieved to be taking off at each other and skirting Nona's sadness, which neither can fix, change, or in the least diminish. A gay lover prepared to lead her to the altar for her father's money is somehow so typical of Nona. Gay, married, uncommitting—those are always Nona's men, the ones who can neither satisfy nor bring her happiness. She is, or seems at times like this one, condemned, a Sisyphus of love.

Nona, drinking scotches, her vision furry, doesn't hear her friends, listening rather to her own voice, to the story she has just told, and remembers how Simon left her as now Magic has done.

13

Cassie intended to confess about Jake, but Nona claimed their full attention. First shattered over Magic, she then delivered the story of Simon—movie material, Eve said afterward to Cassie in the ladies' room, God, so unreal, something up on the screen! The moment was all wrong for Cassie to say, *I'm happy*, in heavy *like* (a Mandy term), maybe falling, sailing in thinning air through clouds of affection, desire, to love. (Oh, not love, she thinks, as if love were bacterial.)

Cassie had gone out with the women semi-confident that Jake isn't fly-by-night, not just a date who will never call again, will breeze off, a man in transit.

Cassie has never had a one-night stand and is obligated to practice what she preaches to patients seeking her help at the clinic: Don't be casual about sex. Sex is more than potent; sex is potentially murderous. So she climbed into her own bed with a man with whom she faintheartedly expects she is having a relationship, and met her friends for dinner to confess it.

Confess is too strong a word; *share* is more like it. *Confess* implies wrongdoing, guilt, and yet Cassie is so uncomfortable keeping secrets that she calls Eve from the clinic, planning to tell her on the phone.

I'm going out with a man whom I like a lot, whom I've gone to bed with.

Oh, God, why does she have to confide at all and let Eve know that she is so normal she is having sex after the long Sahara of loneliness during which she thought all feminine feelings sanded over. When had mores changed from hiding sexual desire—from pretending women never indulged themselves, even so naturally as with their own hand in the dark, never mind in parked cars—to bragging? Cassie remembers a time when the word *orgasm* couldn't be whispered, and *coming* signified only down the stairs or in for dinner, and everyday verbs brought blushes of shame to girlish cheeks. *Do it. Did it.* Only sluts, whores, bad girls said such things and were therefore whispered about and excluded from good-girl sororities. Nice females kept their legs crossed, their blouses buttoned, and fought off groping hands and hot tongues. They never lay down willingly. Or if they had a yearning to and actually indulged in *dirty things* they kept their mouths shut and were both devious and discreet. Don't give yourself away; a girl's reputation is all-important, was what they learned from their mothers. Now, however, a woman who refused to be bedded or couldn't, or went out with a man only to dinner and the movies was weird, to be pitied.

The switchboard pages Eve but she's not in the office. Cassie hangs up to see Barbara standing in the doorway, dressed mid-morning in basic black with pearls.

"What's up?"

"A hellish night. I have a patient with major toxemia over in the hospital and I've been there forever." She lights a cigarette, a sure sign of her distress, since she smokes not at all except when, as she describes it, on the outer limits. "You were already gone when she walked in here, or more accurately waddled, with a hysterical mother-in-law, close to six last night. She's in her seventh month, ankles like balloons and blood pressure that should have sent her into orbit. Damn, she had the works—dizziness, spots before her eyes, epigastric pain. I worked like a coal miner until I finally got her stabilized."

Barbara runs a hand down a dark, silky hip. "Mo had one of his charity occasions so I put on the uniform and bingo, just after the grapefruit I got beeped. My girl was convulsing. *C'est la guerre!* So Mo was in Century City listening to black-tie speeches and I spent a long night fighting nature."

"How is she?"

"Still on the high wire but better than Mo, who is pissed." She sighs. They are all aware how much Barbara's husband resents her doctoring, the time—in his eyes—filched from their marriage, her preoccupation with patients and Magdalene. He needs Barbara, but not as much, she stubbornly insists, as the sick and hurting women she treats with a single-minded devotion that makes them all think Mo will divorce her. *Let him,* she says. *I took an oath to the Greek before I pledged my troth to him.*

"Mo will recover."

"He will until one day he won't, and then," she grins, "I'll get a whopping big settlement and Magdalene will have some much needed improvements."

Cassie shrugs this off, for she suspects that Barbara in her heart of hearts loves Mo and thinks him the one stable element in a life surrounded by pain, disease, and death.

The phone rings. It's Jake. Cassie blushes and swivels around in her chair, supposing Barbara will leave, but Barbara has a cat's curiosity and waits while Cassie, whose lips brush the receiver, says yes, they can have dinner, and yes, if he wants he can cook in her kitchen.

Barbara has stubbed out the cigarette in Cassie's spotted dieffenbachia and settled herself down on the patient's chair. Even the morning after she looks like a high-fashion model in her Valentino, ready to slink down a runway in a panther's glide, like a dark dangerous creature—which she is most surely not.

"Nothing so serious," Cassie says to her. "Just . . ." Just what? She has no name for Jake yet. *Boyfriend* is a term for girls in their teens. *Lover* seems risqué. Does she know Jake well enough to call him friend?

"Love and medicine don't mix, Cassie. As for marriage, well, look at me and poor Mo. Whenever he wants to jet off to Maui for sun and fun I have a baby due." She laughs but her eyes are violet clouds of warning.

Barbara crosses her legs and pauses for Cassie to girl-talk about the man on the phone. But Cassie only cries, "Marriage! No, really, Barbara, it's a date, that's all."

"This date's giving you the preorgasmic prickly flush," she says, and Cassie's cheeks redden more.

The doctors stare at each other until Cassie, tongue-tied as a girl in for birth control information, grabs a folder off the pile in the wire basket. "I'm years behind in paperwork, aren't you?"

"Okay!" Barbara rises with unbearable grace. "But remember, men are only riffs off the main theme." At the door she pauses— Cassie thinking Barbara, like Jena, is a Joan of Arc of medicine, a woman with a mission—and turns back to say, "I've never thought of you as hormone-happy." Then she goes in a breeze of disappointment, leaving Cassie to feel that she's let Barbara down.

Eve misses Cassie's call by minutes. She is taking a couple to see *her* house. At the moment she has several listings but the Iranian's seven-million pie is the one she thinks of as really hers. Not that she could conceive of taking up residence in the large stone building of no coherent style, with its nine thousand square feet of rambling rooms and wide corridors. It looks like an embassy and feels like a mortuary. Steps echo on floors made of marble, and voices drift up to the high ceilings in whispers. In sunny Southern California the light enters surreptitiously and acts embarrassed, touching the walls and the furniture awkwardly.

The couple, however, Koreans, seem to like the house. At least Eve doesn't sense an acute dislike. She finds it difficult to gauge the interest of Orientals and experiences them all, to her chagrin and discomfort, as inscrutable. She's actually made an effort to separate the characteristics of one ethnic group from the others, to be able to tell instantaneously if she's meeting an immigrant from Seoul or Hong Kong or Tokyo, for she prefers tolerance to bigotry. Besides, it's good business. But more than the Pacific isolates her from Far Easterners, and despite her polished exterior she is hopelessly at sea with these foreigners who are buying up a good portion of California real estate. She wishes she understood better what they're doing in Los Angeles and how they have come to be the world's power brokers, the movers and shakers.

Of course she isn't Titus Reynolds, who, if he had his prejudiced way, would sweep them all back into the ocean and let them sail on—if not drown, like boat people—to another country.

"This is the master," she says, opening double doors to a bedroom the size of a small basketball court, and searching for some reaction in flat, dark eyes that are as unrevealing as dinner plates even when confronted by plush purple carpeting and a canopied bed awash in sails of satiny material.

The house, rigidly vertical and horizontal, no curves or arches or bowed windows, no angles softening its barracks-style precision, is decorated enthusiastically. Eve wonders what the owner will do with so much brass, countless ornate mirrors, brocade chairs, wide down-filled couches, fur throws, rugs, cushions, zebra-upholstered chaises, framed pictures of Italian street scenes and Venice canals, china knickknacks, crystal chandeliers with ten thousand tear-drops. The house is as stuffed as auction rooms and the profusion batters at the senses, so it is easy to miss the good pieces, such as a lovely art deco chest lost between swirls of gold-flecked curtains. If the Iranian owns too much, what he does possess is expensive, and the house has the exotic feel of an Arabian bazaar. It hovers on the brink of awful, is blowsy, tarted up, and Eve, embarrassed, explains to the prospective buyers: "Of course you're not seeing it at its best." She tells them: "Try to visualize it empty," painfully aware that it then will resemble the big barn it is, "and redone." Without, Eve means, the flocked wallpaper, the gold and crystal sconces in the bathroom, the speckled mirrored walls, the wall-to-wall carpeting like crushed plums.

The husband nods sagely, as if he can actually see something, perhaps a pared-down structure with tatami mats, silk screens, thin silk-covered cushions for seating. The wife, who has taken a turn around the bedroom and done the bathroom, flushing his and hers toilets experimentally, now is staring out the window. What is she thinking? Eve is dying to ask—Can you see yourself living here, walled up, with your three children?—but won't. Tactically, a good agent suggests improvements or points out what the buyer misses, the superb entertainment flow, for example. None of this does Eve do, however. Her professional patter is forgotten because she is offended by the house, its size, its ugliness, the outrageous price tag it wears like the Hope diamond, and also because she can't imagine these quiet people, placid as lily ponds, in this European fortress. But then, whom does she see buying the house and moving in? Even the Iranian, despite his bringing the house gifts of decoration to cover so much nakedness—lavishing them on *her* as he might a mistress—is not a compatible tenant. He is, like his vacating wife, a tourist. But the house doesn't seem much of a home for anybody. In fact, though Eve knows she will sell it eventually and make a handsome profit, it is as attractive to her as a prison.

"It's chilly. What's the heating system?" the husband asks without the barest trace of an accent. Eve, realizing she lacks even one word of Korean, is mildly humbled as she reels off the details of the house's inner workings, the forced-air furnace, the copper pipes, the impeccable electrical wiring. The house might be a monster but it is a solid monster. The original owner built for a millennium.

They troop through the six bedrooms and five baths more like a defeated unit on a forced march than conquerors, people who can afford seven million or thereabouts. The price, naturally, is negotiable.

When they swing back to the upstairs hall and start down, Eve draws attention to the thick stone walls as she had, going up, to the height of the ceilings. As before, the Koreans offer nothing in response, not even the politest murmur. She thinks they will wander off, perhaps for another inspection of the state-of-the-art granite and stainless-steel kitchen, where the Iranian's cook is preparing a meal that casts off a potpourri of aromas sweet-smelling as flowers. But the couple crowd close to Eve's back and follow her right to the front door.

"Is there anything you'd like to take a second look at?" she asks, feeling, ridiculously, about to steeple her hands at her waist and bow.

"Thank you, no," the husband replies, without questioning his wife, whose face is so unmarked and dreamy she could be framed and hung on a wall. "You've been most kind."

Eve is prim, restraining herself from becoming lyrical about the property along whose circular drive they now curve, three abreast, to her Mercedes. "We can always return for another viewing if you want. The owner is most cooperative."

"That won't be necessary," he says, inclining his chin a fraction of an inch.

Eve waits while the couple settles in the car, the husband in the death seat, the wife behind. At least in this subtlety they've adjusted to American life, or maybe American couples adopted this way of dividing up from the Orientals. Eve can't ever recall taking out a pair of clients where the man sat in back and the woman in front. Does this articulate something about the marital power structure she's missed, never having house-hunted with any of her husbands?

"I might have something else you'd find interesting," Eve says as they drive back to the Booker office. "There's a Mediterranean in Bel Air that has five bedrooms and substantial charm. The kitchen needs upgrading, and the baths, but otherwise it's a very reasonable buy at the asking, eight point nine."

The Koreans are a referral, and though the Iranian's house is the first Eve has shown them, she will, given time and perseverance, find them exactly what they're looking for.

"Also, there's a two-year-old contemporary in Holmby Hills on a three-acre parcel that I'm trying to get us into tomorrow. Unfortunately the owner's been out of the country. A very dramatic four levels, with an elevator, of course, and a pool both inside and out. Quite spectacular but it's just under nine and fairly firm." How preposterous that she talks in millions, as if money is as weightless as snowflakes. "I don't know if that's within your price range." She glances sideways at the Korean's rounded cheek, but he stares straight ahead, letting Eve be his tour guide. The wife is centered in the rearview mirror, no more lifelike than before. But her gaze bores through the glass directly into Eve's eyes. Eve shivers, offers up a sigh that she coughs out, and adds, "Sorry," like an awkward girl. The rich, she thinks, are *so* different, and it matters not a jot if they're white, black, yellow, pink, or polka dot. Richness carries humans beyond color and nationality and gender to a land of Nod, at the end of the brick road, over the rainbow, or far off in a galaxy other mortals will never reach no matter how technologically perfect their spaceships are.

This comes home to Eve like a hammer blow when the husband says, "We'll take it. Offer six million, five hundred thousand dollars, but I am prepared to pay six million, seven hundred and fifty thousand dollars if I must. That is, of course, for your information only." He recites all this without bothering to turn his head, and for an instant Eve thinks he's talking to an invisible genie on the other side of the windshield.

Eve's mouth opens and closes, words momentarily caught at the back of her throat. Being the sole broker means she will clear almost $300,000, with far less effort than Abramson expended crafting a short story and for which he never received more than a few hundred dollars. Certainly William squandered longer hours in one script conference, and Jordan earned less than 10 percent of that commission during their entire marriage. Even as she discusses terms, escrow, and the lighting fixtures which the very aloof client seems determined to keep as part of the package, a turbulent river of discomfort spins up her chest cavity. The thought roars through her mind that no one should buy a house this easily, not for any amount of money, and that an obscenity is being practiced in which she willingly participates, to her shame. She talks calmly, clipped and professional as ever, about geological surveys, title searches, down payments, mortgages, and escrow, both she and the soon-to-be owner aware that his offer will be accepted, if not the six five, then six seventy-five. He appears unconcerned about the extra $250,000, the negotiation to be entered into for form's sake only. Money is no object here, and now her stomach clenches; she finds herself mysteriously afraid. She hears Abramson's voice lecturing that this world she lives in is Orwellian. Leading the couple into her office, she also imagines Jordan agreeing with the bear. She is startled to realize her first two husbands had certain compatible ideas, and both of them would propose, she can just see it, opening the safety deposit boxes of people as rich as the Koreans and scattering a cloud of their wealth to the down-and-out, to the needy, to the homeless.

Of course Magic leaped from her arms to sprint across the parking lot. She cried and raced after him as he darted down a back alley and slipped like a willful outdoor tom between garbage cans to disappear. Nona created just such a scene and rolled it through her mind, rewound and rolled it again until it had actually happened. Having written, directed, and acted in that event, it now assumes the validity of a remembrance, and she grieves officially for a cat who's run off on her. As all her men sooner or later do. Simon, too, for example, or her father, entering a minimum-security facility, where one afternoon he collapsed in "the yard" and could not be resuscitated in the infirmary.

Nona calls Alan to tell him about Magic. She sobs with the stuffed-up unhappiness of a child and he tries to console her. "Don't cry, please!" He promises as a gift to cancel an evening meeting with a client and take her to dinner, to somewhere wonderful, maybe to Valentino's if he can get reservations at the last minute.

Nona's heartbeat should accelerate but she experiences nothing more than a gassy pain in her chest. She begs the afternoon off from Lorraine, who's sour and nervous that George's leg must be reset and that the health club hunk has turned out to be gay. "You're not thoughtful," she says accusingly. "I have my problems, too, and I feel awful." Nona knows this to be true, for Lorraine's herpes has flared up due to stress—George will probably walk down the aisle in a soft cast—and she looks puckered with tension. Nona considers retracting her request but fluish aches now accompany the gas.

When she leaves the mall it is to rush to Dr. Rubin, who pronounces her "healthy as a colt running at Santa Anita."

"There's nothing wrong?"

"No more than usual."

Nona's shoulders sag. The face she sees in the small mirror on the examining room wall is dispirited, for Nona had almost convinced herself these aches were the start of the latest Asian influenza.

At home, in an apartment that is emptier than it ought to be with only a cat dispossessed, Nona climbs into bed just five minutes late for *The McKenzies* and is comforted by the familiar characters' problems right to the last commercial.

She drifts off to sleep wondering if Deirdre will put up her house as collateral for bail money for Helen. Will she help her younger, prettier sister? What would she, Nona, do in Deirdre's position? Nona dreams she acts forgivingly and gently, that loving proves more of a consideration than revenge, and on the misty sets with the camera's red eye blinking, she accepts accolades for being a good person. She stands before the fireplace in Brad's office and tells them all that to give is better than to receive.

When Nona awakens she hasn't even a subtle pain to worry over. Sorrowing, the flu, *The McKenzies*, her nap, have made her late for her date with Alan. If she flies she can arrive at the restaurant within seconds of seven o'clock. But when she comes out there is a red Triumph double-parked at her left rear fender. It will take precious minutes of backing and forthing to extricate her BMW.

The hood of the Triumph is raised and all she can see of the figure beneath it are jean-clad legs. "Hey," he says, pulling out and straightening, "you wouldn't have a set of cables, would you? I need to jump-start her."

"No. And how am I supposed to get out?"

He looks like Mel Gibson, with unruly hair and licorice eyes and the tan of a Point Dune surfer. His smile is an angle of moonlight. "She's dead as the proverbial doornail." Glancing back into the deep mysterious pit under the hood, where, as far as Nona knows, gremlins might be spinning along on flywheels, he adds, "Ten to one it's the battery, but maybe not. It could be the ignition. If I can get her chugging I'll drive over to the gas station on Olympic. Otherwise I'll need a tow."

Nona has the car door unlocked and is about to slip behind the wheel. "That's all very interesting but I need to get my car out from behind your car."

"Ah, don't wrinkle up. It's a piece of cake." He comes forward, crowding Nona. "I'll spring you loose in a second plus. Then, pretty lady, you can ferry me over to the garage. What do you say?" He stands so near, Nona sees herself miniaturized in his eyes. He is only a few inches taller than she is but he fills the space by the car with his presence. The air hums as though someone has struck a tuning fork, and the fine down on Nona's forearms bristles.

Without time for her to say yes or no, to remember *you never get into a car with a strange man,* he commandeers the driver's seat and is introducing himself. "My friends call me Fitz." Nona has no choice but to be a passenger, to tell him her name, and answer the questions he lobs at her. Somehow she's become a captive in her own car, which Fitz casually drives, his arm on the sill of the rolled-down window. He has the negligent attitude of a college student, but isn't all that young. Threaded through his dark hair is a sprinkling of silver.

"You're a princess for doing this," he is saying, as if Nona's an active participant. "A caring Angeleno in a city whose heart is steel. What a rare creature." They stop by a light and Fitz shifts so that she receives the full impact of his smile. " 'Kindness in women, not their beauteous looks, shall win my love,' " he quotes. "And old Will was right-on. Though you're also the most gorgeous female who's ever rushed to my rescue. But it's supposed to be the other way around. I'm the one who should throw down my cape on muddy puddles for you to walk over on your"—he takes a quick look at her legs, her feet—"dainty size sixes. Right?"

"Are you always like this, babbling on?" she asks, embarrassed.

"A regular running brook. But oh, boy, you should meet my mother. 'Son, don't jabber like a mynah bird, least not to fantastic-looking women. They'll think you're a retard.' Do you?"

"What? think you're dumb? Stoned, maybe," she accuses him, hoping not. She is already at risk with the unknown, but more than that she wants Fitz's charm to be authentic and not chemically induced. It's so lovely to hear Shakespeare quoted.

His laughter continues. "Not one joint has touched my lips lo these many hours. My ebullience is completely natural. I'm a high creature as compared to the sour, beetle-browed folk who hump along through life fretting about death and taxes. I worry not and want furiously. Ah, sadness, here's where I leave you." He pulls Nona's car into a Mobil station, switches off the engine, and drops the key in her hand. His face turns serious. "Thank you. For all my joking I really appreciate this." Nona gets out and circles to the driver's side. Fitz holds the door for her. "Fasten your seat belt," he instructs her when she's inside. "And, hey, the truth, this has been my happiest dead battery or bum ignition ever."

In the rearview mirror he is momentarily framed as he stands waving by the gas pumps. Though late, Nona still wants to hesitate, to replay the funny little episode again. And because she does, guilt attacks her. After all, Alan is waiting for her so neatly pressed, together, and more deliberate—not like Fitz, who leaks from the seams with energy and good humor. So Nona presses the gas pedal harder and, going resolutely forward, misses seeing Fitz dogtrotting between the pumps, immediately returning the way they've just come without bothering to ask for help at the station.

She expects Alan to commiserate, to praise her, and struggles not to urge *Say you love me because I love you*. He had arrived ten minutes late at the *nouvelle* Mexican restaurant—Valentino's was booked solid—and kissed her cheek. He complimented her dress, ordered a vodka martini, no twist or olive, and began complaining about the complications in a land fraud case. His client had been made guarantees that never materialized, and now in a shabby maneuver by the opposition he is being countersued. It is all meant to obfuscate the real issues and, to hear Alan tell it, to annoy him.

Nona, listening, realizes Alan could be having this exact conversation with his wife. She could be his wife at home except that naturally she whips up no little dinner in Brentwood but sits here across the table paying dutiful attention. There is no Marjorie; there is Nona, with a diamond band on her ring finger and two children, boys at the Harvard School on the Valley side of Cold-water. Nona's picture framed in silver sits on Alan's desk, and beside her the boys are dark, not towheads.

But before Nona can swim too far out in the deep waters of fantasy Alan beaches her by changing the subject. Marjorie's name creeps into the conversation, the sons he does have and not the two she would have given him (and maybe a daughter). Once again, and so easily, she is the outsider, the waif with her nose pressed against the picture window of someone else's marriage.

The distance widens between Nona and Alan until universes separate them, rather than the space of a white tablecloth, and when she speaks her voice is only a drab echo, though Alan, enjoying his veal *rancheros* with sautéed peppers, never notices. It seems to her it has always been like this, other people passing her in a grand parade, ever in motion, just as Alan and Marjorie and their boys will do on their weekend trips to Tahoe and a borrowed condo.

How can she be one of them and not alone? she wonders, just as she did all those years ago on a Cambridge street corner as waves of protesters swept by her, colorful troops in tie-dyed T-shirts, jeans, granny glasses, printed skirts down to the ankle, headbands, with peace emblems embroidered on their jackets. There was such vitality in the marchers. Arms linked, they chanted, and their voices swelled with music. They were all brothers and sisters, a long-haired, thousand-membered family, and Nona, prim, pressed, and crisp in starched white cotton, longed to join them, to dance barefoot, bells tingling, on the pavement.

Adam emerged from the restaurant behind her just as Nona, in high heels, took a step forward, and he fixed a firm hand to her shoulder. His fingers gripped like talons.

"Bums," Adam spat. "They don't understand a thing about politics or how the world works. They just want to seize the occasion for mayhem. Party time! Infants! The South Vietnamese are our allies," he stormed, as if she hadn't heard this speech many times before. "If we don't put our muscle on the line defending them, where will it stop? Thailand, Laos, Cambodia, eventually India, and all of Asia will topple to the Reds. When Japan falls it will leave China to rule the world. China and Russia. We have our enemies to fight, our way of life to protect."

Nona shut her ears. All she yearned for was as good a time as the girls were having, marching arm in arm with their boys in overalls. If only she could pull loose from her father.

Adam said, "They're not people like us. My God, they never even bathe and they live in filth!" He inclined downward to kiss her, so she smelled the clean lemony scent of his after-shave. His skin was smoothed over sharp bones cold as marble. When she touched him it was like stroking stone, and she wanted warmth, the high-flying exhilaration of the screaming girls levitating on their beliefs and slogans.

Freedom, oh, yeah, all the way . . .

"Oh, yes, oh, wonderful . . . oh, oh, oh!" Her buttocks rise off the bed, and through half-slitted eyes she tries to gauge Alan's pleasure. But his face is contorted. In the throes of his explosions he looks like a gargoyle. His plunging rhythm slows, his guttural cries soften to chirps, and Nona times her motions with more expertise than she will ever admit to. She is conscious of her body as of a ship in which she has sailed out to sea. Only her memory is stirred, and when Alan slides off her, perfunctorily kissing the curve of her neck, it is Adam's face she sees in the emptiness of air—which is not something she can tell Alan, satisfied and soon dressing, or anyone else. To Eve and Cassie, Nona's dead father is yesterday, celebrated in a flowery ceremony, buried in mahogany, forgotten in a Boston graveyard, and not a ghostly presence in her bed.

All their fathers are history; it is something they share. Of course Eve's father still lives, with small puffs of breath and a mind as unmarked as a washed blackboard, but she considers him dead, speaks of him in the past tense, and refers only to her mother. Nona's mother is also dead, and Nona is an orphan at thirty-nine. With no brothers or sisters, no blood relatives to tether her, she is unrestrained by family obligations, and urges Eve to return to New

England for Christmas. She imagines the holiday gathering as a Norman Rockwell painting and sighs enviously. But Eve resists.

The three friends have taken a Sunday ride down to Capistrano. They travel in Eve's white Mercedes, and because Eve is in a foul humor she drives demonically. Her anger derives in part from Nona's fantasies of a white Christmas and because Cassie has finally owned up to seeing a man. The good news comes warped because Cassie held it back, and has stinted on the early details. She and Jake were established—or at least together—before she has even shared "I met a man to whom I'm attracted." What kind of friends are they if they keep secrets?

Cassie is stung by Eve's repeating "Why didn't you tell us before?"

"There wasn't anything important to tell." Of course there was, a history beginning with the grinding of a lawn mower.

"I think it's wonderful, and so romantic," Nona coos. Cassie is one woman whose good fortune Nona enjoys, because Cassie—unlike Lorraine, say—is not forever tripping over men who are panting at the edge of her skirt. This Jake whom she's seeing is a unique occurrence. "When do we get to meet him?"

"Meet him?" It never occurred to Cassie that Nona and Eve will arch their brows in expectation of seeing Jake for themselves, that he is to be brought from a siding onto the main track.

"Maybe we could all come for dinner. You can cook up one of your spectacular meals."

Eve interjects, "I can just see it. The two of us staring him down, treating him to an FBI security check. Were you, or have you ever been . . . ? That sort of mama-papa baloney. Which would serve you right, Cass, for burying him all these weeks in deep freeze."

They stroll the paths of the mission, peeking into the restored rooms, before setting off to the antique stores where Cassie will look for a small Victorian table to position before the living room bay window. Once again she's decided on redecorating, converting the last memories of Doug and her old life to something unusual. And this, too, has to do with Jake. He seems mismatched with the rest of the furniture. Already she has bought new sheets, pale blue, and a finely striped duvet cover. On those nights in his arms she lies more easily on bedding unused by her ex-husband.

Nona asks, "Where are the swallows?"

"Gone by now," Cassie replies.

"Gone where?"

"Where swallows go," Eve says. "Someplace warm. Maybe Mexico or South America." She hunches her shoulders and shoves her hands into her jacket pockets, for the sky is gray as sludge and bursts of wind agitate around them. It's a lie that California weather is always pleasant, bright, and sunshiny. This Sunday afternoon rain seems imminent. They drift into the chapel, admonished by signs to be quiet, for the church isn't a museum but a true house of worship with God in residence. The church, long and narrow, has a high ceiling and the gloomy feel of a tomb. Candles flicker over the few pious kneelers, while Christ hangs on the wall dusty and lackluster.

Eve wonders what they are doing here. She should be in the office catching up on paperwork, though she has no open houses, no clients to shepherd in their search for new homes. In fact, she's the Booker Agency star of the moment for turning over the Iranian's $7 million house as expertly as flipping a penny. It lasted seconds on the market, no mean feat, and Eve is credited with professional legerdemain even by Titus Reynolds. "I couldn't have done better myself," he complimented her, his old eyes watery with dismay. Somehow Titus has forgotten he refused to work with foreigners, that he finds them "sticky" in business dealings. If she had actually passed the Iranian on when he asked for Titus, rather than sitting him by her desk and bringing him coffee while he wept about a lost wife and a house he now hated, Titus would have sniffed. Titus's nostrils would have quivered at the sight of a man crying in public, for Titus can't understand a heart so glutted with love that each beat is painful, any more than he can a house crammed to the beams with gold leaf and crystal and satiny fabrics. Not that Titus knew he was the Iranian's first choice for an agent. What did it matter? In the end, surely, though his sales have dipped to the upper limits of a novice's, Titus would have rejected a foreigner's commission.

No, she has no reason to suffer any guilt pangs. She never stole from Titus or put one over on him. Titus and the Iranian would have hated each other, and Eve can congratulate herself for having done both of them a favor.

"How do the birds know when it's time to go? And when to come back?" Nona asks, curious as a child.

Cassie leads them out of the bone-chilling church and Eve is happy to leave. She can neither sit nor stand in a church with any comfort, nor would she ever, no matter the circumstances, get down on her knees.

"Let's go look for my table, then get a bite to eat before it gets too late," Cassie says.

Eve says, "Remind me why we had to come to Capistrano for this table."

"Wait, I want to stop at the information booth and see what they have on the swallows," Nona says as they pass out of the mission to the sidewalk.

"Forget the damn birds, will you please!" Eve snaps.

Cassie takes Nona's arm. "The antique stores, that's why we're here, and because we planned to have some fun, an outing, a glass of wine, lunch. Remember?"

Eve says broodingly, "It's a long way for lunch."

"Can you imagine what it must have been like when the priest first built the mission? All open land." Nona is trying to read the little booklet she's picked up from a guide and walk at the same time.

"I swear, she's like a second-grader on a class trip," Eve complains, taking Cassie's other arm. "Just wait until she starts doing research on your Jake."

"My Jake! Oh, that makes him sound like a piece of furniture."

"Yes, that's what he is: your Jake, your table. A possession," Eve says. "Think of him that way, as an inanimate object, a thing, and not as a person with power. Then he can't hurt you."

"Why should he hurt me?" Cassie asks, bewildered, as if she isn't trained in unreliable people, as if she doesn't know in how many ways the human being can misfire.

"Why should he? Have you, my dear, forgotten that sterling ex-husband of yours? In the real world of the carnivores, and not the sweet Saint Francis world of swallows, men are beasts. Like Doug. Like Alan."

Nona stops. "My Alan?"

"Your Alan is no more yours than the man in the moon. He belongs to his wife."

"Why is it whenever Alan's name comes up in our conversation, so does his wife's?" Nona is suddenly tearful but whether from emotion or the wind it's hard to discern, at least for Cassie, who squeezes her arm and tilts just so slightly with the desire to hug her.

Eve retorts, "What is his wife's name?"

"Oh, don't!"

"Do you know?" Eve asks Cassie.

Cassie feels tugged by them both. "Let's forget men for a couple of hours, okay? I want to concentrate on furniture, on getting my house in shape." The two women, rebuked, turn their heads away and first Nona, then Eve, releases Cassie.

After a second Nona links her arm with Eve's. "I'm sorry," she says.

Eve sighs. "For what? I'm the bitch of the West today."

"Oh, well, tomorrow it will be me."

"I doubt it."

14

Of the three of them Eve is the most difficult. She accepts that there resides a hard element in her that her friends lack. She wasn't always this way, though even as a young girl she never managed Nona's innocence or Cassie's compassion. The most that could be said of Eve was that she possessed more leniency then. She has firmed up since but still, when ragging either of her two best friends, she isn't such a monster that remorse doesn't touch her. Eve regrets her acid tongue, the razor edge to her comments. It is simply that Nona's naïveté and now Cassie's sogginess over this Jake person outrage her. They are modern women with good heads—Cassie's light-years better than Nona's—on their shoulders. They should act like grown-ups and put their own best interests first.

But who am I to tell them the facts ma'am and not to dirty their petticoats? Eve thinks after she has done just that, and before she will do it again. She is the advocate of biology, a disciple of the flesh, of a woman's following her own sexual pleasure as does a man. What she is not, however, is a pitiful romantic, an eater of Valentine candy, a reader of ladies' weepy novels. Like Nona, and now perhaps Cassie. Can't women understand about distance and how to keep involvements, even commitments, conditional? Why do they fling their heads in the ring along with their hearts? Or, alternatively, why can't they learn from experience, as she has after Jordan, Abramson, and poor William, she thinks, driving to Johnny's.

Johnny rates as a friend, or an almost friend, certainly more than the acquaintance he was when he reappeared in her life looking for a last-minute date for a party. He could have swum back out with the tide after that, not to see Eve again until another year or two has passed, but somehow he has stayed around, held in her orbit by gravitational pull rather than any effort on her part. But he isn't a lover. First of all they haven't gone to bed, not for any particular reason but just because. Eve finds the new Johnny attractive, definitely a more possible sexual partner than the Johnny of yesterday, a man she wouldn't have lain down with if, as the saying goes, he was the last man in the universe.

Because Eve believes a woman chooses—or has the right to—as readily as a man, she can at any moment offer herself to Johnny, but she hasn't. The timing has never been right, and besides, in many ways she likes him too much. Yet with whom should a woman bed down if not a friend? Enemies are the wrong kind of men for sex. That's what she tells Nona and Cassie, though she has secretly practiced what she preaches against, and would be in the mood right now to pick up a stranger if she wasn't going to Johnny's for dinner.

Of the three women she is the only one without a man, and while not begrudging Nona her Alan—why should she want another married man?—or certainly Cassie (at last!) her unknown Jake, Eve is, despite her best intentions, jealous. Their love affairs exacerbate her loneliness, which of course makes Eve feel even worse, a bad friend.

"Hello there!" Johnny swings open the door wearing a large white apron and holding a wooden spoon. He looks like an advertisement: male in the throes of cooking. He helps her out of her coat saying, "We're having spaghetti. The single man's standard dinner when entertaining a lady." He is in a high-flying mood; he is smiling. He kisses her cheek.

"Spaghetti's fattening."

"Slander! Pasta's great for a diet."

"I thought you didn't eat meat, besides."

"Who said anything about meat? I'm making a marinara sauce, from scratch. Aren't you impressed? Fresh tomatoes, fresh basil, fresh everything."

"It smells good," Eve replies.

In the tiny kitchen Johnny pours her wine and clinks his glass of sparkling water—the supermarket's house brand—against hers. "Good health!"

"Aren't we happy tonight." She glances around the apartment, which is easy, for only a tile counter separates the kitchen from the living room. "Very intimate."

Johnny laughs. "That's a euphemism for *small*. If I were still fat I'd bulge out the walls."

"Where's the bedroom?"

"You're standing in it. Or almost. The couch pulls out. That"— he points to a door on the left—"is the midget bathroom. The other is a closet. In fact, the whole place is tinier than a Beverly Hills walk-in. But the rent is five seventy-five, utilities included."

"Very reasonable," Eve says, wandering over to stare out the one large window.

"Even for the wrong side of the tracks." He laughs again and Eve wonders if there is an edge in this explosion of good humor, this expression of making fun of himself, or if she imagines it. She can't believe that under similar circumstances she would not feel rage at life, and at her own stupidity.

All that is visible through the window are a darkened back alley, car ports, the blank wall of another cheap building. This is the sort of area and apartment she once stayed in with Jordan. The furniture, too, is early maturity, except for a leather chair that has lived in better surroundings and an abstract painting in bold earth tones.

Finally Eve has had enough of the dismal view and asks, "What can I do to help with this spaghetti dinner?"

"Nothing. The table's set, the salad's made, and in a second and a half the pasta will be perfectly *al dente*. Wait . . . Parmesan. Here, you can grate it." He hands Eve a hard wedge of cheese and a grater. She sets to work, aware of Johnny bumping into her back or hip as he moves around the tiny kitchen. Steam from the boiling water heats up the air and there is a certain coziness about the confined space that momentarily overwhelms the poverty and confinement Eve senses. She listens to the clang of pots, spoons, the clink of the long-tined fork, and Johnny's sotto voce humming. If she weren't midway into her forties and accustomed to larger rooms, she could temporarily be content. Instead, she has at best the bemused acceptance of a time warp and at worst the agitation of having slid through memory into the wrong place.

Poor Johnny, as far down the ladder as he can go without being right in the muck. Not that he's to be pitied for having blown, smoked, and drunk his good fortune into ashes. Nor does he seem sorry for himself, at least not in the midst of creating this bachelor dinner. Spaghetti marinara, another legacy of youth. It's been years since Eve has had pasta without sun-dried tomatoes or pesto sauce or with cream, primavera, or dressed with seafood.

"That aroma should be bottled by Chanel," Eve says when Johnny pours the sauce into a glass bowl with a chip on the rim. She helps herself to more wine.

"An old family recipe."

"I didn't know you were Italian."

"I'm not. But who says only Italians can make spaghetti? Do only Jews eat bagels? Spaghetti's become as American as apple pie or roast turkey. The same with pizza. Here, inhale. I have to get this to the table," he says, squeezing by her.

"Is this enough cheese?"

Johnny rushes back to the kitchen, which means taking two giant steps. "Fine. Just scrape it into a bowl." He nods toward the cabinet over the stove top. "Up there."

A flowered piece of crockery is the only dish not too large for the few handfuls of cheese. It matches nothing on the table, but all Johnny's dishes come from different sets and are strays, last survivors.

The table with a director's chair at either end is shoehorned into a corner of the room, and Eve has to slip carefully into hers so as not to bump against the TV. But for all the oddities of china and flatware, the meal Johnny has set before her, with the crisp salad and essential garlic bread, is delicious. She finds she is starving and the food couldn't be better if eaten off a Rosenthal plate with a heavy silver fork rather than Target stainless.

Brahms is on the stereo and beyond the tall, graceful candles, still in his apron, with a film of sweat on his brow sits Johnny, as attractive as the polished tuxedo-clad entrepreneur he once was.

After two platefuls Eve pushes back. "Enough. It was wonderful. I couldn't have eaten better in Primi's or Prego." She raises her glass with a teaspoon of red wine left in it. "To a master chef."

"*Grazie*." Johnny smiles, unabashedly happy as a boy. In the amber light he is younger than when she met him for the first time, before his fat and his wealth, before the coke, booze, grass, speed, 'ludes, bennies, acid, 'rooms, angel dust, and ecstasy. His lines have smoothed out and the shadows darken his gray hair.

He refills her glass, emptying the bottle. "You might as well finish it off. I don't have any use for it."

"You mean I drank the whole thing?" she asks, surprised.

"You drank the whole thing." He strings the words out and they both break into laughter.

"Maybe I should go on the wagon."

His smile catches on the edge of his mouth. "That wouldn't be such a bad idea. Liquor's poison—"

"Not another one of your lectures!" she cries peevishly. In the afterglow of the meal, with the alcohol content in her blood just at the balancing level, the ruder aspects of Johnny's decline in fortune mist over, and they don't need to discuss anything so dismal as poison. Eve hates to think of what might kill her, all the carcinogens in the food and air, the fat globules coating anything good to eat that will clog up her arteries, the murderous effects of illegal drugs (and prescription ones, too) that she never indulged in anyway, or hasn't for years. Now, in this present life, she imagines minutes last for lifetimes.

"I guess I natter on," he agrees, and in repentance for diverting him from his pet subject, Eve pats his hand. He grabs her fingers. "Though why shouldn't I?"

"Nobody said you shouldn't. Just don't. The dinner was too lovely for one of your nosedives into seriousness. Right now I'd just prefer not facing down a skull and crossbones. If there's anything that can kill me in what we just ate, I'd rather not know it."

Johnny protests, "Not one molecule! All my vegetables are organic."

Eve giggles, which is more Nona's style than hers and, aware she's out of character, giggles louder. "Orgasmic? Is that what you said?" The last drink has tipped the seesaw and the soft waves of early inebriation float up her backbone. Her head is light as a cotton ball and if, or when, she stands up she will fly if she doesn't fall first. Oh, she thinks, though is still too sober to say it out loud, how sad it is that Johnny won't ever feel like this again.

"See what happens when you drink too much."

"I haven't drunk too much! Stop! You're just a fuddy-duddy!"
Fuddy-duddy? Has she really said *that*? Johnny's brow knits and
Eve is instantly contrite. He is a nice man. Drunk or sober, she
shouldn't tease him. "I'm sorry. I'm not polite making fun of what's
drop-dead serious to you. And this, all this. Such an effort."

Johnny is easily mollified. "That's okay. Apology chalked up. Just
don't get fooled by a plate of pasta."

"Your old mother's recipe. I mean your mother's old recipe."

"Yeah, my mother's Dione Lucas."

"You lied!" Eve rises from her chair.

"Sit down. There's ice cream for dessert and tangerine sauce if
you want it."

"What's tangerine sauce?"

"That is something I learned, not from my mother, who's a
terrible cook, but from my Aunt Dee. She has a restaurant in
Boise, Idaho."

Eve has gotten over to the couch, where she collapses to meet
the springs poking up through the cheap cushions. "I thought you
were from Minneapolis."

"I am. But my Aunt Dee lives in Boise. She's my Uncle Vince's
second wife, now deceased Uncle Vince, which means Dee is
related only by say-so. Anyway, Dee, who comes from Birming-
ham—Alabama, not Michigan—is my age, give or take a year."

Johnny becomes more and more interesting, but whether because of too much wine on Eve's part, or his culinary talents, or a
youngish aunt in Boise, at the mention of whom his tongue darts
out and licks his lower lip—a sure sign of lust or dreams of lust—
she can't decide. Maybe it is her own lust that transforms Johnny,
though she doesn't feel particularly sexy. Or not yet. She just
thinks that she could or might if Johnny plays his part right, the
role of a man who has invited a woman over for a home-cooked
meal, the better, Red Riding Hood, to seduce you.

But Johnny isn't thinking of lust but of ice cream. "It's low-fat,
vanilla. And homemade. One of the few items I managed to save
from the bankruptcy sale was the ice cream maker."

The salvaging of an unnecessary, expensive gadget from grasping
creditors sets Eve to brooding. What will she secrete away if the
banks come after her? Not that she is within calling distance these
days of going broke. The commission on the Iranian's house will

inflate her bank account like helium. She'll have to buy CDs or bonds, maybe some stock if she weren't so leery of the market. There's a small apartment house in West Hollywood—much more upscale than this one—that she can invest in, and a new mini mall down in Redondo.

The filmy curtain clears for several beats as she contemplates how to invest her money, and she opens her mouth to ask Johnny what he thinks, when he sprawls beside her on the groaning couch. "Try this," he says, and hands Eve a dish of ice cream.

"What?"

"Vanilla with tangerine sauce. I told you."

The taste is too sweet and sets Eve's teeth stingingly on edge. "I can't. I'll bust. Burst." She hands him back the dish and in the transfer orange syrup spills on her dress.

"Hey!"

"Oh, wait!"

"Goddam!"

Johnny dabs at the material with a wet sponge. "Take it off and I'll rinse it out."

"Not necessary," she slurs, and adds, "more wine." She needs the tangerine taste washed from her mouth.

"There isn't any, and one bottle should be enough."

"You never said that before you got all straight and Baptist," she retorts, and shivers as Johnny's cool breath blows along the bend of her neck in a track down to her breasts, hanging out in the open. Her dress has been lifted off her in a maneuver that happens so rapidly she doesn't remember it even seconds after. But she won't complain, oh no, not when the taste of Johnny's tongue in her mouth is sweeter than the homemade dessert and sends not queasy feelings to her stomach but electrical charges to her groin. She sighs and stretches and gives herself up to his skillful ministrations.

Johnny groans, "Good . . . better."

What? It doesn't matter. She sinks downward, turns, rears up, and tumbles.

Making love—no, having sex—shouldn't ignite such anger afterward, when she rests, or ought to, in a sleepy warmth. A younger, less experienced woman might be expected to moan that Johnny, ever the fast-moving trader, grabbed his advantage and took Eve against her will. Not true. She was an accomplice from the first kiss. She never pushed him away, said *stop!* or threw up road-blocks. She helpfully took off her clothes and joined the fun. So why is she so filled with regret, to the point of thumping the steering wheel, wanting to strike not at Johnny, whose apartment she's just left, but herself?

And why did she spend the night, when black coffee and cold water splashed on her face would have fixed her well enough to drive home cautiously at twenty miles an hour? She wasn't obliged to burrow into Johnny's bed, née couch, with the poly-filled mattress thin as a wafer and sleep dreamlessly until morning, then again meet Johnny halfway and have sex.

At home, showering and scrubbing her skin with a loofah, rubbing off the night, the smell and feel of Johnny—or trying to—her anger escalates rather than diminishes. She wants to think, despite evidence to the contrary, that Johnny overwhelmed her, victimized her with drink, sweet talk, tangerine sauce on home-made ice cream. Of course he did, and the anger is appropriate. What isn't are the lingering tides of warmth.

I didn't want to! I didn't enjoy his kisses, touch, body next to mine, inside me. No waves of orgasm, oh, no.

Oh, his eyes looking down at me!

She slaps the tile wall, weeps, and remembers what weakness such emotions she now suffers bring. A cellophane woman, torn into shreds—that's what she was with Abramson (though grown smarter and not, therefore, with William), and could, to her horror, be again.

Abramson was an unschooled traveler in the country of love. He hadn't the proper currency and didn't speak the language, but Eve taught him how, her old bear.

"Why is it such a young girl knows more about these things than a grown man, a middle-aged antique?" Abramson asked her. "Did you learn from that young hippie husband of yours?" She was flagrant with confidences, the sharing of secrets, even the tableau stopped in memory, the Tucson *ménage à trois* that had ended her marriage. Only one detail did she hold back, hoping eventually to forget *that* entirely and worrying what the bear would think of her.

"Jordan never understood the least little thing about love. He only knew how to do it."

"Do it? Ah, you mean *make* love. Yes, that's different from loving. Doing it is only physical pleasure, though I haven't *done it* like that for a hundred years, a thousand."

"What do you do with your wife?" Eve asked Abramson as she sat on his lap, teasing his hair up, then combing it forward across the high brow. "Do you do it with her or make love? No"—she put her fingers across his lips—"don't tell me. I can't stand it if you make love with any woman but me."

And he didn't. He wouldn't.

They could have gone on like that forever, Eve thought after, with her being little girl and Abramson daddy. Eve the student, Abramson the professor, except in love, where she was expert.

"Ah, you know so much more about this," he admitted, loving her. "Loving you up," was his expression, shy and joking.

Abramson swore, "You taught me how to have fun in bed, how not to be so serious."

Eve refused to think where it would end, living for the moment. She stood on her head with Abramson, the world topsy-turvy, and was happy, while he groaned with guilt over their loving conspiracy. It wasn't fair to his wife, a nice woman. He wept with his cheek pressed against Eve's bare stomach and promised not to *do it* again, to slip away from her in perpetual mourning, to love her forever, finally to go home with his heart in his hand instead of staying there in Eve's tiny room.

"Go then," she said to him and he took two steps forward, ready to leave Eve with a scream on her lips. But he returned before the door closed, or called the next day.

"I can't not see you," he said, tearful at times, at times severe and dry-eyed, Abramson the writer-professor-scholar.

He was a man possessed but Eve was determined to enjoy him, since he wouldn't divorce his wife. She took that rather well, though she continued to cajole and plead.

"What do you think it's like for me to be alone and know you're home with her, that you have another life?"

"This is my life, too, an important part. The life of my art."

Eve believed him. The alternative was too awful.

So they settled in, their ways becoming familiar, and were

established at the school as a steady affair. They lasted over the summer and into Eve's senior year. *Your friend* is what Abramson's colleagues called Eve to his face; his popsie, tootsie, nookie, plaything, behind his back. They raised their brows and shook their heads, and Bloom, Abramson's equal in age and rank, chided, though enviously, "I never believed it would happen to you. Or that you'd do it, Abe." *Do it* brought a blush to Abramson's cheeks, and he mumbled, as he usually did when forced to view his "friend" as others would, "I have no idea what you mean."

Abramson was a private man, peeking out in public only with his stories and his novel, and he hated everyone's knowing his business. But the reverse was true also: that he took pride in their loving, preened with a young woman stitched adoringly to his flank. Eve gave him a certain stature, and the twinkle in his eyes when they were seen together signaled his masculine satisfaction.

"They wonder about us and say, *Aha, we never thought the old dog had so much spirit in him!*" he'd whisper to her.

"So much sap," she'd say, laughing, and poke him in the ribs. Abramson's face was split in a wide grin. People stopped and gaped at the serious man of letters, Southwestern's panjandrum, dropping his years and acting like a freshman.

It was understood long before Eve appeared in Abramson's life that his wife never came to campus, that she kept herself busy with different concerns in their Los Feliz Spanish. She raised children, now grown, and retired to her knitting.

"She makes scarves and hats and gloves for orphans in cold countries," Abramson boasted proudly. "And she's taking painting at the high school." Mid-semester, after class—Dreiser, Howells, and Crane: Their Influence—Eve found an oil in a bamboo frame on Abramson's wall between the bookcases. A pair of hands in an attitude of semi-prayer. The fingers, long and narrow, greenish tinge, looked like loose strands of algae. Abramson said rather sheepishly, "It won a prize."

Eve commented, "Picasso, move over."

"It is interesting, isn't it," Abramson replied, embarrassed at sharing something of his wife with his mistress. Did he realize the oil was muck, inept and childish?

After their marriage Eve hid all the wife's paintings in the basement, including feet from the same starved sickly person as the hands. Were they her hands and feet? Eve never asked, though she wondered.

In photographs Abramson's wife appeared dimply, a puff-pastry female, not the serious broody hen who threw fits. Later Eve tried to put together the one-dimensional wife she had viewed in albums and the woman of frizzed hair, a rip in her cardigan sleeve, stockinged, sneakered, whom she found on the front porch of the house in West Hollywood where Eve rented a room.

"I can't decide if I should kill you or myself. Maybe I should shoot Abe. Not that I own a gun but I can buy one. It's very easy to get a gun. Just walk into a store and say *sell me a revolver* and give them a number, thirty-eight or forty-five. One of the numbers you hear on television," the wife said as Eve opened the screen door, continuing a conversation they might have been in the middle of, though Eve hadn't spoken a word.

Eve was frightened. In the mottled light of late autumn the woman appeared demented, lipstick smeared on her thin lips. She rubbed bony knuckles over her face, filtering sentences through her fingers. Eve knew right away who this apparition of flesh and bones was, though she had never anticipated Abramson's wife leaving her knitting or her easel to accost her, to threaten. She thought Abramson's wife would stay in the cocoon she had woven for herself, refuse to acknowledge that Abramson's heart lay else-where—if she knew, that is. This wasn't what Eve would have done, but they had flowered in different generations. The wife swayed rudderless, depending on Abramson to give her direction. So Abramson had described their marriage to Eve.

"She'd flounder without me."

Yet somehow she managed to sail west from Los Feliz and beach up on Eve's rooming-house porch, gently gliding on the slatted wooden swing in the dusk. The chains creaked. The woman plucked despair like a snapped guitar string. Her fingers worried the pearl buttons on her cardigan.

Eve thought she had seen all this on television. She thought she could walk down the steps to her car, and the wife would evaporate like a summertime puddle. Then she needn't tell Abramson. . . .

Still, Eve blurted out, "Why don't you divorce him?" Oh, how could she have been so obvious! she'd wonder later.

The wife hummed, swinging toward Eve and retreating. On the

porch beside the glider there were metal chairs, but Eve didn't sit. Somehow to sit would join her in a complicity with Abramson's wife, set the two of them up against him in some way. So she stood and asked again, "Since you know about *us*, why not let him go?" Despite Eve's keeping her distance, they understood each other well enough, that it was up to Abramson's wife to initiate action, rather than Abramson. He was as powerless with his wife as he was with Eve, and they, his women, would decide. But finally seeing the female whom she had repeatedly thrust out of mind, Eve thought the wife had gotten as far as she could go, that little remained in her except the energy to push the glider back and forth.

Eve disbelieved the chatter of guns and shooting people.

"He's an old man. You don't really want him. There are younger men," the wife said matter-of-factly. But she wasn't pleading.

Eve retorted, "Abramson's not old," and was ashamed that the man she so hopelessly loved as a god, as a firm-limbed hero, also loved his graying woman of the torn cardigan.

Her nose was rounded at the bridge, the narrow lips disappeared into wrinkling skin, and Eve wondered what she looked like when young and whether beacons of passion had flashed in her eyes. She plunged into fantasies of Abramson and his wife in bed together, the fur bear's body wrapping itself about this collection of loose bones and draping chamois skin. The visions were pornographic. Together, in Eve's mind, Abramson and his wife were players in a black-and-white skin flick. Her breasts drooped and he wore short black socks.

"You shouldn't have come here," Eve said, stiff, every muscle rigid.

Along the block, cones of murky light dropped from a parade of streetlamps but never reached the porch. Darkness collected in long cloaks around the women. And finally Eve screeched, "What are you here for?"

Soft music from a radio inside the house offered sad lyrics. Down the sidewalk a voice called, *Here Rhett, here baby!* and on the boulevard sirens wailed.

Life continued all around them, as unseen as crickets in the high grass of New Hampshire, and Eve was hungry to get back to it. But the disembodied voice winding out of the darkness as the glider sailed on its far arc held her captive. "What use is an old man to you? He is rotting with age," said the voice.

"He's not old," was all she could think to reply. She wished Abramson's wife resembled Elizabeth Taylor. He deserved a wife of beauty to enhance him and Eve needed a worthy competitor. Often, when Abramson spoke of this person he had married out of graduate school, the young teacher who retired to give him children and provide the creature comforts, Eve saw a twice-weekly bridge player, a silky though wrinkled version of one of her mother's Presbyterian choir compatriots. She never bargained for this time-ravaged settler.

"Go away," Eve ordered, "and I won't tell Abramson."

"Abe shouldn't be upset. It's bad for his ulcer."

"He doesn't have an ulcer," Eve said.

"And hemorrhoids." She gripped her elbows as she glided.

"I want him!" Eve shouted, outraged. "And he wants me! We're meant for each other."

"Oh, well, oh, la di," the woman hummed in a monotone.

And Eve hated Abramson's wife, the mother of his children—a daughter in Potomac, Maryland, a son in San Luis Obispo who afterward hated Eve. They're perturbed; they'll get over it, Abramson promised the next year, but they didn't.

On the porch when she said "our children," Eve thought she could do that, too, with Abramson, only he wouldn't. In more ways than you can count, he cautioned, I'm too far along to start again.

Oh, if she could only reinvent time!

Abramson, in his dusty, cobwebbed moments of sorrow, had said, "You should find a younger man who can give you sons and daughters."

"Don't talk as if I want to found a dynasty, and age is irrelevant. Besides, *you* can."

"I can't."

"You'll never have children with him," the gliding wife promised, smug in her anguish. "He's done all that and we have grandchildren. Has he told you about Charlie, how it was touch and go with him? We prayed through the night, the rabbi right there with us."

They weren't discussing the same person. "Abramson's an agnostic."

"No nonbelievers in hospitals!" she sang.

They argued companionably, two women not friends, from different eras and on alien continents but bridged by their man— old Abramson, sly dog Abramson, his colleague Bloom called him in envy—until Eve ran off, taking the steps in a single leap. She was late for work.

On her break from the cash register in one of the restaurant's calmer moments, she went to the pay phone, deposited a dime, and dialed Abramson's home number. (Why not? The wife was still probably swinging, moving like a shadow in the window.) But Eve hung up on the first ring.

She thought often of telling Abramson, but never did.

Eve gives the Booker switchboard the excuse of stomach flu for not going in. She pulls a Nona and relinquishes herself to an imaginary illness, plumped-up pillows, with a mug of tea and baby food— poached eggs, cottage cheese, applesauce, and buttered toast. She clicks on the answering machine and won't respond to the ringing phone.

The switchboard will hold messages from clients, and talking to Johnny is out of the question. So is talking to Nona or Cassie— Cassie in particular, who can follow the jagged coastline of despair in Eve's voice and will ask, *What's wrong?* Nothing is wrong beyond having been laid, loved up, by a man whom she likes as much as the orgasms he gave her.

The night with Johnny reverberates.

Eve thinks of Abramson, remembers his fumbling love and the gentleness he brought to their bed before his wife came to glide on Eve's porch. Thinking of Abramson, however, is counterproductive, for no amount of love or memory can resurrect the dead or nullify her enjoyment in Johnny's arms. It is hopeless to execute a half-gainer into memory, to plunge for the void, for Abramson dead will continually outstep her, yet Eve chokes with remembering.

"She said not to call me but they did anyway. They don't usually."

Abramson wouldn't hold her. He ventured no nearer the bed

than the desk chair on which he perched, an eagle on a shaky branch, wings stretched, shifting for balance.

Eve huddled with her knees against her breasts, her back against the white iron knobs of the headboard, and stared across at Abramson. From that distance she couldn't see the redness of his eyes that hit her when she answered his knock on her door.

"But it's the second time in a month—that's what decided them, and the fact of her not going to the therapist. A therapist! Oh, my God! What could she say? And why did she do it? She had money in her purse, you know." He inclined his head an inch closer to Eve, as if she doubted his wife went out supplied with cash and credit cards. Eve should know his wife didn't steal out of need.

"And what she took was so silly. Men's underwear in size thirty-two, which wouldn't fit me. A bottle of expensive perfume—"

"What's silly about perfume?"

"She never uses it—only soap and water and some talcum she powders on herself after a bath."

Such an intimate detail turned Eve on her side (makes her turn again, remembering the vision of Abramson's naked wife in the hot steamy bathroom where she, Eve, with her own hand will the next year paint the walls' dusky pink a lyric blue and replace the ruffled curtains with louvered shutters).

"Why would she take perfume and men's underwear?" Eve had to ask Abramson, who repeatedly asked the same question himself.

"They said it's a combination of factors: her age—the menopause syndrome, they called it, only that was over for her seven, eight years ago—and feeling helpless, needing to be validated." His lips pursed at the psycho-babble term. "Rage," he said, "and anger like cancer."

The woman Eve found on the porch seemed as far removed from anger as a galactic star, and that in itself, when Eve thought about it, hinted at madness. And the threats she had been so conversational about. Buy a gun and shoot herself, Eve, Abramson. Eve hadn't believed her, wouldn't, but worried about not saying to her bear, *Watch out!* If he'd lain down next to her and she could have pressed her mouth to his chest, she would have warned him then of a gun, of the open mouth and the muzzle, the bullet that would leave her wrinkled face intact and blow off the back of her skull.

But Abramson kept stubbornly to his chair.

Later she consoled herself that it wouldn't have mattered. No revelations from her and descriptions of the eeriness of his wife's incessant motions, of her rushing from mop and bucket, dishes half-scraped clean, pans unscoured, as if the earth's fault lines widened while she was at the sink and forced her out of a shaky structure, would have changed things. It wasn't Eve's fault that Abramson's wife was caught wandering in Bullock's Wilshire with unpaid-for items in her purse. None of *that* could be laid at Eve's feet or accusations thrown. No *You're responsible!*

More immediate, Abramson explained, "We can't see each other for a while. I have to be with her."

Eve screamed, "You are, every night! You sleep in her bed, not in mine!"

"No, no, you don't understand. I must pay her attention."

Eve went forward, crying, "Who do you think you are, Linda Loman?"

"Don't . . ."

"What about me?"

"My love," he sobbed and crawled over the end of the bed to her. "One last time," he whimpered, and Eve, though frightened, knew that in a matter of weeks, if not days, her bear would be back.

Eve can't sleep or even rest easily. Unlike Nona, she has no patience for soap operas, which she judges silly and morbidly slow.

Several times the phone rings, but not one of the calls is from Johnny, whom she expects to hear from and whom she determines not to talk to, at least not for a couple of days. At which time she can explain, "A mistake's been made." She plans to disabuse Johnny of any notions he might have as to a repeat performance, whether at his Hollywood closet or here in her more comfortable surroundings. This is not to become "a thing," and why don't they just stay platonic friends, providing companionship for each other and dates when social occasions demand a couple rather than a single. A healthy, civilized arrangement. Yes, that's what Eve will tell Johnny, but though she phones his office she can't connect with him and won't leave her name. She won't have him getting the wrong impression, supposing she's calling to oh and ah, to throatily whisper an endearment, to suggest they make love, fuck (no, make love, though fucking would be easy, better, a momentary exchange, as with one of her pickups) again, soon, sooner, soonest.

Eve is too edgy to be sick, to make-believe aches and pains she'd like to have for today, to see her through the aftershock, and she wonders how Nona slides so effortlessly into hypochondria without inspecting her motives. Eve is too conscious of what she does and why, so that by mid afternoon the bed hurts like a medieval rack and she has no choice but to dress and go over to her office at least for an hour.

In the closet she reaches for a silk wraparound and her fingers push through the gauzy image of Abramson's wife swinging on a hanger. It is the linear displacement of light and shadows, the gathering of material, suits, jackets, dresses, the wedge of the shelf extending down, that create the painful phantasm, but no rational explanation can brick up Eve's scream.

I can't decide if I should buy a gun and kill him or you or me. . . .

And when she did, Eve's first reaction was profound gratitude.

I never wanted her to shoot herself, any more than I would have wanted her to shoot either of us, some stranger, a drive-by, oh, why did she have to do *it*, and why not just vanish, leave him, say I can't live with you now, go, be free!

"All over the upholstery. Red with her blood." Abramson wept for weeks, months, at the oddest times and moments, over dinner in restaurants, screaming up from sleep. He never forgot going step by step into their living room, the clock ticking in the front hall, as he called her name, said, *Why are you sitting in the dark?* and *Turn the light on,* and *Is something the matter?* Then the click of the wall switch, which he later fantasized sounded as loud as the gun firing—though who stood there to hear that?—and knowing *this is all wrong*. He couldn't see her temple, from which the bullet exited her skull so untidily. On the right, where she had positioned the muzzle just above her ear, she wore, or so he thought at first, a bright-red ribbon in her hair. How unlike her!

Her face was amazingly serene; the eyes, into which he had looked a thousand times over the years, closed.

The gun had fallen onto her flowered lap and lay in the folds of her housedress like a small dead animal. There was no blood on her that Abramson saw, other than her hair ornament, for the wall nearest the chair in which she ended her life and on which sections of brain splattered in an intricate pattern—that wall angled off into shadows.

"I kept calm," Abramson said to Eve, "for to fall apart would have been self-indulgent. My own priorities at that moment were irrelevant, to cry, to throw myself on the floor, and of course I refused to negate the possibility that she was fine, wasn't—" He always choked on *dead*. Unlike what he would have done in a novel, he described his reactions in cumbersome terminology and language not for the real world of fiction but more for English Department meetings. His anguish in telling and retelling the story to Eve was all the more palpable because of the ponderous words he chose, and she had to bite her tongue not to criticize.

Time, she supposed, would loosen the grip the dead wife held on Abramson's throat, but she was mistaken. Again and again the bear arrived home, shuffling up the short steps, unlocking the front door, calling out, *Hello, are you home?*

Eve tries to bury the memories but she stumbles on Abramson's smile. Once upon a time he told her stories, his and others, and weeping "Oh, Bear!" she sinks to the floor.

Minutes, an hour later, when she's showered and dressed, Johnny finally phones and Eve is grateful.

15

Cassie finds herself in the anomalous position of having gone public about Jake though she has still to show him off. Nona and Eve complain: When are we going to see this marvelous creature, this paragon of masculine virtues, the man who can sweep you—has swept you—off your feet? Beth and Al haven't met Jake either. Beth, dredging up yet another male loosened by divorce, is stopped at the gate with Cassie's *there's someone else*.

Who?

Beth can't know that any Thursday she needs only to glance out her kitchen window to see Jake, over whom she enthusiastically cries, "Bring him to dinner!"

Cassie feels constrained about waltzing Jake around to her friends, of letting them poke and prod him, ask, even if jokingly, what his intentions are? Her reluctance doesn't stem at all from the fact that Jake sports a tattoo, which most likely at the barbecue Beth proposes will soar nakedly in flight, or that he lacks the usual benedictions. Only Eve has cried *The gardener?* but then added *I love it!* It's sexy and literary, a perfect combination, and Cassie thinks Eve is reminded of her favorite husband, Abramson the professor.

No, of course she isn't embarrassed that Jake works with his hands, outside and probably for minimum wage or a little above— not that she asks him so intimate a question as how much money he makes. Her nervousness cuts closer to the bone and depends on how reliable or otherwise Jake is. Can he simply disappear or change his mind? What if he's disappointed, not pleased, slyly shape-shifting, the trickster? Maybe he's decided on a different woman or no woman at all. Is she building castles in the air over a few dates and being taken to bed?

Jake seems offhanded about this relationship—Cassie cringes at the charged word—and seldom calls. Of course, on Thursdays he waits around for her to come home, and so far he has always suggested something for Saturday. Otherwise he pops up, a genie from his lamp, ringing the bell as unexpectedly as Nona, just dropping over as if he has determined she'll be in. What does he presume, that she lies frozen in plastic, activated only by his presence? She thinks of hinting at more ritual. Couldn't they make plans? But fear sucks away Cassie's courage. She can't push him, for men are touchy about pressure and assumptions. That much she knows from listening to Eve and Nona. So she tiptoes around in their *relationship* like a woman in a new house, not certain where anything goes, not even sure what feels right.

What is she to say to him now that he's at the back door, knocking against the window? He is a shadow on the other side of the curtain and she opens the door just as he grabs the knob. They parry in an awkward two-step shuffle that breaks the tension of his arrival and they can smile at each other.

Jake never offers the odd affectionate gesture. His touching is more calculated, so his lips don't brush her cheek, nor will his hand rub in rough warmth along her shoulder. Cassie would have his arms lock about her or his fingers track her chin, smooth unruly strands of hair, but she can't ever ask.

Taking her cues from Jake, Cassie stays within precise territorial borders, playing a cool game, while the girl within wants to launch herself at him, to hug and hold, to climb into his lap, nuzzle his neck.

She asks with a backward glide, "Have you had dinner yet?"

"I thought we might grab a hamburger. What about it?"

He's no stranger anymore in Cassie's kitchen and opens the refrigerator for a beer. Cassie thinks of saying *Can't you kiss me when you come in?* and *Please call*. What if she looks a mess, hair uncombed, a wrinkled dress or shirt? It's not outside the realm of reason that she brings blood home in a stain on her skirt or shirt, her wrist, hand, sleeve.

Instead, Cassie replies, "I'll go change."

He inventories her then. "You're fine."

Is she? What if he lies?

She flies to the downstairs bathroom and the mirror to check her makeup. Her eyes have the pale rabbity look she hates and she hurries upstairs for mascara, wondering if Jake sees her at all. How can he not notice the spot on her sweater, the old slacks? Maybe he is only interested in sex (that ageless cliché), in lying with her with the lights off. She should ask Eve, and if Eve says *biology*, then where will she be? Jake excites butterflies in her stomach, but what does she do to him? Something? Nothing?

What about *love*?

The brush pauses in midair. Static keeps the stray hairs upright. A constriction of Cassie's chest threatens to halt her breathing. *Love?* Oh, no, not really! Weak-kneed and afraid she sits on the toilet seat.

From downstairs she hears Jake whistling a tune that with her unmusical ear she has no chance of identifying. But it is melodic. Jake's not making discordant sounds. He must be happy. Is she? Yes, and yes again, she thinks, not having to decide, and rushes through the fluttery gestures of dressing, remaking her face. Of course she is happy, only out of her element, a lake trout in salt water.

I never thought I'd be in love again. . . .

The word crashes less harshly the more she slides it around in her mouth. Like adjusting to hot peppers, she toughens to it until she stumbles on: But is he in love with me?

"Aren't you ready yet?" His voice drifts impatiently up the steps and Cassie rushes.

"Coming," Cassie flings back down, as the question of love spins infectiously inside her.

Why should it amaze her that she relaxes with Jake after they've been together for a while? But until she adjusts to Jake's being *here* rather than *there*, wherever *there* is—she never visits his apartment in the vague territory of "near downtown"—she shifts and shuffles. He raises wounds of nervousness in her that take time to scab over.

"Some guys have a gig out in the valley for Saturday night," he says. "They've asked me to sit in. A private party, which means we get paid. No big deal, just fifty bucks apiece, but it's something."

She has come to rely on Saturday nights. If Jake plays at Malone's she sits at the bar and listens; then he follows her home in his car. If not, they make dinner together, watch television, or she rents a movie. He likes comedies, old ones in black-and-white, the Marx Brothers, W. C. Fields, Abbott and Costello.

Now a Saturday night alone or with the women aggrieves her. They've come so far, or at least far enough for Cassie to ask "Should I drive with you or go myself?"

"Neither. No friends of the band."

"Oh." She leans back in the booth. *Neither.* Does that mean he doesn't want her, that he's asked someone else? *No friends* . . . He could be telling the truth, or Doug's kind of truth, skewed by his desires.

"Will you come by later?"

She hears the note of pleading in her voice too late to swallow it. Nona would ask a man that question in just that tone, or poor April, she imagines, imprisoned by need rather than passion. She refuses the comparison and quickly slips in before Jake can make his excuses: "Of course not. It will be—what? one, two in the morning? I'll be asleep. Sunday early I'm playing tennis so I have to be up by eight." Tennis! Why is she pretending? She last strolled out on a court three months ago and besides, Barbara, her only partner, sleeps late on Sundays. But tennis is the first explanation of why she can do nicely without Jake—thank you very much, I'll sail in the mainstream of my life—and once she says *tennis* she can't retreat from the commitment. "That's okay," he says. "I thought I would. But, okay. If you can't." Can't, not don't want to, but it's the latter Jake means. The bruising around his eyes might come from a number of conditions, but Cassie seizes on disappointment and her heartbeat accelerates.

"Maybe I can play later, after you go," she says immediately, her hand in a slow crab crawl across the Formica table of the coffee shop in case he wants to take it. But he leaves it lying there and shrugs that she shouldn't change her plans for him.

"It's okay. The afternoon's probably better anyway. Just come over whenever. I'll leave the door open."

"Don't. It's too dangerous. You'd better give me a key."

They advance several steps by this request. A key gives him proprietary rights, and more than hints that he will loosely come and go and expect her not to have other male company. Of course, she has long before confessed there is no one else, but his asking for a key startles Cassie. In various ways a key commits them both.

"I'll have a spare made up tomorrow."

They're quiet now, as if considering the implication of Jake's having such access to Cassie's house, of being able to let himself in without knocking or ringing the bell.

He signals for a coffee refill and asks her what about dessert.

"I can't take the calories."

"Come on, you're not fat. Fat's like this." He spreads his arms.

"I'm five pounds too heavy, or to be honest, ten."

"Get off it—you're perfect," he says, with a mixture of annoyance and pleasure. Cassie doesn't recognize the tone but Eve or Nona could tell her it's the throaty resonance a man gets in his voice when talking to the woman he's steadily sleeping with.

The compliment pleases Cassie, but while she wets her lips over it, she says, "What blarney." It won't do to let him assume she accepts his *perfect*.

Jake shakes his head. "You're a beautiful woman and in bed you feel exactly right."

Heat flames Cassie's cheeks. Eve would probably toss off a smart, sexy remark—*I like the way you look, too, in bed and out*—but Cassie's tongue lies inert in her mouth. She lacks the bravery to admit how much she cares.

"Don't look away."

"I'm not. It's only that you . . . you surprised me."

"By saying you're beautiful?"

Cassie's afraid her awkwardness with the compliment annoys him. But she can't let *beautiful* wash over her the way Nona does. She teethes on the syllables of *beau-ti-ful* like an infant, and then whispers, "Thank you."

He grunts just like her father, like Doug, when not entirely pleased. Men grunt; women seldom do, Cassie's mother once pointed out.

Jake pays the check, waving off her offer of money. Mostly they do go Dutch and Jake doesn't object. In other ways though he is startlingly old-fashioned, holding doors for her, pulling back her chair at the table, being courtly at times with a grace that is almost Victorian. And Cassie enjoys his gestures.

In truth Cassie and Jake are really quite compatible, are in fact—for the moment—happy together, though they never announce their pleasure even to each other. Cassie struggles in learning about happiness and it will be longer still before she adjusts to the condition.

"Thank you for the hamburger," Cassie says when they're on the sidewalk.

Politely, as they get into the car, Jake says, "Don't mention it."

"Next time I'll treat," Cassie promises when Jake starts driving down Wilshire.

"You don't have to."

"Then I'll make dinner."

"You don't have to do that either."

At the next light, where Wilshire slopes just enough to see two blocks ahead, a silver van veers like a misshot arrow and slices diagonally across the outside lane of traffic to explode into an oncoming car. The two vehicles join in an embrace of steel, sprung bumpers and ruptured fenders twisting about each other so that the car and van swerve as one to the right. Together, like lasciviously locked lovers, they collide with a convertible, and the shriek of stepped-on brakes; crunching steel screams.

"My God! Did you see that!" Cassie cries. The crash seems to be something happening on film, a celluloid event.

"We'll take the next right and circle around them."

"What are you talking about? We have to stop."

"What the hell for?"

"To help. There are injured people in those cars!"

"And the paramedics already on their way. That's the job they do, whizzing to the scene with sirens blaring."

"Jake, I'm not going to argue. Just pull up close as you can get." Cassie grips his forearm and might yank his hand from the wheel if he attempts to turn. "I refuse to drive off as if something terrible isn't going on right in front of my face."

"Jesus, the last thing anybody needs are interfering gawkers. We can do a shitload of damage." The sharp angles of light splashing into the car paint Jake's skin a sickly green. His brow and the cleft above his lip gleam with sweat.

"I'm a doctor and I insist you stop *now*. Drive off and leave me if you want, but I'm going to help," Cassie says.

Their argument is sharp and unpleasant, but Jake does double-park four cars down from the mangled knot of steel. The accident is so fresh the wheels on the upended van, halfway across the sidewalk, are still spinning. Cassie can't stop to wonder what's wrong with Jake, why he sweats to speed off, since she's out of the car and running, first to the van, where in the windshield's bulging spiderweb of cracks a man's head is wedged like a red cabbage. A stiletto of glass two thumbs wide sticks out of his jugular. Blood spurts from an uncapped well. As Cassie reaches to do she knows not what, the shocked blue eyes in the bloody face glaze. The van's driver dies as she curses under her breath, feeling helpless.

Traffic on Wilshire at ten o'clock is curiously sparse. Few cars and no pedestrians, and only escalating cries of agony, pitched screams in a forest of sobbing. Cassie spins around and responds to the low keening from a dark slug in denim crawling toward her. She kneels beside him and he collapses by her leg, moaning gently as a baby.

"Here, here," she croons. He can't be more than Mandy's age, if that, and her heart jolts in her chest even as her fingers rapidly work over the boy. He winces when she probes his chest, neck, but he appears more bruised and dazed than seriously broken. Carefully Cassie turns him over, tears off her jacket, and pillows the blond curls against it. "Stay still. Don't move. I have to help the others."

A crowd begins to gather. Cassie scans the onlookers for Jake and finds him hanging on the perimeter. She calls to him but he doesn't hear her, or he refuses to answer.

From the distance comes a warble of sirens and the screech of ambulances and fire trucks, and the night erupts, alive with disharmony.

A fire truck swinging south pulls across both lines of traffic. Two black-and-whites couple to block the east end of Wilshire. The accident scene, set in a tapestry of shining lights, diamondy chips of glass, estuaries of blackness along the macadam, is cordoned off.

Cassie pushes around the paramedics by the convertible. "I'm a doctor," she explains. Without wasting words the two young men accept her. They work in concert over the car's driver, crushed into the steering wheel. The girl from the passenger seat is splayed over the dash, limp as a shadow. Her long hair changes from auburn to dark brown to black in the twirling lights and shrouds her face in a shawl. But when Cassie, having freed the boy, goes to help, she realizes the hair is blondish, turned rubescent by blood. The face has dissolved. A faint flutter wings in her neck, however, and Cassie calls out, "She's still alive!" Hurriedly they loosen the girl from the car. "Clear her air passages," Cassie orders as they rush over the oxygen.

There are six victims in all: the van's dead driver, the couple barely alive in the convertible, and the least injured boy and his two bruised and battered friends from the Chevy.

To Cassie the few feet of Wilshire are a war zone, and she works oblivious to Jake, to whether he still waits with the crowd or has gone off on her. Only time, each lost second and minute, matters. The girl of the bloody hair clings with broken fingers to the ragged edge of life; the convertible's driver has a punctured lung and incalculable internal damage.

At last Cassie steps aside, takes the "Thanks, Doc" from a paramedic with a shrug, and leans against a photographer's store window full of stylized pictures of brides in white gowns and collections of scrubbed children. Unloosening tension sets off convulsive trembles in her legs.

Jake appears out of nowhere, walking over the shadows to say, "Are you okay?"

"Not really. One man's dead, another will probably go soon, and a third is dubious." She raises bleak eyes. "Her face is missing."

"Don't think about it."

"What should I do, go home and watch David Letterman, have a cup of coffee, take a shower, make love with you?" Anger, not at Jake but at the carnage, at her inability to rewind time, to rip out by the throat that one second when the van swerved, uproots the last of Cassie's control.

"Let's go." She sees Jake's lips move, purple in the acid light, but through the blood pounding in her ears she barely hears. He folds an arm about her shoulders and walks her off from the window as she weeps.

———

Jake brews tea, not coffee, and pours a slug of whiskey in it. The mixture tastes awful but he insists she drink it. "You're in shock. Your blood sugar is low."

Cassie's teeth chatter. "I know that."

Her anger refuses to dissipate, even if she does regret the edge in her voice. The hurt she suffers from the bloody accident victims humiliates her, for surely she has seen enough blood in her life to fill all the swimming pools in the Palisades. This is not the first tragedy that has come Cassie's way, but her rotation through the emergency room of St. Luke's, where she interned, was almost twenty years ago, and structured. The broken, cracked, crushed, shot, torn, ripped, sliced, stabbed were never hers alone. She held her place, part of a team; she had procedures to follow. In the white and sea-green and stainless-steel atmosphere of the hospital, there at least seemed a modicum of hope, but on the street, on the front lines, in the first flush of injury, the wrecked bodies were debris. She had only her hands and knowledge, and felt ill-prepared for the accident.

"And where were you?" she asks, enraged.

"Minding my own business."

"You could have helped," she accuses him, lashing out as if he bears some blame for the accident.

"I'm not an M.D. I cut the grass, pull out weeds, and truck the garbage cans to the curb. How's that for not meddling? Because I don't know how, won't, can't. Shit, why do I have to get blood all over my pants?" His voice is scratchy, like a nail on slate, and he seems farther from her than just across the kitchen pouring his own whiskey straight.

"You could have tried to help."

Say you're wrong—say it! She grits her teeth, thinking.

Jake yells, "Leave me alone! I've seen enough spilled guts and brains running like turkey soup! Why the hell do I have to look at any more, even a scratch, a busted little toe?"

He explodes like a sudden squall and his anger wipes Cassie's mind clean of images of mutilated bodies. Instead she scrambles with concern for this man she knows so inadequately, but whom she might love.

"Stop. All right. It's okay. I'm sorry I got carried away."

"Yeah, well, it's been a real fun evening. And your accusing me of being a coward pisses me off." He throws the whiskey down his throat, eyes rolling back in his head, as if he plans to ride a bullet train to the blasted dawn of drunkenness.

"I never said you were a coward." Cassie's hand flies to her mouth. "But you might have done something."

"Done something? Oh, yeah, glued a fucker's head back on his neck. How about that magic trick? Jake Houdini. Or heaving a snake's nest of guts back into a bloody hole and snapping it up with safety pins? What about wading in the muck searching for a pair of loose eyeballs? And—"

She is up from the chair and on him, pressing his face to her breasts, rubbing his hair, the nape of his neck, holding him, rocking in rhythm with the spasms that seem to set the whole house shaking.

He cries into her, through the coarse wool of her sweater and the smooth milk warmth of her skin to her veins: "I never want to see blood again, no arms in ripped sleeves, stubs of blown-off legs—"

"Hush," she whispers, gripping him tighter. "I'm sorry. I never thought."

He yanks back with a swipe upward of his elbow that slams a breast. "Son of a bitch," he curses, in a fury at no one, at everybody. He wipes his eyes with a sleeve, wetting down the sleeping eagle. "I need another drink."

"Here, have my tea."

What does he want with tea? He goes to the sink and plugs the bottle straight to his mouth and drinks until he's had enough. He splashes cold water on his face, over his hair, and dark streaks river his shirt.

"All the shit I saw . . ." He lifts his right hand. "I held a man's heart. It was lying in the slime with nothing except filthy water around it. You don't think that's possible, do you, a heart blown clean out of a guy's chest and just sitting on the ground like a piece of bloody fruit. Well, it isn't possible. Afterward I told one of the medics and he said I must've been juiced, that no way did such shit happen even in Nam. But it did. I had this heart in my hand, and it felt slimy, disgusting." He flings his arm to the side as if he still has contact with the heart.

Cassie keeps space between them, three feet of wide plank

flooring, for to touch him now would be dangerous, a match striking a fuse. He shivers, ready to detonate, take the roof off Cassie's house and fly skyward in a rocket of memory.

"Let's go to bed," she suggests. Let's go to bed, home, have a drink. . . . What inadequacies they offer each other, groping blindly in the dark, tromping with heavy-footed effort to erase pain and right abuses. But blows will not transform into caresses; and healing, Cassie knows in her professional heart, leaves scars.

He allows her to guide him up the stairs to the bedroom, where she undresses him tenderly, passionless as a mother or a physician. Cautiously she eases him under the covers and he lies there stiff with the rigor mortis of remembering. When she is naked herself she winds her arms around him. His flesh is icy and chills Cassie's heart. She thinks he won't sleep and neither will she, but eventually, bound together, they both slide through wintry rivers in dark channels downward.

Jake wakes on the crosscurrent of a shriek and Cassie bellies up out of her dreams. He thrashes and an arm strikes her.

"What is it?" she cries, scrambling for the lamp switch.

"Aaah! aah! aah!" His mouth forms a black hole and he heaves upward, gasping for air. His back arches as though he were in the throes of a seizure until, with one final scream, he collapses in a high fall from the ledge of his nightmare.

Cassie approaches carefully. She rubs his slicked skin and smells fear as ugly as yesterday's garbage. "You're freezing," she says, and draws the quilt up to his chin. He is breathing in low growls like a trapped animal. Cassie holds his hand, which lies light and dead as a whisper in hers.

After several minutes, he croaks, "Sorry."

"Nothing to be sorry about. You had a nightmare. I was having a dream myself, about flying over rooftops on your eagle. Wearing a black skirt and going to a coven." She tries to make him laugh, and when he doesn't, she coaxes him with the same gentle loving she'd give to a child: "Dreams are normal, bad ones, funny ones, all kinds." But she knows that through all the nights yet to come, she will never have so horrific a dream as the one Jake broke out of screaming. She hasn't a clue what monsters populated his landscape, and, cowardly, she hopes never to find out, even as she lies close beside him, waiting for him to describe the fangs and teeth and claws, the brimming horror that lowered his body temperature until he hung at the border of shock.

The swamp of war, body parts, the final degree of fear?

The house feels damp and cold, chillier with Jake's three A.M. terror, and quiet as a graveyard. "I'm just going to turn the heat on," Cassie says. "I'll only be a second." Jake doesn't respond and Cassie hesitates, but then runs naked to the downstairs hall.

He is up and dressing by the time she returns. "Where are you going?"

"Home."

"Home? Why?"

He buttons his shirt. "You've got to have some sleep and I'm going to climb the walls for a while."

"All right. I'll put the kettle on. We'll talk. I don't mind staying up." Liar, she does mind, but less than his leaving.

They stare at each other until she realizes she stands bare as a jaybird, mottled with goose bumps, her thighs unlovely, the back-country roads of fine stretch marks on display across her stomach. She grabs her robe from the arm of a chair, furious with herself.

"You had a nightmare. Well, no surprise. The accident upset you." Is her voice too low? Does she talk to him as if he's a kid, Mandy five, six years ago?

"Lots of things upset me, Cassie."

"You'll feel better if we discuss it. Your nightmare, I mean. Bad dreams fade when you open the shutters and let some light on them. Big point in psychology."

He pulls on his jacket and goes toward her. "My bad dreams are already out in the open. I walk around with them. Okay?"

"Okay what?"

"And I want to be alone."

"Be alone then!" She won't cry. She absolutely will not give in to the down-and-dirty female tactic of tears, except that wetness floods up in her chest. She can't not cry, and twists to the bed so she won't see him retreat.

When Cassie finally glances over her shoulder it is at an empty room. Jake moved as quiet as the wind, a ghost, floating on less than smoke.

Cassie won't sleep either for the rest of the night, the unhappiness, the unfairness of his bolting keeping her up. She lies stiff, wide-eyed, and a thousand miles from sleep, and drifts, wondering where he is, what he's doing, worrying until dawn, when she dresses and leaves early for the clinic.

16

Cassie doesn't hear from Jake. She assumes that he'll call, but the day passes without a word from him and that night at home the phone is obstinately silent.

Has he taken off again? Is he slouched on a plane, train, bus seat, heading away from California, shredding his memories of her as if she's never been? Or is he hampered by twenty-year-old pain, bound and unable even to stumble or cry out? Or does his male pride make him resent her having seen him weakened?

Through the next day she exists out of touch, encased in Saran Wrap and separated from her patients and the other doctors and nurses, who must raise their voices in order to claim Cassie's attention. Doctor, heal thyself! Chris the accountant finally explodes in annoyance when he tries unsuccessfully to get intelligent answers from her on a tax problem. Luckily the clinic day is a serene one, hours of routine, of ordinary ailments, preventive medicine that demands only a quasi-alertness, so she drifts on her ice floe thinking Jake is a phantasm. He hunkers in her mind only as a figment of heated imagination, a dream lover, an incubus, and she quails at even mentioning his name to Nona later on the phone.

Only Eve's name in the schedule of Jena's next day's appointments cracks Cassie's preoccupation. "I didn't know she was your patient," Cassie says to Jena when she captures her at the coffee pot. A cigarette in the corner of Jena's mouth clouds smoke between them.

"She's not. I've never seen her before. Why the interest?"

219

"A friend of mine," Cassie replies, "and I had no idea that she has a problem."

"Probably just the usual Pap smear, et cetera. Don't fret."

"She never said a word to me about coming in to see you."

"Here, have some coffee, and take that I'm-being-snuck-around look off your face. Your friend Eve is just another example of a female happier spreading her legs for a stranger rather than a female she gossips with over bloody Marys. We women are a fidgety bunch of hens about some things."

"I'm not saying I expect Eve to see me as a physician. I thought she used Schwartzman over in Beverly Hills."

"Ben Schwartzman? He's got cancer, prostate. Somebody's taken over his practice but I can't remember who."

"Well, if Eve needs a new gynecologist she could have mentioned it. I don't see anything wrong in her saying she's booked in to see you."

"Pet," Jena sighs, "when she comes in tomorrow, you girls can let down your hair on the subject. But my advice is, be thankful. Friends are a burden." Jena is a believer only in medical relationships. As far as anyone at Magdalene knows she exists alone, without chains to the world outside.

"It's just so secret."

"And the whole business is bothering you too much. What's really up?"

The problem with being evenly balanced and never tripping, no matter what emotional upheaval sets off seismic cracks, is that after a while others always expect such equilibrium. Nothing is ever supposed to cause Cassie to miss a step.

"Just life in general, I guess."

"PMS?" Jena asks.

Cassie shakes her head no and returns to her office to call Eve, whose answering machine responds. The Booker switchboard reports that she is out of the office. Can they take a message?

"No, I'll catch her later," Cassie says, her voice up an octave. She resents Eve's not being available.

Cassie's next patient is ready and she puts both Eve and Jake out of her mind. Jake, after all, is conditional. No strings tie him to her, no promises, and when he arrives to garden he'll tell her some story, even if it's no more explicit than *I've been busy*.

She continues to try to get Eve, however, on and off until eleven that night. In asperity she finally shouts down the machine, "For the tenth time, Eve, where are you? And would you please give me a call. Otherwise I'll see you at the clinic tomorrow before or after your appointment with Jena."

"I didn't want to say anything to you until I had some idea what was wrong. In case I'm hyperventilating over squat. The usual female twinge. Besides, I hate how Nona runs to you with all her little boo-boos, crying wolf."

"You're not Nona."

"Lord, no. Three inches shorter and without those bones." Eve's front teeth, in that slight overbite men find sexy, nibble her bottom lip. In the patient chair, hugging her elbows—a position Cassie has seen countless other women assume—Eve sits, trying not to appear worried. There is such distance between them now, more than a matter of feet, a chasm that spreads from doctor to patient and is unbridgeable.

Cassie repeats, "You're as different from Nona as night from dawn. Nona needs to hurt and ache, to find things wrong with her body, or at least hope poor Dr. Rubin will."

"Do you think it's serious?"

Cassie thinks, you might not be Nona but you ask her questions with the same trapped-rabbit look in your eyes. If you sit still as a post, hold your breath, maybe the wind will shift and carry off the scent of bad news.

"Jena wants you to have an ultrasound," Cassie equivocates. Eve has a tumor on the left ovary, about the size of a large walnut, give or take a centimeter. They plan the usual, but when the results are in, Cassie's betting there won't be a choice.

Jena isn't a cutter and disparages male gynecologists who rip out female organs as offhandedly as weed pullers in the garden. "I believe in saving as much of the equipment God gave us in the beginning as is humanly possible," Jena the atheist is fond of saying. But if Jena proves right, Eve's tumor won't dissolve and each month her periods will gush like Niagara. The pain will escalate.

Eve, her chin lifted, is asking, "Is it cancer?"

The dreaded word flowers in ugliness as it leaves Eve's lips.

221

Cassie struggles not to rush around the desk and hug Eve and, holding her, to cast a future that might be a lie. Instead she forces a yogic calm into her voice, that especially serene tone she uses when doing rounds: "Don't worry. From what Jena can tell now it appears to be benign. After the ultrasound we'll know more."

"But what do you think, Cassie?"

"I didn't examine you." Eve's presumption is endemic to every patient told *something's wrong* instead of *everything's fine*—even a friend who knows that under the white coat is a human body, the same heart, brains, liver. A physician should have a divine instinct.

"Right. That would be, oh, well . . ." Eve, staring up at the ceiling, searches for a word.

Cassie reassures her. "I understand. Embarrassing."

Eve suddenly claps her hands and hoots with laughter. "Can't you just see it! Me with my thing out in the open and you poking and pushing around like a miner digging for gold." She bends over, hiccoughing, and thumps her chest.

Now Cassie *is* embarrassed and says stiffly, "It is difficult for nonmedical people to accept that at times the physical is just a matter of flesh, tissue, blood vessels, and unrelated to the individual."

"My tissues are fairly individual to me, thank you very much." Eve laughs and breaks into tears on the upswing. "And I don't want to be sick!"

In her khaki Ralph Lauren suit and crisp cotton shirt, looped in gold chains at the neck and both wrists, hoop earrings with diamond chips, Charles Jourdan pumps of polished leather, Eve transmogrifies into a frightened child. She melts like a candle and her fear importunes Cassie, who must leave the high-backed doctor's chair to take Eve's hand and croon, "Nobody's said a thing about cancer, so hush now."

"Will I be all right?"

"After the tests we'll decide what's best, but it is possible you might need a hysterectomy."

Eve tightens. "Is that the downside?"

They search for lies in each other's eyes and Cassie thinks how all the patients in the world want only to hear *You're a hundred percent; you'll live forever*. And though she realizes she might be offering Eve less than the truth, that there is often a wild card, she replies, "Yes. You'll be fine. I promise."

Eve takes Cassie's *yes* home with her like a fish in Lucite. It hangs suspended, unlatticed by bracings. Sure she'll be all right. Sure, insure, assure . . . The pressure of *tumor* ignites Eve's tears as she drives.

Cassie would never misrepresent the facts. Cassie cleaves to the truth more than to the ground that supports her, and lying not only abuses their friendship but, worse, violates her physician's oath. No, Eve thinks, Cassie flies above the lies that some doctors tell in order to banish terror.

Yes, Cassie said.

And Eve hungers to be relieved, not to jettison her tumor but simply to forget about it, at least until it's captured by sound waves. After which imaging they (who? Jena? not Cassie, of course) will excise the feminine part of her, the clockwork of her sexuality. Not that she needs the plumbing. For what? A child?

"Don't be an ass!" she cries aloud, swabbing her tears with a tissue.

She's universes apart from her sisters with their progeny and mothering, their lost mittens and wrapped presents, lollipops, sullen teenagers, hugs and kisses. Right then she is too scared of the ultimate dark herself, longing for the nest of her own mother's lap, that scrawny pea creature of splintery bones and lace hankies and *wear your best panties when you go traveling,* to worry about the barren void that will collapse inward like a black hole.

I am out in the world, somebody you don't know. . . .

Dust motes of memory coalesce in the passenger seat as Eve weeps, banging a ringed hand on the steering wheel. In the next lane a curious driver watches her before speeding off past a light.

No child, children, and no tulip organs, delicate stemwork. Nothing inside. Vacancy. Nobody's home.

The sentence to be issued, spoken already as far as Eve is concerned—Cassie's *you might need* as good as an edict—shames Eve, to her surprise. The tears run down her cheeks at the stunned realization of how normally she is reacting to her female organs' being cut out, reacting with utter horror, as she knows her sisters would.

What can it possibly matter? As long as, dear God in whom I only now remember I believe, please don't let it be malignant.

Cancer.

The word tastes foul, and Eve—conservatively tailored, successfully designed and dressed—spits a large white glob of disgust in a splatter on the dash.

Nothing rots in her. There are no maddened cells gobbling healthy flesh like video game baddies, so why should she worry? All that's necessary is to relinquish what she has no need for anyway, and why not? There's even a plus side: no messiness each month, forget the pain blazing in a four alarm fire, the tiger chewing her up, and sex without any contraception.

Somehow she has gotten to the beach, unconscious, flying blind. She turns onto the Pacific Coast Highway and drives until the tears dry in crusted patterns on her cheeks. Then she swings into the first seaside restaurant she arrives at.

With a glass of wine Eve walks down to the surf. She slips off her pumps and steps through the chilly water in stockinged feet, and pearls foam around her toes. She walks, drinking the wine, with the wind in her face until she outmaneuvers it. When it curls at her back it raises tendrils of hair. She walks for such a long way that the last drops of wine dry in the glass.

Cassie struggles out of sleep hoping that the water will be running, streams gullying in the flower beds, splashing on the concrete, errant drops tinkling in xylophone notes on the windows, but she awakes to crisp silence.

Of course she hears nothing. Jake comes late in the afternoon, his last stop, but in the first moments, as the black scarf of sleep retreats, she half dreams him on the grass shirtless and sweaty, the pelt of curly hairs on his chest glistening.

But she still must wait, and the day creeps, an inch in an hour, taking forever. By four her palms prickle. She asks Barbara to take her last patient.

At home, she showers, applies makeup with a loving care Nona would approve of, twirls her hair, hates the frothy girlish look and brushes it straight, chooses a green blouse, then a blue sweater, bursts into tears.

"You're a fool, an aging female, oh, hell. . . !" she shouts at the mirror.

The phone rings.

"Mom."

"What's wrong?"

"Mom, why do you think there's something wrong just because I call you?"

"Mandy, I'm sorry. I've had a hard day."

"I've had a hard day too. I think I've flunked my bio test. It was gruesome," Mandy complains as Cassie listens for Jake's truck. Any minute he will drive up and she guiltily wants Mandy off the phone. She rehearses *I'll call later,* waiting to slide it in between murmurs and motherly responses. Meanwhile she climbs the upgrade of a roller coaster, death-defying, on the edge of her chair, to be plunged by Jake's arrival off the tracks and out into space.

And there, *now,* the slam of a truck door. She cries, "Mandy, someone's here. I'll have to call you back."

"Who's there?" Mandy is not so preoccupied that she misses the tear in her mother's voice.

"I don't know."

"Mom, put the phone down and go see. Then you can—"

"Mandy, please! I love you!" Cassie says and hangs up just as she sees Yang through the kitchen window.

"Yang, how are you? It's been a long time."

The stooped little man, wrinkled as a roasted chestnut, lifts his head. "Dr. Morgan. Have you been well?"

"Yes, fine. And you?"

"Perfect, thanks to God's good grace." Yang is, as he once explained to her, an observant Christian, grateful to the missionaries with whom he went to school. Clean-thinking people, they imbued him with spirit so substantial that he survived outrages of endless war. As he fell through despair, a merciful Lord and the Bible comprised a safety net, and he floated, as Cassie understood it, to freedom on faith.

"Mandy, she is happy at school?" Yang asks, holding the hose, prepared to enjoy the civilities. He has the polite demeanor of a courtier.

"Yes. She likes it quite a lot," Cassie replies, her eyes searching the small yard until she must ask, "Where's Jake? I mean, why are you here this week instead of him?" She blushes in response to Yang's blank stare. "Not that I'm unhappy to see you, Yang. Of course not. It's always a pleasure to see you. Jake does a wonderful job though. I'm not complaining. Please don't think I have anything against him." She babbles on, painfully certain as the minutes tick off that the old gardener is here alone, and that he is only too aware what gear shifts, what cogs and wheels of disappointment drive her chattering.

"I am glad you're so happy with my friend Jake."

Yang's eyes, small black nuggets of darkness nesting in wrinkles, are hard to read. With an otherworldly courtesy he never stares at her directly, but watches the aura about her head like a soothsayer who knows the future and the past, who can dissect what she says more skillfully than Cassie herself a woman's malignant growth during surgery. So naturally he is alerted to the way her tongue touches *Jake*, the slow slump of her shoulders, the collapse of lines at the corners of her mouth as he says, "Jake is sick. He could not do his gardening today, yesterday, the day before."

Worry unravels in Cassie, leaving dangling strands of fear. "What's wrong with him?"

"Not your kind of sick, Dr. Morgan," Yang says.

Her smile elicits no response from the gardener, over whose face time and culture have thrown a mask. Cassie thinks he won't tell her more, but he adds, "Jake has old problems. Sometimes they make him sick."

"I'm sorry to hear that," she replies inanely, wanting Yang to explain, needing to hear more.

Yang's delicacy bends him over a flower bed. He plucks an invisible weed, pads the dirt about a clump of azaleas with velvet fingers. "We should reseed the lawn, Doctor," he says.

"If you think so," Cassie agrees, withdrawing to the kitchen, where she leans by the sink.

Old problems.

The cadence of war is imaginary for Cassie. Movies describe it pictorially. Actors play their parts and die temporarily. In books and newspapers, words carry the battles, air strikes, recon search-and-destroy missions on their syllables. But whatever efforts Cassie employs to comprehend what happened in Southeast Asia, the military action that wasn't officially a war, she remains stateside, once removed. She knows what she knows secondhand.

She has charted Jake's "old problems" only by the symptoms he displays, the sour-smelling sweat, lowered body temperature, the rise in his pulse rate. Flames reflect in his pupils, and his memory on fire sends his blood pressure soaring. From her side of the equation of Jake and Cassie, Cassie is only an observer. What kind of love is that when she is forced outside like a Dickensian waif into the cold? Not much of a love, and she would complain to Jake if they were confronting each other.

You're guilty of bad faith. If you don't believe in me, or trust me, what does it all mean?

He hasn't said he loves her, never says much at all. Jake is a quiet dog—no, cat, padding on silent paws, slipping around briefly opened doors and leaping out upraised windows. Now he's skulked off with his wounds, his "old problems," and Cassie sits in her kitchen worrying so intently she barely hears Yang's knock on the screen.

"I only want to tell you, Doctor, that possibly it will be I who comes next week. Perhaps, but again perhaps not. A rearranging of the schedule. We must see. My friend Jake is . . ." Yang's lips press each other and disappear. His disapproval is heavy as chalk. He adds, "My friend Jake could be going off."

"Off? Off where?" Cassie's worry that Jake refuses to be taken into her life and made at home climbs, and she wants him back so ardently she tastes the saltiness of his skin.

"Who can tell?" Yang replies.

Cassie restrains the urge to tear through the mesh of the screen with her hands and grab the mysterious old man. She would shake some satisfaction out of him if she could.

"Why?"

"*Why* and *why not* for Jake mean the same thing, Doctor. He is a man in pieces. How do the young people put it? He can't get it together." Yang is solemn. "The war was a bad time for a good man. Jake isn't the only one. When my country was turned inside out like a beggar's coat so you saw the rips in the lining, many men lost their souls. Death became what we lived by, not life. My own son was dead in a ditch with no arms, Doctor," Yang says before Cassie can stop him.

She sees Yang down in the road, kneeling, and hears a woman's high keening scream, while at the same time, through the faint crosshatching of the screen, Yang's face is a bomb's crater.

"I'm sorry," she says, helpless and hating herself, humiliated for so inadequate a word. She should slap a hand over her mouth, push back *sorry* behind her teeth. How insulting is regret, and compassion after the fact won't stand Yang's son on his feet and give him arms.

Yang confides without emotion, "Jake has seen many such children, been—between us, Doctor—responsible for deaths just so terrible. No man of humankind can give away his soul so easily, not if he is of good heart."

Over the time Yang has tended her lawn and flowers, the imperial palm, they have had scattered conversations of so few words Cassie could collect them all in a salt shaker. She lacks, she realizes with a pang, any information about Yang beyond the missionaries and the continuing faith he drapes about him like a cloak.

Who was he back there, home, in Asia?

"Most of us try to forget. Some succeed; others fail. The past is a terrible burden, Dr. Morgan. I myself have nightmares occasionally, for which I drink hot milk and read a few passages of Deuteronomy. But my friend Jake has no faith. He speaks blasphemously of a void, of there not being a guiding light and wisdom." Jake's lack of belief saddens Yang, draws more years into the grooves by his mouth. "But I forgive him. Besides, only the Lord Almighty can pass judgment."

"Where is he?" Cassie asks, not at all assured that Yang isn't judging her this very moment.

"In his heart he is in a dark place, a cramped, gloomy cave." Yang sighs and rolls his eyes, the whites muddied, and he seems about to grab the pulpit for a sermon. "He attempts to emerge into the light, but it is difficult without *His* guidance. I have tried to instruct him, for we have known one another a long time. He was good to me in Saigon. Why? Who can tell. He found for me papers."

"Papers?"

"Papers in the last days were more valuable than gold. No one could do anything without the proper documents."

"And Jake got you some?"

"Good ones. Proper ones. Not counterfeit. The U.S. government was very alert to the bogus."

"And with those papers you came to America?"

"Yes, thank the Lord."

Which means, Cassie thinks, that Yang isn't Yang, if the story is true. Of course it's true. Why would Yang lie? But why would he tell her he's an impostor?

Yang glances around the yard as if seeing what remains to be done for the week or checking that he's actually here on U.S. soil. He returns finally to Cassie. "So you see, I must repay the favor which was more than a favor. I give Jake a job when he comes to ask me. Even after all the years that flowed between us like river water I don't forget. To do so would be very bad karma." What is karma to a Christian living once, dying forever, redeemed or damned to eternal fires? Important enough to Yang, apparently, for his actions to be governed by a possible rebirth.

"That was generous of you, Yang," Cassie agrees, and shivers with the irrational terror that it was Jake who left Yang's son in that ditch.

Yang shrugs with a motion that carries centuries of acceptance in the rise and fall of his bones. He moves to his truck and lifts down the lawn mower. "We are meant to help one another if we can."

Cassie the doctor can clap her hands to that.

"I want to help Jake too."

Yang isn't an innocent. Though he understands Cassie's feelings as if they have sat down in a confessional, with tears and hot tea, he straightens and pretends. "Many people have spoken to Jake. I have myself. Other doctors, too, from the time in the hospital—"

"What hospital?"

"Have I dishonored a confidence?" Yang asks but doesn't sound worried. There is an Oriental evenness in his voice, a smooth, silky quality Cassie finds soothing even as she is agitated by what Yang says.

"I was just wondering which hospital, that's all. For instance, was he in the Veterans here, over in Westwood?" Late in the game she tries for a professional tone.

"I must be finishing. My dinner will be on the table and I won't be there to eat it." He actually smiles at her as if he's made a joke, and maybe he has. For all Cassie knows, Yang disappears down a dark hole from week to week. Until now she's never thought about where he goes or what he does or with whom. Has he other children, ones he brought across the Pacific with him? A wife? Grandchildren maybe?

Yang backs down the steps.

"The fox and the fish cannot swim together or run at each other's side in the woods," Yang says. "And give my regards to lovely young Mandy, Doctor."

"Yang!"

But Yang has resolutely grasped the handles of the mower and is pushing it to the far edge of the grass.

Cassie has no desire to go out for dinner but she can't stay home, locked in an empty house, a tomb without even whispers in it, waiting to hear from a man who most likely won't call. She shouldn't want to hear from him anyway. In that longing lies madness. Common sense dictates that she cut out Jake from her mind and heart, relegate him to the category of past mistakes. Except that her heart is more than tough muscle. So until Nona calls, Cassie figuratively wrings her hands, while in actuality she sits at the kitchen table sipping her ritual glass of "winding down" wine, the newspaper spread out before her, bloody with the daily disasters: PLANE CRASH IN THE SIERRAS; 7 CHILDREN DIE IN HOME FIRE; TOXIC CLOUD OVER VALLEY. The tears spilling onto the newsprint are as much for her own unhappiness as the agony of others, which doesn't make Cassie feel at all guilty, though Nona's "She must be so depressed and the least we can do is take her out for dinner, cheer her up" does. A bad friend, self-absorbed, she has momentarily forgotten Eve's tumor. The treachery of a woman longing for a man abuses Cassie's self-respect, and she wants to flagellate herself for whining no differently from any other female in heartbreak. She could be, is, April, Nona, Mandy, which so displeases her—this awareness that she has no special resistance to the viral infection of love—that she speeds on the way to Westwood, to a woody restaurant of hanging ferns, sawdust floors, flagons of icy beer, and is stopped by a motorcycle cop and given a ticket.

_____

Nona, posing ridiculously as the mother of them all, pats Eve's hand and says, "Cassie can tell you there's nothing, just soap bubbles, in those old wives' tales. You're not going to grow hair on your chin and crawl around for weeks afterward as bent as a safety pin."

"I never thought I was. A hysterectomy is just another operation. Yank out the old rusty parts and junk them." Eve is her usual prickly self except for her pallor and the way her freckles have swum to the surface from under her makeup.

"I wish you wouldn't smoke," Cassie says as Eve lights a cigarette, having defiantly decided to take up smoking in earnest now, thumbing her nose at unknown destiny. "We don't know for sure yet if you need a hysterectomy. So wait before you start worrying up a storm."

That isn't a lie, since no decision has been made by anyone, meaning Jena, that the best way, the only way, is via surgery. Only it will be when the tests are in and the conversations over, Cassie's medical instinct tells her.

Nona is excited as a child at Christmas, expectant and prepared for disappointment as she faces at one remove a real physical problem that the doctors take seriously. It would be too much to say that she wishes she were the one going under the knife, the authentically sick person, but she plans to enjoy Eve's experience.

"How long will she have to be in the hospital?"

Cassie answers, "Five days is the usual now."

"Five days!" Nona exclaims, disappointed. "That doesn't seem like enough time."

"*If* we do the operation . . ."

"I can live without it, in case anybody's wondering," Eve says.

"It's your decision, of course," Cassie points out.

"Sure it is," Eve agrees bleakly.

Cassie insists, "It is."

"None of us gets to decide anything, just to dance around from one horror to the next. We pretend, darlings—that's the old bottom line. Pretend that we've got life under control when it's a continual escrow. The deal can sour at any time."

Cassie's throat scratches, raw with grief, but she can't expel

Jake's name, won't offer up her unhappiness for the women's meditation if Eve doesn't ask. But she does. "How's the gardener?"

Eve has designated Jake a lark. Cassie's folly, a low-down roll in the hay. She hasn't come straight out and called it slumming, but that's what she means. To Eve, Cassie is playing around out of her class, not so much demeaning herself but being foolish.

"Still having a good time, which is the way it ought to be? You need some fun, a little no-sweat rock and rolling," Eve says, believing that Cassie would be better off with a cardiologist or a surgeon.

A tear slides down Cassie's cheek.

"Damn!" Eve breathes, crushing out the smoldering cigarette.

Nona quivers with concern. "What happened?"

"Nothing."

"You're not crying over nothing," Eve snaps.

"What did he do to you, Cassie?" Something really awful that they can cry over, get drunk on?

"He hasn't been awful. He's just changed his mind. At least I think he has. Anyway, I haven't heard from him."

Eve nods. "The to-be-expected no telephone calls. Welcome to the land of heartbreak, my dear. It's where men perennially take you."

Eve drapes her own experiences over them, nailing not only them but all women to the ground, wrapping their loves in chains, and Nona feels put upon. "Not every romance ends unhappily. Don't listen to her, Cassie. Jake will come back."

"Oh, hearts and flowers, Pollyanna. Why," Eve asks, "are there some women who simply must think the best of men, who'll insist a mass-produced print is equal to an original Rembrandt?"

"You're not being fair," Nona, stung, retorts. "Just because I'm not negative."

"Oh, well, negative! My darling with a heart of pure platinum, every romance is an affair, and you're walking proof of that. In fact, you've got so many scars you're the tattooed lady in the circus."

Eve in her fright needs to grind someone with her fury, but Nona, for once, is wise to her tactics. She sniffs and says she's not about to listen or be criticized, and besides, they have to concentrate on Cassie's problem.

Cassie, however, can't traffic in Jake's memories. What he shared was in confidence and the pain he suffers she refuses to offer her best friends while they toy with their hamburgers. So the story she tells comes with gaps, spaces wide enough to drive several diesel rigs down the center line.

Nona and Eve are skeptical. To Eve, "It's not a matter of my disbelieving you, but something's lost in translation. Why would he just wake up in the middle of the night and run off with no reason?"

Nona interjects, "He had his reasons but we don't know what they are."

"Naturally, unless the man's a padded-room case, which we trust to Dr. Morgan's good judgment that he's not. So there's some explanation for his behaving like a loose Ping-Pong ball." She stares down Cassie with a look of *Don't try to fool me*.

"Bad dreams," Cassie confesses.

"The old bad dreams up from the swamp, scaly and with fangs," Eve says.

Cassie wants to change the subject. "I think I'll order a slice of their pecan pie. With a scoop of vanilla. Anybody want to share with me?"

But Eve isn't buying. "What kind of bad dreams?"

"About Vietnam," Cassie finally admits, for the women will wait forever.

"But that was such a long time ago!" Nona cries.

"Some nightmares last forever," Eve says.

If Cassie thought talking about Jake would lighten the iron weight of despair and transform it to feathers, she was mistaken. She feels worse now than before and asks as plaintively as any of her patients, "What should I do?"

"Call him up," Nona suggests. "See how he's feeling. Have him come over and talk. I bet he'll be grateful that he has somebody so sensible."

"Last I heard, men weren't in the market for sensible women," Eve says.

"Why are you being so mean to Cassie?" Nona wrinkles her perfect nose as if smelling something sour, and forgetting it's because of Eve, not Cassie, that they're all out for dinner. Eve is the one tonight who needs a steady hand, an arm up, cheering.

"You don't know your Jake any better than one of these waiters," Eve says, leaning over and poking a finger at Cassie. "A fly-by-night! A sneeze in the wind! This isn't a relationship—it's a pit stop!"

"Don't say such things!" Nona cries, slapping the air around Eve, trying to fan her criticism in another direction.

Eve ignores her and says, "You're better off, Cass, seeing that Jake isn't the prize in the Cracker Jack box."

If Eve intends to drive the women to distant corners, she succeeds, for Cassie is angry. "Stop badmouthing him, Eve. He's . . . he's . . ." *Wonderful* catches on her tongue, but, abashed, she forces herself to say it because he is, and she wants him back, or in contact, on the phone, mowing the lawn, by the sink drinking a beer, in her bed with his arms wrapping her up like Christmas ribbon.

"He's not for you, a gardener who has nightmares about Vietnam, who runs out at three A.M. and never calls. A man who could live in a packing crate on Main Street, or might have, given his background."

"There's nothing wrong with his background!" Cassie's voice rises.

"Forget him. Find someone more appropriate," Eve advises Cassie like a grown-up, a sensible female herself, the way Cassie would if the situation were reversed and Eve mooned over a man who had blown into her life like a Santa Ana and as easily blew out again.

"I can't."

"You're stubborn. The truth is you don't want to."

"Okay. I don't, then."

Nona, her breath clouding on vapors of tears, understands. "Poor Cassie."

Their hands are busy on the table, rearranging silverware, salt and pepper shakers, glasses with melting ice cubes, dishes with unwanted food.

Cassie says, "Let's go." She is eager to be home and out from under their eyes, grieving in private.

"Hey, how are you?"

The women, startled, look up at a man in jeans and a leather jacket shifting from one foot to the other beside the table, focusing on Nona with the steady gaze of a cinematographer.

"Remember me?" he asks. "You were my angel of mercy, and I was the prince in distress." He grins and with his crooked front tooth he is the boy next door, the junior-prom date waiting under the porch light with a gardenia corsage. "Come on, I can't be all that forgettable!"

"I remember," Nona replies hastily. She introduces Fitz to the women, now solemn as owls, and they listen politely to how his car broke down, to Nona's driving him to the garage, then demur as he orders a round of drinks for the table. With casual grace he's pulled up a chair, joined them, learned their names and professions, all the while intent on Nona, and finally asks, when Nona agrees with Cassie that it's time to go, "Do you like to dance?"

"Sure."

"Great. There's a little club just over in North Hollywood that has the best jukebox in the state. Come with me and we'll do a Fred and Ginger." Nona hesitates. "Please."

Nona glances at the women, and Eve—who decides this man, unknown that he is with all his superficial charm, must be an improvement over married Alan—urges, "Go on."

"I don't know."

"Would you laugh at me if I said the night's young and you're so beautiful?" Fitz asks. Nona giggles. "Good. You're even prettier when you laugh."

Both Cassie and Eve are embarrassed by Fitz's public wooing of Nona, by what seems to be reverence in his eyes, yet stirred too. They touch themselves, Cassie smoothing her blouse, Eve patting the hair pushed behind an ear, as if Fitz's interest laps in waves and they sail on it. His glow spreads around the table and they wax when Nona sighs with *yes*. Saying quick good-nights, they exchange mothy kisses, lips to cheeks, and their pleasure dims only when each is alone in her car with the slow draft of warm air for company.

17

Alan swears, storms, angrily inflates inch by inch until his head scrapes the ceiling. "I fly back on an earlier flight *expressly* to be with you. Now, now . . ." He has seen them from the window, or heard Fitz's *One for the road? his Coffee? tea? you and me?* Heard Nona's laughter, which Fitz has aroused all evening like the fine hairs on her arms.

"How could you be so unfaithful?" Alan groans with tears in his voice, his eyes.

That Nona pleads, "Nothing went on. He's just a man," has no impact.

"A man. Just a man. Lincoln was just a man, Billy the Kid, Clark Gable. I'm only a man, too, remember."

"I'm sorry."

"But what kind of a man? Where did you meet him? Did you pick him up in a bar?"

"Don't be crude!"

"I just want the truth," he insists, when he wants nothing of the sort, only for Nona to be at home in the long silk dressing gown he bought her in Magnin's, when his flight lands, when he calls, when he drops by in the spare moment, when he has time, in a convenient half hour between the office and dinner. The idea of Fitz (or anybody) taking her out, telling jokes, buying her drinks, dancing cheek-to-cheek with her (not that she will tell him any of the latter), the sheer possibility of another man drives him to an explosion that shatters glass. Just as in a hundred movies, he theatrically throws the tumbler of scotch in the fireplace and outyells the crash: "I thought we had a relationship!"

"We do!"

Alan assumes Nona's guilty, which she is, of both surprising and inconveniencing him. He picks at his hurt until the scab bleeds. Nona follows him around the couch while he gathers up his things and whispers with genuine hurt in his voice, "I thought you loved me, that this was something more than the casual—"

Nona cuts him off. "I do love you, Alan! And I've done nothing wrong." She grabs for his sleeve. "But you can't expect me to sit home like faithful Penelope—"

"Have you gone to bed with him?" Jealousy and fear mesh in his voice.

How has she gotten so in the wrong?

Don't panic. Sit quietly. Be careful. *Think!*

Nona perches on the edge of the bentwood rocker. "Alan, I have to go out some time. I mean, it's not fair for you to want me to wait here, just wait, while you're out with your wife." Nona knows this is sensible, and Alan's eyes reflect that he knows it too. Still she flails in the sticky web he weaves around her. Alan's clever, and with his silver tongue he whips up closing arguments of a case he maintains is hers but isn't. He contends he's caught her with a smoking gun, a corpse at her feet, and in the face of his indignation Nona believes that though she never committed any sin, she surely could have. So she begs his forgiveness, and besides, he's leaving quietly, no longer yelling, which frightens Nona more than his curses and accusations.

"I love you," she repeats like a mantra as he moves through the veil of her tears, a misty figure.

"Nona, I'm not a monster," he says sadly. "I realize wanting you for myself, not being willing to share you even casually, is asking a lot. But I love you and when you do love someone you have certain expectations."

"What about your wife?"

His sigh ruffles the curtains on the windows. "That's different."

"Alan . . ."

He shakes his head. "Maybe this is all for the best. Sooner or later . . ." His broad shoulders rise and fall. Then, like a bit player striving for stardom, he exits from Nona's apartment. The door hushes closed and Nona, though weeping, knows that if this scene were to be described by Eve or Cassie or any other woman, she'd call Alan awful, that she'd proclaim this woman—now digging nails into her palms so as not to run after him—dumb.

Nona cries bitter tears, for she loves Alan (or is convinced she does), needs him, thinks of how he might have left Marjorie and their sons for the house, children, marriage, that were hers in dreams.

She comes away from the door, and the silent apartment—even the air seems packed in Styrofoam—accuses her. She moves noiselessly on the wall-to-wall carpeting, an automaton taking off her clothes, understanding nothing, not what to do, beyond weeping, not what, if anything, she might barter the pain for. Another man has sailed out of her life when she wanted him to harbor.

Nona is too tired even to argue with fate.

In the closet she hangs up her dress and hears something tinkle, a remembered silvery sound. On the floor between two brown boots there is a glitter. Nona bends and finds Magic's catnip mouse with its collar of bells.

The toy undoes her and sends her to her knees. "Magic!" she cries, going up and down the scales with regret, touching higher notes each time. The harmonics of her grief for the cat mix with those for Alan.

The telephone rings for a long time before Nona on the closet floor realizes it.

"I know it's late and you're probably in bed, but I had to call. Just to say what a great time I had and how I want to—Nona? *Nona?*" Her tears have dripped through the wires and fall in droplets around him. "What's wrong?"

"Nothing. I'm okay."

"Look, I'm coming over. You're not okay."

"No, don't. I'm fine."

"I don't know if you're fine, but you're upset. What, half an hour, an hour ago I left you laughing and now you're crying, and maybe it's my fault—"

"It's got nothing to do with you!" Why do men always think a woman's tears rise from the seeds they so recklessly sow? She could be crying about a hundred different hurts, she almost screams at Fitz before she is drawn up short. She does cry because of a man, but not him.

"Fitz?" She holds a dead phone. He is making good on his promise—or threat—to rush to her aid despite Nona's refusal of his offer.

Quickly she washes off the tracks on her cheeks and re-creates her eyes. She ties a red kerchief around her hair that makes her into a gypsy, so she looks far jauntier than she feels. She swallows—along with a Valium—several long, slow, meditative breaths during which she resolutely thinks of the sea on a calm day, rather than Alan roaring like a dragon out of her apartment, her life, and she is ready to be comforted when Fitz rings the bell.

At the sight of him she wails, tripping right over her good intentions to keep a firm grip on her emotions, and lets his arms close about her. The warmth of another person and the shattering of the quiet excite more tears.

Nona planned to tell Fitz—since she needs some reason for coming unhinged—about Magic. How she lost him, and just as he called had found the toy in the closet. All of which is true. But Fitz is less concerned with what upset her so that she hangs around his neck, drenching his shirt collar, than with how to turn off her tears.

He launches himself into consoling her, stroking the ridges of her spine, kissing her neck, breathing murmurs of nonsense into her ear, until he possesses her salt-slicked lips and kisses the storm back into her throat. Nona considers stopping him, but then he might go, and the night stretches like a transcontinental highway in front of her. The darkness will last a hundred hours before dawn crawls up the bedroom wall. She'll never sleep, no matter how many pills she swallows, or if she does, she'll dream. So she dances again with Fitz, this time into the bedroom, into bed, and lets him lavish his desire on her while she hides in his arms.

"Thank your lucky stars. Kiss the ground. Offer hosannas to the patron saint of single women. Out with the old, in with the new. Do you know how many females would be grateful?" At the mall's French bistro Eve clicks her cup of decaf with Nona's Diet Coke. "Cheers. Fitz is a vast improvement over the married attorney."

"You can't say that. You never even met Alan. Besides, I love him."

"Love is a will-o'-the-wisp. It flows like the tide. Talk to me next July about who you love."

"I'll be forty by then."

"Forty's not the worst thing that can happen," says Eve, who has seen forty come and go, who thinks now of her mortality.

Nona starts, "I want—"

"Don't tell me about babies."

Eve's vehemence shakes Nona loose from her sticky self-absorption. She protests, "I wasn't!" when babies, husband, home, family, Sunday dinners, were about to fall from her lips like pearls.

Eve straightens her cuffs, evens them whitely below the navy jacket sleeves, and checks her watch, unable to face Nona squarely. Nona displays no effects of a shattered night, heartbreak, and pain; she glows like a model in a cold-cream ad. So seldom does emotional upheaval work over her face that Eve, while loving Nona, resents her. She seems inhumanly young, a vampire's luscious victim.

Why is she complaining? True, she's been given the heave-ho, but already another acceptable man replaces the old. Eve tells her as much, but Nona bleats of love again, though more quietly.

"Love, love!" Eve slides around on her chair as if there is one comfortable position she must struggle to find. "Love is an ox collar. A man locks it around your neck and then you trudge through the muck, not looking right or left. A beast of burden, that's what a woman in love is."

Nona thinks it's unfair that Eve is entitled to her unhappiness while refusing Nona the same right.

Mostly Eve appears calm in the face of catastrophic possibilities. Of course she worries about the tumor. Is it really benign? But all in all she can't be criticized for how she handles her fear. She might even let go, at least once, in the release of hysterical crying, and Nona hopes she does before being wheeled into the operating room. Such a loss of control will shrink Eve and make her, for Nona, a little less perfect and awesome.

Eve intimidates Nona at times, though she is one of Nona's best friends, if not the first on a short list. Eve is always so together, her emotions as tailored as her clothes, and Nona can't imagine her making sloppy puddles of her affairs. Even if she has had three marriages, they all know Eve to this day would be Mrs. Abramson if the professor hadn't keeled over, *dead as a rock*, Eve always says when she relates the story.

Dead as the book he was reading, the words on the page, as the ball-points in the Mason jars by his blotter, dead as a thing, Eve thinks, thought then, her fingers on the nape of Abramson's neck, the pale exposed slit of skin where the guillotine's blade would just fit. Dead. . . .

She thinks, too, that her "illness"—which she considers a malfunction of a nonvital component—pulls Abramson nearer. She would welcome him now (though there are few times in the angry years since his death when she would not have opened her arms to him) and forgive him for dying on her. He leaped from life with a blowout in the heart while she sat a floor below by the washing machine, watching a bubbling brew of sheets and towels and wondering how to tell the bear she wanted to move. His wife's ghost—which Eve certainly couldn't see, since the dead were forever dead as dirt, but did—chased sunbeams down the upstairs hall. His wife's ghost haunted Eve, who thought she must be certifiable.

Eve spent the first months living in the Abramson house trying not to scream when periodically—and without warning—a cold chill crept around her neck like a noose. The specter of a woman wronged climbed up the stairs and down again, sat primly in the back hall, stepped from closets. She could be anywhere.

My bad conscience was Eve's explanation, and if she were able to get on her knees and confess, maybe, just maybe . . . But confess what? Love? Was it my fault, she argued with herself, if I loved a man already married?

She blew herself to hell, Eve thought. I never shoved a gun in her mouth.

And above her head, in his book-lined professorial study, Abramson's death was blossoming. For a second the chrysalis of his dying sent a sizzle down her back, but then his death was full-grown, and as the machine geared into the spin cycle, he subsided. Afterward she swore and cursed; she should have known.

Eve stepped over faint footprints to the second floor, inched open the double doors, and said, "Let's talk. We have a problem."

What irony!

If Abramson's blood hadn't minutes before taken the last journey, he would have laughed.

She supposed he was sleeping, his head on his chest, the book fallen to the carpet. He was reading, of all things, Augustine's *Confessions*.

Where then and when did I experience my happy life, that I should remember, and love, and long for it?

"Abramson, wake up!"

He stared at a leaf in the border of the rug with eyes of marble.

"Bear, stop fooling around!"

When her screams began they hurtled about the room and seemed to last forever, but she finally ran out of air.

She closed the leatherbound volume that he'd had since graduate school and placed it carefully on top of the desk, the red strip of silk marking his place. As if he meant to pick it up again. . . .

"I'll never forgive you," she promised.

Then she called the paramedics, who attempted useless strategies to resurrect a dead man. It had been past his time when Eve found Abramson. His flesh was already cold as he settled earthward. He no longer posed a struggle with gravity, and when Eve buried him it was—ignoring his children's protests—without ceremony.

Abramson returns to her unbidden, as he usually does, taking up residence in her memory, saying in his dead voice *I will love you forever*. . . . Eve carries him safely, pretending, though she is a different woman now.

If Abramson lived on the earth, standing up, she wouldn't be so scared. But Abramson exists without substance and he can't put his arms around her, calm her, promise it will be fine . . . don't you worry.

She considers saying to Johnny, I'll be out of commission for a while. An operation. Female. But she holds off.

Johnny takes her to dinner at an inexpensive bistro on Pico where the couples are youngish, the newly marrieds on their first house, plus a scattering of older, wrinkled husbands and wives probably from Rancho Park. Johnny takes forever, as always, ordering, studious as a yeshiva scholar over the menu. When he turns around to call the waiter, Eve can't ignore the bald spot like a monk's tonsure at the apex of his skull. It is no disfigurement to a man rich as Johnny once was, but now it reminds her of a baby's bottom. Eve looks away and right at—unhappily—a woman alone, at the farthest table to the back, behind a book.

Once, out with William, Eve recalls a lone woman in Bistro Gardens, neat, with diamond earrings, quietly eating soup and weeping. The tears fell on her spoon, and though she never screamed or threw a bread roll, was in fact decorous, Eve felt herself witnessing an obscene event and had the captain change their table.

The gentle rain of a woman's tears on a lonely evening at dinner . . .

Now here is another woman.

A woman without company for dinner could have much to cry about, and Eve experiences a sudden chill thinking of how Johnny—tonsure and vegetarian habits—fills up hours of her social time that were empty spaces before. She is both grateful and ashamed of her gratitude, while wondering if she is nice enough to him. Right now, if he wandered out of her life she would be bereft, for she needs someone to hold her hand and Johnny is a decent, acceptable hand-holder. Though frayed by life and not a great, not even a minor love, Johnny isn't to be dismissed. She should take him seriously, perhaps even settle for him or with him, make a commitment. Of course he never implies that he loves her, or that he needs more with her than he already enjoys.

"What are you having?" he asks as she is about to say it's time they had a serious discussion.

"Chicken paillard," she says instead.

"That's not too bad," he says smugly, as though he's computing the effect he's having on her.

His pleasure with himself annoys Eve just enough for her to back off from the discussion she is ready to start. And she won't tell him about the operation either. Maybe later she'll get him talking and see just how much he's willing to give, and how much she can bring herself to offer. Maybe she'll suggest that they spend more time at her apartment, three or four nights a week, that they try a closer arrangement on a temporary basis, that they practice.

Certainly he will be happier at her place, more in the style of his old life, or perhaps they can even get something larger. She'll have to look.

Which is what Eve is doing, at her desk, a finger running down a list of new condo listings, when Titus Reynolds, his potato-white skin flaking about the mouth, stops by her client chair. His glance ricochets off Eve. He looks whittled, too worn to be dangerous, but Eve distrusts Titus and therefore isn't surprised when he comes around with "That Iranian's house . . . I understand it was referred to me from Wattman at First Federal."

"Really, Titus? I thought you have a thing about foreigners."

"What are you talking about?" he peeps, rising on his little toes.

Eve reminds him he asked her before to handle an Israeli searching for a perfect condo around half a million.

Titus neither confirms nor denies this, but his nervous flutters are about to lift him off the gray industrial carpet. He will fly with a squawk in the subdued hush of the Booker office.

It is only the arrival of a client that saves Eve.

Later she hears from one of the other agents that Titus is in a dither. He's lost two sales this week and a major prospect's gone to the Monrovia people. His inner sanctum lies in jeopardy and can possibly be foreclosed.

Eve's mouth waters at the news and in an opportune moment she takes herself by Tom Holloway's office just to chat, gauging his reaction as they banter. Tom is gracious, crossing his legs, offering her a Pellgrino from his refrigerator—a good sign. Eve lights a cigarette, though she knows Tom loathes smokers, to see if he'll suggest that she restrain her urge. But he barely grimaces and Eve smiles, even saying how uncomfortable she is with just a desk, how cramped. No room to spread out. Not enough file space. Slave's quarters, really.

"We'd hate for you to be unhappy," Tom agrees. Time enough to tell him that she'll need a month off—hopefully she can keep the operation at bay until Christmas, the worst season for properties—and perhaps by then she'll have Titus's office, where Eve is convinced he merely rattles like a loose marble. Surely she has earned it, her commissions topping Titus's for five months in a row.

Eve is half inclined to push further with Tom Holloway, to mention Monrovia, the Herman Agency, to whisper of broadening her base. But the soft sell is Eve's best tactic. Don't overdo it, she cautions herself, when she's paged for a call and leaves Tom.

Her body, now without the familiar knifing pain, the excess bleeding, feels so reassuringly the same that she forgets its malfunctions, allowing her to hum and think how she will redecorate Titus's office, lighten it up with earth tones and perhaps a painting by the newest in artists, Manuel Swacz, who does brilliant abstracts. She can afford an oil, even at gallery prices. Besides, it will be an investment.

Eve answers her call bright as a penny, the future strobe-lit and glowing. She might buy a Rolls this year (used of course). Why not? What's money for? Give it away, Jordan said, though Abramson's *Eve, we have to be careful* is the advice she most often heeds.

Eve promised Abramson she'd earn them a bigger house, a new car instead of his old clunker and her creaky Ford, a sabbatical in the South of France, on the beach, the Négresco, the Grand. *Oh, Eve,* he would laugh, *money means less than windsong!*

"Eve, good to hear your voice. You sound terrific and are, I hope."

"William?"

How often she misplaces her third husband, the might-as-well-not-have-been husband for the marks he left on her psyche. Now she's not even sure how she came to marry William, except by error. If they hadn't been three sheets high and sailing into the wind on Armagnac in Las Vegas one weekend, plus giddy with blackjack winnings, would they have stopped off at the Orange Blossom, two in the morning, and exploded in laughter as they said to the bathrobed little justice of the peace, *Go, do it*?

It was a joke, the tumbly wife in pink hair curlers and the teenager matted by sleep for witnesses. The JP's sonorous voice, so incongruous in his pinched ferrety face with its icicle nose and wire-rims, bound them together, Eve and William, while photos of other smiling couples watched like recording angels, saints, and martyrs.

The wedding was the most momentous event of their short marriage, which took them just to the edge of a year before Eve bailed out as William mourned her. He yearned to keep her, for complicated reasons he couldn't unravel. But though she doesn't dislike him—William is too placid and suety actually to elicit a strong emotion—she never loved him, and love seemed crucial. He sank in the bear's shadow, and maybe their marriage was an act of revenge, an unconscious flailing out at Abramson dead. Oh, even though years had passed, she was so angry with Abramson for flickering out on her, disappearing while she washed his underwear, that she married when drunk a man for whom she didn't care enough.

The memory of the wedding rides in on William's voice, the plastic flowers, the sullen daughter's coughing fit, the mother's pear liquor, a heart of stale Valentine's candy William bought her, and Eve smiles because she still likes William—liked him, too, when she married him, for that matter.

Like newly introduced strangers they make small talk before getting down to business. William hasn't phoned on a whim.

"I want to sell the house and thought it only fair that I give the listing to you."

"I appreciate that, William." And she does, for William owes her nothing. As Eve remembers their marriage, he got much the worst of it. On the other hand, as various divorcées remind her, she never asked for alimony, took only a few choice pieces of furniture, her car, and books, and left William's finances in the same shape as she found them.

They discuss the relatively good market, as Eve wonders why William seeks to sell. She asks him directly for a reason and he counters with an invitation to drop by later and have a drink. Eve's curiosity is pricked but William has a mulish streak and nothing will result from Eve's pressing him further. She exacts a penalty, though, by saying, "Not today. I'm booked to the last minute. How's tomorrow?"

Not having given any thought to William for so many days, weeks, months, she must wrestle with her memory to recapture his fair hair and polished cheeks, the veins too near the surface, eyes beagle-brown and thinly lashed. He is a handsome enough man, if one likes the type, rather drawing room English, reminiscent of Leslie Howard as Ashley. William's looks aren't in fashion and he has a different aspect to him, a more muted softness, than either of Eve's other two husbands.

William is so slight that, slicing through the spill of radiant light as he brings her a drink, he seems transparent. Yet Eve recalls with a rather embarrassed jolt how skillfully William performed between the covers.

"Well, here we are," William says, as though she's a first-time visitor.

The house—a heron on skinny steel legs—rises off an upper canyon ridge. Cantilevered over dead space, it feels to Eve as impermanent as the marriage. When she lived in its spacious rooms, a different view from each, she never forgot that there were few underpinnings.

William gazes around as if he can possibly see his house through her eyes. "I had the floors refinished, but otherwise it's the same. Don't you think so?"

"Oh, yes." She is as polite with William as with any other client.

She takes his word that the house is exactly the one she lived in with him, but in truth she can't remember. Yes, the house feels familiar, though impersonal, like a motel room. Nothing touches a chord, no symphonies of joy or, on the other hand, regret soar as she wanders about, mentally jotting notes.

"I have to make up a list of selling points."

"You should know them already," William says, sounding resentful. "You oughtn't to have to think about what's a plus in this house."

Their marriage meant more—much—to William than it did to Eve. In hindsight she understood she had never intended to marry again, that both her prior trips to the altar had worn her emotions raw. She preferred—if not for time immemorial, at least for years and years—to be fancy free, her own person and not in debt to a man for her psychological well-being. Really, in the months she lived with William in this house he now wants Eve to sell, she suffered moments of sheer embarrassment over the foolishness that a laugh and a kiss of whiskey breath had bound her to. William in the light of day confused her. Of course they barely knew each other, but more importantly, Eve discovered when she surfaced for air—joke's over!—that she disliked the idea of being any more intimate with William the stranger than she was already. Never mind the sex, or that he turned out to be—after a flashy, Hollywood first acquaintance—a marshmallow-timid soul and *a nice person,* not plastic clear through. He simply wasn't the man she wished to see on the other side of the bed when she rolled over in the morning. An affair would have been pleasant, but *forever* silvered her bones with ice.

As they tour the rooms, bits and pieces bob up in Eve's memory. She recognizes a sketch they bought together one Saturday in Laguna, a limpid nude with eyes of polished steel. Her mother's one birthday gift to William, a leather humidor, still sits on an end table. A silver ashtray. Cracked light splinters on the master bath mirror. The king-size brass headboard.

Most of all, however, Eve is reminded of how the sun angles into the house. With so much glass, waves of light enter at morning and stay whether wanted or not. Even louvered blinds can't entirely exclude it. Yes, it's the light—a prime selling point—that comes to her and whispers on the hardwood: *Why weren't you happy here?*

William, by her shoulder, might be saying, as he had before, that he loved her, that he never thought he would care so much. His devotion was—and now Eve remembers this too—tenderly offered.

Oh, the ridiculousness of it all, of getting married as a lark, a fun sport, as if they were teenagers, and then William's growing serious. The whole episode, Las Vegas, the marriage, could have been a movie with Claudette Colbert and—who? Fred Mac-Murray? Robert Cummings? What about Cary Grant? But unlike a thirties film, no happy ending came prior to the credits. For that she would have had to love William, too, and the most she ever dredged out of her heart was mild affection.

Abramson took too much of her into heaven or hell or wherever his soul had traipsed off to on its panicked flight for Eve to surrender any of what was left. She couldn't reciprocate even a fraction of William's feeling. What she bartered instead was tolerance and lust. Neither was sufficient.

I want your heart, he said once too often, and she left.

"So, William." Eve smiles. They are back in the dining room sitting at a Swedish pine table a hundred and fifty years old. "Why do you want to sell? Are you buying another house?"

"Not exactly." He steeples his hands over his mouth and his voice comes out muffled.

Eve waits. With silence she always extracted from William whatever he hesitated to say, what he might have wished to stay quiet about. Her stillness rubbed at him like sandpaper, wearing down any resolve he had, burnishing his secrets, which were few. He is an honest man and Eve forever wondered how he made his deals, what promises were ground from his bones. She never asked William business questions, out of fear of discovering he had been taken advantage of by a studio, a director, a star, and his weakness would shame her. The affection she felt was so frail she needed to protect it and not let even William's minor imperfections scrape it away.

"I'm not in the market for another place," William says, staring over her head through the windowed wall onto a slope of Monopoly houses three or four miles away. In that moment he might actually be playing Ashley about to inform Melanie that he is off to war in the morning.

Business problems, Eve decides. "Do you need the money?"

"Money? Oh, no. Things are shipshape. I've got three pictures in development and I earned quite a few shekels from *Bad Dreams*." His gaze travels to her and stops above her hairline. "You wouldn't have seen it. Exploitation. Awful garbage. But it will do twenty-five, twenty-six million with foreign distribution," he says decisively.

She won't ask *So why are you moving if it isn't money?* but she wonders. As Eve remembers it, William liked the house, his before Las Vegas, his for those eleven months with no evidence of her in it besides cosmetics on the bathroom counter, clothes in the closet, a few books and magazines scattered about. No, she can simply sit and let the sun warm her face and drowse like a cat, as she once did on this same chair. William makes her sleepy, and she suddenly also recalls that she had uninterrupted nights here. She dreamed few horrors and when she cried it was during the day and she was alone.

"Well, I'm moving."

"I know that, William. I don't see you roaming the hills in your Mercedes and camping in the parks. But where?"

"To Alicia's."

"Who's Alicia?"

"The only woman I've ever loved, the woman I am planning to

marry next month on the tenth," he declares, standing up as straight as one of the house's steel beams. He is a gladiator announcing his intention.

The *planning to marry* Eve could congratulate William about, express sincere pleasure; but that he needs to preface his plans with *the only woman I've ever loved* strikes at her venomously. How can he love for the first time when during their marriage he was in love with her? Has he forgotten or is he being cruel?

She ought to swallow any retort and remember it hadn't mattered back then and matters less now whether William loved her or not, or was making the best of an unwise impulse. But Eve won't listen to her inner voice of caution. It's as though William slaps her, and she rises, rebuked, with "What utter nonsense. Love for the first time. Honestly, William, you're fifty years old and you've loved countless women, me included. You said you loved me to death, to the stars and beyond. That's what you babbled about, night and day, a leaky faucet, in this house, at this very table over intimate little candlelit dinners." She's said too much already but continues to plummet, all engines sparking out. "And who is this wondrous Alicia anyway? A twenty-five-year-old starlet, I bet; a pop-eyed blonde eager to make her break in pictures by working off her back. Well, tell her, William, that you're not Sidney Lumet or Steven Spielberg, that you've never made a picture over four million and only have balcony seats for the Academy Awards."

Eve is breathless with indignation. Her heart pounds alarmingly, a fist hammering against her ribs. A sour taste coats the back of her mouth. Her teeth ache with anger.

"Were you lying to me? Or did you make it up? I never suspected you of duplicity, of nattering on about love as if it was nothing more than a subject for dialogue." What difference can it make, especially so many years after the fact? she thinks spitefully. But William's love, which had little relevance when he was indulging himself with it, had been a given, a rock embedded in the mountains of the past. Eve *assumed* it.

He confronts not Eve but the view and says, "I've worked that out in therapy. I'm cured."

"Cured of what? Me? What was I, William, a disease?" She points an accusatory finger, and arrows of light collide on the diamond she bought herself last Christmas. For a second Eve wonders where her wedding ring has vanished to—not the real one of small stones and platinum William had made specially but a cheap turquoise band from the casino cigarette gift counter that he slipped on her finger. It isn't something she should have been so careless about.

William nervously plucks the buttons of his shirt. He has allowed himself to come to rest in the living room and Eve follows, only she can't sit calmly and hear about Alicia, whom William feels forced to defend. No, Alicia isn't a teeny-bopper; she's a fortyish divorcée with children and a large Normandy in Beverly Hills. William pronounces this love substantial, and Eve laughs shrilly. "I suppose that means fat."

"Why are you acting so bitchy, Eve? I'm doing the nice thing. I'm making the right gesture by giving you the house to sell."

"Oh, thank you very much, William. How big of you! But I don't need your house. I earn more than enough without your mercy fuck!"

He winces. "There's no reason for that kind of language."

"There's no reason for you to gratuitously backhand me with *the only woman I ever loved*. Who asked you?"

William bends practically in half with his arms on his legs, a man in pain. "I've always told you the truth and you never appreciated it. But then you never cared much for me or our marriage," he says bitterly.

Is William finally getting his own back, settling an old I.O.U. that Eve has all but forgotten? Has his anger and resentment lasted this long? But she can't think clearly with the sudden pressure along her left hip that intends, as it has before, to crawl over the bone, slither along the soft curve of her belly, and fire. Blood is going to flow, she thinks hysterically, and, her legs shaking, she collapses at the edge of the couch. "We're not talking about *that*, but about you denying you loved me. For no reason . . . no reason." As if she'd never harmed William by loving Abramson while living in this house, crying for her dead bear, wanting him alive and William gone. The deals she would have forged with the Devil are devious and without number.

Had William known her heart was elsewhere?

"We could have made a go of it, you know," William is saying.

"We could fly right off the deck if we were airplanes," she snaps back.

Pain builds along her side and Eve imagines it will lift her right out in midair, over the gullies of the canyon and the red roofs below.

"I tried, God knows I did. I struggled like a demented person to hold us together. But you weren't serious."

"An Orange Blossom wedding in Las Vegas! You think I should have given weight to that?" As if where they were legally joined, flesh unto flesh, was what kept them apart; as if a church ceremony with some Higher Power officiating would have bound them in chains. Eve tastes the futility of a marriage that shouldn't have happened at all, and is filled with bile.

William has saved up for this face-off a long time, years, and the resentment has brewed into poison in his system. Now, flushed and sweaty, he rocks with it. "No matter how hard I worked, how I struggled, you were a slab of stone, concrete. Emotionless, like the living dead. You weren't there, Eve."

He is right, of course. Eve had occupied this space but lived someplace else, in a marriage ended against her will, ended by death.

Abramson celebrated her and she entered him like the sun. She owned a home in Abramson. With William she only rented a house, glass walls, uncluttered light.

Of course she wasn't *there*.

"Nobody can blame me," William protests.

"No one is," Eve says, just wanting to leave. She would, too, if it weren't for the commission. Every sale matters if she is to unseat Titus Reynolds from his office.

"I asked you to see somebody with me, to talk things out. Resolve our differences. I suggested it over and over."

"Yes, you did, William. You're very big on taking your problems to professionals and saying here, solve them for me." Spite grows in Eve along with the pain. Will she leave blood on William's leather couch? *Will she?*

". . . a child . . ."

Eve misses his words, for his voice fades in and out, a faulty radio signal. She must leave, *now*, and never mind the commission.

"But you were so adamant about children. Why, Eve? I never

understood your aversion. A child would have given us the glue to stay together. We could have been a family, and had important elements." Agitated, he ruffles his hair, pulls at an earlobe.

A child, he says, then repeats himself until the word bounces against the sliding doors, hits the glass over and over, rising with the beat of pain in Eve's ovary.

A child, a child, a child . . .

And it seems she's not in William's living room but in a narrow cubicle with white walls reaching to infinity, where she screamed from the same pulsing, the flight uphill to a pinnacle of hurting so intense she fragmented in a shower of blood. She bellowed like a cow, cursed Jordan and damned him to hell, damned all men and would have ripped life out by its roots to get rid of *that thing* tearing her apart.

Only Eve's long red nails digging into the leather cushions, on which she will leave bloody tracks, shamed by her sex, her pain, the terrible infirmity of gender, keep her in the here and now and out of *then*, the delivery room as William's child—no, never!—as Jordan's fights to leave her.

Eve yells, blowing a torrent of hate into William's face. "I had enough of children, babies! Once was enough. Do you think I'd go through that again? What for? That pain? This?"

"What baby? What are you talking about?"

"So you could abandon me, too, William? So I could play the great earth mother all by myself?"

"You had a baby?" William's mouth is a terrible hole in his face. "You always said you wouldn't, that you didn't want a child. You said . . ."

But Eve doesn't hear what she said way back when, for a spear shoves into her belly with such force she is finally unmoored from the smooth leather.

"You had a baby and gave it away? Is that what you're telling me?"

Has she confessed any such thing?

William, as drained of color as a dead man, stumbles to his feet. Eve elbows by him, running from the screams and shrieks and the loud insistent wail of a baby.

"Stop! stop! stop!" she cries, her hands over her ears, accused for not being one of her sisters or a woman like Cassie, for wanting nothing to do with that baby, hating it, Jordan, all men but the bear.

Mother, where are you. . . ?

In a nursing home sitting by the bed of a wandering man with a mind of loose syllables.

No, that's not Eve. That's *her* mother, and the baby is gone, somewhere else, somebody else, no connection to her now, and therefore this pain, which she drags to the car—William yelling at her back—should vanish too. The delivery is over. The creature's out in the open.

"Take him away! I don't want to hear him crying!"

William yanks her arm. "What did you do to me, Eve?" he asks, as if even now he isn't sure, as if time never explained the paltry life of the marriage, the larger death. He asks as if he cares, despite his loving for the first time, as if he never means to sell the house and marry Alicia.

As if the baby's his.

"What?"

Eve pulls from him, fighting hands that hold her down and the harsh crow voices ordering *Breathe* and *Don't be a baby* and *Every woman goes through this* and *Hush up* and *You'll wake the dead. Be a good girl!*

"Leave me alone! I don't want you. I never loved you." With a final shove she frees herself and for an instant there is clarity so sharp that the vivid blue sky, a backdrop beyond the ridge, cracks, with fine splinters in it. She sees William fall backward and sit shocked on the gravel.

Eve is in the car, grinding gears, slamming the Mercedes out of the drive. She hears a crack and the tinkling shatter of fragments, glass against the cement wall buttressing the hill. She's smashed the headlight but doesn't stop to look, for the pain is clawing again, a flame from her groin to her stomach. The pitch increases as she sweeps down the hill and around curves on two wheels, braking with a screech. She will fly away from the hurting and from the baby, now a boy fully formed, sitting on the seat beside her. His tousled hair is Jordan's.

The road winds like a rattler though the brush and the car going too fast for the turns slithers on it. Miraculously she misses a station wagon, a ditch, a dog leaping out of nowhere and saved by a frenzied cabriole.

Tears smear her vision and the light pours in a torrent. The pain passes her midsection and climbs with hooked nails up to her throat, almost choking her. She feels the blood now, wet on her legs, gumming her stockings. Her slip sticks to her and the skirt is drenched.

I won't have you! she calls to the boy shimmering in the wind blowing through the open window.

You have . . .

And Eve weeps.

She knows, speeding down the long hill, turning, twisting, that she might have made the best of it. But her anger against Jordan drove a shaft ten miles deep into her heart and she gave part of herself away.

And they took him so quickly. She saw him only once after the delivery room, not of course that she cared, not that he meant anything to her. Just a baby.

Liar!

She is pulled as she descends into remembering. . . .

. . . How they had an hour together. She marveled—such little hands, feet. Perfection. His skin really was like silk. She could have stretched that one hour when she held him into forever. But finally a nurse swept in to carry him off.

She shouldn't even have had that long, but the nurses were rushed off their feet and somebody forgot. After all, Eve had signed papers with a flourish for the tall, aristocratic woman who had iron in her voice as she proclaimed Eve was doing the right thing; that by putting the welfare of the child first she would never be sorry. *Liar!* Who said her son was better off with strangers?

She handed him over, sinking her feelings in concrete, thinking she was wise and smart, and thinking *Fuck you, Jordan. Now we're even.* Oh, but cocooned in his blue blanket, he looked back at her and she turned into stone.

Now, as she careens out of control he is with her again, grown-up or nearly, in the passenger seat. The same liquid brown eyes, heavily fringed.

No, she cries, go away! And she swings her head from side to side, wishing she had confessed to Abramson, who, if he couldn't offer her absolution, would have been kind. He'd understand how there were black moments when she'd be stabbed by desolation. Abramson would have kissed the palms of her hands and cradled her. . . .

Except that she hears her bear accuse: *You killed my wife too*. "No! I never did!"

A gun, the gliding woman said.

"A gun. She's bought a gun. She's going to do something awful with it," Eve cries aloud, swerving away from a jacaranda. Bruised leaves fall against the windshield.

The car lurches and Eve wrestles the wheel. Even the Mercedes is against her now, an enemy, with the fading boy at her side, Abramson's wife on the backseat bleeding.

Why was Abramson reading Augustine?

She shakes so violently that when the road widens, so little strength remains in her hands that she can't keep the car from smacking up against a long black Cadillac parked by the curb. Her neck snaps back; her head butts the steering wheel.

The impact stops the car and in the ringing silence Eve fights darkness on whose slippery surface she slides as if on ice. Pain buoys her up and she crawls hand over hand out of the car to cross the empty road. She walks purposively when the tide retreats, in that pause before the pain gathers, roars back in a new attack.

She sinks on a bench in the small park and has the peculiar notion that roots anchor her, that she is a prisoner run wearily to ground. Little children—dark-haired, dark-eyed, toddlers on tricycles, baby boys banging tin pails—crowd the walks and sandboxes only to torment her.

The warmth of a tiny body pressing her breast, his rosebud mouth on the nipple tugging . . . She remembers the curve of his cheek, the pink shell ear, the mothy lashes quivering as the contractions continue to rip and tear, producing now nothing but blood and more blood.

Red drops trickle over the wood and fall onto the ground, wetting the dust. Black stars form by Eve's feet, and rocking, she tries to cry them away, unable to straighten even as a whitely starched female stops at her knees and asks, "Are you feeling ill?"

She wants to tell the woman *I have lost so much of my life to mistakes*, but she won't speak, for to open her mouth would let the pain loose in a howl, and she would lose the baby who is so surely in her womb kicking and struggling to be born. The baby whom she knows in the unfired part of her mind is only a chimera. There is no baby and no haunting boy, and if Abramson's wife hangs herself up in Eve's closet as brilliantly vivid as she did when walking the halls of Eve's marriage to the bear, it is only bad conscience that enlivens her—the same conscience, riddled with guilt, that put the boy grown in the passenger seat or, just as easily unborn, back in her womb.

"She's drunk!"

"Oh, no!"

"A stoned addict, even here. Cocaine."

"Don't be silly—"

"Look at—"

"Are you sick?"

"I think there's something . . ."

"Definitely wrong."

"Is that blood?"

"Oh, dear, yes. Poor thing, she's bleeding."

The voices raise an umbrella over Eve's head and sing songs of worry, for which she wants to express tearful gratitude but can't. The pain swells and fills the universe and she is wrapped like a mummy in its winding sheets.

18

Later Cassie tells the story to Nona as it was related to her, of starched nannies, zealously guarding their charges, rushing to phone the police and report Eve, the dangerous intruder, mental, a vagrant though well-dressed. Only a clear-headed young mother cited the blood as evidence that they should help her rather than protect themselves and the children. She called the paramedics. So, an ambulance, which Eve entered no more willingly than she might a patrol car, brought her to Cedars-Sinai, where she gives Cassie's name not only as her physician but her next of kin.

You're not related at all, Nona will protest. Why say you are? And Cassie reminds Nona that she's not even Eve's doctor; Jena is—none of which matters. The blood loss and a good whack on the head confused Eve.

The emergency room physician, a boy so young-looking he seems an impostor, urges Eve to stay in for observation. While not on the staff, Cassie has privileges and she reads Eve's chart and agrees.

"No."

Eve lies on a cot in a curtained cubicle. Her face is as white as drawing paper and her voice whispers between swollen lips, "I want to go home." She angles up on her elbows as Cassie advises against leaving.

Eve is insistent. Her head throbs and the swelling on her forehead is tender as an overripe spot on fruit, but she is only mildly concussed. X-rays reveal no fracture. Still Cassie equivocates, for she has learned of Eve's confusion, the crying fit of a woman in torment, though now the streaming tears have slowed to a trickle. Even these Eve appears unaware of.

The bleeding continues along with some pain, though nothing like that which dragged her down the hill out of control. But Cassie and the young doctor concur on no medication. Nothing prescribed with a head injury.

"Who can tell?" Cassie says, urging Eve back on the thin pillow. She strokes her hand and automatically records Eve's pulse beating rapidly under her fingers. A frail bird seems trapped in the narrow wrist, and she feels a pang at Eve's vulnerability.

Cassie says, in the professional tone of a stranger, "You're going to have to take it easy for the next couple of days. Stay in bed."

"I can't be away from the office."

"The office will wait."

She brushes Eve's hair off her brow. Eve is a mess. In all the years she and Cassie have been friends, Cassie has never seen her so undone. Wrinkles pleat her skirt, ladders ripple up her stockings, and blood plus dirt smear stains in an archipelago on her blouse.

"Help me home, Cassie, please. I can't stay here. I just can't!" She is begging, wounded, Cassie realizes, in unseen places. Protests, an order to stay put, are what Cassie should say. But Eve can simply sign herself out despite them, go off alone, refusing to listen to any warning.

"This is a mistake. You should stay under observation," Cassie says, even as she is helping Eve up on unsteady legs.

Barbara agrees to cover for Cassie at Magdalene, so Cassie sees Eve home to bed, tenderly tucking her in, as she has done in the past with Mandy. She makes them both a pot of strong tea and urges on Eve two perfectly poached eggs with wheat toast.

Eve accepts Cassie's ministrations in silence but fans off her offer to stay overnight.

"You'd feel better if somebody's here."

"No, I hate sleep-overs, always did. Sharing a room with Louise still makes me covet space, my own." Eve's eyebrows ride high and she tries her usual deprecating smile, but the exhaustion defeats her.

She is humiliated. Washed and bathed, in a granny gown of

259

ruffled cotton, her hair slicked smooth and held by barrettes, the girl she once was peeks through the bruises of a woman hurting. Plainly she regrets Cassie's witnessing her disgrace, but nothing will be made right even if Cassie says *Forget it*. They're all entitled to their bad moments, those occasions when emotions run off the rails. In her practice Cassie beholds all manner of distress, women drowning in silent outrage, women finally sparked into outbursts, women who during brief eclipses lose their minds (often the better to retrieve them). Because Cassie has intuition about herself and professional expertise with so many other women, she disbelieves the claims that women and men are not so different, their biology no more than alternate methods of plumbing. Both PMS and menopause issue cards of transit to foreign territories where men are aliens. And surely during pregnancy women move by tidal patterns men can never experience.

Cassie pulls up a chair to the side of the bed, though Eve obviously wants her to leave. "What you're going through isn't so strange. It's not exceptional. Because it's happening to you it seems outrageous, but other women have suffered the exact same things, thousands, no, probably millions. It's endemic to being female."

Eve fires back: "Everybody dies but that doesn't mean I have to like it when it's me."

"You're not dying. Don't be an ass."

"I'm hemorrhaging."

"Heavy bleeding, not hemorrhaging. From a large ovarian tumor. Unpleasant but ordinary." Cassie is clipped, medical, but her expert's stance affects Eve no more than would loving concern.

Eve is silent and Cassie listens to the distant hum of traffic far below on Wilshire. Then Eve sighs, when Cassie had been expecting an angry howl. "You can't understand, because it's not *your* body that's betraying you. Your insides haven't gone to war and made you the enemy." A shudder ruffles the material on Eve's breasts. "If you can't trust your own body, who, what, do you trust?"

"That's too elaborate" is all Cassie can think to say.

"Is it? Maybe, but right now I'm two people. I'm the 'I' in my head, the trapped creature who peers out of a cage, the one who hears, has emotions. And then there's the other me, the one full of physical pain, the one who hurts so much I could scream the teeth out of my jaw. That one's maimed, broken down, rotting, diseased—"

"Enough!" Horrible though what Eve's been through is, Cassie thinks she veers too close to the dramatic.

"That's the traitor, the one who's going to die—"

"You're *not* going to die from this, Eve. I keep telling you that!"

If Eve catches the annoyance in Cassie's voice it doesn't affect her. Relentlessly she continues. "That one will take this one, the 'I' with it, her. Should I say *her*? Me? Two mes, yes."

"You've absolutely lost me with this confusion of pronouns. Drink some more tea, then try to sleep for a while. If you can't, watch some television or listen to music." Cassie whirls through a list of remedies for Eve's morbidness, but Eve obdurately remains grim. She is sunk into a mood too somber for lightening, and for the first time Cassie wonders if there was something more to Eve's accident than a spasm of pain so severe she lost control of the car. Where had she been? Or where was she going? Cassie hesitates to ask.

Eve is quiet. Her fingers cease their nervous plucking at the sheets. Her breathing grows shallow. As Cassie watches, Eve finally falls asleep. Cassie should leave but for several minutes sits there, a quiet guardian, and considers her feelings for the woman she hopes is dreaming no black dreams.

There is nothing extraordinary about the friendship. It goes back years, but some women she has known much longer, girls from home, sorority sisters from college, to whom she writes at Christmas and who visit on their trips to California. Barbara and Jena have been in Cassie's life for more time than Eve, and Nona for only a year or two less. Time in a friendship means little except as a container of stored, shared experiences. It's not time but love that excites her to worrying about Eve.

How diminished she would be without Eve in her life! Eve is more than a woman whose birthday Cassie circles on the calendar, more than another walking-talking female person to have dinner with or take in a movie. She has had long woolly conversations with the woman sleeping on a lace-edged pillow before her, lashes penciled against the pale cheeks, and weepy sessions that begin with *I can't go on* but end in a calm of acceptance. She has relied on her common sense, and if Eve's approach is occasionally harsh, still she shelters no unkindness. Eve will rise at any time—even from sleep or when feeling lousy—and come rushing to Cassie's aid if Cassie asks. She is quintessentially the one to call at two A.M. when the rest of the world vanishes in darkness and the blinds of all the houses are shuttered.

Nothing will go wrong with Eve, no freak episodes of the sort that prove medicine is an inexact science with a margin for luck, hope, and prayer. Nothing, Cassie promises, quietly slipping from the edge of the bed and tiptoeing out through the last of the afternoon light, as if she were empowered to make such decisions.

The fragility of a woman she viewed as steel leaves Cassie shaken. Every body disintegrates sooner or later. We're all meant to be worm food, her father used to joke. Cassie thinks not of Eve's death, but just simply of dying, of time moving like wind across the face of the clock.

She is, on leaving Eve's glitzy building, partly a child ready to cry out in fear, and furiously adult, Super Woman. She wants to battle, to issue a demand that her days of sitting, waiting, doing nothing, being female-as-object are over. How dare Jake drop through a hole in space on her! And how stupid, snivelingly weak-kneed of Cassie to let him.

Enough! she thinks, and drives down to Pico, into the first gas station on the right. From the pay phone she calls Yang, who isn't at home, but a tinny little voice obligingly gives Cassie the address.

On the freeway, traffic crawls forward by inches. Cotton-candy clouds tinged pink as flamingoes float lazily in the West. Silk light slides slowly down the sky until the last of the blue has darkened to navy by the time she turns off the exit ramp, leaving the unbroken trail of cars behind.

Yang's house isn't easy to find and she must stop twice for directions. When she eventually pulls up to the muffled shape of his truck in the drive, it is night. Without a moon, and only one pale lamp at the end of the block, the street is a shadowy culvert. Cassie carefully picks her way over the grass, across earth recently watered and spongy beneath her feet.

She climbs three steps to a wide porch. Her knuckles barely touch the wood before Yang is there inclining his head. "Dr. Morgan."

Cassie listens for surprise in Yang's voice as he invites her in, offers her a seat on either one of the stuffed chairs or the sofa of the three-piece matching living room set, but she hears none. Has he foreseen her arrival or is it simply his Oriental mien, an almost ethereal politeness, that keeps him from showing emotion?

"I'd like Jake's address, Yang. Please."

"Can I offer you some tea, Dr. Morgan?" Yang parries.

The house has the sepulchral silence of a mausoleum and Cassie wonders briefly about Yang's family. Was it a wife or a child who answered the phone?

Chafing to be gone from the very moment she has walked through Yang's front door, Cassie understands there are rituals to be performed. She must be calm. Only she's overcome by longing. Too much time has been wasted and now she obsesses about tracing the line of Jake's jaw, kissing his eyelids, shuddering when his lips grace the curve of her neck. Like a lovesick girl she needs his arms around her. *I'm sorry*, she will say to him, though she can't quite think sorry for what.

"No, thank you, Yang," she finally decides, feeling feverish. She lowers herself to the couch and when she settles, Yang sits on her left at the very edge of a chair. "I thought I'd check on Jake, see how he's doing. Maybe"—she coughs in her fist—"he needs something."

Yang's gaze meets hers for the first time Cassie can remember, and the flat brown look, as unrevealing as a slab of stone, alarms her. The walls move in suddenly, the room narrowing until there is little air left between them. She hears a clock ticking wildly. Or is it her heart?

She bursts out with "How is he?"

"I don't know, Doctor. Fine, I suppose."

"He'll come back to work in a few days?"

"Perhaps, though perhaps not. Jake moves around. He's a restless man; he likes to travel. He could just pack his things and go. This is such a big country. There are so many places in it."

Why is Yang frightening her? She knows about Jake's wanderlust, if that's what to call it. But even the most determined traveler tires after a while. Even a man running eventually slows to a halt. And Jake has come as far as the Pacific. There's only water now, and if

Jake hopes to stay on land he'll have to turn around and retrace his steps. Cassie says as much to Yang, who nods.

A pause, two beats, and then Cassie cries out, "I can't understand why you won't tell me where he is."

"Please, Doctor, I'm not hiding anything. It's none of my business, only . . ." He lifts a hand, which hangs in midair until he thoughtfully replaces it, like an object not a part of himself, on a bony denim knee.

"Only what?"

"None of my business," Yang repeats.

Of course it is no business of his why she asks for Jake's address or what they are to each other, though Yang knows well enough. Cassie wears her feelings out in the open like a blouse or shirt and would be embarrassed at such shameless revelations before anyone, but particularly a stranger, someone who works for her, the gardener! (isn't Jake a gardener?), if she weren't so impatient. Time, however, falls away into nothingness, echoed by the clock's metronoming. She loses minutes of her life while the little man opposite rests sedately, able to exist for an eternity on his chair, simply occupying space and staring.

She wishes she had accepted the offer of tea so her hands weren't protuberances with nowhere to light, so she wouldn't be out of place in the small room with a gallery of religious pictures covering the walls. Christ at Cana. Adam and Eve fleeing the garden. A metallic Last Supper reflecting the light, the shiny beams bouncing off a table.

What if Yang won't tell her, if he refuses to say another word? Or if he lies and swears he has no idea where Jake lives?

Naturally she won't beg, but her voice quivers when she says, "I have to get there before it's too late." She amends this, for it sounds as if she is to discover some awfulness at Jake's. "I mean, it's almost eight."

"It's not for me to say whether or not you should do this, Doctor, but please reconsider. You and Jake . . ." He waits and Cassie holds her breath.

Abruptly Yang stands and, going to a small rattan desk in the corner, writes something on a slip of paper. When he passes it to her he says, "Please ask Jake to let me know when he will return to work—if he will, of course."

"Thank you, Yang."

The address Yang has given her is far east in Hollywood. It will take Cassie a while to zigzag across town, even if traffic has thinned out, but now that she knows where Jake is, the rush to reach him slows to a shuffle. She drives slowly, making deliberate stops, pulls in for gas at a Mobil station, though she has half a tank, drinks a Pepsi after she fills up, and searches during a long few moments for stars in the sky.

Just having Jake's address calms her.

She stops again, this time at a Denny's for a cheeseburger and coffee and to think about what Yang has said. Is he right—are they too different? Her mind spins with the spoon she swirls around in her cup.

Foolish, foolish, foolish . . . You've asked these questions before, she tells herself, wishing she wouldn't agonize so. Let him go! or keep him! But get on with it, she thinks, and orders a dish of chocolate ice cream.

Either he is in my life or not! Either way . . .

Cassie's head is hurting. A smart woman would turn around and go home, but she gets back in her car, studies the address Yang so carefully wrote down, and continues driving east . . .

. . . having forgotten she and Nona were on for dinner.

Nona calls and gets Cassie's service, which hasn't heard from her in hours. They'll take a message but Nona replies no, it's not important. She must have misunderstood, thinking their date definite when it was tentative. Nona always assumes the mistake is hers, so feels no animosity toward Cassie for standing her up, just disappointment. She needs to talk, to replay yet again the last scene with Alan, plus a varied assortment of their dates before that. Has she told Cassie how tender Alan was, how he once brought her a gardenia, called her his sorority girl, shared his most interesting cases, as he never did with anyone else? Does Cassie realize that Alan loved her?

She won't call Eve, who pushes Fitz as if he were an Oscar winner, while Cassie says, *Wait, take a breather*. Not that Fitz isn't nice enough, not that she doesn't like Fitz, because she certainly finds him attractive, though her memory of sleeping with him is blurry and indistinct, sifted through cheesecloth. She was so upset she forgot everything but Alan going out the door. Which is probably just as well, since she can't count on Fitz returning. He has such a breezy style he could be here today, tomorrow in Santa Barbara heading north. He reminds her, in fact, of the boys she saw marching in Cambridge, boys with important plans for the future, and laughing all the while.

Fitz is younger than she is too. She's never gone out with anybody younger and just the idea makes her feel old, illuminates forty, fast approaching, in neon. She's as afraid of that treacherous number as if the four and the zero together are actual things, welded into a real weapon of steel, a machine, a horror-movie machine that can crunch up her bones.

So when Fitz phones just minutes after her last call to Cassie, Nona nibbles at her bottom lip. He tries to cajole her out for a pizza, maybe a flick.

"Come on, Nona, we'll have fun. We're meant for good times. We're soul mates."

"You're goofy. You don't know me at all." Only he does, or has in the biblical sense, though he left her unsatisfied or must have, for surely she would have remembered *that*. She has experienced so few orgasms in her life she can count them on one hand, and there have been far, far fewer of them than men who have tried. Which of course she would never confide, not to the men or to her best female friends. Nona, the great pretender, is sorrowfully embarrassed about how little pleasure she has ever received in bed.

Fitz won't take no for an answer, or maybe she is just too easy. Besides, she needs to get out of the apartment, to go someplace where the lights are bright and other voices collide. And he is cute, with that dimple in his chin. They'll talk, he'll make her laugh, and after a few glasses of wine she can stop thinking of Alan.

"Okay."

"I'll be there in fifteen minutes."

Only after Nona hangs up does she think he should have called earlier, at least a day or two before, because—she remembers Marian lecturing—you never go out with a boy at the last minute.

———

Cassie's mother never instructed her in the social etiquette of male-female relations. If she had any preconceived notions about how a woman behaved she failed to pass them on to Cassie, but surely she wouldn't have approved of her daughter's chasing after a man who stopped calling, simply because he makes her heart pound faster. Her mother had said, however, don't be cheap with yourself, and Cassie hands down the same advice to Mandy, and Mandy laughs that they are different generations. There's no such thing as being cheap anymore.

Cassie consoles herself that she's modern, assertive, too, that she merely is going after what pleases her. She acts like a man who won't give up, she thinks, arriving on Jake's doorstep.

Jake lives in a tiny, self-contained cottage behind a larger main house, on a run-down side street in Hollywood. Even at night, when darkness shelters the peeling paint and sagging porches, neglect tarnishes the neighborhood.

"Cassie, what are you doing here?"

At the sight of him, conflicting emotions assault her—relief that he hasn't disappeared and humiliation at needing to track him down. She steps away in the swing of changing her mind, but Jake, opening the door, reaches through to grip her arm. As he pulls her forward she trips on the lintel and needs to be steadied.

The house is as square as a packing crate, sparse as a monk's cell and just as neat. Light spills from a gooseneck lamp beside a frayed and lumpy wing chair but barely shifts the darkness gathered between walls in need of paint.

Cassie feels as if she were in a cave, buried thousands of feet in the belly of the earth. Here it will be impossible to tell when the sun's at the zenith, and in Jake's house neither night nor day has impact; it must always be three in the morning.

"I came to see how you are. The other night you were pretty upset. Then, I didn't hear from you. You never showed up on Thursday. Yang said you were sick. He also said maybe you wouldn't be back working." Cassie talks too fast. Now that she is actually in the same space with Jake, within arm's length, though he has dropped his hold on her, anxiety makes her babble. "I thought you might need something, or if you're really sick, well, I'm a doctor. Free medical care, okay, even if you're not female.

267

Or I guess we could just talk. We didn't say much the other night about the accident, how it affected you."

"You mean about getting whacked-out." His laugh is ragged. "I had what's called a flashback. Like, for who-the-hell-knows how long, I was *there*, in Nam, when, shit, we know I wasn't. I was in your house in California in the middle of a night twenty years after the fact."

He looks awful, a man who's been on a three-day bender. His eyes are burnt to cinders. Cassie, filled with what might be love or pity, or both brewed into a lethal mixture, turns away to the room he lives in for clues as to what he's been doing. But he might have walked in only moments before she did. There's no beer can out, no coffee cup, plate, or saucer. No book or magazine lies open by the chair, and the little television set on a wooden ledge is off.

He must just have been sitting in the shabby chair, just sitting.

"I'm sorry," Cassie says.

"Sorry about what? This has nothing to do with you." He hooks his thumbs into the belt loops of his jeans and stands, legs spread, macho, a marine, a cop, a biker. It only now occurs to Cassie that Jake would have resented her seeing him sweaty and terrified, freaking out.

"You didn't start the war or kill anybody, or try to keep your ass in one piece in the middle of a firestorm. You probably were here in the old U.S. of A. on a protest march shouting about GIs killing slant-eyed babies."

"You never killed any children!" she objects, as if she had been there, at his side, as if she knows this truth for a fact.

"Two different sides."

Of course he's right, but Cassie can only say "It was a long time ago. And now all I want to do is help."

"Help? How? Roll twenty years out of the way? Raise the dead? Change those bad times into picnics? What the fuck do you think you can do for me that will *help*?"

Jake's anger shrinks the room and sets off echoes that hurt her ears.

"Love you," she says, as if into a vacuum. "Relieve your pain. I can't stand to see you hurt."

"I'm not one of your lady patients."

Cassie has no control over the fractured feeling inside her, but still, this is a poor excuse to love anybody, even Jake with his broken good looks, his unhealed wounds, his unspoken cry. Cassie swears she hears *Fix me!*

Run, the clear voice of reason whispers in her ear, escape, get back to your own side of town, continue with the endless blind dates, join Great Expectations, answer ads in *Los Angeles* magazine, look over the men on barstools and keep searching for another male who turns your female parts to jelly.

What Cassie definitely shouldn't do is stay here so near to Jake, in this confined space dark as a pit, airless and with the dangerous consequences of an iron maiden, and say, as if life is a fairy tale, "I can love you. I will, forever."

Jake explodes. "Jesus, women! You're all the same. You think love can change black into white. 'All you have to do is love, baby'!" He parodies the song, waving his arms, striking out and hitting a wall. "You should meet my ex-wife. Boy, was she ever a class-A lover, and where did it get her? Or me either." He whips around and leans in menacingly close to Cassie, but she holds her ground and refuses to step back. "One night I busted up all the furniture. Threw a fucking dining room chair through the front window. Nice?"

"I wasn't there."

"And you weren't around when I busted up so many cars that Texas yanked my license."

"What do you want me to say, Jake? That you behaved stupidly? That you needed help?"

"Don't say a frigging thing to me! Be like my kids, so shit-scared they walked around the walls."

Cassie insists, half-believing herself, "I'm not scared."

"Yeah, well you should be, because I was a real prick as a father, a husband, and you better get away from me now. If Emily kicked me out in the beginning before I dumped her, the three of them would've been better off. But oh, no, Emily was a lady with a mission. Hurray for love, Cassie. Do you think you can do any better?"

Cassie cries. She stands rooted in Jake's little squalid chicken coop, so near him his anger sprays spittle on her cheeks to mix with her tears, and cries silently. The liquid leaks from her eyes as if Jake's fury turns her heart to water.

269

"Can you?" he shouts.

"I thought we were having good times together. I was happy. I thought—"

"You didn't think. You sit in your pretty house, drink a ten-dollar bottle of wine, cook up a gourmet meal, play some classy music on the stereo that costs more than I made some years, and okay, the world's picture postcard perfect. You live in a fucking commercial!" He sinks suddenly into the chair and squeezes his head as if it will come loose, off his neck, and leaves Cassie standing in a puddle of tears.

"Things just felt right, and there hasn't been anybody else. Not since Doug. You said—"

Jake interrupts with a yell that rocks Cassie in its high wind. "I never said a damn thing! Don't put words in my mouth!"

Cassie is on a wild roller-coaster ride, careering need and rocketing emotion hurtling her around curves and down plunging slopes. "You felt good too. I know you did. You can't have made all that up. Those times when we were laughing, when we made love . . ."

"Cassie, oh, Cassie, don't." His anger slowly deflates, leaving him flaccid.

"I never asked you for anything."

"You did—do. With every gesture you try to bring me up to your level. You're a woman a man has to measure himself against, and shit, I'm a double amputee. I walk around on stumps, for Christ's sake."

"No." She is winning, and a rush of adrenaline makes her almost high.

"Listen, there always comes that moment when I bolt, when things turn into garbage and I'm hanging by my heels upside down in time. It's not now; it's way back when. I fall into some frigging time warp and forget L.A. It's the DMZ all over again, like I've never left. We're down by a river, almost buried in nipple palms, holding our heads because the world is vomiting up all around us. That brown mucky water is spraying in geysers and throwing a shower on the opposite bank. Mud, water pound down on us. We're locked in. There's some fat cat pumping away to the left of us and if anybody sticks up his head he's dead meat. This fucker has us in a hole, and mortar fire is thundering from hell and back.

And the sky is raw liver. Like it is coming apart. A hand falls from somewhere and lands in my lap. A goddam hand with hair growing up the fingers. It's a stupid joke. Can't be real. But there are guys we don't even know ripped into jigsaw pieces and dropping down out of the clouds. A big sick joke, but whose? God's?"

There's no sense in his telling her all this, in forever heaving it up until his insides are on fire, his psyche catching him on a tide he can't get free of. As he says, he relives each moment so that every one becomes an hour, a day, a year.

"It's over. The past. Let it go, Jake."

"Yeah, sure. Like I'm holding on because it's such fun to wake up screaming, or to freeze like a Popsicle when something presses the trigger."

"Everybody—"

"Don't say it. Everybody has his monkey."

He sinks back in the chair and she sees in the lines already scoring his face the old man he will grow into.

"When I was a kid," he says, "I had this friend, Kevin, down the block. Kevin didn't have a left arm. He was just born without one for some reason nobody ever explained, if they could've. Kevin came out half-baked, like a broken cookie. I never thought it was any big deal. Neither did Kevin, who had no idea what two arms were. His reality was a one-armed world and it was okay by him. But whenever kids came along and saw Kevin for the first time they were awed, like he was a geek. They'd go all red and shuffle their Keds and look anywhere except at the empty sleeve flapping in the breeze if Kevin forgot to pin it up. They'd stare google-eyed at where everybody else had a left arm, like it was just hiding and would pop out any second. And lots of times a kid would zero in on Kevin and drive him nuts with questions. How'd it happen? What did it feel like? That kind of shit.

"That no arm was Kevin's monkey. I used to think it would have been worse if he was born with two arms and then lost one—like then he'd have something to cry over and feel rotten about losing. But you can't grieve about something you never had. Once I asked Kevin, and he said it didn't make a frigging difference because when you got down to it he still would have ended up with only one arm."

Jake wipes a hand over his face and pulls himself up from the chair. "Want a beer?" The storm inside him seems to be ebbing. When he passes Cassie on the way to the minuscule kitchen he rubs her shoulder.

Cassie shivers. "I could use a beer. My throat's dry."

"Old Kevin at least didn't have to go to the war. So something good came from his monkey."

Jake pours her a Corona and waits for the foam to settle before handing it over. "You know, for a while I thought there was some payoff for all that time, all that grief that went down, but *nada*. I drift and things will be fair, no big hassle, and I'll start to pull together, and then bingo, a Claymore goes off under me." He returns to his chair, and Cassie, following, sits on the couch.

"The accident."

"It doesn't even take blood running in the streets like the accident. Before, it could be a couple of rainy days in a row, a heat wave where your skin bubbles, a muggy Santa Ana. A dream, a program on the TV. Once there was this woman, Vietnamese, in the grocery store. Guys used to say all gooks look the same. Seen one, seen them all. But they're crazy. The Vietnamese are like everybody else, tall, short, fat, skinny, pretty, ugly mothers, big-eyed, piggy-eyed, little noses, big ones. I mean, like white people, blacks, they're not all from the same cookie cutter. Anyway, I was in a Piggly Wiggly in Baton Rouge where like, hey, what's new, I was passing through. I passed through so much of the fucking country I could write a travel book. Anyway, I had done some construction so I was fairly flush with some change and just wasting time before I moved on. I had a little apartment and did my own cooking, and this one morning I went over to the grocery for some stuff, and there was this girl, about twenty or so, just standing in line. Pretty, with polished skin like rare wood, only she had this terrible scar, wide as a nail file laid right across her mouth and chin. Her lips looked like a crazy had sliced them with a hatchet, just chopped the bottom of her face in two, and one side was up, the other down, the two pieces of her lips way out of sync. And the minute I saw that, while I'm staring at her, she explodes right in front of me, just blows up.

"Yeah, I know a bomb didn't send the Piggly Wiggly sky high, but that girl flying to pieces was as real as anything I ever saw in my whole life."

Cassie wants to create a new language, words other than *that's awful, how terrible, what pain, poor man*, but there aren't any. She nods and listens professionally, sits with her knees shaking, without a hope of writing a prescription or authorizing tests, suggesting a medical procedure.

"That was the end of Baton Rouge, which was haunted. Only the country is full of ghosts—not the Vietnamese so much, but guys in wheelchairs who don't have to tell me where their legs are, and guys with canes who've got sewed-up eye sockets.

"I thought maybe I could bury them with booze or dope, but getting smashed or stoned is temporary. Comes the dawn and for a little while anyway you got to be sober. Then the light is like a firestorm; you're absolutely blinded and scared to your toes. And I got so tired being in gaga land, so bored with nodding off or throwing up. I wanted my mind back in one piece. I wanted to think without falling on my ass. Only by that time, when I hated myself so much I was either going to get sober or swallow the pipe, Emily was long gone with the girls and close to two decades of my life was history."

"Jake, you're starting over."

"I'm always starting over. It just takes something like that accident to set all the sirens screaming."

"That accident was horrible. People were killed. Anybody would have gotten sick from seeing that." She hurries on, determined to convince him. "Okay, not me, but I'm a doctor. I had a turn in a city emergency room, which is like the front lines, and I learned to put the human destruction *out there* so I could do what had to be done. I was trained."

"Florence Nightingale."

Cassie can't wait any longer. She leaves the couch to sit on the floor—with her long legs awkward as a heron's—by Jake's chair. She puts her head against his knee and wills his hand to alight softly on her hair.

"Florence, find yourself a nice doctor."

"My Jewish mother."

"Cassie, seriously, I'm not for you. Trust me. I'm a loose cannon."

"Not always."

"Yeah, well, I'm also unemployable except to my good buddy

Yang, the bastard, who pays me a buck an hour over minimum wage and to whom I'm profoundly grateful. I've been on the street; I'll probably be on the street again. And you saw what it was like when I have a bad dream."

"It doesn't matter."

His fingers tighten in her hair. "Women in love are idiots. You're too smart, Cassie, to love me, to do anything with me except say *see you around*."

His voice lulls her, a murmur. She rides in her old bed again, in her room in Landry. Soft rain patters at the window, and under the eiderdown, on a mound of pillows, she dreams safely, unafraid. She is comforted as if by music.

"Take me to bed, Jake," Cassie says, for the first time in her life asking a man to touch her, hold her, love her. For a moment she fears she's gone too far, that he'll say no and push her aside, run even farther than he has already. But Jake doesn't.

19

Jake walks over the grass in Cassie's dream. Before they fell asleep in the snug little bedroom tight as a ship's berth he told her the story of Washington. Cassie has never seen the monument for herself, only sections in pictures, and imagines it set on an endless open plain flanked by an honor guard of rolling hills in the background. One long stone grave-marker with the list of the dead in memory buried beneath it.

The monument is a creation of the living, an actual physical *thing* to which the survivors can make a pilgrimage, as Jake has, driving nonstop but for short catnaps on the Honda's backseat all the way from California. It was time, which is all he can say about why he went. And he arrives with three days' growth of beard and gritty eyes, with a sour, metallic taste in his mouth.

He traces the names he knows, some with his fingertips, and each touch returns a boy to life momentarily. None of those Jake remembers were fully grown men, only children. They all had far more years in front of them than the few they had lived.

Hello and goodbye, Jake says in the rain, cold as the granite, chillier than tears.

Cassie cries in her sleep, awakening with a hard ball of sound knotted in her throat and unexpelled. She doesn't know where she is, the sun's blade of first light nowhere near the window.

She has never in her whole life spent the night at a man's, and the morning is misshapen. She is cold clear through and, all elbows, moves as cautiously as a cat. Maybe it is the dream sprung loose from Jake's memory that makes her feel an achy dampness in her joints.

He drove to D.C. for an exorcism, to lay the dead to rest in memory, and with their entombment chase off his ghosts. It works in books, he laughed bitterly, in movies. But in real life seeing their names—as if a name is a person instead of only what a person is called by—means nothing.

No ritual can snatch those lost from out of the void, and certainly not time. Over time the dead only grow hoarier.

To Cassie, an investor in the future with savings accounts, CDs, government bonds, who even as a child built toy houses methodically, one block firmly anchored on top of another, Jake's credo— live for the moment—while not heresy, is unmanageable. Cassie's thoughts fly around corners; she needs to know the prognosis.

Jake brews her a strong cup of black coffee that a spoon can stand up in and says, as she's ready to leave, "I can't make you promises, Cassie."

She ducks her head when she asks, "Can you come over to-night?"

"Quite a lot of calls from yesterday afternoon and last night, Dr. Morgan," the crisp, anonymous voice of Cassie's service informs her. "Do you have a pencil?"

"Go ahead."

Nona phoned and Mandy, but there was no word from Eve. The clinic's service also phoned, and Jena rang twice. But it is the calls from April that frighten Cassie. She draws a circle around the phone number the operator gives her and asks, "Did she say what she wanted?"

"There's nothing written down, Doctor."

"Okay. Thanks."

Not once has April tried to contact Cassie. Their relationship has been strictly visits to the clinic, and as Cassie dials, a clammy feeling creeps up the back of her neck.

"Answer, damn it!" she whispers as the ringing continues.

Cassie swings around in her chair just as Jena closes the door. Jena stuffs both hands into the pockets of her white coat and rises on her toes. Her anger fans across the office in such heat that Cassie, surprised, hangs up the phone.

"What's wrong?"

"You left early yesterday."

Cassie explains about Eve. "I was going to stop by your office after I cleared up some stuff."

"Stuff! Stuff! What about yesterday's stuff?"

"What's bothering you, Jena? I had no *stuff* from yesterday. Barbara covered for me. Ask her."

"That's irrelevant. Nobody, including Barbara, could find you. You're a physician, Cassie, and you know better than to drop out of sight even for a few hours."

"Jena, I don't have any patients in the last trimester, so what is the problem?"

But she knows, feels the coldness in her belly, even as Jena, her face tight as a fist, says, "One of your patients was very disturbed. She finally got in touch with me to see if I knew where you were. Nobody but Dr. Morgan would satisfy her."

"April DeVito. I've just been calling her but there's no answer. What did she say?" My husband beat me, Cassie imagines, but if he was on one of his periodic tangents from sanity, where was April this morning with her bruises? Were they so bad she went to the hospital emergency room?

"She wouldn't tell me piss-all, only kept asking where could she find Dr. Morgan. As if I had you hidden in my bottom drawer."

Cassie sweats at the base of her spine, an uncomfortable warmth that indicates her closeness to panic. "Incoherent?"

"The opposite. Cold as an ice pop. Eerie. Is she mental?"

"No, not at all. Her husband's an abuser. Every full, half, and quarter moon he gets soused and beats her up."

"Another bully boy," Jena says with scorn.

"Let me try her again." But still there is only the continuous ringing at the other end. "No luck."

"You should have been available when she needed you, Cassie, rather than picking up the pieces now."

Cassie can offer no legitimate excuse. Jena's right.

"You don't just disappear without even bothering to check your service. You don't drop off the ends of the earth. You have responsibilities." Jena pacing the carpet is a stern schoolmistress, a biblical prophet, Cassie's conscience.

"I know."

"Where were you?" Jena stops moving to ask.

None of your business, Cassie could tell her, but Jena won't leave without an explanation. "Personal," she says finally.

Jena laughs. "Oh, a man. I should have known. It's always a man, isn't it?"

"No, it's not. Or not with me. And you know that, Jena," Cassie protests. She has a vision of herself in reverse, as Jena, who is back by the door once more, sees her, and it is a woman with her hair standing on edge, a woman so obsessed she sizzles with electricity.

"A man, even an occasional one, doesn't excuse not being available when a patient needs you. A man is a man is a man, Cassie," Jena says, licking sarcasm off her lips.

"I don't need a lecture, thank you very much!"

They glare at each other as Barbara opens the door and sticks her head in. "Doctors, we can hear you all the way over in the pharmacy." Jena storms past Barbara and out of the office. "Well, well, well, what were you two having such loud words about?"

"I thought you heard every syllable."

"Not every single one. Just a stray vowel or consonant here and there."

Again Cassie punches out April's number and says as she anxiously waits, "I was incommunicado for several hours. Jena rightly called me on it. I was wrong, no question, but she is so damn officious that—Oh, shit!" She slams down the unanswered phone.

"Several hours. Like all night several hours?"

Cassie avoids Barbara's eyes and feints with "For quite a while."

Barbara's lips curl. "Well, if a man is at the bottom of your mystery, Cassie, I hope you were sensible and kept quiet. Jena's preferences, et cetera and so forth, don't make her think kindly of a man as an excuse."

"It's not her preferences, whatever they may be—and none of us knows; we just gossip scurrilously—but her point is that I should have been reachable. And she's right." Somehow Cassie's gotten turned around to defending Jena for yelling at her.

"Let her who is without sin toss the first brick," Barbara says, but Cassie knows she is umbilically attached to the clinic at all times. Barbara punctiliously remembers she is a doctor first, a woman and wife second.

Up to last night Cassie would have described herself as unimpeachable in her conduct, like both Barbara and Jena. What was she thinking of? Jake . . .

"Look," she says, "do me one more favor. See whoever I have scheduled next."

"I won't say this is becoming a habit, Cassie, but it—Okay."

"April DeVito called five times last night and now she's not answering the phone."

"I said okay, Cassie."

A fourplex of stucco with a carport beneath in an open mouth, the building squats mid-block, identical neighbors to either side. A concrete walk ribbons down one flank between limp, dust-speckled bushes in need of watering. April's is the last unit in the rear, just off the alley.

The silence of the noon neighborhood, with most of the residents elsewhere, is broken by an unharmonious voice shouting "I wanna hold your hand!" and the rapid drumming of an inexpert musician.

Cassie presses the bell, impatient for April to call out *just a minute,* or a child's cry, a sign of someone inside. But there is nothing, no sound, only a feeling of emptiness.

Cassie rings again, knocks, and then finds to her surprise when she turns the knob that the door is unlocked. "April?" she calls into a silence so dense it has substance.

Stepping carefully, one foot before the other, she moves off the cement step onto yellow shag carpet. From his position in a beanbag chair, a teddy bear watches her glassy-eyed.

"April, are you home?"

The apartment faces west and the day isn't far enough gone for sunlight to have found its way through the windows, yet heat thickens and the air has a yeasty smell to it.

Get out. You're trespassing. Inside without an invitation. If the husband comes down the stairs . . . Cassie thinks of the demon whose darkened image has no clear face, no features beyond the burnt-out anger, like a collapsing structure that fire has gutted, lethally dangerous because so unreliable. She can see him striking her, too, as he has hit April.

"Is anybody here?"

In spite of the carpeting the stairs creak. Cassie is walking on bones, just as two generations, year after year, stepped over the women in Santa Monica. She would run but for being squeezed so painfully by guilt.

Above, something fetid taints the air, growing worse as Cassie climbs upward. She knows and already is heavy with regret.

Oh, April, she grieves even before seeing her, crushed like discarded clothing in a corner of the children's bedroom. A crib lies on its side. A lamp is shadeless on the floor, the filaments of the smashed bulb exposed. April's two children are welded onto her body, one at each hip, the younger asleep, head drooping like a too-heavy iris on a brittle stalk. The boy—six, Cassie remembers—has eyes blank as pebbles. As for April, she is a riotous abstract of dark colors, purplish contusions, blood dried to magenta.

"Oh, April!" Cassie cries aloud, releasing her hold on the jamb. The room, as she struggles across it, seems filled with water and her feet are heavy, with weights attached to the ankles.

Only when Cassie folds down to her level do April's eyes focus. A flash of fear splits the dark pupils, but then April recognizes her, and the bruised face shifts in an earth slide.

The sleeping child whispers a dream sound and burrows with animal neediness farther into April, as if she could tunnel back inside the body that once contained her. The boy, however, doesn't shift, staying locked next to his mother.

Gently Cassie touches April's sharp little chin, and turns her head, examining the ruined face.

April whispers, "I called you."

"I'm so sorry I wasn't there, that— Oh, forgive me!"

Confronted by the wreckage of April's face, as fragile as a child's and replicated on the little boy, Cassie is hushed with anguish. She doesn't need to ask April for details, for the story gushes out of her like bile. She has rolled herself up into a ball with the children just waiting for someone, for Cassie, to come and listen.

"His drinking got worse, and the TV was up. The neighbors hammered on the walls and then I asked him, turn it down, we're creating a nuisance. And he hit me. The kids were crying. I'm holding on to the baby and he gives her one on the ear."

Cassie gently sweeps the hair from the soft little baby face to reveal a dark stain stretching along the cheek. She probes the ridge of the cheekbone and a fluty whimper comes from the baby, though she remains asleep.

April keeps talking even as Cassie says, "I have to get you all out of here. Before he gets back."

"No." April screeches like a small rodent stepped on.

"Where is he?" It is the boy's sidelong glance, even more frightening than April's cry, that tells her. "Here? In the apartment?"

"Hurt the baby . . . I ran downstairs . . . a knife . . ."

"Oh, my God!"

Cassie abandons April to her monologue, the tape of the night before looping around: "He was going to get up . . . and then he would've done all of us in . . . not just me but Frankie and the baby . . . and if it was just me it's okay . . . I can live with it . . . but not them and . . . I let him have it then . . . him just laying there . . ."

"April!" Cassie screams from the doorway.

". . . called you, kept calling . . . talked to that other doctor . . . have to call you because he's so mad . . . the TV going on . . . him four sheets, ugly . . . the neighbors banging on the wall and . . ."

The sour smell stinks up in a great brew at the other bedroom, where Cassie is being dragged without her compliance, knowing she is going to get her first and last look at the husband. The mad dog, she thought of him, when April would turn up at Magdalene swearing to falls, convoluted accidents, an innate clumsiness. Mad dog, take him out on a leash and lose him, her anger would dictate, while she professionally cautioned herself: Abusers are sick, wounded themselves, usually victims as children. Treatment, reprogramming, therapy, training. Lose him; get rid of the mad dog, she still thinks, compassionless, her instincts at war with her intelligence.

Now someone has done worse and all Cassie thinks of is that in all the time April's been her patient not once has she heard his name. It is always *husband, he, him*. His identity lay under a shade, shadowed from the light by the fear he ignited, fanned, kept in flames. His fury, craziness of rage, made him invisible. Rage changed him, Jekyll to Hyde, a werewolf by the full moon; rage swallowed him whole and made the man hateful.

Did.

Cassie lays a finger to the cold neck. No pulse has beaten for hours below skin that feels closer to stone now than to anything living.

The blood—surprisingly little—that bubbled up from the intrusion of a wood-handled kitchen knife in his back has congealed. Yellow stains the white sheet, discolors his khaki chinos, but the urine has dried. Only the smell remains, pungent and ugly.

The body (now the husband, he, him, undergoes a further metamorphosis from person to thing) angles on its side. The head is profiled against the pillow; one eye marble and unreal as the stuffed bear's, staring wide open at nothing. The puckered skin below the lower lid is unnaturally dark, but otherwise the skin is smooth and unmarked on the ordinary face, more good-looking than not.

He's small, a much littler man than Cassie envisioned. It is hard to tell with him lying down, legs pulled up, as if in the last moments he contracted into the fetus he once was, but he can't measure more than five six, seven. Cassie had expected a behemoth, the wicked giant of fairy tales, and there is only this pitifully small human male. Even alive he can't have been much, and dead he is nothing.

Slowly Cassie removes herself, going backward the way she's come and hearing a scream that trails on and on, persistent as wind; but it is only inside her head.

20

Lorraine's temper is honed to a knife's edge. She slashes out these days at the least provocation. George's leg is mending too slowly for her purposes and the wedding plans are floundering. Everyone is out to get her, she complains. So at Flora's, Nona walks on tiptoes, quiet and compliant, taking her criticisms on the bias. The customers, however, are not so pliant and lose their footing on Lorraine's iciness.

Nona takes pity on just the sort of woman Lorraine would as soon send down the mall to a cheaper, less chic shop. A timid, colorless creature, drab as a peahen, who will probably finger the material and sidle out once she glimpses a price tag. But even so, Lorraine shouldn't hike a frosty shoulder against a hushed question and shake out a sleeve after the woman explores it.

"Can I help you?" Nona smiles.

The top of the woman's head barely edges Nona's collar. "I need a dress," she says.

"What kind of a dress? Casual? Daytime?"

"Oh, something special, something just right!" Her glance rests on Nona limpid as raindrops.

"Well, why don't you tell me what you need it for and then I can make some suggestions," Nona says kindly, Lorraine's hostility carving up her back. She won't buy anything! You're wasting your time! Flora's time!

Though the woman might be less obtrusive in medium-priced dresses at one of the department stores, it is Nona's time, and no other customers crowd Flora's but old faithful Mrs. Jorgansen, whom Lorraine has under control in a dressing room with two Missoni knits.

"My sister is getting married," the woman confides, bending closer, exposing to the light her gray, untinted roots.

"Then it's for the wedding."

"Oh, not yet. This is just the engagement party," she says, then adds confidentially, "She's marrying a man from a very good family."

"And where's the party going to be held?"

"At Matthew's house. I mean his parents' house, which is very large, with grounds. They have two in help."

"Afternoon or evening?"

"Cocktails," she says with a frown.

"All right." Nona guides her to a rack along one wall. "You're very tiny—a four or six, I think."

"Nothing ever looks good on me."

"Let's think positively. I'm sure there's something that will be absolutely smashing."

"Oh, smashing." She wrinkles her nose as if the idea of *smashing* is beyond her. "I just want to be sure that it's *proper*."

"Proper?"

"I mean that it's the *right* dress, the kind all the other women will be wearing."

Nona whisks out a beige silk and holds it under the woman's chin. "It's just a matter of developing a style, that's all. You have to learn what your colors are and if you need a defined waist—which I think would be best for you—and the proper length."

"Skirts go up, then come down, and I'm always in the wrong year."

"Right at the knees. That's the safest, especially if you're short."

Nona hangs up the beige. "What about this?" She pulls out a blue dress with cap sleeves. "I like the color on you, exactly the shade of your eyes. And the print isn't overwhelming. Why don't you try it on and I'll gather up a few other possibilities." Nona edges her toward the alcove in the back, past Lorraine, who curls like a snake, hissing—"That's a Nipon for five hundred and fifty dollars!"

Once Nona has the woman safely occupied she flips through her collections as fast as a casino dealer. Lorraine, diagonally across the floor, seems about to give her a stern talking-to on the sort of customers she never encourages, or perhaps about wilting the merchandise, but Mrs. Jorgansen sets sail with both Missonis and Lorraine has to ring up the charge. Furthermore, for just under a thousand dollars she is obliged to defrost enough to form a smile on her mouth, though it is like an ice flower on a winter window.

While Mrs. Jorgansen holds Lorraine at bay Nona returns to the dressing room with a deep-peach crepe of simple lines, and a black-and-white moiré that might work. She is betting on the blue, however, and it does fit the little woman perfectly, the gored skirt giving her needed fullness.

"That looks lovely."

"Do you think so?" The woman is a totem stiffened before the mirror.

"Turn around and take a look at the back." The woman shifts obediently, easy as a child. Though it is difficult to pinpoint her age Nona guesses she is midway through her forties. A spinsterish aura clings to her like lint to velvet, and she's added years with short, wavy hair hennaed one color, a solid, too-harsh reddish brown—the sign of a do-it-herselfer. Nona will tactfully suggest Joseph's, down on the second tier, and gold highlights. She might also hint at a tone-down on the lipstick and a whisk of mascara. Really, with care, the woman could be attractive.

"Now straighten your back so the material doesn't gather. There, that's it," Nona says, having grasped her firmly by the shoulders and inched her up. "What do you think?"

"I don't know," she replies, staring at her reflection as though at a stranger's. "Is it too much? I mean the print. Prints always seem wrong for me."

"This one's lovely on you. But try the peach and see what you think."

"Nona!"

There is a flurry at the front of the store. Three customers wander in out of nowhere. Lorraine waves Nona forward. "I'll be back in a second," Nona promises the woman.

"Stop encouraging that one. You know she'll never buy anything."

Nona shrugs. "She needs a dress and that Nipon is perfect."

"You're a fool, do you know that? In all the time you've worked for me, you have learned absolutely nothing, not even who buys a Nipon and who just tries one on because she has nothing to do in her lunch hour!" Flares of color rouge Lorraine's cheeks and she is about to soar in a rage, but the customer taps Nona's arm.

"I think this is good."

Rescued from Lorraine's outburst Nona guides her gently back to the mirror. "Let me have a real look."

Behind their backs Lorraine snaps, "Déclassé!" Nona hopes the little woman fails to understand, that the insult passes over her head.

"I like the color," the customer says. "Do you?" She glances at Nona in the mirror, eager for her approval.

The peach accentuates the sallowness of the woman's complexion, but Nona murmurs a kindly "hmmm," and narrows her eyes. "Attractive, but try on the black-and-white before we make up our minds."

She should avoid the plural, demeaning somehow, an adult talking down to a child, even if her diminutive customer arouses protective feelings in Nona, particularly with Lorraine out to banish her to a cheaper shop.

As Nona suspected, the black-and-white is wrong, and the customer slips the blue on again, saying, "It does look nice."

"And it's perfect for an afternoon party."

In a sudden reversal, for which women buying clothes are famous, the customer turns from being dubious to loving the dress. "It is gorgeous," she says. Picking up her courage she asks, "It fits me too. Yes, you're right, this is just the dress to wear to Carol's party. How much is it?"

"Five fifty," Nona replies.

The woman's pupils dilate. She is awed. "Five hundred and fifty dollars?"

All at once Nona worries not that the woman won't buy the dress, but convinced that the dress is the only dress to do for Carol (or not to shame her sister), she must have it at all costs, and $550 is far more than she can afford. Passion flames in her eyes. Rent . . . car payments . . . three months of lunches? In the heat of the moment she is liable to give anything up.

"I'm sure we can arrange layaway," Nona says hurriedly.

"The party is a week from Sunday," the woman counters grimly.

Nona prays she isn't over the limit on her Visa or MasterCard, that she won't pen Flora's a bad check.

Dressed in her own skirt and blouse the woman reverently hands the Nipon over to Nona and says, fervent as a communicant, "Wrap it up, please."

The little wren buying one of Flora's dresses angers Lorraine more than if the woman had slunk out, tail between her skinny shanks, and headed for J. C. Penney. So she looms like a storm over Nona's shoulder while Nona checks the woman's Visa. Further, Lorraine inspects the woman's driver's license, carefully comparing the photo to the peaked face at the counter. She is not about to be put in the wrong, to authorize a mistake, her own.

In an angry whisper Lorraine promises Nona: "She'll bring it back after she gets home and realizes what she's done. Or worse"— here Lorraine clenches her teeth—"she'll wear the dress and then try to return it."

Nona argues, "She won't do that."

"I'm realistic, which you never are. You live in a dream world where everyone is wonderful!"

The insult stings and Nona is ready to retort, but a customer claims her attention with a request to see the gold earrings in the window.

By the time Nona and Lorraine are again alone in Flora's, Nona has digested the insult and considers how often it is that she is swept away in the swell of intense feelings. Look at Alan, how crazy she was about him. Of course she made a terrible error in judgment thinking Alan was *him,* since Fitz has come into her life and she now just adores the ground he walks on. She and Fitz are so in sync, and Fitz is single. And good to her, better than Alan, who squeezed her in between office and home.

Fitz, on the other hand, is at Nona's for a leisurely dinner. He even cooks.

"You're not to lift one delicious finger, angel. Just park your gorgeous ass on the stool and talk to me. Here, a glass of Chardonnay to keep you oiled."

"Can't I help?" She is strangely dispossessed, a guest in her own home, while Fitz bustles around the kitchen wearing an old checked apron of hers.

"Nope. I have my paella down to a system."

"I love paella."

Fitz says what every man cooking on occasion does: "You never had any like mine." He grins. "And never in Boston. You old New Englanders are into baked beans and clam chowder. Bet your mother had some dynamite recipes passed down in the family since the Revolution. Right?"

"Oh, my mother never cooked. She only found the kitchen because it was next to the dining room."

"Who did then?"

"Cook."

Fitz slaps his forehead. "Of course. My little rich girl with the wonderful childhood."

Nona sips her wine. "It was just an ordinary childhood, nothing elaborate."

"That I don't believe."

"It's true."

"Pretty little rich girl from Boston."

"Don't tease me," she says, uncomfortable with Fitz's laughing at her.

He senses he's put a foot wrong and swoops around from the stove to kiss her cheek and lightly lick her neck down to the shoulder. He whispers, "Sorry. But I want to know everything about you, each moment in your life before we met. I am enamored with you, smitten, Nona love."

How she wants to believe him!

His eyes do shine when he moves off so he can look at her. Is that hunger she sees, lust? Could it be love?

Her discomfort butts against fear and moves close to panic. She says, "Tell me about you first."

"Anything at all. What do you want to know?"

She's bone-ignorant about Fitz, not even exactly sure how he earns a living. Between careers is what he is. In the business— meaning Hollywood, TV, movies. Working on a deal. "I'm getting it together, Nona."

She has never been to Fitz's apartment, a pit, the black hole of Calcutta. Not as nice by a mile as hers. "One of these days I'll invite the cleaning crew in and when the place isn't knee-deep in debris, fit for a princess, we'll spend the night there."

"You don't have to go to all that trouble."

"You're adorable, do you know that? Just the prettiest thing imaginable." He kisses the tip of her nose and offers her a shrimp on a fork. "Try this." He watches her as she nibbles. "You must have been a beautiful little girl. Got pictures?"

"Somewhere."

"I've got to see them. You in lace on Daddy's lap. And riding your pony."

"I never had a pony."

Fitz is disappointed. "I expected this shot of you on a pony with your hair in pigtails. Daddy holding the reins, smiling up at his little girl. Very *Town and Country*."

He brings the large pot to the table, pours them both more wine, and lights the candles. "Come on, sit down and tell me what a great cook I am."

The paella is okay, though the rice is mushy and the chicken bloody around the bones, but all the same Nona swears she has never tasted better. She eats and smiles and says what Fitz wants to hear, but when Fitz clears the table she has to go to the bathroom and bring up the undigested meal into the toilet bowl.

"To us were his exact words."

Two nights prior to Eve's hysterectomy the women have not quite a celebratory dinner (what's there to rejoice in?) but a meal to mark the upcoming "event." Nona and Cassie are closing ranks around Eve, circling the wagon train, lighting bonfires. They agreed beforehand that some solid statement is necessary besides the flowers they will bring to the hospital, the magazines and humorous greeting cards. So Cassie whips together Eve's favorite meal, which surprisingly isn't anything *nouvelle* or chic, but leg of lamb, Caesar salad, chocolate cream pie with a graham cracker crust. The condemned woman's last real feed before the intravenous bottle, Eve says jokingly, but the good-will gesture consoles her.

"Only why do women always think they should feed people in stressful situations or crises?" she asks at Cassie's table. She'd rather talk about herself and the impending operation than hear about Fitz and this ominous *us*. All Nona's past experiences at coupling, at making an us with a man have taken her down the garden path. Right now Eve wants to stop worrying—at least for a while—over whether Nona will get shattered. Which has to happen.

Eve has forgotten how she told Nona to be grateful for Fitz, what a jewel he is after that swine Alan.

"Shut up and eat your salad," Cassie says, eyeing Nona's slender fingers making incantatory motions over the lettuce and darting in on the croutons. Nona has few food passions, but garlicky, oil-soaked croutons are one of them. Cassie recalls past Caesar salads that Nona denuded.

Nona says, "I'm in love." Cassie slaps her hand and Nona sits back, chin up, regal.

"Pleased with ourselves, aren't we?" Eve says.

Cassie frowns. "You're always in love."

"This time it's the real thing. Crisscross my heart!" Nona swears with childish intensity, marking her sweater with polished nails. She is urgent to have the women accept her declaration as the truest of true statements.

Eve groans, "Give me a break!"

"You have to get to know Fitz."

Eve has a proprietary interest in Nona, regarding her as a little sister. She admits that she cares as much for her as for Louise or JoAnne—if not more than for those distant, alien blood siblings with whom she has a history. It's the ones we choose that count, not those people we're saddled with. But she lacks any interest in getting to be chums with Fitz, for, if history draws blueprints for the future, Eve expects to come out of the hospital and find Nona smitten with a different man altogether, to have her raise a shoulder and curl a lip at Fitz, as she now does at Alan. When Eve climbs to her feet again, Fitz will probably be swallowed by a black hole in Nona's memory.

"Three weeks at home," Eve reminds them, returning to her own concerns. Anticipation, a certain fear—she admits it—makes her circle back to the operation. She dwells on post-op pain, sees her body as bent as a paper clip as she shuffles in an old womanish two-step.

"It's not like that at all," Cassie counsels her, but Eve is remembering her mother so long before.

One morning when Eve was eight, her mother casually over breakfast announced she'd be away a few weeks. Out of sorts, resting up, was what she said, echoed by her sister Daisy—a smaller, looser version of their mother—who came to stay. From their father they got worried looks and silence.

Each night after dinner their father went off in his Sunday suit. Old Spice masked any lingering smell of paint or turpentine. He had scrubbed his hands to the raw pinkness of a baby pig, and dug out the flecks of paint from under his nails. His hair was slicked to his scalp and he moved with a serious weightiness, as though he had lead in his shoes. He carried off their drawings and cut flowers from the garden, paper hearts, a box of candy, and promised that one time soon when he drove off to the hospital, their mother would come home with him.

When at last she did return she was bent over, a stoop-shouldered stranger, dragging along like the hound hit by a car Eve had seen the previous summer. Louise cried and hid under the dining room table.

Aunt Daisy cautioned them to be quiet. "You kids have got to help out. No bothering your mother."

Eve carried up her tea every morning, though her mother asked for coffee. Tea's best, Aunt Daisy said. JoAnne read her the headlines in the afternoon paper, showing off. Louise was a baby who curled next to her, on top of the spread, sucking a thumb.

When she walked, Eve's mother took slow, faltering steps, a hand laid protectively over her belly. Her smile tightened in a crescent moon. She was sick, Eve thought, forever.

It can't have been just a plain hysterectomy, if Eve's remembering correctly, if there's no distortion in a child's memory, but she won't phone New Hampshire to ask. She hesitates to tell anybody in the family she's suffering, not tough Eve, down for the count.

"Did you call the agency?" Cassie is asking.

"What agency?" Nona dives after the last crouton, licking her fingers. She has a little cat tongue, red and pointy. Cassie, who before Jake never thought of other people's sexual moments, who is embarrassed by the idea of anyone naked in bed, heaving, stifling mewish cries, groaning in pleasure, thinks that men must love Nona when they have her undressed. Nona manages to be both slender and voluptuous at the same time, like one of Raphael's madonnas.

"For a home attendant," Cassie explains briskly, blushing at her imagination's stripping Nona to the buff.

Nona's eyebrows triangle. "I thought we were going to take care of you."

"How can you take care of me? You both work all day." Being a victim and not in control sends Eve's voice up. "And you"—she pokes at Nona—"have this Fitz love of your life, these moon/June stars in your eyes, to keep happy! And let's not overlook Cassie's Jake!" Eve laughs but she is only half kidding.

Cassie's and Nona's worried glances cross. This won't be easy, they both think.

Nona fears an argument and hastily changes the subject. "How is Jake?" she asks Cassie. "When do we meet him?"

"Thanksgiving," Cassie replies, only momentarily sidetracked. "Eve, one of us will stop in every day."

"Sure we will!" Nona agrees.

"But you should call the agency. For the first week you're home it's not a terrible idea to have somebody around. You're not going to feel so wonderful."

"I'll feel like shit. If I don't die, of course."

Cassie yells, "You're not going to die!"

Nona's napkin flies to her mouth. She *knows* Eve can go under and never surface, but it's nothing to talk about. It's bad luck to bring the possibility of Eve's dying into the open.

Eve subsides, sobered by the appalling truth of what she has thrown out to frighten her friends, to twist their arms into accepting the awfulness of the operation. They've been too casual about her insides being ripped out, her *femaleness* uprooted.

"Of course I can die. People do, from a reaction to the anesthesia. My heart can just stop—"

Cassie interrupts: "Not likely."

"What about a hemorrhage?"

"What about a lot of things?"

"Eve, stop looking at the negatives."

Cassie and Nona both talk to her, in tandem, together, their words lapping over each other. All of which Eve listens to but doesn't hear. Cleft in half, as if there are two selves under one skin, ever since the afternoon with William, she is unbalanced by her hormones. There are moments when Eve's not precisely in her right mind, but outside it, winging about like a separate entity, like the ghost of Abramson's wife. She is ectoplasm floating.

Then she weeps, crying at the oddest times, hysterical for no apparent reason, as in the park. How humiliating to frighten little children.

Eve bursts out, "Neither of you would be alone. You'd have a warm body on the premises." To her own ears her voice sounds amplified. Another symptom of rampaging cells?

Nona breathes in and does her cheerleader's best to reassure Eve. "You're not alone. We're there for you. We are *committed*."

"And there is Johnny," Cassie points out.

Nona agrees. "He's going to be around—wait and see if he won't."

Eve almost confesses that as far as Johnny knows, she is in the prime of health. But they'll leap on her, harping that she has to tell Johnny this very minute, call him right up on the phone. Eve can just hear Nona: *Sharing is the essence of any decent relationship*.

Cassie slices the lamb, which falls away from the knife silky pink and tender. She wishes they'd stop talking about Eve's hysterectomy, even if that's the reason for the best china and silver, the expensive Pouilly Fuissé, and leave Nona's Fitz alone also. She has an inordinate desire for silence, just the food in her mouth and Beethoven on the stereo. She wants only to savor her sensations: taste, sound, to enjoy the artful arrangement of lamb and carrots and new potatoes on the white plates.

For if Cassie fails to concentrate on the moment, up pops April's husband, a jack-in-the-box. Up comes April, too, draggy-haired, gape-mouthed, a hundred and twenty years old after defending herself and the children. April might as well have killed her own youth.

Cassie hands around the plates and pushes April back into the darkness with a shudder.

And Nona says, "Men are peculiar about sickness. Some are truly Florence Nightingale, bringing you peppermint tea and fluffing the pillows, but most of them get squeamish. Only I just know Johnny will be one of the great ones."

Eve slaps the table, rattling the silverware. "And how do you know? You've said what, ten words to him? But because he wears pants with a fly he's wonderful. Wonderful, wonderful. Fitz is wonderful. Alan was wonderful. I am going to wash that word out of your mouth with Lysol." Nona's eyes brim with easy tears, and immediately Eve's conscience is pricked. "Damn it, Nonnie, I'm sorry. You mean well. Just, please, stop thinking the best of the whole world. That's how you get hurt. You have no discrimination. If someone smiles at you, he's your friend for life."

"You make me sound like a fool."

"What Eve means is that you don't look at people squarely. You never make judgments and you forgive everyone," Cassie says, as if Eve needs a translator.

"There's nothing wrong with Fitz. Why do you think there is?" Eve says, "History."

"I know him, you don't, and he's—" She stops, *wonderful* on her tongue.

Eve flushes with triumph. "See? That's what we're talking about. Come on, swear you won't say that word for a week." She grabs Nona's wrist.

"Let's eat. The food's getting cold," Cassie says.

It might be Eve's favorite dinner, but she picks at it. Nothing tastes right anymore. Jena says she's stressed out and has prescribed vitamins. As if pills will do her any good. She finishes her wine and pours another glass to the brim. No alcohol, that's Jena's advice, too, along with fresh fruits and vegetables, whole grains, and plenty of sleep.

"I want this over with," Eve says, staring at the meat, heaviness under her breastbone. All of a sudden she's sickened at the thought of eating flesh. Johnny's diatribes, which she lets sail over her head, must have dropped a seed or two.

"It will all take place quicker than you think," Cassie sympathizes.

"To be on the other side . . ."

"The other side of what?" Cassie is worried that Eve is only poking at her dinner.

"Life. Age. Old, without possibilities." Eve wrinkles up, depression layering years on her face.

Nona, frightened by this long look into the future, rushes into eating. She compliments the lamb, the mint jelly. Cassie passes Eve the French bread. They're quiet until Nona exclaims, "My

God, I forgot to tell you. I had this terrible dream about your murder—I mean the one you found. I don't remember the details but I woke up shaking."

"It wasn't murder," Cassie defends April.

"The husband's dead, which comes to the same thing," Eve says with a shrug. Neither the dead man nor his killer have any relevance for her. Since her accident she drifts, at a remove from the world around her, from what isn't connected to her own body.

But the killings stimulate Nona, though she will deny it. Prime-time television in real life. She coaxes the story out of Cassie several times, until she can faithfully describe "the crime scene" to Fitz, and how the police arrived, questioning Cassie for over an hour.

"Fitz thinks that you were heroic to even go into that apartment, with the door unlocked and nobody answering."

"Why? I couldn't know he was dead."

"Well, April had stabbed him, and she might have been crazy enough to hurt you."

"Temporary insanity," Eve says, waiting for Cassie to protect April with *She wasn't responsible*.

Cassie is less willing to talk about April and the dead husband than she is Eve's hysterectomy, and launches into promises, when up to now she has acted prudently. The facts, truth unembellished, is a practice of Magdalene, and Cassie adheres to the principle of a woman's need to know. It is her body, after all, and not a vehicle, with a physician the mechanic. She should be informed, told whatever there is to tell. Cassie remembers old Dr. Ormond from Landry with his "hmmms" and "ahs" and his "Don't worry." With a mane of white hair and an imperial Roman profile, he was a Caesar Augustus of medicine who lulled patients from the cradle to the grave as ignorant as sows and twice as sleepy. That isn't Cassie's style, nor that of the other doctors at the clinic, but her love for Eve makes her want to fabricate, to minimize the pain, the ups and downs of recovery, the sudden jolt to her system.

"And think of the plus side," Nona chimes in. "No periods. Won't that be a relief." Though not to Nona, it is apparent from the glare of terror in her eyes. No uterus, no ovaries, no precious babies, husband at the breakfast table, lovely picture-postcard home, Christmas tree, all the appurtenances that decorate her daydreams. No matter what cheery tone Nona sings, if Eve's impending loss were her own she would die. Curl up her toes and sprout daisies. Cassie sees that and she's sure Eve can, too, but Eve allows Nona to flow on like a river.

"I'm forty-five," Eve says, pushing her plate aside. "A nowhere age, so much time behind but enough in front. Enough to be happy in, anyway. If I am going to be happy again."

"I can't stand this!" Cassie cries.

"Cassie!" Nona is shocked, since Cassie ordinarily sympathizes.

"You make me feel guilty, Eve, because I am happy now and healthy."

"Just give Cassie a man." There is resentment in Eve's voice, and something more, an edge. She feels, ridiculously, betrayed.

Cassie, struggling with love, shamelessly inept, wishes she had kept her usual quiet. Now she is forced to say, "Happiness doesn't depend on having a man in your life—"

"Not just any man, Cassie!" Nona chides her.

"Naturally not just any man."

"But you certainly are in an up mode since Jake arrived to mow the lawn," Eve points out.

From childhood Cassie's mother had drilled her, though nicely, in a soft, ladylike fashion, to do something, to go out in the world and earn her own living. Naturally a woman marries, has children, but, her mother advised, she has a skill, a way of taking care of herself. Where, Cassie wonders for the thousandth time, did her mother even get the idea? Not because her father was an ogre, or tight with a dollar.

If her mother hadn't encouraged her, would she be back in Ohio canning peaches and running rummage sales for the Eastern Star? Would she be working part time, for Christmas Club money, at the telephone company?

Marriage, family, profession, not just a job. In her mother's lexicon there was no *divorce*, nor cooling your heels waiting for the *right man*.

"The right man." Cassie wrinkles her nose. "Women get so fixated on this creature who appears, if at all, in fairy tales."

Eve looks at Nona. "Did we bring up the subject of Prince Charming? I mean, Mr. Right?" Nona shakes her head.

Cassie cries, "Oh, stop! Jake's just . . . just a guy! And we have a

good time together. I like him. I'm happy when I'm with him."
Cassie feels silly defending herself.

"I can't believe what I'm hearing. *Happiness* and *man* in the
same sentence from Dr. Morgan."

"Oh, shut up, Eve. Don't make such a big deal out of a couple
of statements. I'm just telling you both how I feel. I'm not starting
a new religion."

"Just preaching the old one, the one Nona and I have been
telling you about for years. The having-a-man faith, oh, Jesus save
us. Down on the knees, thank the Lord, confess!" Nona rocks with
laughter as Eve pounds the table and singsongs, "Better to be with
somebody than alone, I tell you that, oh, my faithful communi-
cants! Hear me and you shall be saved!"

Cassie won't laugh. If the joke's on her she won't accept it. "This
isn't a matter of dating a man with a nice car to take me out for
dinner. We aren't talking about a man like that. I care about Jake."

Eve sobers and retorts angrily, "From what you said you probably pick up the check more times than he does. And I bet you he's
not driving a BMW."

Nona is agitated. Her nerves spark and misfire with their quar-
reling. She can't stand for the women to argue, even a little bit,
even over silly things such as their different philosophies of life. If
there's no harmony with us, then where will there be? She gives
enormous weight to the three of them holding tightly together.

"I'm not an idiot," Cassie is saying.

"Please, let's not fight," Nona cries. "What if Eve has cancer?"

"*What?*" Both women stare at her.

"What are you talking about?"

"Who said I had cancer? Cass, are you hiding from me?"

"Of course not. Magdalene policy is to tell the patient everything—you know that."

"I just meant"—Nona is scrambling to explain—"that we
shouldn't argue in case Eve— Oh, God!" She stops. It's not the
first time that Nona, meaning well, has made things worse. Her
knack, opposite to her intent, is for confusion.

"What about forgetting to mention a detail or two?"

"That's the same thing, Eve. You don't have cancer as far as we
know. As far as any of the tests indicate."

"But I could?"

The barometric pressure drops in the room. A round, doll-faced Early American child hanging over the sideboard smiles enigmatically.

Nona just about screams, "Of course you couldn't. Wash that thought out of your mind!" Carelessly having carried them to this point, Nona tries to erase the indelible, to white out *cancer* before it actually flourishes.

"Could I, Cassie?"

"Anybody can unknowingly have cancer. It's simply a condition of normal cells suddenly proliferating, going out of control."

"Thank you, I know very well what cancer is," Eve says. "And you haven't answered my question. You back around it, over it, under it, but come on, Cass, stop on the dime."

Cassie throws her head back, staring up at the ceiling. "Of course you could have some malignancy." She lets the statement drift upward. "It's unlikely, very unlikely—so unlikely it's not even a factor. Or much of one. But it's a possibility because it's always a possibility. There, are you satisfied?" Cassie is furious at Eve for having pushed her to this admission.

Having yanked the truth out of Cassie like an abscessed tooth, Eve wishes Cassie had lied. What is this sudden obsession she has with the truth? Eve would give anything if Nona hadn't brought up *cancer* like vomit.

So would Nona. There is an ugliness in the room now, not only the word, the disease, the "could be," but anger and unfriendliness. Tears climbing up her throat, she leaps from her chair. "I have to go. Fitz will probably call. Maybe come over. I can't let him just hang. You know. Men get fidgety."

"Cassie doesn't know anything about that—the delicacy a woman needs, the skills—but she's learning, aren't you, darling?" Eve says.

Cassie is stony-faced, watching Nona's last-minute flutters, lifting her cold cheek for a butterfly kiss.

"You have no right to deride me the way you do," Cassie says when the door closes.

Eve realizes she has crumbled a whole chunk of bread. "I can't sit here with you another minute," she says.

"Because you want the truth and when I give it to you it's nastiness time."

"I suppose so," Eve admits. Then, "Oh, Cass, you're just too *good*."

"What a lot of rot!" Cassie pours the last of the wine.

"You cooked this fantastic dinner that we've barely touched."

"There's still pie."

"I can't, honestly. I'm sorry." What a mess she's made of this evening, Eve thinks. She should try and reclaim at least something, stay, have pie and coffee, but that's impossible. A buzz saw is going off in her head and in another moment or two she will scream so loudly all the windows will shoot up.

"Stay and we'll have espresso."

"Not tonight."

Cassie doesn't argue. She sits quietly, watching Eve collect her things, put on her leather jacket, and zip up. Only at the last minute, when Eve thinks Cassie means to let her leave without another word, does she get up. She follows Eve to the door and gives her a hug. "I'm sorry," Cassie whispers.

Eve shrugs. "I don't know for what."

21

Nona is in love. Her bones are as light as air. Her breath seems torn right from her lungs. She hums as she moves in graceful, winding dance steps until Lorraine admonishes her to be quiet. Lorraine complains that Nona is distracting. She gives her a headache.

Of course Lorraine realizes Nona's in love; everybody does. Nona can't keep still and sees no need to. Thank you, she says to thin air in the morning, before Fitz shows up at her apartment, when she hangs up the phone. Thank you to nobody, perhaps to God.

"If you're so in love how come the two of you aren't living together? Why do you see him only a couple of nights in the week?" Lorraine asks. Spite sets her thin nose quivering. She has a cold, which prods her to be even nastier.

Lorraine implies something off-kilter, *a situation*. Nona hears her but ignores the criticism. She'll have no clouds in her blue sky, no auspicious fingerprints on her crystal happiness.

Of course Nona wonders what Fitz does with the rest of his time.

Fitz calls her Nonnie, just as Adam did, and her heart goes out to him when he discusses putting together a deal. He has things brewing, things on various burners. It's all, according to Fitz, a matter of wait and see, and then again *mucho* complicated.

Nona thinks of movies, of a series for television. This is Hollywood, after all, where the waiters are actors, and girls scooping Häagen-Dazs daydream of discovery. Gas station attendants have scripts, as do doctors and dentists. Every accountant searches for investors in low-budget films and housewives sit over morning coffee thinking up ideas for another *I Love Lucy*.

"He's working on several projects in various stages of development," Nona confides to Eve, having extrapolated "projects" and "stages" and "development" from what she's imagined Fitz has said.

Nona is at the hospital on her lunch hour. The operation is a day old and Eve lies high up on a white bed in a white room, colorless as the rough sheets on which her hands—the nails stripped of their bright-red polish—scrabble like field mice. Her hair has lost its body and droops in limp strands about her pale face. She seems to have dwindled to half the size she is when standing up and, in impeccably tailored confidence, selling houses. Substance has been sliced away from her along with the tumor and the organs around which it wound like a pulpy tropical fruit.

"Water, please." Eve's voice crinkles like tissue paper.

Nona fills a glass and hands it to her with an elbowed plastic straw. "I love straws," she says, watching Eve drink. "You use straws on good times, picnics, the movies, at the beach."

Eve is not having a good time. But she isn't having as bad a time as she had anticipated before surgery. The pain fails to live up to its advance notices. And since it's possible to regulate the narcotic dripping through the intravenous, Eve, while not taking advantage, stays in control. She allows the pain to build up, like a masonry wall, until she can barely see over the top, until there's no hope of swinging a leg up, gaining leverage, and falling free on the far side. Only then does she press the button, release the flow, deep-breathe and relax, having earned the high float, the stoned, muzzy drift that obliterates the hurting.

Eve's eyes are cloudy. She has sedated herself only a few minutes before Nona arrives, just long enough to be carried from the pain, the Queen of Sheba on a litter. She doesn't care what Nona talks about, though the sound of her voice is nice, a low buzzing of summer insects outside the screen.

To Nona, Eve appears only marginally improved from the evening before. She still resembles a woman who's been violated.

Some symptoms have consequences, Nona is reminded. Not all dark-of-the-night aches and pains leave at dawn. It has been weeks since she's seen Dr. Rubin and maybe Eve's operation is an omen and she should stop in for a physical.

While Eve drops off to sleep, Nona worries about her own health and inventories her body, probing all the unseen innards, testing, calling out to them like a pilot in space—*Are you okay?*—until she leaps up and reshuffles the arrangement of phone, tissue box, water glass, and carafe on Eve's bedside table.

Eve jerks awake suddenly and Nona asks, "Has Cassie been in today?"

"Yesterday . . . in the afternoon."

Nona knows for a fact that the previous day Cassie didn't show up at the hospital until six, but she won't refute Eve's scrambled sense of time. "Well, she'll come later. Don't worry."

"Hmmm." Eve lacks any interest in Cassie. In orbit on Demerol, she can't grab a firm hold on any subject. Images tend to peel away, a nose here, an ear, misplaced as in a Picasso. Her inner vision is piecemeal. There are more loose fragments than in a junkyard. But that doesn't upset her. Sailing as she is, death would seem only another way station in space.

Her mother, whom Eve can't remember informing but must have, calls from New Hampshire and says the Baptists are praying for Eve, that *if the worst happens there's another side, across the river where . . .*

Abramson waits.

Of course he does. There are shades that don't evaporate, that swing free—Abramson's wife for example—electrical impulses, or molecules retaining the shape of the substance when the body ceases to exist. There is *something*. Eve, drugged, needs no convincing. Once sober, on her feet, and selling a two-million-dollar house in Beverly Hills, she will—perfectly made-up and clunking heavy gold jewelry—laugh at the hospital reveries. But that's then; this is now, and Eve's not laughing. She's thinking of dying, or swimming out with the salty tide, just letting go.

She opens her clenched fist and spreads her fingers on the sheet.

Nona assumes Eve wants to hold her hand and obliges, squeezing. What Eve wants, however, is to be gone, back to the dream so vivid she confused sleep with waking, unreality with the hard-edged world of doors, desks, chairs, windows.

The dream is simple as a Chinese carved puzzle when the neat wood pieces fit snugly together.

Eve trails down a long road winding through a flat brown landscape. There are smooth rolling hills like the folds of a quilt, land without trees or rocks. No jagged wounds spoil the dream's geometry.

From a distance the hills appear soft as breasts. Newly fallen dust lies in a mossy ground cover and Abramson, flapping along in worn-down carpet slippers, leaves no footprints.

It is Abramson dead, but other than being pared down, thin and bonier inside his favorite flannel shirt and rumpled cords and as gray as the land, gray as ash, he is the same man.

Be careful of getting what you want, Abramson says.

Does she want to be dead? To be with Abramson means—

"Oh, Eve, honey!" her mother cries all that long way gone to New Hampshire.

—crossing over.

They stop in the road within a foot of each other. Nothing between them, nothing to ford, not a stream, a street, a concrete bridge. Eve has only to turn and walk the same way Abramson goes, slipping and slapping.

But she doesn't, didn't. She thinks she chose not to die—which is nonsense, she repeats over and over in a litany, before the pain climbs too high to fight, before the junk drops a net over her, taming the beast.

It was only a dream. . . .

Forget how sharp Abramson's face is, the pores on his misshapen nose, the long, stray hairs, the red routings in the whites of his eyes, Eve thinks she is telling Nona, but the conversation, like the meeting with her lost husband, happens only in ether.

Nona, unaware that she is engaged with Eve in a dialogue, listens to the hospital music, all the beeps and buzzes, a funereal voice on the P.A. system paging doctors, the clatter of food carts, the soft shoe-tapping of aides, the hum of the library wagon. Nona's hands are clammy. She imagines herself a patient, flat in bed, immobile, minus volition. Her legs, arms, nose have tubes in them.

Coming to see Eve makes Nona nervous, but she won't leave yet. She arranges the sprigs of baby orchids and irises she's brought in a green glass vase an aide has found for her. She putters about the broad window ledge, positioning the calla lilies, the roses, the bunch of yellow daisies in a straw hat from Johnny—told only the night before the operation—the balloon with a Garfield grinning GET WELL!, Titus Reynolds's small clutch of violets that fit perfectly in a toothglass. Eve has enough flowers for a wake and she's been in the hospital less than forty-eight hours. They'll need a truck to get her home. Who will? Nona supposes she and Cassie can use Cassie's station wagon. They'll come together. Single women, women without men, rely on one another. Not that she's exactly unattached, not with Fitz in her life, nor is Cassie either.

Poor Eve.

Nona smooths out the coverlet upon which the restless fingers now lie still and smiles at an Eve whose eyes are shut in sleep. At last she can leave. She hears Fitz's voice on her answering machine, sees him leaning outside her door, and can't wait, though he shrugged that tonight he'd be tied up with business. Still, plans are subject to change, and meetings sometimes end early.

Oh, how Nona loves to have him in her bed, to sleep pushed up against his chest, the mat of hair cushioning her cheek. He is a great warm animal sharing heat, and when he's not there on the other pillow Nona sleeps in a sea, miles from shore. The nights without Fitz last forever. How easily she's grown adjusted to that other body, that man showing up, calling, arriving for dinner with a bottle of wine. That familiar face. He is sweetness to her, and though he hasn't said anything of a future, made no plans, promises, commitments, Nona thinks of their being attached, like Siamese twins at the hip, breastbone, forehead, until death.

She's learned—oh, yes, she has, finally—not to ask anything, not to hint about permanence. The Devil himself couldn't yank such words as *commit* and *forever* out of Nona's teeth. It is a fact of life, she's at last accepted, that the men ask the questions. *Will you?* is a man's province. So she waits for Fitz, quiet as a mouse. And happy. Of course she is.

Beth Levinson comes around and plops spreading her hips on Cassie's back steps, clutching a gin and tonic, getting mellow while her turkey roasts.

Cassie's not in the best of moods, since she'll be celebrating

Thanksgiving on Saturday rather than today. Tonight she'll bring a pasta casserole over to Eve's for dinner, because this year Tracy's old grandmother flew in from Salt Lake and Doug asked, with that little-boy lilt Cassie once found so attractive but which now grates, if he could have Mandy for the holiday.

Cassie told Doug she had already made plans, and besides, didn't it depend on what Mandy wanted? Mandy wasn't a little girl whom they could push around in a stroller. Mandy had definite opinions. And Doug replied that they should ask her. He hinted that Mandy would know what was fair, that she spent every holiday except the Fourth of July with Cassie, so one Thanksgiving wasn't such a sacrifice.

Tasting the sourness of temper on her tongue, and hating how Doug was trying to sweet-talk her, Cassie came within a hair of saying out loud what she was thinking. Damn you to hell and Tracy and her old grandmother!

Cassie considered not asking Mandy at all, but Doug must have called up to Portland immediately, because within the hour Mandy was on the phone announcing that she was going to Daddy's for Thanksgiving. She sounded enthusiastic, as if Tracy would order in from the local pizza joint, or maybe pick up McDonald's.

Beth knows all this and has campaigned—still does—for Cassie and Jake to sit down and have turkey with them. But the casserole meal with Eve is already planned, and Jake is dropping in on Yang for a Vietnamese version of thank you, God. Beth, strong-willed, hates to compromise, but she finally does and agrees that she and Al will join the late celebration on Saturday.

"You can still change your mind," Beth says, wanting the company to set between her and Al at the long table, since Tony has gone off, up the coast. Also, they like Jake, whom they have formally entertained at a Sunday dinner. Jake wore a white shirt, no tie, and a corduroy blazer, and Beth oohed. She whispered in the kitchen to Cassie that Cassie had snared a live one.

Tony happened to be momentarily in residence that week, between jobs, apartments, girlfriends. Jake and Tony hit it off, old friends in minutes, two houses afire, recognizing something familiar in each other. *In sync from a previous karma* was Beth's reaction as the two men talked music, clinked bottles of Corona, and churned up some laughter that eventually included the others.

Such good humor set Al purring, curled in his chair as happy as an old fireside tabby.

The Levinsons have decided that Jake will be around for the duration, which equates in Beth's mind with marriage.

Cassie protests, "People live together eons these days without benefit of—"

"I know, clergy." Beth thrusts out a narrow bottom lip when she drinks. Her eyelids flutter. She enjoys the gin a bit too much, savors it earlier in the day than she should.

"We don't have to get married."

"But are you? That's what I want to know, not can you *not* get married. You can *not* be Hindu, too, if it comes to that."

"Oh, who can tell!" Cassie cries, agitated, still not easy with Jake's return. She hates to confront the possibility that he will disappear again, and even when she is warm in his arms, a tight little voice in her head murmurs: What if the day comes when you don't want to keep him? Since Doug's departure Cassie has learned it is okay if she evaluates, if she reviews a relationship and stops being so accommodating. She can find fault, slide into unhappiness, and make a break. Of course, up until Jake arrived in her life, Cassie hadn't a man on whom to practice what she considers valuable lessons. Now, though involved nonstop with Jake, from time to time airborne and out of control, in love, heady with passion, silly as a schoolgirl, there is still a niggling discomfort. Jake is prickly and she must be careful. He reminds her of a wool sweater that itches and leaves a faint rash on her skin.

"He hasn't asked you, that's what it is," Beth says, having a firm hold on the subject of marriage and reluctant to let go. "You've got to finagle him into it. That's all." She rattles the ice cubes like dice in the glass.

"That's all!" Cassie is indignant. "What if I don't want to?"

"What, finagle him or have him ask you?"

Cassie shifts on the step, feeling mean enough to tell her forever-married friend and neighbor: Not every woman drools for a *Mrs.* in front of her name. But Beth has drunk just the right amount to remember Cassie's crying through lost midnights—and to say so.

Beth will say anything. There's no governor on her tongue, Al more than once points out. She has hoisted even him, often, on the horned truth of her comments.

306

The slope of the step or maybe Beth's condition—a previous gin and tonic while rolling out the pie crust?—sets her stumbling as she stands. Cassie grabs for her hand; then she's up also.

It seems for a minute as if Beth will follow her into the kitchen. Upstairs, too, through open doorways, into the shower? Beth can stick like tape on paper, and Cassie isn't in the mood for further grilling about Jake.

Holding the screen door, Cassie is suddenly envious of Beth because Al isn't an alien to her, or vice versa. Blindfolded they could find one another in the dark. She will never have that togetherness with Jake and knows it.

"Got to go. Eve will be starving."

Beth rubs the moist glass against her flushed cheek. "If you won't change your mind . . . ? We could drive over and scoop up Eve."

"Can't do, Beth." Cassie feels as though she is apologizing because Beth seems so unhappy.

Which she never was, Cassie explains to Eve.

"You always used to say that Beth Levinson was too happy. She oozed."

"I never did. Not 'too happy.' I don't think anybody can be so euphoric that it's somehow wrong, not unless they're stoned on drugs."

"What about Nona?" Eve asks. "She just flies away like a helium balloon someone's taken the string off of."

"That's not happiness."

They have finished dinner and Eve is stretched out on the couch. Cassie drapes an afghan across Eve's legs. "Well, I don't know about happy," Eve says, "but I'm pleased, very." As she should be, since Jena pronounces her a hundred percent and Cassie concurs. The pulpy mass proved to be fibrous tissue. No maniacal cells are, this moment, eating Eve alive.

Eve emits a long sigh and closes her eyes. The light is always too bright now. Like a mole she ferries her reality through the dark. She slips to the edge of sleep, then shakes herself awake and asks Cassie to repeat whatever she's just said.

"Only that I think you're looking pretty good."

"Oh, sure. I'm a real beauty queen these days," Eve scoffs. If anybody but Cassie complimented her on her looks now, since the operation, she'd suspect their sincerity, for she feels as attractive as an old sock.

"True," Cassie insists.

"What about these roots?" She fluffs her short-cropped hair.

"Forget your roots. Every female has roots."

Eve grins. "What would you say if I didn't bother from now on? And let it all go gray, I mean."

"Why not? Very becoming with your coloring, your eyes." But Cassie is surprised. For Eve to give in to a visible sign of age is out of character.

Cassie stretches, pats her hair, and reaches for her shoulder bag, preparing to go. It's only nine-thirty and Eve pre-hysterectomy would have asked her to stay on, have another drink, coffee, a game of backgammon. That Eve of "before" hated empty space, but this Eve is different. As if one woman was rolled into the O.R., into the glare of lights, and another, a softer, easier woman, was brought out. Such an idea is unscientific, utterly ridiculous, but as Cassie kisses Eve's cheek she almost asks her *Who are you?*

There's no need for Eve to see her to the door. Cassie can find her own way out. Eve won't argue. And Cassie, with a last glance flung over her shoulder, thinks maybe she should stay longer. But then, she really should go.

Why is it she never knows her own mind anymore?

She has arranged her time, slicing down the minutes, so as to miss Doug. Mandy will already be home, upstairs, and Jake will arrive a minute after. That's the way Cassie schedules it in her head, but of course it works out totally differently. For one, she and Doug pull up almost at the same moment, the lights of his BMW blinding her when she comes out of the garage. She is stripped naked in the glare, every bulge exposed, and can just hear Tracy snickering. But Doug has brought Mandy home alone.

They had a *tiff*, Mandy, Miss Pleased, tells Cassie later. She's decided this visit that her teeny-bopper stepmother is a woozy— whatever that means.

Doug, all bonhomie, gets out of the car, turning off the engine as if he has intentions. Mandy comes around the other side and wedges in between her parents. For a brief second they are that old trinity and Mandy nudges a hip at her mother, rubs an arm against her father. Cassie half expects her to say *Let's make a sandwich*.

"Hello, sweetheart." Cassie kisses Mandy's cheek, tugs her ever so gently closer to her and away from Doug.

"We had a great day. What about you?" Doug asks with the curl to the corners of his mouth that he passes off as a smile with strangers.

Cassie wonders if Mandy has mentioned Jake. Mom's got a boyfriend. Will Doug stiffen? Reply *God damn*? Or *It's about time*? *What's he like*?

Surely Doug won't tell Mandy that *he'll do your mother good*. She's too uptight. *Can't you ever relax, Cass? Take things easy. Lie back. . . .*

In the dark driveway Cassie's memories make her edgy. She tries to hunch her shoulders against the past and concentrate on all the slapdash phrases Doug might throw around, the criticisms. Certainly not: *Gee, I'm pleased. Good for her. Hope she's happy.* She can't imagine Doug wishing her well when he bent her so far backward doing her harm.

He did her in with a younger woman, and how many others were there before Tracy? Ones who didn't want to marry Doug, or couldn't seduce him into marrying them? Was she always sharing this man, whose wrinkles are pronounced in the updraft of harsh light?

"Nothing like a good roast turkey." Doug is chatty, determined to stand around and swap small talk, though so far the talk is all his.

Jake's car, parked farther up the street, parallels the curb. Cassie glances toward the house, searching for him behind the muzzy film of front window curtains, but he is invisible. Has Doug any idea another man is inside the house they bought together, where they lived, painted the kitchen themselves, stripped the old banister, worked flower-patterned paper from the walls? Has he any feelings for the house, any memories? Or is the house, like her, disposable?

Alternatively, is Jake looking through a slit between the curtains at them?

"Quite a girl we've got here. I've been hearing all about school. Wow!"

"Wow what?" Cassie asks. Doug sounds like an insurance sales-man.

"She's fabulous."

"Oh, Daddy!" Mandy groans. It can be worse. Doug is capable of saying, for fabulous, *fabulosa!*

The year Mandy turned eight Cassie realized she had only one child when she had fantasized a houseful, and proposed to Doug that they have another. *Proposed* is wrong. More subtly, she propositioned her then husband. She had her hair done, cut, feathered—as they described it in the salon—wore pearl polish on her nails, bought a long silk thing that draped over the too-rounded parts of her.

She set out to seduce her husband with candlelight, a good wine, soft music—Sinatra, Tony Bennett on the stereo. "My God!" he yelped. "Where did you unearth that hoary stuff?"

"Dance with me," she said and held out her arms.

Of course she cooked him up a prize Julia Child accomplishment.

Doug blew out the candles, turned up the lights, ate. "Like to see what's on the plate," he said.

Cassie brought the cognac in crystal on a silver tray to the living room.

"You're up to something," he accused her, not being in the least a stupid man. He scratched his ear and waited for her to ask. A week in Maui? Or was she crying uncle on her Mustang and petitioning for a Mercedes, a BMW, maybe a Jag? A mink? No, not Cassie.

She wove patterns of deception on Doug because she knew if asked outright, *Do you want another child?* he'd bark, as he did when he figured out what the soft music and candlelight were all about: *No! Absolutely not!* One was enough. And wasn't he busting his balls to support an only daughter with braces, camp, private school, tennis lessons, ballet? (As if, Cassie would think years later, she didn't do her part.)

Besides, he attacked, he didn't need any more children to make him happy. For him the house couldn't be too quiet.

He countered Cassie's suggestion with the offer of a trip to Europe in the fall. Or maybe Rio next February, where he had a yen to go for Mardi Gras.

Cassie's seduction fizzled, and if she thought of dropping the pill down the toilet instead of her throat, she was too honorable for such a deception. So the sole child she has, they have, is the one standing by her shoulder, now an inch taller than Cassie, bearing a shadowy, furtive resemblance to her father. And she will only ever have half of her.

Cassie's resentment, which she has never expressed in a long, ear-splitting scream, gives her the gassy feeling of indigestion. She would have been better off if just once she had kicked Doug, punched him in the mouth, or left long bloody scratches down his cheeks. But Cassie, sly as a teenager, harmed only herself. She took to biting her nails, nipping at the corners, tearing the index finger on her left hand to the quick until it bled. She chewed away, and Jena, repelled, ordered her to stop. If divorce so dislocated her, she needed a psychiatrist. Jena's disapproval frightened Cassie into letting her nails alone, but now a thumb is homing in toward her teeth.

Her bitterness increases. Doug is dressed in a white crewneck sweater tied jauntily around his shoulders, over a dark shirt unbuttoned beyond the level of discretion. He is a Ralph Lauren ad, a Calvin Klein model, a successful yachtsman selling single-malt whiskey in the slick pages of *GQ*. He is not the man to whom she has been attached since college.

How has he changed so rapidly? or is she just this moment noticing?

She searches for his eyes—surely *they're* the same—but they sink below an overhang of shadow.

How has he come to be this repository of stock phrases, talking to Mandy as though the three of them appear weekly on a television half-hour of good humor, chuckles, a tear or two, entitled *Divorce*?

Having gotten Mandy home he should be going back to Tracy, but his feet seem stuck to the driveway as she paints the air with puffs of conversation. There's a reason for his trying to edge Cassie up the walk into the house, as if for a glass of port, one of his after-dinner rituals. Some revelation is prodding him and he's going to tell her if she lets him. But Cassie pushes away from her old husband, who seems an impossible man to have ever belonged to her. He reaches arbitrarily across Mandy and catches hold of her arm.

"I thought we could have a cuppa, or what about a toast of good cheer? You still have any of that port my Aunt Tildy sent us from England?"

"No, I don't!" Cassie cries, pulling free. "That was years ago. It's long gone."

"Sorree!" He backs up a step. "I never knew you liked it so much."

Cassie veers to the left and circles around Doug on her way into the house. She is not going to explain that she poured the port down the kitchen sink. "I have to go. I'm busy."

"Going out again?"

"That's really none of your business." Cassie turns on him as though he's a snarling dog snapping too close to her heels. The light is behind him, though, and she can see nothing of his face. He is the featureless stranger of one's nightmare.

Imagine sitting down and having coffee or port as though they might discuss the situation in the Middle East. As if the divorce hadn't been acrimonious. *Why can't you and Mandy live in a condo? Tracy and I are. That house is a valuable piece of community property.* Which he now wants to enter, to sprawl around the kitchen, as if he hadn't struggled to snatch it out from under Cassie's feet, as if he won't pant hungrily for the proceeds at Mandy's twenty-first birthday when Cassie must sell.

It's three years since Doug dropped his *There's another woman*, and he hasn't spoken a decent word to her since. Now, with Jake waiting, probably watching TV in the den, he's decided this is the very moment he wants a social visit.

"I don't see any reason for us to be friends," Cassie states bluntly.

"That's uncalled-for!" Doug protests, sounding hurt, as if he hasn't any notion why she's angry with him.

"Good night, Doug. Mandy, I'll see you inside."

"Don't try and drag Mandy with you."

"Mandy can stay out here and have a loving father-and-daughter conversation until dawn, Doug." Cassie starts again for the steps.

"Wait, Cass, I've got to tell you something."

"Next time." What next time? It is months since she's seen

Doug, and this encounter is unwanted as a summer flu. "Call me," she adds. "You know the number."

"Cassie, you're a hard woman. You always were, always will be."

"Hard? *Me?*" she says to Jake, upstairs in the den with the latest issue of *Time*. Oh, no, she is the dawn, suds on a beer, the lightest dew on the grass. "I have a heart like a feather bed. If I had been hard he would never have gotten off with Miss Gidget. Hard women come out on top; they don't get tossed on the wind, gum wrappers, debris—"

"He's putting tacks on your chair." Jake laughs at her. "Exes do that. If they didn't we'd all still be married."

"Oh, I suppose so."

There's the slam of the kitchen door and the thump of Mandy's sneakers on the stairs. She gives Jake a sidelong cat look as she says, "You weren't very nice to Daddy. He tried to be friendly."

"He might be your father, Mandy, but he is still my ex-husband, remember, and he's got a reason for buddying up to me. He could have taken you to Swenson's and sat debating life issues over ice cream sodas. But to want to chitchat in *my* kitchen with *me*, he's got a purpose."

"He says the house is half his."

"Does he want to cart his half off to the Marina?"

"You're so suspicious, Mom." *But not suspicious enough*—is that what you're not saying? Cassie wonders as Mandy glances away from Jake, apparently at ease in an old swayback chair she intends to throw out one day.

Jake and Mandy, having met this weekend, unceremoniously and offhandedly on the stairs, clashed on impact. Both immovable, of course they can't forge an instant relationship. Time must pass before they trust each other, before Mandy understands no man will ever come thundering between her and her mother. No man will ever change what they have.

Stay and see the news with us. . . . Go to your room. . . . Cassie can't think what she wants Mandy to do. Jake goes back to his magazine and isn't any help.

Mandy plonks down on the day bed they use for company and tucks up her legs. "What are you doing tomorrow?"

"Get your feet off the furniture."

"It's just an old piece of junk," she complains, but complies.

"I'm working, of course. Why?"

"I thought maybe we could go shopping." Mandy, who hates to shop with Cassie, acts as though Jake were not in the room.

"Let's see what time I can get away."

"We could go at night. The stores are open late. And then we can have dinner. Or a movie. We haven't seen a movie together, Mom, since before the summer."

"Maybe."

"Why not?"

"Mandy, let's talk about this tomorrow. Okay?" Ants dance under Cassie's skin.

"If you don't want to, just say so."

"I never said I didn't want to."

"You sound like it." She uncoils and sits up primly. "I can tell when I'm not wanted."

"Who said you're not wanted?"

Mandy scowls at Jake, whose head stays firmly lowered over *Time*. "I think it's time for me to go to bed," she says.

I love you best in the whole world, Cassie repeats silently, widening her arms with the exuberance of the game they played when Mandy was just learning to walk. And she says aloud, "Get a good night's sleep. We'll talk in the morning." Cassie offers up a cheek but Mandy avoids her, flouncing off without a word. Cassie asks, "Why do you do that?"

"What?"

"Act like Mandy isn't here. She pretends you're furniture and you look right through her."

He holds up the magazine, a screen for bullets. "I'm reading."

"You could have talked to her."

"Leave her alone, Cassie." He means not *her* but *me*.

"I want you both to get along."

"We will. These things don't fall into shape overnight." She remembers his own daughters, the lost unphotographed faces he left behind in Texas, the girls of no name. Under the circumstances, why should he be interested in her Mandy?

And what, anyway, is she doing with a man who's gone good-bye on his children, who probably hasn't ever sent a card for birthdays, or at the most offers a call on Christmas Eve?

He pushes himself out of his chair. "Come on, it's late. Bedtime."

Cassie, angry, is about to flog him with *You can't spend the night*, but she's undecided. The question has bobbed in her mind all day and only gets resolved now as he urges her along the upstairs hall right into her own bedroom.

The door no sooner closes than Jake unbuttons her white silk blouse, lifting up wrists too slender to flower into such strong hands. Freeing first one cuff, then the other, he kisses her palms, flicking his tongue along the lifelines. Slipping the blouse off, he brings his lips to the pulse in her neck and nips the flesh. He circles her with his arms and expertly (oh, so expertly!) flips the catch on her new, lacy bra, while just on the other side of the wall Mandy creaks the floorboards.

Cassie tenses. She thinks she should stop him, say not tonight, send him home. But she is oh, so weak, liquefying under his touch. And even after he waltzes her to the bed, lowers her across the quilt, it is still possible to cry out, *No! I can't!* But all she does is make soft, mewing sounds as he steps back for a second to shuck his clothes.

When he returns to the bed his lips press down on hers. Cassie's cry of protest is mixed with one of hunger as Jake's breath fills her mouth.

Still, she struggles against pleasure, not to give in, and what words she suddenly brings up he hushes down her throat. Then he is inside her, reaching for her breasts, rising urgently, pulling Cassie with him in his climb. And Cassie must juggle woman and mother, let go, falter even though she can imagine, can *see*, the fine veins in the shell of Mandy's ear pressed against the violet-patterned wallpaper.

22

"The nerve of him! The absolute nerve!"

Cassie's hands shake and hot coffee splashes over the rim of her mug, but she is too agitated to feel the pain. Anger and hurt are running through her, out the soles of her feet onto the floor.

In the doctors' lounge, Cassie and Barbara are sprawled across vinyl-padded chairs like college students. Barbara, smoking a cigarette pinched between her right thumb and index finger, stares squinty-eyed through the spiral of smoke. She is flat and lacquered, a Technicolor version of Theda Bara and not at all the person Cassie would have chosen to lose it with. But so much is circumstantial.

"Expect nothing and don't be disappointed," Barbara advises.

"I never expected anything. But *this*!"

"Well, you *did* divorce him. If he'd been wonderful, the prince of charmers, you'd have kept him, hmmm?"

Cassie won't remind Barbara that it was Doug who went, that given the choice, she intended to hold on to him, let him husband her down through time, through the years they both have left. She'd never planned on his running off. But had she really been satisfied? Now it seems as if she must have lived half-asleep, the marriage a fandango of deceit, a farce, but in truth it had thrived just fine, thank you, a garden if not of delights, at least without weeds.

Cassie swings around to sit up straight with her knees together. Earnestly, she answers Barbara, who hasn't asked, "I'm not going to tell her. Let him tell her himself. And how dare he even think it's my job?"

"He does have a nerve. You're right."

"Boy, does he ever! 'Listen, Cassie,' he said, 'it would be easier to hear from you that Tracy's going to have a baby than from me.' And why would that be? Because he's scared shitless Mandy will throw a bird."

"Throw a bird. Are the kids still saying that?"

Cassie ignores Barbara's question. "So he'll let me take the fall. As if it's *my* baby!" Oh, that it were! And what a further betrayal, never wanting another child with her but now one with Tracy. She wishes Doug were chopped into little pieces. Lucky him that he didn't beard her in the kitchen last night. She thinks she might have run him through with a butcher knife, and immediately remembers April's husband. His blood wasn't let's pretend, his death so real Cassie smells again the stench of decaying flesh.

No, no, no. . . .

"And jealousy is a disease," Barbara pontificates. She is Nefertiti, with that straight, perfect nose. Cassie just knows she's never suffered a jealous moment in her life. Mo would rip away his right testicle at the roots before he'd blink in the direction of another woman. His plaint is not too much of Barbara but too little.

Cassie replies, *pro forma,* "I'm not jealous." Yet one hand creeps furtively around to her stomach, as if to feel the flutter of fetal feet like angel wings. Barbara, who has no desire for children, never did, observes her silently, one brow raised.

"Why in God's name should I be jealous? Mandy's eighteen. To have a child at my age—how silly. And the risks! I'd be forty-five. Haven't you read Kasmir's paper on late pregnancies?"

Barbara says nothing. What's there to say, since she knows Cassie is fast-dancing. Cassie closes up, all at once itchy with embarrassment. She should have saved Doug's news, *his request!* for Nona or Eve. It occurs to her that if it's a sign of friendship to soothe, to offer palliatives, Barbara isn't much of a friend. She says whatever enters her mind, though surely she could offer up a spoonful of sympathy, Cassie thinks, feeling needy. But then Cassie aches to fight, even with Barbara, who habitually walks off—as she is doing this minute—when the smell of an argument is on the wind.

It is an irony that sets Cassie's teeth further on edge that her next patient is infertile. A woman of thirty-seven hearing, like Nona, the near-deafening tick of biological clocks, and with a primitive hunger wanting, wanting, *wanting*, but month after month producing nothing. Cassie suspects ovarian dysfunction, and after all the usual lab tests come back normal, now plans to test the woman's estrogen levels.

The patient pants like a jogger after a hard five miles as Cassie explains. With eyes blank as slate, she is not listening. She is here at Magdalene to be pronounced fit, or to be promised that whatever is malfunctioning can be fixed. Easily. With surgery if necessary.

"Well, what *is* wrong?" she asks belligerently, for Cassie is the soothsayer, the priest, the priestess. Nothing has been gained by replacing the male authority with a female figure if the oracle speaks in twisted tongues or delivers only doom. This patient will beam death rays at Cassie, too, if she can't change nature.

It's not yet the moment of *no hope whatsoever* and Cassie, sympathizing, coaxes the wrinkles smooth in the patient's forehead and woos a sigh out of her. "Doctor, please. I need a baby *so much*. . . .

Cassie gives no guarantees. Nor does she do what she did to Doug, which was to scream *no!* down the line.

Back home, facing Mandy's profile in the bathroom, Cassie blurts out, because she has to, "The reason your father was so determined to come in last night was to ask me to tell you that he and Tracy are having a baby. He called me this morning at the clinic and I told him no, I wouldn't; but if I don't tell you now, he won't, probably, until the baby is an established fact. And I think you need time to adjust. Oh!" she cries when Mandy turns to her with eyes like a sea serpent's, black and hooded, "oh, I've done this all wrong. I knew I would, but I thought I'd do it better than your father. Or I would do it, at least. I'm thinking of you, Mandy, only. Always."

"That's . . . that's . . ." Mandy shudders.

Cassie leans against the door, lightheaded, as if she's the one three months gone and not Tracy. Please let Tracy ruin her perfect figure, spread like a toad, sprout varicose veins, have stretch marks two inches high engraved across her stomach. May she gain sixty pounds and only lose twenty!

Mandy says, "It's ridiculous, Daddy having a baby. And what about me? Why should he love me anymore when he has a brand-new baby to start all over with?" She slaps a theatrical hand over her heart but Cassie understands she isn't playing to any gallery. The pain digs mine shafts into her.

"Of course he'll love you, always!" Cassie cries, logy with worry. Maybe Doug *will* forget Mandy, she thinks with ice in her heart. Not altogether but enough to hurt this child of *hers*, for whom she now reaches.

Mandy throws up a hand to back Cassie off. No hugs and placating gestures, kisses and tickles under the chin are going to dry up these tears.

"Honey, I *am* sorry," Cassie rushes on, so near to crying herself she has to stiffen her jaw. Adding her sobs to Mandy's will verify Mandy's fears. Instead she must staunchly deny that Doug could possibly neglect Mandy in favor of this unborn child.

Liar, liar! How do you know?

"Because," she blurts, answering her own silent question, "if he wasn't so concerned about you, would he have been doing such a song-and-dance last night when he brought you home? Would he have been wheedling for me to tell you if he wasn't afraid you'd be upset? And," she adds almost in triumph, "if you didn't come first in Daddy's heart, he'd just say, with one of those shrugs of his, 'Oh, by the way. . . .'"

Mandy sucks in her breath, her eyes growing wide. Cassie readies herself for a bloodcurdling shriek that will shake the house as dramatically as a five-point quake, but just on the brink Mandy pulls back.

Slower now, rubbing an arm, which Mandy stiffly allows, Cassie says softly, "It will be hard for a little bit. Then things will be okay. Nobody can take away what you have had with your father, sweetheart, what you still have." And why, she asks herself, in a sweat to save Mandy from despair, wasn't Doug satisfied with playing swinging single? Oh, how much she despises him. If there's justice in the world Tracy will run off—baby and all—with a gorgeous blond lifeguard.

Mandy's hysteria appears to be subsiding, but just as Cassie begins to relax, Mandy—tears starting up again—shoves out of the bathroom wailing, "Everybody's going to laugh at me."

God, there's that, too. Cassie shudders as they run in tandem to Mandy's room. "Wait!" Cassie says, catching hold of her sleeve before Mandy abruptly pulls loose and bolts. The door slams in Cassie's face; the key turns.

"Leave me alone!" Mandy yells when Cassie rattles the knob.

"All right, honey. Whatever you want," Cassie cries against the wood before retreating. But she doesn't take half a dozen steps along the hall before Mandy's crashed the door open and is yelling, "You're as bad as Daddy! With *him*! Can't you wait until I'm back in school? Or maybe you want me to go now. Maybe I'm ruining your scene."

"Mandy, stop! Let's talk about this." And say what? Cassie wonders, though she is willing to apologize for taking a man into her bed. Motivated by guilt, she has no choice but to cry *I'm sorry!* Only Mandy doesn't give her a chance. Flying on anger, she is down the stairs, ignoring her mother's protests winging after her. Cassie starts to follow but Mandy is so much faster. In seconds she is outside, and by the time Cassie reaches the kitchen door, Mandy is driving off.

Cassie's called Jake and warned him about coming over. If she expected him to be warm and understanding, she's mistaken. He is distant and as cold as winter.

Mandy needs to get adjusted, Cassie explains. Everything's hit her all at once. Jake . . . Tracy having a baby.

Jake says that's not the point. She gives in to a kid; she coddles Mandy. She has to live her own life, he criticizes, and for a moment she wonders if he's talking not about her so much as about himself. But she immediately puts such a disloyal thought aside, at the same time remembering that Jake's a father come and gone.

Cassie longs for Jake to hold her hand, but she can't go to his house either. She must be home when Mandy returns, she tells Eve when Eve calls to invite her over. They could all get together at Cassie's, but Nona has a date with Fitz. She does, however, pick up Eve, still advised not to drive yet, and transport her.

"What fun, my first outing," Eve says to Cassie when they arrive. "The aging grandmother!"

Cassie can't stand this jokey manner of Eve's, which is another strange effect of the surgery.

"Have to go," Nona says. She stands with a hand on her hip, and in a black cape, wearing a light-gray wool skirt, high suede boots, she looks divine, queen of the night. Both Eve and Cassie say so.

"Love conquers all," Eve cheers, for once not disapproving.

Nona rolls her eyes. "You are so weird these days."

"Am I?" Eve asks, genuinely surprised.

Nona is off to meet Fitz back at her apartment. He has a key—so you never have to wait out front if I'm not there, she's explained to him in case he worries that she's trying to trap him—but even so, Nona hates to have him hanging around until she arrives. Only, he assures her with a smile, a kiss, a bear hug that creaks her bones, he doesn't mind.

Marian's credo was: If you please a man he'll please you, give you what you want, a home, marriage, security. And though Nona knows such beliefs are atrociously out of date, that there is something shameful about bending a knee to her mother's faith, she can't help herself.

Once in a while Nona thinks she allows herself to work too hard to please the men who have passed through her life. But fear always stops up her throat at the moment of saying *no*. Even as they're leaving she's afraid to make any definitive statements. Watch and wait; be shy and quiet. Do what they, he, wants.

Magic pads through her memory, and shivering, Nona drives on. Fitz is waiting, but that's okay. He'll have a beer, stretch out on the couch, be there with reaching arms when she puts her key in the lock.

"I thought we were going out," she says when she walks in on him in the kitchen.

"Fantastic new Chinese restaurant down on Pico. I just picked up a bunch of stuff." He smiles, slides a kiss along her neck with the skill of a downhill racer.

She has a new Anne Klein jacket, trimmed in gold braid, studded in gold knot buttons, that she planned to wear, moss-green to complement her favorite wool crepe pants and white silk turtleneck. She wants to dance, thought she'd wear her hair in braids, fuchsia lipstick, which is all the rage.

"You're luscious, babe." He squeezes a breast and she moves sideways into the pressure of his hand.

"Chinese is great."

"And, surprise, surprise, I've got some Thai grass that's to die. Whoopee-do, it will blow the cobwebs out. Great, you know what. You'll see."

Drugs frighten Nona; they always have. Marijuana stirs large cloudy currents that channel through memories, stirring up sludge she is afraid of disturbing. The few times she's been stoned she slipped too loose, but confronting Fitz's pleasure she shrugs. "Okay. Maybe."

"What's the matter?"

"Nothing, but—" She expected something special. Suddenly she rises up on her tiptoes. "Let's go to your apartment."

"My hole in the wall?"

"It can't be that bad. You're just trying to spare my"—she giggles—"good taste maybe?"

"Well, it's not the Taj Mahal, that's true. Only a way station between before and after. And nowhere as nice as this. Not fit for you, princess." He dumps fried rice into a pottery bowl. "Money problems, the wrong investments, a matter of listening to a snake-oil salesman with super earnings, but unfortunately on margin. So be it, babe. Things are changing. I've got a major deal in the works." His eyes have sparkles in them, good humor. Nona thinks she's home at last, here, with a man who can take life's upheavals with a smile, a puff of laughter soft as a June breeze. This is what she needs and she hugs gratefully against his chest.

"Hey, let's eat first."

"Just affectionate," she says shyly.

He pats her shoulder. "Here, Chinese beers." He puts her arms aside and uncaps two bottles. "Tonight we shine," he says. And all of a sudden Nona feels awkward, as if Fitz were putting on a show for her. There seems to be an extra, a theatrical, carny flourish to the way he sets the table, ladles out the food on her plate, drapes a napkin across her knee. He coaxes another beer on her, encourages her to highs of delight with smiles and little tweaks, with wandering fingers walking up her arm, along her cheek. But for what? To eat Chinese food that tastes unexceptional to Nona, and to drink the bitter beer. Most of all, so determinedly to relax. Get with it.

"We should be comfortable with each other, easy." Fitz writes *easy* in the air with a chopstick. "That's what everything means, right?"

"Sure."

"And listen, I know so little about you. I have to know you, babe, inside out, from A to omega, from day one to now, every-thing. I need"—he leans over and grips her hands, gazes deep into her eyes—"to take you inside me, to be inside you." His intensity raises the temperature in the kitchen until Nona can barely breathe.

"When you were little, didn't you have secret fantasies to be somebody else, to slip in and out of other bodies and see the world from another person's eyes? I did, but that's because I was a fat kid with two left feet. God, I cornered the market in zits!"

Nona laughs. "You! I don't believe it."

"Make fun. You were probably perfect. A perfect little girl in lace and ribbons sitting on Daddy's knee. You ruled the world."

Nona blushes. "I wasn't that bad."

"Bad! I bet you were wonderful." Fitz offers up a shrimp between his chopsticks to her lips. Obediently she takes the morsel. He watches her chew with a scientist's curiosity. "Tell me everything, about being a kid, growing up, every moment from the day you were born. I want to hear it all and see the world out of your beautiful eyes."

Nona has never connected with another human, male or female, who desired her so intimately. Fitz flatters her, and yet his intensity is a brush fire, burning out of control, too close, and throughout the meal she digs ditches to forestall him. She thinks to lead him into talking about himself, a safe trick she's used many times before. But Fitz is wilier than Nona's usual men. He's told her enough, too much personal flotsam, and now he tracks after her for the endless years of details. He will gobble her down, incorporate her essentials and spit out the bones. For the briefest moment, a breath, Nona distends with anger. *What right has he?*

She reaches for the empty cartons. "Nope, this dinner's on me," he says. "I'm cleaning up. You get into the living room. Here, take a couple of beers. I'll be there in a few minutes." Nona, the puff of anger vanishing, is hustled out of her own kitchen. She goes, obedient but not resentful, drinking beer and letting Fitz's concern, love, lighten her.

"I haven't had grass like this since I was at Berkeley. And that was a hundred years ago." Fitz is on the couch at her feet, the joint in the center of his mouth. He strikes a kitchen match on the sole of his work boot and drags until the joint flames. "Oh, man, this is mother-loving pungent stuff. Try it." Nona hesitates. "Come on, it will mellow you out."

Nona takes the joint between her lips, though Fitz continues to hold it. When she finally releases the pent-up smoke he urges another drag. With his free hand he rubs her stockinged toes and a hum of pleasure travels up her leg in the faintest sizzle of current.

Nona won't admit it but she's never been much of a grass smoker, even when turning on was essential. She can drink but she can't do dope without a rush of panic. Fear lashes her that she will be swept away in an altogether different wave than the tide that washes over her in sex. Not that she ever totally loses control then, for all of her bedroom acrobatics. Though she moans, she is more involved in listening to a man's groans spiral to a crescendo.

"What was it like, growing up in a big house, all those servants?"

"Not so many. Cook, Nanny, then a woman to clean in the mornings."

Fitz roars, falls off the couch to the floor, then runs his lips up her leg to the knee. "Oh, princess, that was an army. My mother thought a Hoover was God's gift to the housewife!"

Fitz's hand marches on up under her skirt, and Nona tenses, but down it goes, returning to her foot, which he kneads as he talks about Marian and Adam as if he knew them.

Grass sends Nona into a tight little room, behind high walls, in front of clear, polished windows. She hears herself describing the house, her room, downstairs. She tells Fitz she sat on Adam's lap. "He'd bounce me, ho-ho horse, up and down. Sing me songs. He whispers, see right here." She points to the curve of her neck. "Then he tucks me in, not Marian, tucks me up to my chin. Here." She prods her bottom lip. "Over the Alps, magic carpet ride. Wind in my hair."

He smooths his fingers on her mouth before she inhales from the joint, a new one. "Dead, isn't he? Your old man?"

"Poor Daddy. He never deserved all that to happen to him." With her eyes closed she keeps the smoke a long stoned minute before letting it escape. "In the yard! The yard! Some yard. Hundred of them. Men. I saw it, not it, that one, but in the movies."

"What yard?" He crowds her vision, fills it so there's nothing but Fitz, blurred, out of focus.

"Dead in the yard. Dead before he hit the ground, they told my mother. They." She angles up on her elbows. "They were all *they* if you know what I mean."

"Sure, sugar. Here, have another hit."

They pass the joint back and forth, Nona floating like an astronaut buoyed in the weightlessness of space. She turns, tumbling over, feet up, legs spread.

"What was he in for?"

"What?"

"Your old man. How come he was in the slammer? What did he do?"

"Nothing. They lied about him." Again she thinks to lever up but her arms melt, are watery. "They were wrong. A thousand percent. He wouldn't have, not believing the things he did, the way he did. He never . . ."

"Course not."

Nona flops down, spaghetti arms and legs. "Right." She makes a disordered move toward sitting up, bright all at once with suspicion. "Don't pretend just like everybody else about believing him."

"Never. I wouldn't do that, not to you."

"Wicked people, throwing rotten eggs and tomatoes at the car."

"What car?"

The light blurs into a mist that shapes the solid granite outlines of the courthouse out of Nona's living room. "To court," she says, "up the steps and down again." She thinks she's falling out of the house she grew up in, tumbling from an upstairs window to a hotel in the Back Bay, than another more anonymous hotel with black window shades.

"We never went home again, and my mother died up in Maine, thirty miles from where she ran away. Did I tell you that before?"

Fitz says no, but he is so easy, sliding along her, graceful as a dancer, that it doesn't seem possible he can't remember how she cried. "In Bangor, not even in Bar Harbor. Like she hadn't traveled all that way. Never to L.A.—Don't say L.A., that's soooo common. Los Ang-e-les." Nona turns her head from side to side on the cushion, moving Marian from chair to chair in this very room, dressing her in a tailored suit, a print dress, white linen, just as she would a paper doll. Her mother haunts her.

"Room's turning upside down," she says. "Take me to bed."

"In a minute, hon. Have one more hit, seal over all the rough spots. Get feeling perfecto. Your daddy would want that. Loved you, even if he did that thing that got him in the slammer."

Nona travels on her own wave with the next drag, and the one after that. "Marian said nobody'd forgive. Never forget. Said it was a good thing I never married Simon."

"You never told me about Simon."

"Not to worry. No true love like you." Nona giggles and stretches for him, swallows his mouth, licks at his face, takes a hit, blows the smoke finally released from her lungs over his lips, his cheeks.

"To bed then. And don't call me Simon."

"Simon's long gone."

Fitz, with his arms wrapped around Nona, waltzes her into the bedroom. They fumble with each other's buttons, Fitz far more deft than Nona, whose fingers are jelly. "Oh, I am the blob, running runny!"

He gets her across the quilt, then under it, and trails kisses, which he knows she dies for, in a path along her neck, over her shoulder to her breasts.

"Simon," Fitz whispers.

"Simon's up on the Vineyard, old sailor, no hair, I bet, and bony like his father. Adam promised he'd be his father from toes to top and it was a good thing we weren't—Oh, do that again, please. Yes . . ."

He licks, touches, strokes, and little by little she is looking through a window again, past the diaphanous curtains fluttering in the breeze, tendrils of light off the bedroom floor lamp curling against Simon.

"Pretty Simon," she says. "Called me names. Nasty things which were all lies. Adam was going to kill him. No, Simon . . . Touched me."

"Who touched you?"

"Who . . ."

"Like this?"

"Yes, oh, please. No, don't stop!"

"Tell me first. Who touched you? How? Why did Simon call you names?"

"Please, Daddy. Don't. Daddy, just a little bit."

"Did Adam do it like *this*?"

Nona goes slipping under Fitz, down a chute to the sea in her grass high, swimming across a mosaic of time past. There is Simon's face hanging like stained glass in the window. Simon on the second-floor porch behind the curtain. Simon yelling . . .

His voice pounds worse than the sea in her ear. His voice crashes.

Daddy, she says, *please don't. Daddy. Get up*.

All the words are inside her mouth. The words are memory and nobody hears her.

Saturday night Nona again drives Eve over to Cassie's for the postponed Thanksgiving dinner. Eve isn't ready when Nona stops to pick her up.

"I can't decide what to wear. Now isn't that silly?"

There's a cheesy softness to Eve's face, a loosening around her mouth, so the smile shifts on her lips unanchored. "I thought about this white dress." She brings out a long-sleeved silk print with red poppies. "I bought it from you ages ago and never wore it. Time is fleeting, Charlie Brown. I could have died, you know. So"—she takes a small two-step, swinging the dress disembodied on the hanger—"I gotta wear all my clothes."

Eve being silly, acting half-witted, to say nothing of aging in minutes right before Nona's eyes, makes Nona so nervous she acts uncharacteristically impatient.

"Don't wear the white. It's lucious but too dressy. Cassie will be in pants and Mandy jeans—"

"Mandy's a child," Eve says, but without vehemence.

"And see, I'm only wearing a sweater and skirt."

"What about dear Jake? And dear Fitz? If we're having a fashion lineup. Where is dear Fitz, by the way? Isn't he riding with you?"

Nona thought he was, but awoke in an empty bed. No sign of Fitz. No note. In the living room the coffee table was littered with beer bottles, dirty glasses, an ashtray with dead joints in it. *Fitz*, she called and called again, having glided out of sleep with the image of Simon superimposed on the window. She dreamed of torn scenery, of Simon on the porch, behind the gauzy breeze of the nighttime curtains. She dreamed of Simon watching her with red ruby eyes.

Eve has her arm and is gently shaking it. "Are you okay? Is something wrong between you and Fitz?"

"No. I'm fine. Just some crossed wires, that's all."

"What's that mean?"

That she has no idea where Fitz is, why all she gets when calling his number is the robotic voice on the answering machine, that's what she's thinking, but what she says is: "I was sure I mentioned dinner at Cassie's, but I guess I screwed up." Screwed up like always, she thinks.

What did she tell Fitz that made him disappear without a sign, a last kiss?

23

Even a noncook can put together a Thanksgiving dinner—turkey, dressing, candied yams, mashed potatoes, pumpkin pie. It's all so uncomplicated. Cassie, a traditionalist, never deviates from the menus she remembers back through time to all those Landry feasts, and serves up the exact same meal to Eve, Nona, Jake, the Levinsons, and Mandy. Johnny is flying back from Santa Fe and will come over when his plane lands. Don't wait, he advised Eve, but Cassie is in no hurry. There is wine to drink, a blue-cheese mold with crackers, her own country pâté on crusty French bread. Dinner, starting at five, should be a slow banquet, and Cassie can pretend it's Thursday, not Saturday.

The air, however, vibrates with charged ions of tension, as if a storm on the horizon were gathering force. Even Al Levinson, though half dozing, is on edge. The epicenter is Jake, though he acts oblivious to the attention focused on him. He ignores Eve's and Nona's curiosity like someone who moves invisibly, as if he's not the one they cast covetous glances at and whisper about behind their hands and with bent heads to Cassie.

He's so good-looking.

Where did you say the tattoo was?

Those eyes—my dear, you didn't let on by half.

Jake moves back and forth easily between the living room, dining room, and kitchen. He's at home, knowing where the best china and silver are kept, which serving bowls Cassie prefers to use for company.

"Refreshing to see a man who doesn't lie around taking up time and space and letting the little woman carry all the burden of dinner," Eve says to Cassie in the kitchen while Jake carries another bottle of Chardonnay out to the coffee table.

Nona is slicing cucumbers. "Eve, you should be sitting down," she says.

Eve pushes a strand of hair back from her forehead. Cassie can't see any gray and is about to mention that Eve wasn't going to color it, but she is distracted by Nona's mutilating the cucumber. "No, not like that. The slices should be thin." Cassie takes away the knife and demonstrates.

Eve leans against the counter, purposely staying on her feet. "How's Mandy taking the boyfriend?" she asks.

Cassie wishes Eve's question had a simple answer, or that she could shrug it away.

"Can't talk about it now," she says finally, wishing there weren't anything to talk about, wishing Mandy could be laid-back and accepting of her mother's possessing a lover. *A lover* . . . Oh, Lord, why shouldn't Mandy be swept up in a tornado when Cassie herself feels strangely displaced. I'm not the sort of female who takes *lovers*, Cassie thinks for the hundredth time, especially now when the man who has come to occupy her bed on a regular basis—and they all know this—is sitting on the edge of the couch spreading cheese on a cracker.

Cassie has brought out the pâté and the chunks of French bread warm from the oven. She offers a sample to Beth, sitting by Jake's elbow and telling him the latest on Tony. Al, soporifically pleasant, leans into a conversation with Mandy that is all one-sided. And as he has done for years, he asks her about school, though now it is college rather than kindergarten. But Mandy, who once ran in and out of the Levinson house as she did her own, announced to Cassie the night before that she can't stand their neighbors. This is all part, Cassie reasons, of Mandy's toxic reaction to her life at the moment, to Jake, her father, Tracy. Though with the perverse logic of a teenager, Mandy has this very morning driven over to Marina del Rey and behaved as sweetly as a milkmaid to her expecting stepmother. She has even dealt tolerantly with her father, who subsequently called up Cassie and reported that things were just fine. That in worrying so about how Mandy would face having a half-sibling at this stage of her life, they overreacted. Cassie doesn't bother telling Doug that Mandy's still mad as piss, only the burden of her resentment falls nearer home. On Cassie. Kill the messenger! And through Cassie onto Jake, who is already involved in the unforgivable. Jake, having captured her mother's attention and affection, becomes the convenient villain of all Mandy's scenarios, and Cassie can't think how to change that.

Cassie has put some pâté on a piece of bread and stretched across the coffee table to hand it to Mandy. "I'm on a diet," Mandy says, turning away.

"Kiddo, nobody diets on Thanksgiving, It's un-American. The FBI carts you off to the slammer for subversive activity," Al teases her, not aware that he's poking a stick at a hornet's nest, that Mandy is just waiting for a reason to go off into orbit.

She narrows her eyes at Al. "Being fat is not something to laugh at."

"Who's fat? Not you." Al Levinson genuinely likes Mandy, has known her since she was—as he likes to say—knee-high to a grasshopper. He pushed her thousands of times on the backyard swing, gave her countless hot dogs and hamburgers from his barbecue, candy apples for her Halloween trick-or-treat bag, and, along with Beth, presents each Christmas and birthday. He has pictures of Mandy almost every year of her life in his photo albums, and once he took a wasp stinger out of her arm when she was five and screaming blue murder and Doug had turned green. So he will be destroyed if he learns that Mandy no longer cares for him— says now she never has—and that their easy friendship rests not on bedrock but on shifting sand. But while Al isn't aware of Mandy's rejection, something unnerves him enough to struggle forward to the edge of his chair, from where he can reach out and grab Beth's hand for a squeeze. Beth's tongue continues to move in her mouth, but she rewards Al with a loving glance and lets him entwine his fingers with hers.

Eve, now back in a cushioned living room chair, witnesses the gesture and is reminded—as she is by so much—of Abramson. But whereas before when she has seen Al and Beth behave so lovingly and been inflamed with jealousy, this Saturday she suffers no envy. She feels a simple pleasure at their love for each other after so many years of marriage, and an even greater pleasure at her own lack of resentment.

Abramson would have liked these two placid, middle-aged people, would have responded to their warmth. The most important human trait, he always said, was kindness.

Eve's softness in this post-op period not only raises Cassie's eyebrows and has Nona asking *what's happened to you?* but amuses Eve herself. She bellied up out of the anesthesia an armadillo now unplated, but she can never counter Nona's question with any other response than laughter, a shrug, or "Nothing. I'm the same." The truth, unfortunately, has the coloring of science fiction to it.

Though Eve won't ask Jena or even Cassie, she has no doubt that at some moment during the operation, or perhaps just afterward, she veered dangerously near to death, set a foot in the river, and did in actuality—not in a dream—meet Abramson on the road. And the bear presented her with a choice: to stay or go. That she went is no betrayal, and Abramson forgives her for not joining him then. What's important is the knowledge of Abramson sequestered in some quarter of space and in no-time, and how he waits. The corniness of this revelation, the Sunday sermon babble proving to be true, tickles Eve as much as it delights her. Santa Claus is real, Virginia. But who'd believe her?

That Deity, Mind, or Power Who strung together the intricacies of the universe hasn't given her a special gift, chosen her out of millions. No, Eve isn't so presumptuous as to think that. Her returning from the other side with memory intact is simply a mistake. The most perfect of creations has, it seems, margin for error.

Eve makes no plans for this knowledge. No soapboxes in MacArthur Park, no best-seller *I Came Back!*, no establishing a new faith for eager disciples. If it's selfishness to secrete revealed truth, so be it. Softer she might have become from learning there still is a future with her bear, but not soft-headed.

Eve is smug.

Preoccupied, she fails to take in a rearrangement of the guests. Beth finally relinquishes Jake to Al, who pats Mandy's knee before he turns away and so never catches the girl trying to scrub his touch off her skirt. Already Beth is halfway into Eve's operation, or rather her own hysterectomy, thankfully with a somewhat lowered voice so that only every third word is audible across the room to the men talking basketball.

"The hormones help with the sweats, and those terrible mood swings! They even you out, like tranks."

Eve smiles.

"They should have started you already."

Along with having her insides vacuum-cleaned comes membership in this sisterly society. Eve nods and Beth barrels on.

"You don't have any bad reactions, do you? I've had friends who've gotten sick to their stomachs, another with leg cramps, and then a gal I know from my aerobics class swears they give you cancer and won't take one if you beat on her with a hammer. Says all the upheavals are nature's way and it's best to lie down like a tired dog and submit. I ask you!" Beth waxes indignant.

"Who can tell?" is all Eve will say. She'd rather stare at the ceiling than indulge in more conversation about her body.

Al lumbers to his feet. "Before dinner I better see a man about a horse." He is off to the downstairs bathroom.

Beth sees Mandy's grimace. "He always says that. You've heard him a thousand times." She swings around again to Eve. "Men don't have our problems, the lucky beasts. Though Al's prostate troubles have not been a picnic, let me tell you."

Jake scoops a mound of pâté onto a cracker and holds it out to Mandy. "Want some?"

"Nobody believes me when I say I'm dieting."

"Al's got a point. Thanksgiving is a day for eating, not fasting."

"It's not Thanksgiving," Mandy pedantically points out. "That was Thursday. This is Saturday night. I spent Thanksgiving at my father's." The look Mandy shoots at Jake is so lethal it should be registered with the police department.

Jake's mouth curls slightly upward, as if Mandy is a small dog who has performed a trick. Two nights before he said to Cassie that Mandy will come around or she won't, and the way he acts with her now makes Cassie think he cares not in the least whether Mandy decides on peace or warfare.

What Jake does do is get up and go into the kitchen for a beer instead of the wine, which everybody else (not Mandy, who in her pique won't even touch a Diet Pepsi) is drinking.

The women all watch Jake go, as if he's onstage and exiting, until the spell is broken by Beth's saying, "Cass, this cheese stuff is terrific, just like always."

Cassie laughs. "I guess I do make it a lot."

"Beth's giving you a compliment, Mom. Why can't you let people say nice things without going through your oh-no-not-me routine?"

"Stop knocking your mother," Jake says, entering like John Wayne to the rescue. He's holding a beer can, and Cassie wishes he would use a glass, which, she realizes, is not only ridiculous but not important. He has defended her and that secretly pleases Cassie, who must keep from smiling, since Mandy watches. Though really, there's no need for him to leap between her and Mandy, to remind Mandy that "Your mother's done heavy duty putting this meal together."

Mandy's face squeezes up and for a moment it seems certain she'll either burst into tears or blow sky high, but before she can, Beth cries, "And a wonderful dinner it is too!"

Mandy turns, rounding on what—given her scowl—she apprehends as yet another attacker. "We haven't eaten yet, so how do you know it's so wonderful?"

"Wonderful or not, let's eat. I'm starving," Eve says, hoping to save Cassie, and herself. She shrinks from a scene, any unpleasantness, as dismayed as Nona always is by raised voices. And that's new too.

But Mandy's not in a mood to let anyone escape her bad temper. "Now how come you're jumping in, Eve? You're supposed to relax. Mom says nobody's to bother you. I mean, have I ever bothered you?"

Nona shouts from the kitchen, "Help, Cass! The mold is stuck!"

Cassie rushes, appreciating any crisis that takes her from the room, calling back, "We'll eat in exactly two minutes. Jake, come carve, please," she adds, though she can expertly carve a turkey herself.

Mandy's anger scalds them all, though everyone's conscious that she is a kid having to adjust, that from her point of view both her mother and father are doing her in. Still, not even Al, who has returned from the bathroom, wants to stay in the living room with Mandy. So they move, practically in a group, to the kitchen.

Beth lifts the mold out of Nona's hands and, with a no-nonsense tap to its bottom, frees the cranberries. Al hangs at Jake's elbow to add his nickel to the ritual turkey carving. Though there is a clatter of voices with everybody talking at once, Jake says nothing. Cassie hopes he is concentrating on the bird and that Mandy hasn't been able to make inroads on his own temper. She worries that he is mad at Mandy (well, Mandy is acting obnoxiously, so that's okay), and because of Mandy, at her. It's the *at her* that Cassie chews over, and the taste is off.

Eve takes the basket of rolls and the little butter dishes off the counter and heads for the table, announcing, "I'm fit to walk ten feet and I need the exercise. Exercise," she calls back over her shoulder to anyone listening, "according to the hospital gestapo that dragged me up and down the halls when I was half asleep, is the key to a healthy recovery."

All Cassie's friends paint over Mandy's outburst, pretending for Cassie's sake that no cracks mar this holiday celebration, this Thanksgiving on a Saturday; that it is an ordinary, television-perfect happy occasion.

Eve smiles at Cassie. Nona floats by her and drops a quick hug. Al tells a joke about a man and an umbrella, but Cassie, scooping stuffing into a serving bowl, fails to follow it. She's busy cautioning herself that Mandy's feeling lost and that, as the adult, she must stay calm.

Amid all the activity in the kitchen Mandy stands by the back door with her arms folded. Her head's turned and the sharp angles of her profile give her the look of an older, hungry woman. She stares out the window at nothing, ready to bolt, Cassie fears, if the wrong word is spoken. Please, Cassie offers in silent prayer, don't let her just run off and ruin everything!

Yet she's poised to fly like an angry crow. To where? Jennifer's house, Pepe's Pizza Parlor? to Harve's or Dom's or June's or a friend's I've never met before? And come home with beer on her breath, the smell of grass in her hair?

Cassie drops a dish.

"Oh, dear, that's Depression glass," Beth cries, falling to her knees. Her hands flutter in incantatory gestures over the shattered pieces, as if regret were a magic ritual.

"Stop, Beth. You're not the one who broke it."

"A bowl is a bowl," Nona says, and calls, "Mandy, get the dustpan and broom."

Strangely the breaking of a bowl, over which Beth continues to lament and which Eve thinks can be fixed, defuses the tension. Nona reminds everyone, in case they don't know, that a thing is just a thing no matter how pretty or valuable, that her mother had a houseful, all of which were sold or lost. Movable property can just vanish. Nona is feeling for once wiser than the other women, to whom she most often dips a shoulder like a child, and lectures that things have little if any meaning unless they're true art, a "Guernica" or the "Mona Lisa."

"Things aren't people," she continues as they sit down at the table. If Fitz were next to her he'd tell them the story of the Karman Ghia that almost took him off a bridge once but he jumped at the last split-second, of the house his parents lived in that burned to the foundations when they were off at the beach. Fitz blossoms like a jacaranda with his stories. His real-life adventures flower. He glows. Oh, she wishes he were here beside her. He would never sit stoically, like a traveler in a foreign restaurant, like Jake with his head hanging over his plate.

Conversation lurches in awkward fits and starts, never picking up steam. Cassie offers one topic after another to her guests along with the turkey, broccoli, cranberries, yams, and homemade rolls, but no one, not even Beth, has much to say. Cassie persuades herself it's the food, that they're all too involved in eating, which is fine, no problem, but Eve blames Jake. He's out of his pond and there's Mandy, just aching to chop him off at the knees. The two of them will never synchronize, Eve predicts.

Just when the silence is becoming strained Johnny arrives, walking in without waiting for Cassie to answer his ring. He is a fresh wind from the desert and Eve isn't the only one happy to see him, because his presence shifts the mood. The clouds pull loose and voices rise again as introductions are made, for Johnny knows only the women. In the transition Mandy's anger, which has held them all captive, is shunted to a side track.

Only Jake fails to unbend. Eve already hears Cassie's excuses: He's shy; it takes time for him to warm up.

Eve wishes Cassie, finally finding a man, had unearthed some other specimen.

When the meal winds down at last to pie and coffee, weariness sandbags Eve. The coffee cup, a delicate china, is suddenly too heavy to hold. Her neck can barely support her head. A hopeless feeling collects around her bones.

Cassie notices and asks, "Do you want to lie down for a little bit?"

"No. But I think it's time to fold my tent."

Johnny is up as if shot. "You overdid."

"My nurse," Eve laughs.

"Come on, I'm taking you home."

"I can if you're—" Nona starts to volunteer. "I mean, you're just in from Phoenix—"

"Santa Fe," Johnny sniffs, put out, since he's spent ten minutes telling the table about his trip.

"Do you have your car?"

They negotiate over Eve's head while Cassie says, "I'm giving you some turkey and pie for tomorrow."

"Don't expect me to say no. Just throw in a tub of your cranberry mold."

Beth can't keep still. "Cassie is the best cook."

Al cocks a finger at Jake. "You're some lucky mister. Brains, beauty, and Julia Child in one package."

Mandy flings down her napkin and runs out of the room, pounding up the stairs to the second floor.

"You were the straw," Beth says, slapping her husband's arm. Al looks around the table surprised. "What did I do?" he asks.

Nestled in the corner of the front seat of Johnny's car, Eve meditates on Mandy, on Cassie and Jake. How difficult it is for people to shape their lives around one another. Most times they bounce around like billiard balls.

She thinks of the involvements in her life that worked out well, the ones she'd never be persuaded to regret, as Johnny drives carefully because he doesn't want to subject her to any sudden stops, starts, any bumps. Johnny keeps both hands on the wheel and does a monologue about his New Mexico holiday, his growing son tall as a cactus, on a horse no less. God, he is something. She's got to see him.

Eve smiles and nods and puts in a word when necessary, but thinks of her sisters. Holidays stir up a family brew, memories that stick in her mind. But in the California night New Hampshire is as distant as Jupiter and her sisters are only faces in old pictures. Eve moves on to her friends, to Johnny, Nona, Cassie. There are also a few from the long ago, like Mae Horton, another waitress the summer Eve met Jordan, Mae six feet tall and now the mother of seven. And then she has the shadowy women here in Los Angeles, women like Allie, good for a midweek dinner, a gossipy phone call, Saturday lunch at Neiman's and an hour's shopping.

"I wouldn't have been a great mother," Eve suddenly hears herself saying. Yet the memory that she savors, and savors for the first time without guilt and tears of both pain and rage, is of the few minutes she held that baby. Buster, she remembers she called him in the seconds they were together. *Buster,* she thinks, *go away,* but she means it nicely. *Be free* is what she should say. And me, too, she sighs, leaning her head back against the seat.

". . . the best in the world," Johnny is saying, intending to compliment Eve but only riling her. Has he forgotten, even while he's careful not to hit any potholes in the road, that she can't have a child anymore even if out of the blue she develops a desperate desire to be a mother?

"I hate the idea of being torn apart, being shoved out on a ledge like Cassie."

"It doesn't have to be like that."

"You missed most of the show. Mandy's holding Cass prisoner. She threatens her with—oh, I don't know what, withdrawal of love maybe, running to Doug even though Tracy is in the family way. I suppose, just tormenting Cassie with the possibility of her leaving."

"There are more nightmares than that," Johnny says with a shudder. "I bad-dream of car crashes, ODing, his getting shot in a Seven-Eleven. When he flew out here I swear to God I didn't breathe until the plane taxied up to the gate. You wouldn't believe the worries I can conjure up. I'm a real magician when it comes to my kid." In a shaft of white street light Eve sees a nerve tremble across Johnny's cheek. "There are millions of kids in the world but the bottom line is only one or two or three, how many *you* have. Only yours."

Eve feels sorry for Johnny, as she does for Cassie, the two of them such hostages to fate. She was right, she tells herself for the thousandth time.

Limply she lets her hand lie on Johnny's leg as they travel the rest of the way.

24

Of course she's being stupid. There is a reason for Fitz's absence and when she gets him on the phone he'll laugh and explain. Or will the very moment he calls back. Nona leaves countless messages on his answering machine, which plays night and day. Fitz's tinny voice greets Nona with *Hi, I'm not here right now,* at three in the morning.

He must be out of town. A sudden business opportunity. A death in the family. Please, our Father who art in heaven, don't let him be sick, lying in a coma, tubes in his arms, alive mechanically. Don't let him be lost where I can't find him.

"Fitz took a hike," Eve pronounces. She is not completely transmogrified into sweetness and light. She has stopped by at Flora's to look at a dress Nona's been holding for her.

"I love you in blue," Nona declares, standing to the side of Eve, reflected three ways in the mirror.

"These ruffles. Aren't they overwhelming for me?"

"Absolutely not. *Trés chic.*"

"Oh, you think lamb chops are *trés chic!*" Eve teases.

She's dubious about the dress but buys it anyway, as penance for her cynicism. Fitz has probably gone bye-bye on Nona, but Eve decides she won't be the one to say so. Not that it matters, since Nona won't listen to her. Nona clings to how happy they were. They never had a disagreement, never mind a fight, nothing to set him walking. They ate Chinese food and made love. Fitz should have been in Nona's bed that following morning, but then

340

his phone has no right to be permanently connected to the answering machine either.

Fitz should be available but isn't.

A day, two, three, four, a week. Time folds over, hour by hour. Dusk discolors the sky earlier and earlier as autumn creeps toward winter.

It is impossible that Fitz would just disappear, poof, the white rabbit. Over dinner, Nona discusses notifying the police with Eve and Cassie.

"The police!" Cassie slides back in the caned chair. Her napkin slides off her lap onto the tile floor. The police are connected in her mind with April, with the husband's stiffened body, with those two poor little kids.

"Have you been to his apartment?" Eve asks.

"No."

"Why not?"

"Because I don't know where he lives," Nona admits, lowering her face over a wineglass.

Eve lifts an eyebrow at Cassie. "Can you believe? She doesn't learn. And I need a drink."

The old dread of not being able to find Jake takes hold of Cassie again. But if she confesses how she needed to ask Yang for Jake's address, how really she's no different from Nona, both women will think her soft and tissuey.

Eve orders a scotch and soda.

"Have wine," Cassie suggests.

"I need something with more kick in it."

"Wine's kicky enough. Listen to me. I'm your doctor."

But she isn't. Jena is still Eve's doctor, performing whatever checkups are necessary, and they both know it. Besides, a real drink, a scotch and soda, won't kill Eve. Why should it? Except for being minus her female organs she is as normal as Nona and Cassie. But reluctant to be sucked into Nona's latest romantic mess, Cassie and Eve rear up as easily as an old married couple and engage in untidy bickering.

Neither woman cares to speculate what went wrong *this time*. Fitz offered such promise, single as he was, good-looking, and— according to Nona, who has an unreliable sense of such matters— attentive. When Nona goes to the ladies' room Eve leans over the table and whispers, "What on earth happens with that woman, drop-dead gorgeous, sweet as a Hershey bar, that each affair becomes as poisonous as cyanide?"

"She really should have some therapy."

"Oh, forget that." Eve waves a hand in disgust, then digs around in her purse for a cigarette. "She uses that old Dr. Rubin as a shrink."

"He's an internist."

A middle-aged woman with purple lipstick, sitting at a table to the left, taps Eve on the arm the minute she brings a match to her Winston. "This is a no-smoking section."

"God damn," Eve swears, looking more like the old Eve in readiness to do battle, but she does nothing overtly hostile except to actually light up and take one long drag. Then she puts the cigarette out in an empty wineglass.

"That's disgusting," Cassie criticizes.

"Do you want me to step on it instead?"

Cassie starts to suggest they stop sniping at each other when Nona returns and asks straight out, "What should I do?"

Eve doesn't miss a beat. She clangs a fork to her plate and sings out, "Forget him!"

Nona's shoulders droop and Cassie rushes in: "Give him time." As Nona sucks in her lips like a hurt child, Cassie offers what she realizes is inadequate advice. "Maybe it will work out after all if you just let him come around when he's ready."

The table the women are squeezed in at, elbow to elbow, is on the glassed-in patio fronting a wide street of imperial palms. Beyond, its thundering unheard by the diners, the Pacific pounds up the sand. The transparent wall screens out almost all sound, but not the crushed face that suddenly presses against it. Snakes of hair in tiny braids radiate from a primeval face, ancient and misshapen.

"Shoo! Scat!" A waiter has darted outside and flaps a starched white napkin at the old woman who is fixed in front of them with a shopping cart crammed full of belongings. "Get away!" He thrusts at her, a clumsy matador, until she drags along and places herself against the glass before the next table and then the next. The waiter, flapping his arms, chases her off at last.

"She's hungry. We can't let her walk away without some food. Some money," Nona says.

"If you want to feed her, why not bring her in, sit her down—"

"Eve, that's foolish!" Cassie interrupts, though she has heard the sardonic note in Eve's voice. She doesn't think Eve will rush out for the old woman and dance her inside. Maybe back in her Jordan days she would have. But by Abramson's time she was taking a defensive stance toward outrageous radical gestures. With Abramson, whose heart was in the right place but who displayed a certain timidity about going on the barricades, she settled for giving money and signing petitions.

Nona, however, has taken Eve's impulsive suggestion seriously and before either woman can stop her is up and out of the restaurant. Cassie can't decide if she should follow her or not.

"I don't believe this."

"You gave her the idea."

"But does she have to listen to me? Can't she discriminate between what's done and what's simply conversation?"

Cassie watches Nona come around the side of the restaurant and up to the old woman. "Sometimes I think she really does confuse reality and fantasy," she says. Nona's hand darts out for the creature's ragged cardigan sleeve; the woman shakes her loose.

Nona and the shopping-cart lady are within feet of the glass, but except for Cassie and Eve, the other diners ignore them, as if the wall were solid stone, admitting no unpleasant images of the homeless. The friends watch the pantomime warily. Will they need to hurry to Nona's rescue? The conversation between such disparate species—Nona tall, slim, and lithe; the woman, who might even be young beneath the dirt and madness, as round as a pillow—goes nowhere, however. Moving suddenly against the traffic light, the woman lumbers off the curb.

For a second it's possible that Nona means to gallop after her. Cassie cries, "Oh no!" and Eve half-rises. But Nona returns, though not dragging her feet or chagrined, as both women silently agree she ought to be. She takes long strides and, swinging her arms, finally draws attention. The man of the couple at the next table comments to his companion, "Pretty woman."

Nona's chair clatters as she reclaims it and the women say

nothing. Nona might simply have left the table to powder her nose.

Cassie encourages Nona to eat. The garlic soup is first-rate here, but Nona wrinkles her nose at garlic. She'll smell, and maybe Fitz will be waiting, so she should be careful.

"You're demented!" Eve cries.

At this discovery that Fitz has a key, Cassie almost orders Nona to get the locks changed at nine the next morning, but Nona digs in her heels. She shoves out her chin and reminds Cassie of Mandy. Mandy is back in Portland and suspiciously silent. In other circumstances Cassie can see calling Doug to ask what he's heard, but while that would have been hard before, now it's out of the question.

Nona orders shrimp salad for dinner. "Low in calories," she states defiantly, as if she has a weight problem. She expects Eve to yell at her about this too. Of course Eve raises her voice because she loves Nona, but still Nona hates the criticism, which falls on her like a handful of stones.

Across the street, on the park side, the shopping-cart woman is standing under a streetlamp. Nona turns away and moves her chair, crowding in closer to Cassie. She is still wounded by the derelict's refusal to let her be kind.

I have nothing in common with her, nothing, Nona thinks, and the very idea, so silly, brings tears welling up in her eyes. A breadstick she doesn't even realize she's picked up snaps between her fingers.

Cassie touches her shoulder and says, "There's always tomorrow."

Eve explodes in laughter. "My God! What tripe! You are straight out of afternoon TV."

"Well, at least you sound more like your old self, all snitty and difficult," Cassie retorts, embarrassed.

But Eve has managed to pull a smile out of Nona, who reminds them that *The McKenzies* is a part of her life. "To the soaps then!" Eve says and raises her wineglass for a toast.

"I'm worried about her," Cassie phones Eve to say.

"You can't always."

"Before this there was married Alan, and before him—"

"Her sister's keeper."

"You make me sound imbecilic," Cassie says and, when she hangs up the phone, tries to put Nona and her problems out of her mind. But then she begins worrying about April.

She feels responsible for April, and guilty because she should have done more, but what? and how? The husband was already dead when April called, so Cassie's being near a phone wouldn't have saved his life. Still . . .

The police were kinder to April than Cassie expected them to be. Though they took her off to jail, no matter how loudly Cassie cried *self defense!*, they waited until her sister drove up from Whittier to claim the children.

Afterward, April said that they were quiet with their questions, that they gave her coffee and Kleenex, that they let her go to the bathroom, though with a matron. And most importantly, to Cassie's thinking, they contacted Legal Aid. April, now out on bail, has a lawyer, a smart redhead from Stanford who burns with indignation. She plans to put Cassie on the stand as her star witness. He beat her, Cassie will say. He pushed her down the steps. He raped her.

April has been allowed by the court to stay at her sister's until the trial, which is scheduled for early in the new year. Cassie talks to her on the phone once a week and when she does, April remembers. No more excuses, bouts of amnesia. She describes to Cassie each slap, each push, every punch and poke, the cigarette burns on her feet. April remembers and Cassie longs to forget. She tells April she wishes none of it happened. Well, it did, April tells Cassie back, and—she is learning from the firebrand lawyer—I was driven crazy.

The things men can do to women, Cassie thinks each time she hangs up from a call with April, and again with Nona.

"Will you quit drooping?" Lorraine, hands on her hips, legs spread—she-devilish as a kung-fu instructor—accosts Nona before the three-way mirror. One of the day's periodic lulls has marooned the two of them alone. Lorraine, whose eyes have been as red-rimmed as chinaberries since Nona arrived that morning—though Nona is afraid to ask why—wants to fight.

Nona falls into Lorraine's net before she can shut her mouth, and says, "I'm not drooping."

"You're scrunched in like a turtle."

"I'm not."

"Don't argue with me, Nona, especially since you're supposed to give our customers confidence. When they shop at Flora's they have a right to the best."

Lorraine makes the store first cousin to a cathedral, and if Nona hadn't just caught her unhappy face sliding across a wedge of mirror, she might have squared off with her manager this once and said, *Lorraine, you're a fool*. But she's the fool. Droopy. Lorraine's right.

She simply can't find Fitz. His listing in the phone book appears minus address. Venice is where he said he lived, and on Sunday, Nona tours it from one end of the boardwalk to the other. Though it is winter, the weather is indistinguishable from late spring. The sun blazes from an unblemished blue sky, and a faint breeze blows off the water, so Venice is jammed with nearly nude bathers, gawking tourists, bulging weight lifters oiled and sweaty, dangerously fast roller-skaters. Girls in G-string bikinis are so plentiful they barely draw admiring glances. A midget, elegant as a bridegroom in a white suit, shirt, tie, shoes, drags a heavy wood cross from one end of the strip to the other in his weekend ritual.

A lonesome pine, growing out of a tub in the sand, wears colored balls, tinsel, and angel hair. An old woman on a folding chair keeps trying to straighten the lopsided gold star at its top.

All of Los Angeles seems to be on the Venice boardwalk, except for Fitz.

Nona broods again about calling the police and reporting him missing. Or hiring a private detective. The idea of a detective entertains her while she decides if she'd rather he look like Paul Newman or Robert Mitchum when younger. A private eye is thrilling, and she can just see herself climbing a flight of creaky stairs to a plain office where the ratty carpet has coffee stains and cigarette burns dotting it, and where she hires a man in a shiny suit, a man wearing a hat, though he has all his hair.

The adventure of a detective continues all the way home from Venice to Westwood. Nona enters the quiet apartment, which feels as vacant as a for-sale condo. How different coming home was when Fitz waited, or when she knew he'd be over later.

He's gone, lost, abducted, missing, or maybe he just doesn't care anymore, she thinks, and starts crying from the knobby hurt in her chest. He's got to resurface in her life because she wants him so. She's done nothing wrong. . . .

I want to know you inside out. Tell me . . .

No, I never, Nona shivers, frightened. Nothing, only revisionist history, one of her stories, sanitized details, that's all she ever said.

She grabs a Diet Sprite and turns up Michael Jackson on the stereo until the slats on her blinds quiver. She walks around and around her living room, refusing to remember what she might have done or said, stoned on grass and too much wine.

"I wouldn't," she cries aloud in the few beats of silence between "Thriller" and "Beat It." "I couldn't have told him anything true!"

The possibility that she's been foolish sticks in her mind, and later she calls Fitz's answering machine to leave a message. But after the buzz she can't think how to explain and she hangs up.

When Jake's fingers still on the guitar strings, Cassie asks him what he thinks about Fitz's slipping out on the tide, leaving not so much as a note in a bottle, not even a thank-you for all the lovely memories.

Jake has been playing a country tune about lost babies and angels. The words, he told her, weren't important. It was the melody. Cassie doesn't care which she is supposed to listen for, just enjoying Jake's filling her bedroom with music. No one has ever serenaded Cassie before, though Jake plays as much for himself as for her. He sits on the end of the old plaid chaise longue by the window and lets the music carry him off into another dimension. Since the room is long and the bedside lamps cast little light beyond the puddles that splash on the hardwood just to the end of the bed, Jake is bathed in shadows. From where she leans against the headboard, letting his sad song float around her like smoke, Cassie can hear him better than she can see him.

All his songs seem to be sad ones, though once when Cassie accused Jake of this, he denied it. Then, the next time he played for her—as if to prove her wrong—he sang only of protest (though never songs from *his* war), and the following week he made her laugh with comic tunes. But eventually he returned to the slow unhappy songs that he is most comfortable with.

Nona and Fitz—or more specifically Nona—could be the subject of one of Jake's songs. Jake maintains, "It's no big deal to write a song about anything or anybody if you've got the right melody."

Cassie shakes her head, thinking of Nona's latest romance set to music. "Why do you suppose he did it, just went off on her like that?"

"How do I know? I never met the guy."

"Just as a man, what do you think?"

Cassie decides he's being stubborn. She says, "A man is more clued in to other men. I mean you should be able to at least guess what's with Fitz. Besides . . ." She leaves him an opening to bring up his running away on her and how she had to go after him, to entice him back into her life. Since that night the question—which maybe now, in this discussion of Fitz, Jake might satisfactorily answer—is: Would he have returned on his own?

"Look, I'm one guy, not the whole hetero population of L.A. Don't start believing I can tap in to a male unconscious anymore than you can with women." She has amused him and he smiles at her.

"In terms of emotions I have a better than good idea what goes on in most female minds." Does she? Sometimes she's not even sure what goes on in her own head, but she won't say that to Jake, for she understands him less than anyone. In many ways he's still a stranger to her, and if her trust is misplaced she won't find out until their affair is over.

"Play some more," Cassie says, feeling safe with Jake when he is involved with his music.

"No, I'm tired." He stands and lays the guitar carefully on the chaise. From the distance it seems as though there's another person in the room with them, someone else stretched out for sleep. The way Jake touches the instrument heightens Cassie's fantasy.

"For what it's worth, my bet is on Nona's friend having done the good-bye boogie and he's chickenshit about saying so. If he keeps incommunicado long enough, Nona will cool down and nobody will have to have a confrontation. Men hate confrontations," Jake says, taking off his shirt, getting ready for bed in her room with the ease of a man who's been here before, who expects to spend the night again in the future.

"You just said you can only speak for yourself," Cassie reminds him, wondering, even as the sight of his naked body pleases her, whether she wants him to be so comfortable in her house. *At home*, Beth commented, and Nona and Eve agreed.

He pulls back the covers and slips between the sheets. "Okay, *I* hate confrontations."

"Then we'll never have them," she promises bravely, certain as she will ever be that when Jake goes out of her life it is going to be in much the same way that Fitz has vanished from Nona's. Oh, she believes he'll say good-bye but he'll be brief and he'll hurry.

Jake curls on his side and Cassie leans toward him, but his back is firmly to her and she can't see his eyes. Not that his eyes will tell her any secrets.

Jake lets slip no more than he has in the past. In fact, these days they talk less. Cassie waits to hear about the war, Vietnam, friends killed or maimed in action, his wanderlust and unsatisfying travels. But if she swerves too close to the personal, he changes direction. He has suffered more than enough and she has no right to layer up questions like bricks around him.

Often, with Jake, Cassie bites her tongue and keeps quiet.

With his spine rounded, his legs pulled up, and his arms looped about his knees, Jake's vulnerable middle is protected. This is his serious sleeping position, and if Cassie nudges up, runs a tentative hand over his exposed skin, a ripple that she fears is terror will shiver through him.

When they sleep, a Gaza Strip must run down the center of the bed separating them.

Now, with the covers up to the ridge of his cheekbone, she listens to the soft ruffle of Jake's breath and knows he has fallen— as he always does—instantaneously asleep. She wishes he would wake up, though even needing to crawl into the space his arms provide, needing to make love, she won't wake him.

Moving silently, she readies for bed, for sleep. When she switches off the light the darkness, for the first few seconds, is total. Then her eyes adjust to the grayness along the window, the grainy texture beneath the door. In a little while, she thinks, she'll drift off, but instead she lies awake for hours.

It finally becomes obvious even to Nona that Fitz has gone underground, that he's folded his tent and sneaked out o her life, though she can't think why. She stops asking his mechanical voice to return her call. If her fingers still tremble when she opens her box in the mail room off the lobby, it's because a letter takes time; a letter, therefore, is possible. Writing, though, is more a woman's thing. Writing is what Nona thinks of when she struggles to restore a frayed connection. It is the act of writing, almost more than what is down on paper, that's important. A letter casts a bridge across space.

Nona spends forty minutes of her lunch hour picking out a Christmas card for Fitz in one of the mall's stores. A cheery Santa on a beach, sprawled in a deck chair, sipping a drink from a frosted glass with a paper umbrella in it. *There's more than one way to spend Christmas*. Underneath Nona dashes off in violet ink, *Have an absolutely terrific holiday!* But of course she can't mail it because she has no idea where he is. The card remains in her night-table drawer while she waits for a card from Fitz. But she receives nothing.

"It could be the post office." On the phone with Eve she is hopeful. "They're notoriously bad during the holidays."

"He's not giving you a card, a call, anything. And don't hold your breath for a diamond necklace to be delivered by limo from Cartier's. The shit is passé, last month's male. He's a rat and you're better off without him."

"But it's Christmas!"

Eve ignores the holidays. She gives what business presents are mandatory, a check to her mother, fruit baskets to important clients, small gifts—under fifty dollars—to both Nona and Cassie. Usually she buys Mandy a sweatshirt, a bottle of teenage cologne, a junk jewelry bracelet. She does this because it pleases Cassie, especially since the divorce. This year, if Eve follows her instincts, she'll give Mandy a spanking with a paddle.

Nona, on the other hand, loves a fuss. She puts up a tree each year and has a small group of friends over for eggnog and carols on Christmas Eve. But as the holiday approaches she thinks for a while of forgoing the ritual, of letting the season wash over her and pretending it isn't happening. As if that's possible. The mall is a gaudy carnival, with elaborate decorations and a tree that soars two stories high. There are carolers in Dickensian dress, corduroy knickers and striped scarves, and a Santa on a throne for the little children. Shop windows have artificial snow or candy canes or small sleighs piled high with gaily wrapped boxes. The presents look beautiful but are empty boxes beneath their glossy paper and bows.

Mostly in the Crystal Mall at this time of year there are crowds with a purposeful lift to their push and shove, a glow of determination in their eyes. People are intent on spending money.

Usually Nona has a slight buzz on all through the season. She floats, naturally high on the glitter and communal cheer. This Christmas, however, she sinks. Her spirits unravel and she drags, physically weary, feeling as though she is being tugged into the ground. She stops at Dr. Rubin's to have him examine her. He announces that she has a very common syndrome. Not to worry. She will be much improved by the second week in January. If not, he prescribes a weekend skiing where she can concentrate on not breaking a leg. Nona realizes Dr. Rubin isn't being sympathetic and wonders if she should consider switching physicians, finding a doctor to whom she's not old hat. But lethargy keeps her from making any immediate decision and she goes ahead with the annual party. More energy is involved in breaking tradition than continuing. Eve plans to bring Johnny, and Jake is invited to accompany Cassie and Mandy, though Mandy will undoubtedly drive herself.

"A fly in paradise," Eve says when the three women meet for a quick bite on the third floor of the mall. They snatch fifteen minutes to rest their feet in the midst of Christmas shopping.

"All right," Cassie, confronted, shrugs. "Mandy's uncomfortable with Jake around."

"Downright hostile, if you ask me," Eve says, shredding her roll so she won't have to eat the crust.

"No, don't make it worse," Cassie counters. "It's just that they're uneasy. They pass each other like ghosts."

Nona empties half a bottle of ketchup on her hamburger. "She's tense," Nona says, "with the man, with a man in her mother's life. Sounds normal to me."

"Are you actually going to try and shove that thing in your

mouth?" Eve asks as Nona lifts the large soggy mess of meat and bun, lettuce, tomato, relish, and ketchup.

"I start to ask her about Jake, why she becomes a dark cloud when he's around—and she's only seen him, what? four or five times—but she clams up. From the second she got off the plane the standard remark is there's nothing to talk about."

"God, Nona, you've got goop on your chin."

Nona wipes her face unconcerned and takes another enormous wedge of hamburger into her mouth. "Stop watching me," she says, trying to chew and talk. "You know I get all piggy with cheap burgers."

Eve says, "We've noticed."

Nona goes back to Mandy. "Has she given any hints about her feelings?"

"Just the same drill—nothing to talk about."

"Of course there is. You don't like him."

"Did I say I don't like him, Mother?" Mandy using *Mother* is a bad sign.

She draws up and away from Cassie, leaner now since she has lost weight, fifteen pounds, which is too much for the few short weeks between Thanksgiving and Christmas. So Cassie worries over her daughter, who leaves the room with a rigid spine, haughty as a British duchess.

The next morning she catches Mandy at breakfast. "I care about Jake," she says, sitting down on the opposite chair.

Mandy scowls over oatmeal and sliced apples. "Good for you."

"And I want you to be friends with him."

"I think I'm old enough to pick my own friends. I do go away to school and live somewhere else most of the time."

"You live here. This is home." Cassie is more adamant than she means to be.

"I think home's where I usually am, not where I come for vacations."

Cassie slams her cup on the saucer, and coffee splatters her cuff. Even as she rushes to wash the muddy stain out of the silk she knows it's useless, that there will always be a faded blotch.

The following night Cassie knocks on Mandy's door and asks if they can talk.

She perches tentatively on the edge of the desk chair, ready for flight, though she has determined to have "this" out with her daughter. Why should Jake bother Mandy so when, as Cassie promises, "He's never going to come between us. He's not a Tracy."

"Mother, Tracy and Daddy are *married*."

"That's what I mean." Cassie bows forward, so ardent she feels she might snap in half. There's a tight knot in her stomach. "I'm not going to marry Jake." Of course I'm not! The declaration, blurted out without a moment's consideration surprises Cassie and she broods over it. When did she decide so firmly that Jake wasn't to have a permanent, an established position in her life? The other night she thought about his going and that he was the kind of man (what does she know about *kinds* of men?) who, like Fitz, was destined to get out the door before she would even realize it had creaked open. But wasn't she just scaring herself? She isn't determined that he'll leave, or have to—rather the opposite. In fact Jake's not being in her life makes Cassie want to do something dramatic, like punch a wall or run up and down the sidewalk yelling. But she knows that eventually he will be, to use one of Eve's expressions, *sayonara*.

"I care about Jake. I guess you could say I love him." Cassie swallows painfully. "But we'll never get married, or even be together for always." As Cassie fumbles in expressing her feelings to Mandy, who shouldn't be told too much according to all the books Cassie has read—a child is a child and not a best friend!— Mandy, looking bored as milk, spreads *Cosmo* across her chest. "You're obsessed," she says. "Nothing bothers me. Just forget I'm here and go about your little love affair. I'm just trying to survive Christmas, read all my assignments, and see my friends. Have a great time. I'm happy for you." She closes her mouth in a narrow line of disapproval. How have I raised such a puritanical daughter? Cassie wonders.

The conversation is heading nowhere, though Cassie persists in talking on for another few minutes. Mandy seems just as unconvinced by Cassie's confidences as she was before she made them. Or maybe there's bad chemistry between Mandy and Jake and she *sincerely* dislikes him. But why? "It's not a requirement of life to like everybody you come across," Mandy replies when Cassie asks her.

"Sometimes I think I'm butting my head against a stone wall with you . . . honey." She tacks on the "honey" so Mandy won't think she's angry.

"Then give it up, Mom." *Mom* instead of *Mother*. Well, at least they've advanced that far. Mandy resumes reading her magazine, and Cassie, leaving the room, decides to quit while she's ahead.

Cassie continues to fret over Christmas Eve, though as it turns out they all drive their own cars. So when she's in line by the cash register at the liquor store and shrieks "Oh, my God!" neither Jake nor Mandy is beside her to ask "What's wrong?"

The picture at the bottom right of the muckraking, scandal-happy tabloid explodes in front of her. The entire bundle of papers might as easily burst into flames. Cassie snatches up the top one and reads: DAUGHTER MOLESTED BY AMERICA'S FIRST SUPER SPY!, which is the caption under a grainy yellow-tinted photo of Nona, smiling that waif smile that makes people want to say *Hush, honey* and take her home. She is standing at an angle, staring back over her shoulder and wearing her Calvin Klein denim jacket and a T-shirt.

Cassie drops the champagne she's clutching—a domestic vintage selected by price rather than name—and the bottle shatters on the floor. The man ahead of Cassie jumps and yells "God damn!" accusingly, but Cassie, riveted by Nona's picture, is too shocked to notice.

Nona molested? Spy? Her father?

Nona's father was a staid, buttoned-down businessman who died of a coronary. Her father, she'd said more than once, was elegant.

"Lady, that's a twenty-five-buck bottle of champagne you broke. *Lady?*" says the man behind the counter.

"What? Oh, I'm sorry."

"Sorry! Jeez! The holidays bring 'em out of the walls."

"I'll pay."

"Twenty-five plus tax."

Cassie hands over the money, moves aside, and still shaking, reads a story which—though there are threads of familiarity woven into it—finally is weaving a tapestry as strange as a map of alien outer space. This isn't her Nona, it can't be, never mind the picture, Boston, Adam the entrepreneur, Marian, a big white house with pillars.

Engels? Nona Engels?

There's a terrible mistake—this scandal sheet screeching in large type. Nona's name isn't Engels, hasn't been, never was, at least not all the years Cassie's known her.

They must retract such garbage: sexual molestation. Cassie gags and doesn't hear the cashier until he raises his voice and repeats, "And that's fifty cents for the *Insider*."

Adam Engels, America's pin-striped spy. A faint bell rings in Cassie's memory as she reads of secrets sold for a small fortune, political friends, bad business deals, traded information, a high life of antiques, caviar, Dom Perignon, a Silver Cloud.

Engels was the flashiest of spies, not drab like the Rosenbergs, or ordinary like the more recent Walkers. Engels was a high-living scoundrel with a broad smile, a superb businessman, a CEO, a member of various charity boards, an elegant party giver, and according to the leering *Insider* reporter, a man who had sex with his daughter.

He used his only child to fulfill vile desires. Engels perverted the lovely girl, as beautiful as a flower. For years Nona Engels moved in a stupor. Even her fiancé, once aware of how depraved Engels had made her, couldn't bring himself to marry Nona. Though he loved her and has been quoted more than once as remarking that she was "the equal to a young Elizabeth Taylor," he severed their engagement.

Coming upon Engels and the girl on the night of a sumptuous party in the aristocratic enclave of . . .

The prose is as thick as treacle, and out in the car Cassie devours every word. The story, as unbelievable as science fiction, is, however, Cassie thinks, at least true in checkable details.

Engels, Cassie discovers reading further, died in prison. (*Died just like that*, Nona said of her father. He never knew. Dead as he collapsed.)

There are pictures of Nona on the inside pages that erase any doubt Cassie might have. Nona caught in tentative half-step at the front of the federal courthouse. Again, next to a car before a large house matching descriptions Cassie has heard often enough. Another of Nona, arm in arm, very *Town and Country*, with Adam Engels, a handsome, decidedly virile man on a sloping lawn.

Adam Engels looks younger than reported and, with his arm around Nona's waist, more lover than father. Which the *Insider* scurrilously asserts he was.

"I'm not saying what I saw; I'm merely saying *no comment!*" Simon Anderson, Nona's ex-fiancé, retorted heatedly to the *Insider* writer.

Who was the witness? The actors? Which were onstage?

I saw Simon and his best friend . . .

Cassie struggles to remember the long-ago, lost, supposedly too loving friend but loses his name.

"The innocent boy came upon the girl he adored and Adam Engels, who was to blaze a trail in infamy, embracing in the bedroom. Engels was fondling his daughter's . . ."

Nauseated, Cassie cannot read any more. The tabloid's style verges on camp, a parody, yet the writer is skillfully descriptive. Cassie can almost see the scene, reversed from the one Nona laid out on a table.

How like Nona to invert the horror of discovery, to stand the story on its head. It's Simon in Nona's version who's the betrayer, who engages in the awful behavior.

Cassie doesn't blame her. The lie is stained with pain, with blood. She sees the young teenage girls of the clinic, confused and bewildered. It's Adam Engels and the writer of the *Insider* article who should be hung by their toes.

Cassie flips to the front page and finally reads the byline of the writer, revealed as unabashedly as if he had signed his name to an article in *Esquire*.

She's not surprised. In hindsight the brittle, icy light in Fitz's eyes signaled malevolence. He was a beast with a handsome face, yet they should have known. He showed far too many teeth when he smiled.

And he preyed on Nona as mercilessly as did her father.

She and Eve recommended him to Nona on the basis of his

singleness. After Alan he shone, and, along with Nona, they were hopeful. He trailed no marriage with him, though he might have that, too: a wife, even children. Who can tell? Not that it matters. In the collection of Fitz's sins adultery is minor.

So many procedures, routines, pills, syrups, sprays, so much machinery of one sort or another, wires, tubes, vials, to alleviate physical anguish, and yet nothing Cassie can write a prescription for will help this. Well, she could throw the tabloid into the trash, go on to Nona's as if these past fifteen minutes never happened, and pray.

Recklessly she considers not turning up for eggnog, bouillabaisse, salad, raspberry torte, but it's only a fleeting thought. When has she ever ducked the unpleasant? Besides, Mandy and Jake are there.

Cassie checks her watch. She should hurry. In other years she was always early, helping Nona set up. Nona adores all the delicate gestures, a doily under the petits fours, the napkins folded like origami. Slices of lemon are decorated with mint sprigs. She'd ice the champagne glasses if the freezer were big enough.

This Christmas Eve, Cassie would rather travel on her knees in a pilgrimage from Nazareth to Bethlehem than attend Nona's party. The kiss she'll place on Nona's cheek is the kiss of Judas. How will she make small talk, eat, drink, raise her glass in a toast to health, friends, good times always, Tiny Tim!

Cassie sits so long in the car, parked directly opposite the liquor store door, that the clerk comes to the window to stare at her. He's scowling, with no Christmas spirit in his heart. Yet to give him his due, maybe Cassie means to rob him. There are baby bandits and grandmotherly thieves and pairs of pretty girls. Cassie's looks and the knit suit, pearl eye shadow, and diamond studs in her ears are no guarantee.

As their glances clash through two thicknesses of glass, Cassie anticipates his finger on the trigger.

She crushes the paper in her hands. The *Insider* isn't the *Times*, or even *People*. It's not at all the style of news anyone Cassie—or Nona—knows reads, except while waiting in the supermarket line to pay for groceries. Scurrilous gossip and incredible stories— THREE-HEADED DWARF RAPES MOTHER! SEVEN-YEAR-OLD GIVES

BIRTH TO ALIEN! TV TALK SHOW HOST REINCARNATION OF REM-
BRANDT!—are not for them. Nona and friends could, theoretically,
get by without seeing DAUGHTER MOLESTED BY AMERICA'S FIRST
SUPER SPY!

I didn't . . .

The clerk moves to the glass doors and positions himself with
the macho spread-leg stance of a state trooper. In a minute he'll
be out after her. She can't procrastinate much longer.

25

"I didn't say I don't like him."

"Well, do you?"

Nona backs off two steps from the pantry counter, where the trays of hors d'oeuvres wait, ready to be ferried into the living room. Mandy has arrived early, maybe to help but more likely to talk.

"He's not up to her. You know what I mean?"

"Because he's no doctor or a lawyer like your father?"

Mandy wrinkles her nose. "That sounds racist."

"Racist?" Nona asks.

"Like I don't like him because he doesn't have any money. And that's not it. Money is irrelevant. Tacky. I mean thinking about it."

Nona wonders if she ever sounded quite so silly with her rich parents and a life in which no one ever mentioned how much things cost. She supposes all sheltered children—and Mandy is surely that—are more than a little foolish.

"Let's get the deviled eggs out of the fridge. They have to be arranged on a plate."

"That long glass one? It's the one we used last year."

Nona is pleased. "You remember."

"Why shouldn't I? I'm not a lamebrain," Mandy replies testily. She suspects that her mother's friends, even Nona, think her crazy over boys, makeup, clothes, with having a good time and partying. They probably even think she takes drugs, which she doesn't except for recreational grass offered at every party Mandy attends.

Grass is as common as beer and pretzels and no more a drug in Mandy's mind than aspirin.

Mandy sees herself as an essentially serious person. At certain moments, it's true, she is lost in the woods, unable to separate the individual trees, but this happens to everyone who's not a moron. She crosses her heart and swears she's alert, but in fact much information bounces off her. More placid than prickly, she has never been a child who automatically responds to a *yes* with a *no*. Only recently has she reacted negatively even to her mother, though, since Jake, she couldn't agree with Cassie if her life depended on it. She has fantasies where she and Cassie are in a burning house or on a sinking ship and Cassie tells her what to do to save herself but Mandy won't listen or does the opposite and dies.

Mandy has recently come to realize that Cassie has no idea, absolutely none, who she, Mandy, is and even less hope of finding out—information she shares with Nona. "So if I'm a black hole in space to her, how can she understand about *him*?"

Nona doesn't get the connection and itches to change the subject. There is a certain disloyalty in discussing Cassie with Mandy.

When Nona was a teenager adults avoided any topic even faintly unpleasant. At least the grown-ups in her life did. Marian in particular walked off in the middle of a sentence if Nona discomfited her. Certain subjects simply weren't to be talked about, were as off-limits as enemy territory behind barbed wire.

Nona thinks of closed doors, Marian's pinched face coming at her in a mirror. She hears Adam's laughter as if he were in the next room rather than the grave, and she shivers.

"He could be an ax murderer even," Mandy continues, refusing to let Jake go.

Nona lifts her head. "He's not, and you can say his name without making a commitment to like the man."

Mandy rocks on the balls of her feet. "You're making fun of me."

"Nope, but you're juvenile, sweet, to say *him* for *Jake*. Let the man have his name."

It's difficult for Mandy to back off, but this is Nona. She relents. "Oh, I guess you're right. It's just that he's crawling around in our lives like a snake."

"What is it about him that you object to?" She hands Mandy the cheese platter to carry into the next room.

"He's not substantial," Mandy calls back.

"He's very good-looking."

Mandy returns for the deviled eggs. "I don't think so. He needs a shave whenever I see him."

"Lots of men have heavy beards." Nona follows with the dip.

"Why doesn't he shave more often then?"

"Oh, stop! His beard has nothing to do with why you don't like him."

Mandy's shoulders come up. *"Don't like* is extreme."

"Stop fussing," Nona says, lightly touching Mandy's arm as if to gentle her, "and count the glasses."

Mandy protests but Nona leaves her at the wet bar to make a quick inventory in the powder-room mirror. She tucks an errant hair in place, smooths a line by her mouth that won't go away, and finally satisfied, circles around to the kitchen.

The secret of the annual party's success is an excess of food, which—but for the eggs—Nona buys at the best takeout shop in Beverly Hills. Traditionally she has enough leftovers to feed another complete party.

Marian, Nona never forgets, was profligate with food.

"Which of your big squeezes did you invite?"

Nona twists to the side quickly. "Don't sneak up on me like that!"

"I'm not sneaking," Mandy says.

"I didn't hear you."

"Yeah, well, who has carpet in the kitchen?"

Nona replies defensively, "It's the latest thing."

"Eve's suggestion, I bet."

"No, Eve hates it."

Mandy runs hot and cold on Eve, though since the operation she is, if not bullish, at least less resentful of her. The currents of Mandy's likes and displeasures are often storm-tossed and, except for Jake, not worth bothering about. A sudden shift in the wind often changes her feelings. Nona hopes, for Cassie's sake, this will eventually be true for Jake, too, but gut instinct makes her doubt it.

"So, who is he?"

"Who?"

"The grand passion you've got coming tonight."

Mandy pictures Nona's life as straight out of *Dynasty*. If not exactly on a Hollywood fast track with stars and power brokers, she rides near enough. Nona has never had the heart to disillusion her.

"I'm on my own tonight."

"Didn't Mom tell me there was this love of your life?"

"*Was* is a big word." Nona shrugs, clenching her jaw and vowing not to cry. The twenty years' difference in their ages, and being a mother figure for Mandy as much as a friend, preclude Nona's coming unglued. She imagines one of *her* mother's friends flying into wails and shrieking of heartbreak and how she'd have wanted to crawl under the coffee table.

The ringing doorbell allows Nona to fend off Mandy's curiosity with a smile. She rushes to the first guests, relieved, remembering as she accepts a brightly wrapped present that she plans to enjoy her party though she is miserably unhappy. Another Christmas alone without husband and children, without a lover against whose warmth she can curl in bed.

Cassie shifts with anger. A nervous prickle inches down her spine and she drives off from the liquor store, from the squinty-eyed clerk whose annoyance was so visible. She drives nowhere in particular, not exactly toward Nona's apartment but not in the opposite direction either. Circling, that's what Cassie's doing, ringing around the flames of her rage and grief.

Of course she is mad at Fitz, James Fitzgerald, with his sweet Huck Finn, ah-shucks grin, the endearing way (according to unreliable Nona) he ruffled his hair. Oh, how he cared! How he listened with his head at an angle!

Of course he listened, after plying the dummy with questions, getting her drunk probably, yanking her past unfaithfully out of her. He used forceps and tore tissue.

Naturally men have taken advantage of Nona before, leaving footprints on her back, wringing her heart like a dishrag, behaving scandalously, as men only do with women they decide not to keep for the long haul. Nona is a born fool, beauty being no bulwark against outright bad use of her body and good nature, but (to Cassie's knowledge) no man has ever dissected her from cerebellum to Achilles tendon.

Cassie stops at a light. A dark shadow crosses from corner to corner, nearly brushing the bumper. Without a moment of moral hesitation, if that sliding shape were Fitz, her foot would descend on the gas.

Not only Fitz, however, stokes Cassie's anger. She is mad at Nona too for having fallen victim to a man whose sole purpose in her life was to get a good story. And she is furious because she's the one who has seen the *Insider*. She no more wants to possess this lethal knowledge than she would want to stand up in front of a firing squad.

Now she must show Nona the tabloid. She must.

Over in Westwood they're all gathering. Maybe Mandy is at Nona's already. If Jake arrives and finds she's not there he'll back into a corner. Her friends make him uncomfortable. *I'm the wrong man in the wrong place* is all he says, and Cassie feels lucky if Jake turns up at all. She hates to lie, to manufacture a sudden flu or a car breakdown.

Her anger feeds on itself. She grows furious with Jake, with Mandy, even with Eve, for not coming across the *Insider* first. Why is she always the one to break the bad news?

The first time Cassie had to announce a patient's death she thought, I can't do this forever, saying words people slap useless hands over their ears not to hear. I can't be the messenger of the worst of bad tidings.

She couldn't beg off, because she was too conscious of being a female and vulnerable to taunts of weakness. She had to bear burdens equal to those of her male colleagues. She needed to prove to the other resident and the attending surgeon in the O.R., where a young boy injured in a freak fall out a second-story schoolhouse window died, that she was able to say *I'm sorry but your son just passed away*.

Still in a scrub suit, her mask dangling loose at her neck, she padded to the lounge, where, face to face with the tear-streaked strangers, she recoiled.

My God, I'm out of my mind. *Died, passed away, we lost him, never regained consciousness*—all the words Cassie considered dried up in her mouth.

What she managed was "I'm sorry." Sorry! Bleeding heart! As if sorry changes *up* to *down*. As if they cared for *sorry*.

Even now each moment limps past in slow motion as she remembers that wrenching encounter.

It was late afternoon. The hospital hummed with the comings and goings of visiting hours, the outside world toting in gifts of magazines and flowers, the well hunching to hide exuberance and health from the ill.

The lounge near Recovery where families waited was painted bright orange and yellow. A paler yellow, almost white linoleum spread across the floor. An optimistic administrator believed a warm environment prodded time into passing more easily and faster.

The mother and father, old parents for the boy already wheeled under a sheet through a back hall and into a service elevator down to the morgue in the subbasement, held hands like teenage lovers. They clung to each other, oblivious to the framed Utrillo prints on the wall, the sloping cobbled streets, the muddy country walls, even to the light in outrageous splendor at the window. They stood up, terrified, as Cassie slapped toward them in her paper booties.

They were unremarkable, the man in a nondescript brown suit such as Cassie's father wore, the woman in a wrinkled two-tone purple print. They were everyday people holding their breath for Cassie to inform them that the structure of their lives had collapsed.

Beforehand she had determined not to sidle, take half steps, avert her eyes from the sting of the parents' anguish. She would look at them straightforwardly, but then she saw them first inching to the edges of their identical plastic chairs, slowly rising, taking so long to stand up they frightened her. What made her think so arrogantly that she had the strength to rip their son out of their arms? As long as she kept her mouth shut he remained alive, would possibly survive to be well again, maybe scarred but undamaged. The moment she voiced *passed away*, their illusions would vaporize and they would no longer be parents terrified by their boy's accident but bludgeoned mourners.

A reddish purple stain near the waistband marked the mother's dress. The father's striped tie was loosened, his collar unbuttoned. His shoes were scuffed and needed a shine.

(Cassie, years after the fact, is still awash with details. Her memory faithfully snapped photographs she would just as soon lock away in the dark.)

As it happened—and would in numbing repetition her whole professional life—she had only to start with *I'm sorry* for the father to shake his head from side to side and the mother to seize the tail of grief and kite high in a shriek.

I'm sorry, Cassie said that first time, and added as the mother staggered back in her chair, flinging out the words in a rush of panic at the shocked parents: *We tried*.

Though Cassie is no longer hypnotized by tragedy, tongue-tied in the face of grief and despair, she can't, just can't, when showing Nona the *Insider*, throw out stock, meaningless phrases. No *I'm sorry, the truth's out*. But what can she say?

Distracted, Cassie lets the car wander from its lane, crossing the white line in front of a Cadillac. The screech of a horn jerks her back into place. The near miss sets her hands shaking and she pulls off at the entrance of a high-rise. She sits hyperventilating until she can say out loud, "I'm tired of being the grown-up."

Bear up, Cassie, everybody said when Doug got his itch and ran off, just like a kid deciding to play. Doug didn't stay home because of obligations, oaths sworn, because Cassie was a good wife and helpmate. He absconded in a swoon for long, firm legs, a swollen mouth, and breasts like peaches.

Doug wouldn't consider for a minute doing anything but throwing the *Insider* into the trash and sallying on to Nona's party as if he hadn't read it. Not my problem. Or alternatively he'd rush in and holler, *Hey, what's this, your father was Adam Engels the spy?* He'd salivate for details, though not even Doug could ask flat out, *Did the two of you have sex together?*

By the time Cassie gets herself to Nona's, the party is half over. Mandy meets her at the door with raised brows, her eyes brimming with worry that Cassie is too rattled to recognize. "Where have you been?" Mandy demands.

"Busy."

Jake is on Mandy's far side. "I was just going to split." Cassie hasn't heard the expression *to split* in years and the anachronism scrapes against her bad temper.

"You should have called," Mandy says, claiming her mother's right arm.

"I couldn't."

"You need a car phone. I bet you're the only doctor in Los Angeles who doesn't have one."

"She's right," Jake adds, as if either female asked him.

For once Mandy and Jake are in agreement, but Cassie has no desire to discuss car phones with them. "I'd love a glass of wine," she says and moves farther into the room.

"Mom, you're acting peculiar." Mandy trails Cassie. "And where's the champagne you were bringing?"

Jake has gone off to get her a drink from the bar and when he returns Cassie downs it greedily. Jake expects her to sit and be still but she keeps going to Eve on the couch. She squeezes Eve's shoulder and whispers, "We've got to talk."

"Talk?"

"Alone."

Cassie feels like a sneaky kid, slyly creeping off to the bathroom. Tears bead her lashes and the mascara stings her eyes. The color has been nibbled off her bottom lip and the edges of her two front teeth are stained with Pink Passion.

When the door is closed and locked, and Eve is sitting on the rim of the tub, Cassie pulls out the crumpled *Insider* from her bag.

"What's this? Such secrecy."

"You don't know. Here, read."

The headline and prominent photograph startle a curse out of Eve: "God damn!" Cassie chews on a thumbnail while Eve reads the article. When she finishes she's flushed with anger. "Why did you have to show me this?"

"Thanks a lot. That's a big help."

"Oh, Lord!" Eve drops the paper and puts her head in her hands. "This will kill her."

"That's what people always say when they can't think of something original. Kill her! It won't kill her. Human beings don't drop dead so easily, not from bad news or twenty-year-old secrets out of the closet and going public in a supermarket sleaze sheet. Human beings, usually women, are more resilient."

"Right, until the whole enchilada becomes too much, like the case of your April," Eve reminds her.

"This is different."

"Well, if you're asking me, she has just as good a reason to skewer his liver, dear beloved Fitz. Oh he's so adorable! Like Attila the Hun was adorable. The prick!"

"Great, Eve. This is some help, sitting here and cursing out Fitz." Cassie's voice is shrill.

"Don't take it out on me. It's not my fault that this shit has gotten in the papers."

"Why hasn't she ever told us?" Cassie drinks a handful of tepid water from the tap, wishing she'd brought another glass of wine into the bathroom. Eve lights a cigarette. "Now you're going to poison me."

"I can't get through this without nicotine." Eve's tone is defiant.

"You're hooked again."

"Don't get all medical on me. I'm not hooked."

Cassie shrugs. "We can't sit in here all night and argue about your smoking. We have to do something. Nona's got to be prepared to see her face on the rack in the supermarket. I'm surprised nobody's out there waving copies of the *Insider*."

"Maybe nobody will say anything."

"You're being stupid."

"And you're impossible!"

They are both standing, shouting at each other. Cassie sees a red-faced stranger glowering from the mirror, and two beats pass before she realizes it's herself. "I don't like this," she says, turning away. "Being put in this position. I am tired of worrying, of catering to people, of figuring out where the emotional bandages go. I'm a gynecologist, an obstetrician, not a psychiatrist. My territory is the physical. But oh, no, that's not enough. Old Cassie had to soothe all the boo-boos. I have to be the calm one. Trust Cassie to fix it! I am so tired of—"

Eve is clapping her hands, the cigarette bobbing up and down in her mouth. "At last!"

Nona calls out, knocking repeatedly at the door. "What's going on in there?"

It is the worst Christmas ever, gray as a funeral, though the sun shines. It is an even more depressing and unhappy day than the first Christmas Cassie and Mandy dragged through without Doug. Religiously they stick to the rituals. Mandy, as always, gets up first and sneaks downstairs to the presents clustered about the base of the blue spruce. Forget that Mandy is grown up, able to fend for herself. "Mother, I'm not a child anymore!" On Christmas she demands a child's pleasures, the security of events falling like dominoes in the same predictable patterns. Any change is threatening, all the more so since her father vacated the big easy chair by the window, no longer sitting there in his bathrobe smiling as he drinks black coffee.

This Christmas especially, change is banished, not allowed to put a foot in the front door with its wreath of pine cones—meaning no Jake will sit cross-legged with Mandy and Cassie to open presents. Christmas Eve at Nona's had enough space in it for strangers, and Christmas dinner can be at the Levinsons' or Eve's or at some friend's with whom neither Cassie nor Mandy ever celebrated a holiday before. Christmas dinner is negotiable as long as there is a baked ham and mince pie. But from the moment they arrive home on Christmas Eve until dinner the next day, there are the small familiarities Mandy can't do without.

She pulls up the covers of her canopied bed on Christmas Eve the same little girl who expected Santa to come down the chimney, though she no longer puts cookies and milk on the mantel. She takes with her into sleep candy-cane dreams of surprises under the tree, the thrill of foil paper and bows, mysterious boxes and tissue paper.

A hand-knit stocking to fit the foot of a Brobdingnagian hangs on a hook between the bricks of the fireplace and will yield up treats of candy and bubble gum, licorice strings, pencils, memo pads, sharpeners in the shape of hot dogs or hamburgers, tiny bottles of perfume, lipsticks, round plastic boxes of makeup, cotton scarves, tennis socks, lace bikinis, a wind-up pair of smacking lips, a miniature rubber Snoopy.

Traditionally Mandy sits on the couch and dumps out the stocking's treasures before they get down to the business of opening serious presents. One or two at the most are tagged for Cassie; the rest are Mandy's.

Of course Cassie knows she overdoes, but she has no brakes at Christmas.

This year is no exception. Making Mandy happy has weighed heavily on Cassie since the divorce. But there's no triumph for her in Mandy's cries of delight. Time and again she is yanked back twelve hours to the night before.

To Nona, staring at her photograph and the blaring headline as they, miserable and helpless, watched her evolve into a homely woman with hard bones and loose skin. Her face was as colorless as floor wax, and against such paleness the bright red of her lips seemed obscene. There in her bathroom between Cassie and Eve she was no beauty, not even attractive.

"Nonsense!"

"Such garbage!"

"You can sue of course."

"And get yourself a nice nest egg."

Eve and Cassie couldn't keep still. They fought against Nona's silence, babbling—as they agreed later—like silly brooks.

Eve touched Nona's hand and it was so cold it chilled Eve's fingertips. Cassie tried an arm around her shoulder but there was concrete troweled over her bones.

They had assumed wailing and weeping. Perhaps Nona's fist smashing the bathroom mirror. Cassie was prepared to run to the car for the emergency bag she carried in the trunk. She hoped physical damage of some sort would take place, thereby allowing her to make it better. Medical skill would pull Nona through. Instead, Nona sank into the silence of withdrawal. She seemed to shrivel and, though almost catatonic, was drenched in sweat.

"We don't have to talk about this." Eve bowed her head.

Cassie rubbed moist palms on her thighs. "We won't, not tonight, not ever. Whatever makes you feel the best."

Nona had no answer. She arched over the sink, the paper spread below her. Slowly she read, word by word, her past made public in Fitz's article.

"Whatever you want," Cassie repeated, as if she might heal this wound with a promise. If only there were a process for the selective erasure of memory.

"Anything," Eve said, avoiding the slice of her own face in the mirror, focusing on Nona, preparing to catch her if she fell.

Nona said not a word, as if her voice had been sucked down her throat, as if her mind had disappeared altogether.

Eve poked Cassie. "Give her a shot."

"What kind of shot? Certainly not a tranquilizer," Cassie said, meaning that any calmer, Nona would be dead.

"Some magic juju juice. You're the doctor."

"We're not going to argue," Cassie replied, refusing to slip into the routine they did so well when with one another and stressed.

"Let's send everyone home. Party's over. She can't go back out there, and we're not in the hearty celebrating mood."

Cassie had had more than enough of the party herself. Just walking from the front door to the bathroom had made her want to turn for home.

"Adeste Fidelis" in wobbly, wine-soaked tones drifted through the keyhole and under the door. The convivial fun from the rest of the apartment shoved at Cassie like a sliding wall of earth. Hurriedly she asked, "Do you want us to say you've gotten sick?"

"Yes, please," Nona rasped. Just the sound of her voice set Cassie and Eve smiling. The sound gave them hope.

"Don't worry about this crappy article. Today's news, tomorrow's garbage wrapping. And who reads this shit anyway? Moth brains. Nobody we know," Eve said, ignoring the fact that it was Cassie who brought the *Insider*.

"Eve's right. Nobody who's your friend will ever pick it up," Cassie swore, willing to lie, to pretend, to light candles before any god available if it meant that Nona would rest easier.

"Besides, the photo looks as much like you as I do. That could be a thousand women."

They puffed at her, windy blowhards, struggling to turn straw into gold. And not once did they ask Nona about Adam Engels. Though certainly curious, neither mouthed a single question. The ominous glitter of spying, illicit millions, federal trials, the penitentiary, the lowdown that fixed viewers in theater seats put them off. This was happening, had happened, to one of them. Unbelievable, Cassie would say at another time—several times in fact—that it was Nona and not a stranger or a character in some television drama.

As for the "sexual intimacy" Fitz sketched with evil intent, the women left it lying between the lines. They agreed, as Eve said, on not needing to know. Of course things go on in the world. But who wanted to discuss *it*, even think about *it*?

Eve and Cassie, crowding against each other, careful when they bumped hips and elbows, treating each other with uncommon delicacy, as if they were china and could shatter, were afraid Nona had. Right then, without discussion, as if psychically in tune, they decided Nona had to put her life's secrets, done up with photographs and nationally circulated, at a distance. Bury the past, erect a tombstone, they urgently suggested. This is a tempest, over tomorrow.

Embarrassed by finally knowing too much, Cassie and Eve were ashamed of their reaction.

Nona hadn't shed a tear but Eve handed her a tissue as Cassie went out to send the guests on their way.

"Nona's not feeling well. A flu she's been fighting all day. As her doctor I'm ordering her right into bed." Though clad in silk, Cassie, her shoulders squared, fingering the air by her neck as if in search of a stethoscope, had the guests convinced without the faintest doubt, had them offering regrets and leaving as quietly as Santa's elves.

Cassie saw all the partygoers on their way, Mandy along with Jake, though both suggested they stay. She kissed their cheeks and said "No, thanks," and that she'd be home later.

Though Cassie struggles, a pall hangs over Christmas morning. Mandy hasn't a clue what causes the ashes in the air, why her mother's smile slips its anchor every time she thinks she's unobserved. Why is there such a false brightness to her?

The presents unwrapped and duly exclaimed over, they have muffins and bacon and shirred eggs in the dining room, semiformal befitting the occasion. Cassie assures Mandy she loves the pink button-down sweater, that it will be perfect with her white pleated skirt. Mandy admires again the gold bracelet she already wears and says she'll try on the painter jeans the minute they finish breakfast.

The effort works after a fashion, and for a little while they are just two females, girls talking things over, rather than mother and daughter. The strain of a blood relationship, of one evolving from the other, is temporarily absent as they drink their coffee.

Cassie mentions dinner at the Levinsons', four o'clock. Drinks first. Mandy is free from obligations until then.

"Is Jake going?"

Cassie inches the basket of blueberry muffins across the table, store-bought, not fresh baked, which gives her a twinge of guilt. She'd never prod Mandy to diet on Christmas. "They're pretty good for out of a package."

"Mother!"

"Well, they are."

"You're evading the question." Mandy gives her the fishy-eyed look of a parent rather than a child.

"Jake's been invited," Cassie admits with a sigh, as guilty about including him as she is about the muffins.

"Why?"

"Don't be silly, Mandy. You know why. Because I want him there. Jake and I have—"

Mandy interrupts. "Mom, don't start. Don't give me all those bullshit words like *relationship* and *commitment*. I mean, if you say *I'm involved with him* I'll puke."

Cassie flushes. "I am. Involved."

"Oh, Mom, you sound single! Just like Eve or Nona."

"Of course I'm single. I'm not married. I'm a divorced woman. Once married. What are you talking about?"

"You're my mother!" Mandy glares at Cassie and the intensity of her disapproval practically lifts Cassie, chair and all, away from the table. Mandy would sail her out through the wide window, across the street, up and over the opposite house, send her flying. She would displace her, because at the moment Cassie is the square peg.

"I was a living, breathing human being, Mandy, long before I was your mother. And I am many other things besides. A doctor, for example. I am a woman, a friend, a citizen, a taxpayer, a female who is having a relationship with a man she cares about." Oh, God, why doesn't someone put a cork in my mouth! Cassie thinks, unable to stop her ranting. Mandy covers her ears. "Of course I'm your mother. Top of the list. But that's not all I am." There, rub her nose in it. Make her day, Cassie, you fool! Cassie chastises herself. But the anger churning since the night before splashes over the top. Cassie shouts, "I am a person!"

Mandy enters the select company of those Cassie is mad at. Perversely, Mandy, whom Cassie fears the most to upset, is the only one Cassie can safely lose control with. Mandy, no matter what, is always connected to her as if a cord of flesh still linked them. Mandy won't walk off. Oh, she can run to her room; down to Doug in the Marina; away, like a statistic on a police blotter. But any severing between them is artificial. Cassie will always be Mandy's mother if they exchange no more than three words a year (which Cassie doesn't believe for a second is possible), and Mandy is her daughter absolutely. Eve's biology, though not what Eve means.

So when Cassie stretches even in her fury, when she says *I love you* along with *I have got my rights, too*, to Mandy, who draws away, throwing the ladder-back chair on its side, it is only for these few minutes the end of the world.

26

The week between Christmas and New Year's, Johnny flies to New Mexico to see his son. They spend the time—quality time, in Johnny's words—driving through the desert looking at ghost towns. All expensive property these days, Johnny informs Eve on his return. Artsy-craftsy, with lots of candle shops, homemade fudge, cowboy outfitters, hand-tooled boots (he lifts a leg to show her), local artists big on sage and western sunsets. All the natives wear jeans, fringed suede, gingham, calico. A fun way to earn a buck, swinging the past into the present. Johnny laughs. He loved every mile of wooden sidewalk.

"And," Eve points out, "people are hot for property. A tiny bit of land, a thimble of dirt. I remember when I was a little girl my great-grandfather stayed with us for a while. I suppose Gramps was out of his own house and being passed around between my mother and her four brothers. Here for a month, down to Salem after the holidays, over to Rhode Island for a couple of weeks. Anyway, at our house he slept in my mother's sewing room, which is just a glassed-in second-floor porch, and on the sill next to his bed, alongside his teeth in a glass, he had a small jar of dirt. Plain old dirt that he carried over from the old country when he came at the turn of the century. From his village with a name that's all consonants. He used to say if he never went back he still always had his home with him."

"And do you have a secret vial of New Hampshire grit in your lingerie drawer?" Johnny kids her.

"I'm not the sentimental type. Trees have roots, not me."

374

Johnny has more than a tourist's interest in the sun-bleached relics. "About a dozen more are ripe for development. I found one I like a whole lot." He outlines what it takes to convert the time-battered wrecks into suitable locations for midsummer art shows and winter movie festivals.

"You're serious about this!"

The suntan he acquired enhances the green of his eyes and he's better-looking than he's ever been. Already there's an outdoorsy quality to him, a desert squint, so Eve's not particularly surprised (and why should she care?) at his answer. "About redeveloping? Yeah, I am."

"Down what tube did the simple salaried, nine-to-five life flush?"

"There's one town, not so far north, nearer Las Cruces. Just sitting at the end of a dirt road. A real plum. Right out of a Howard Hawks western. It's perfect. And not in such horrendous shape. Some of the buildings are still sound."

Johnny glides on enthusiastically and a hot flush drenches the back of Eve's sweater. Estrogen keeps the flushes at bay but there is a steamy sweat nonetheless. Is it hormones or Johnny's eagerness that raises her temperature and burns in her cheeks?

Fools are born every minute, she plans to say to him when, if ever, he pauses for breath. Fools—and how *dare* he think of going away? Don't they have a practical, a comfortable arrangement? Does he think, even with the crowds of single women baying like hounds in despair, that he'll find another relationship so *easy*? They are, miraculously, just about conflict-free.

"I'm not going without you."

"What are you talking about?" Are her thoughts suddenly audible?

"You're coming to New Mexico. The two of us. Together, Eve." He laughs like the fat man he once was when she retorts that he is a walking greeting card.

She tells Cassie, who sounds surprised. "Is he asking you to marry him?"

Johnny has mentioned no impending nuptials, says nothing of making the arrangement he proposes legal. Just "I want you with me."

Is he used to her, as she is to him, and averse to beginning in New Mexico with a stranger?

"I've adjusted, if that's how you have to put it. I've grown loose with you." He squints with the honest effort of finding the right sentiments.

"You're not a particularly difficult person, you know that," she replies. "And I mean that honestly. I'm not bullshitting you."

"Stoned—"

"Well, stoned, that's different. But stoned was then, remember?"

Johnny is readying himself to leave Los Angeles, preparing to finish this life and start up that one faster than Eve can turn out a housewife's quickie soufflé. Opportunities exist in the desert and Eve, being in real estate, should appreciate land.

"Being in real estate in Los Angeles is mighty different, pardner, than hoisting buckets of sand five miles from nowhere."

He has taken her out to dinner, not his standard moderately priced restaurant but a trendy Argentinian café with a mirrored ceiling and glass flowers decorating the walls. It is early, and they are afloat in a sea of empty tables and unoccupied wicker chairs. The waiters with their slicked-back hair and black tunics remind Eve of tango dancers. The whole restaurant is arranged for an event, a loud and boisterous party, but except for another couple in a far corner, Eve and Johnny are the only ones eating. The clink of their silverware crashes through the silence like cymbals.

Johnny orders chicken.

"Chicken's meat," she tells him. She isn't going to let him get away with this, an upscale restaurant *and* chicken.

"I tend to chicken once a month."

"Since when? You never had anything but negative words for chicken, at least for eating it. Once a month, my ass. You're making this up. You said—"

"I know my regimen. Chicken's acceptable occasionally." He bristles with the on-fire impatience of his commodity days. Is Johnny reverting to who he once was, someone hungry to get on with things, to speed ahead of the pack, to fly high in the clouds minus a plane? Not that she supposes he's into junk, only chicken.

Johnny decides Eve is more than curious, swimming toward

suspicion or, worse, censure, so their conversation breaks down to the clatter and rustle, shift and slide of their eating.

For a moment at dessert Johnny freezes with desire over a chocolate mousse cake. He plays a tattoo on the table. The waiter, a sun-tanned surfer, recites the list of sugary confections once, twice, three times while Johnny listens. His sigh is moist with grief and he lusts like a man at the end of his rope.

"I would," he admits to Eve, "but you keep me honest. I can't order a thousand calories—"

"And pure poison," she interrupts triumphantly.

"And pure poison, with you opposite me."

Eve is so sympathetic she orders decaf coffee, no cream, and passes up a piece of lemon pie that makes her mouth water.

After dinner they walk along Melrose in the first surge of early evening strollers. The night gentles around them, slowly settling into a rhythm. Open stores have SALE signs in their after-Christmas windows. There is a cool tang to the air, like sherbet. Eve buttons her coat, leery of colds, the flu, of disorganizing her body. She is reminded daily that she's poised tentatively on a window ledge; she can go either way. Sleeping, she hears thunderous horse hooves, which are heartbeats, her own.

In her dreams Abramson stands down the road calling.

As they wander along the sidewalk Eve swings the crushed-leather bag, from Magnin's, that Johnny gave her for Christmas. It is a costly present, though not quite as expensive as the suede jacket Eve bought him. Still, he's made a statement—of affection, Eve judged on unwrapping the silver paper. Now she wonders. It's a present Johnny might have given a woman in his previous life. Understated. Good design. From a prestige store.

Is the bag a warning of his itchiness to make another grab for the gold ring?

A ghost town! Oh, sweet Jesus!

Eve needs no convincing that Johnny will make a success of his schemes, turn the quiet of the desert into a chichi resort, oh so quaint. Already her teeth are on edge. The idea of history reconstructed into a page from the Sears catalogue depresses her.

She is about to remind him that sleeping dogs are best left lying when, in the middle of the block, they come on a long, boat-finned Cadillac, flagrantly red and outfitted with neon designs. Palm trees sway over the doors, and a blue ocean waving across the trunk practically sets the car in motion.

A crowd, spilling into the street, forces cautious drivers to slow around them, and the gawkers in moving cars crane their necks as if there's an accident of twisted wreckage, broken bodies, rivers of blood.

"Why would anyone go to the trouble of doing that?" Johnny asks.

Eve can say the same of his ghost town, but answers, "It's funky."

"I've heard that word, *funky*, for years, and I'm still not positive what it means. It's not art and it's nothing you can give your mother for her birthday."

"I'm talking about fun, while you're after substantial."

"My ghost town is fun."

"Your ghost town will be a hoot. An amusement for overweight mothers, fathers in Bermuda shorts, sticky kiddies. It's just not you, that's my objection."

The shuffling crowd urges them on and they separate for a black leather trio, come together, and part again around an old woman pushing a young man in a wheelchair. When they do join, Eve's hand doesn't quite twist with Johnny's. The fingers meet and as easily slip away.

"It's a business deal, that's me. Do you think I should just let a solid gold opportunity like this one slide by because—" He pulls up abruptly. Now it's their turn to interrupt the tide. "What's wrong with making some money?"

"And where do you think you'll get investors? Who's going to loan you the millions—God, millions!—it will take?" Why does anger taste so foul in her mouth, as if the meal they've recently finished were tainted? If Johnny asks her, can she answer that she hates for him to change? She likes him just as he is, lean as a Great Dane, if not as a whippet. With the fat melted from his face, his bones are prominent. He is as stripped-down as a fast car, not cluttered like the Caddy, as he once was when a rich Rockefeller on the Malibu sand.

Johnny unrolls an elaborate plan as they start walking again. With the street noises and the night's confusion, and with her reluctance to take Johnny seriously, Eve hears only snatches. But what floats to her on the breeze is far-fetched, almost farcical.

"Your ex-wife's current husband?"

"Actually it's his father."

"Your ex-wife's father-in-law is going to bankroll this venture?"

"Don't give me that 'I don't believe you.' Harvey runs an investment syndicate and we're on the same wavelength."

An alien is in possession of Johnny's mind and body, because the Johnny she knows wouldn't say "on the same wavelength" if hung by his thumbs. Her Johnny, peculiar about his eating habits and nervously energized to convert the country to vegetarianism, to flush vitamin supplements down the water supply, to throw smokers in jail for the duration, drags no fake words behind him. Or at least he hasn't up to now, not till his admission that he harbors designs on a New Mexico plot of worthless dirt.

Johnny is about to walk out of the clatter of Melrose, away from freeways and West L.A. manicured lawns, from beaches and shopping malls, from too many restaurants. He'll clop along wooden sidewalks in fancy high-heeled boots. He'll wear a fringed vest, western shirt, a battered cowboy hat that his horse stomped on, and worn, not prefaded, jeans. Johnny is about to command his domain—the shiny old/new town as polished as wax fruit—with Wyatt Earp authority. He'll be rich again, undoubtedly famous, and living a ten-year-old's fantasy.

"So, will you or not?" He's asking her once more to go east with him. "It won't be much at first. We'll live in Albuquerque, and then get a trailer on the site once work starts." In his anxiety he takes Eve's silence for a comment on the trailer, because he spins into a sales spiel, citing a bevy of luxury appointments. According to Johnny all the vehicle lacks are gold bathroom faucets. "You don't even know you're on wheels," he swears.

"This is for real, isn't it?"

They blunder to a halt by a yogurt store that must be giving away free sundaes because a line of people trails out the door and three stores down.

"Do you want to have yogurt or are you going back to ice cream too? I remember when ice cream was one step away from sin. Now I bet, Johnny, if you do eat yogurt it won't be low-fat. You'll go all out and get two, three flavors and top the mess with chocolate sauce and sprinkles. And what about whipped cream?"

"Who cares about yogurt? You want a sundae? A cone? After that meal we ate?"

"Stop taking giant steps backwards!" she cries and crosses the street, cutting between cars as if she were hallowed, immune to damage. Not that Eve thinks so. She feels like a pulsing wound, an unhealed strip of skin so sensitive to the touch air brings the blood to a boil.

Johnny runs after her shouting, "Do you want to get killed?"

Does she? Is she angry at Johnny because he's kept her alive, kept her at least interested enough so that she won't join Abramson just yet? Now he's leaving her, or demanding *Will she? Won't she?*

Johnny trots beside her, half-dragging her to safety.

"I've made peace, Johnny!" she shouts.

"Made peace! You were almost made *into* pieces. Jesus, for a smart woman you are awfully stupid. Didn't your mother tell you not to walk out into the middle of the street without looking, even if the pedestrian has the right of way in Los Angeles?" He rants as though she had been in immediate danger, a car screeching within inches of her swinging skirt.

"Don't lecture me!" she yells and throws a fist to his chest. Even thinned to knobbiness he looms so much bigger than Eve that she only thumps her knuckles.

Johnny grabs her wrists and holds them together. With ease he could lift her up, trussed as a turkey, but he only shakes her gently and his glare has more pain than anger in it. "Why are you mad at me? What have I done?"

Eve sucks on her lips not to howl: You had chicken for dinner and almost ordered dessert and are changing like The Blob into someone else right before my eyes.

"I've had enough of men changing," she says when she catches her breath. Going dead, she suddenly realizes she means, dying on her. Or, if staying alive, becoming some other woman's lover.

In the cone of street light, elongated shadows stream over Johnny's face. A trickster moves and shifts before her.

"I'm just going on instead of standing still," Johnny apologizes. "I won't ever again use myself as a testing ground for nuclear warheads, but Jesus, Eve, I can't spend many more days in a little cubby putting together facts and figures for other guys. I've been hiding, head under the bed. No risks. No surprises."

As Johnny defends himself to her, Eve backs up against a bookstore window. She thinks, horrified, *I love this man!*

After Johnny runs out of words Eve simply nods, and with his arm about her shoulders they walk in step back to the car.

Eve is afraid to inform Nona. It seems best to bypass the truth, to shy from specific confessions, at least until things are better arranged.

The two women meet for an early movie, then a pickup dinner. Eve chats about real estate, the sluggish season, the prime rate, the Asians making a fiefdom of downtown office buildings. She has urged Nona into choosing the movie, and now coaxes her to eat until, like a gawky child, Nona snaps, "Stop hovering. I am not on the brink of death!"

"So help me God!" Eve swears and orders another glass of wine.

Nona is being difficult but that's an improvement on Nona glassy-eyed and almost comatose, which she was most of the holiday season, when Cassie gave her tranquilizers.

Eve spent Christmas day sitting in Nona's living room, checking every few minutes on Nona curled in bed. Nona never asked for her company, for Cassie's pills, for the food they spooned into her, the Bach they played by the hour, the kindness. Their concern fell on her like rain.

We can't babysit forever, Eve complained, but they clung to her as fast as barnacles for as many hours as they could spare. They went in shifts, as if it were the most natural thing in the world, as if Nona had been operated on like Eve.

Surprisingly, Nona gets up every morning, dresses, manages her makeup.

If anyone Nona has more than a nodding acquaintance with has seen the article, they are amazingly discreet. Since the name she now uses (legally? the women wonder but don't dare ask her) was published in the tabloid, however, several creeps do dial her number and spit out a combination of hate and obscenities. Nona's solution is to leave the receiver off the hook but Cassie, more practical, persuades her to get an unlisted phone.

"Am I losing my mind or is that the beauty you brought to one of my parties?" Allie phones Eve to inquire. "You know I'm a dunce about names but the face is familiar."

Eve's instinctive retort is "A mistake. She's suing, of course. The writer has her mixed up with someone else. And the *Insider* is the worst of the scandal sheets. How come you happened to pick it up?"

"Imagine, sex with her father and she looks like a Popsicle won't melt on her lips" is Allie's comeback. She doesn't believe Eve's disclaimer. Most of Nona's friends don't. That the *Insider* is trash everyone acknowledges, but they take what's written about Nona for at least semi-gospel. Where there's smoke, Jake reminds Cassie, people expect fire.

A reporter from *People* materializes on Nona's doorstep one morning. She returns to the apartment, locking him out, and calls in sick.

In the best of possible worlds Lorraine would be on vacation in Mexico the week the *Insider* fouls the racks. But the fates are malevolent. Lorraine must have the *Insider* delivered, because she is immediately onto Nona the day after Christmas. Her fang teeth drip venom, as if she intends to puncture Nona's neck.

Nona counts the cash in the register.

"Aren't you going to make some comment? Now that you're famous? Are you just going to pretend everything's the same?"

Nona's mouth is a wound but she has nothing to say to Lorraine. She goes about the morning routine, checking bags and boxes, credit card slips. When she circles through the store to the back room Lorraine follows, tottering on her high heels. "I really thought twice about letting you come in to work this morning."

The unopened store is chilly and under the sleeves of her cotton sweater goose bumps rise on Nona's skin. She rubs her arms, making believe that Lorraine is in Alaska and not two steps to the rear, talking loudly as if to someone with impaired hearing.

"Of course it wouldn't have shocked me if you stayed home. If you didn't even bother to—"

"Lower your voice," Nona says, turning sharply, cutting in front of Lorraine.

"What?"

"You're shouting."

Lorraine tenses, as if Nona means to attack. "I am not!"

"Yes, you are. You're shouting at me because of that dirty scandal sheet."

Lorraine juts out a hip as Nona gathers a stack of boxes and returns to the front. Never a quitter, Lorraine trails in Nona's wake. "What do you expect, that normal people won't be curious? We're not saints—at least I'm not. Let's just hope nobody recognizes you."

Nona's shoulder dips and she banks, sliding about. "I'm not a bank robber. I didn't do anything wrong."

Did do, did to, a younger voice at a higher pitch whines in her ear. The scratchiness in her throat signals how easily tears can rush up. She bears down hard not to burst into sobs, scared of weakening with Lorraine when she should, when she must, have a spine of iron.

"That's a matter of opinion," Lorraine says.

Nona chews the inside of her cheek so as not to lose control. The pain keeps her clearheaded as Lorraine frets, angrily buzzing at Nona, shuffling between gutter curiosity, fury, and resentment that—scandal sheet or not—Nona's face is public property.

Nona's training with anyone in a pique, riddled with unhappiness, riding the updraft of a fiery temper, is to behave sympathetically. You catch more flies with honey, Marian drilled into her, though Nona, unlike her mother, is sincere.

Be a lady always was Adam's order.

Why did she ever listen to the silly things they said?

Daddy loves you. . . . Nona tastes blood in her mouth. How stupid to think Adam ever did anything wrong; how wicked for Fitz to pretend she said so. I never! she screams in her head, shouting against a wall of darkness.

What if she doesn't remember?

Lorraine refuses to ease off, glaring out of snake's eyes, and Nona grips the counter in order not to slap her. She won't feel the sting to her palm one little bit, not like her teeth biting off a soft, fleshy piece of her mouth. She will send Lorraine's head snapping like a lily on a stem and experience at least as much pleasure as she does with a man in bed.

Tides of shoppers pass along the mall's walkways. One minute by the wall clock and Nona will open the double doors, swing them back, latching them to the hooks in the floor. Customers can wander easily into Flora's; they can browse. They can also stand about and point fingers. *Spy's daughter. Father and daughter. In love's embrace.*

Lorraine finally pushes too close to her, arriving with hot breath and a cloud of Opium. Nona pivots and jabs her index finger in the bony terrain between Lorraine's breasts. "Leave me alone. My private life has nothing to do with Flora's."

Lorraine squeaks with indignation. "I think it does and I'm the manager. Leonard and Howard agree with me too."

"You told them."

"This isn't some silly prank, some misdemeanor, Nona. The *Insider* is sold in Orange County too. By this time they must have seen it."

"Not everybody buys filth," Nona snaps. She wants Lorraine's throat between her teeth; she salivates to bite into the woman's jugular. Already blood drips over Lorraine's white Liz Claiborne. Lorraine is dead on the floor. Nona's foot is placed on her belly triumphantly. *I won't let anybody hurt me anymore!* she cries, raising her flag of independence.

The two women are frozen in their angry stances until, out of the mall's rising hum, a customer intrudes demanding help. She is a fussy woman, no doubt with a houseful at her command, for she arches her back when there seems a moment the women won't snap to attention. Lorraine's rage temporarily banks and Nona's fantasies fade as Lorraine tends to business. Apparently Flora's has been highly recommended by one of Lorraine's best customers, so the time spent catering to the woman's many whims is doubly important. Nona, waiting on lesser mortals over the next hour, rocks with private delight at Lorraine's swinging in the breeze of the customer's snottiness.

Serves her right, Nona thinks, and hopes Lorraine is wringing wet from the sharp demands that go on until lunch hour. Nona herself has a quieter morning. Still, she needs a drink. Her tongue is dry.

She never drinks during the day except for a glass of wine sometimes, but now her mouth waters at the idea of gin, though she can't quite remember what gin tastes like. But then her memory is faulty, broken-down, a wreck. Her memory has been stashed out back with the trash barrels.

He never . . . I never, Daddy . . .

"Yes?"

A long, thin woman with artful eyes and skin smoothed wrinkle-less by surgery is asking, "Have we met?"

Nona inclines her head like a bird but refuses to bend a knee and curtsy, as she once did before dinner parties. This is a Marian kind of friend, a raven hanging over a Sèvres plate counting asparagus.

"I'm sure I know you from somewhere."

If Lorraine hears, she will assume the woman connects Nona's face with the *Insider* photograph, though Nona has her hair pushed back tight to her scalp and has heightened her makeup. A resemblance exists, but under the brash lights Nona assures the woman, without saying so, that she's mistaken. She lies effortlessly, with more skill than she had ever been capable of before, rolling off a list of names, citing the theater, the museum, the opera.

"Last week, *La Bohème*, of course. I knew I had seen you somewhere. I pride myself on never forgetting a face." The woman chats amiably with Nona, having placed her one notch out of the service class and into that group who sits center orchestra at the opera—where Nona's never been.

A few other customers stare at Nona, stand back and regard her, but no one suggests *You're the one who. . . .* Los Angeles is awash with supporting actors and actresses and after a while the whole world appears as familiar as Wonderbread.

Nona strides through the store not at all wary or worried for five minutes, then suddenly finds herself shaking. Her emotions go from high boil to low simmer. She's frightened one second, choking off a scream, and lulled into thinking she's invisible the next. She needs a drug or a drink potent enough to file down the edges, but one that won't put her to sleep, keep her out of Flora's, and hand Lorraine a gilt-edged reason for firing her. Nona has no intention of quitting, or exposing her neck like a fool on the steps to the guillotine.

Her stomach aches constantly, but instead of going to Dr. Rubin she calls Fitz's answering machine. "I don't love you! I never did!" She calls once more, at three in the morning and, after the beep, puts the receiver against a stereo speaker while turning to high the volume on U2.

When she can't sleep she lulls herself with *I will survive*, words she gripped years before while Marian wept.

Adam's trial, Nona dreams, takes place under water. She swims in and out of the courthouse. The judge is a fish, the prosecutor an eel. Marian has tentacles heavy with rings.

In actuality Marian was quietly tailored. She barely moved, and walked with exaggerated care, one well-shod foot before the other. The lawyers cautioned: Be discreet! But Marian's eyes were wild. The lawyers feared her coming unhinged, so Nona parceled out Miltown with Marian's morning coffee. She doped her mother during the day into presenting the frozen demeanor of a sleepwalker, and at night when she started to unfrost, poured her into a drunken slumber with stiff martinis.

For herself during Adam's trial it was all paint-by-numbers. Assiduously she followed a program of denial. Let's pretend. *My father is innocent,* she said with her head lifted to one of Adam's lawyers, and because Nona looked like a nymph he longed to believe her.

She spent long hours staring straight ahead, usually at the blank wall behind the judge or, alternatively, at the corner of the high window latticed with mesh. Against the opaque glass the light lay flat, and was the color of oatmeal.

My father is dead, she practiced saying aloud in the shower (the only place no one could hear her). Died in the war. In a crash on Storrow Drive. After a long, debilitating illness.

But Nona was incapable of bringing it off. Adam appeared each day, so handsome and elegant, so cleanshaven, so lemon-smelling, though she wasn't near enough to catch his scent. He turned repeatedly and nodded in their direction.

They were—Nona and Marian—leggy, good-looking women, the subject of much interest.

Adam's need made Marian a wreck. She begged not to go to the trial and refused to visit her husband in jail.

Why didn't Fitz write of that, put down how Marian screamed *No, no, no?*

Because I never told him . . . never told him the other, either, not Adam with his hand on my breast, the wavy hairs over the knuckles.

Under Lorraine's scrutiny, right in Flora's during an empty

fifteen minutes, Nona refolds messed-up scarves, spangled T-shirts, and heaves into Adam's arms. Memory stokes his warmth. She climbs onto his lap, and out in the garden as she curls in toward him, his tweed jacket scratches her cheek.

No matter what Nona said to him, Fitz made an elaborate deception out of crumbs, and now Nona mines through clouds of time, unburies memories, and works next to her father. She strives to get his touch right, to adjust his husky whispers. Aligning rows of lace-appliquéd cardigans, Nona says without moving her lips, *I should kill him, Daddy*.

Nona neatens the hanging belts, fusses with stacked shirts on the chrome-and-glass *étagère*, and purposely stays in eyeshot of Lorraine. What Lorraine misses, however, is Nona presenting Fitz's head on a plate to her father. She hangs a Kenzo two-piece on a wire frame and hisses against her teeth, *beast*.

Dirt collects in Nona's mouth, and pebbles, slimy water. But she'll choke on it before asking Fitz: *Why did you play at loving me? Why, like a spy—just as they accused Daddy of being—did you steal all my secrets and sell them to the enemy?*

"No one person knows everything about someone, especially a woman about a man," a stray dinner guest said at drinks, urging kindness on Marian. Only the three of them—Nona, Marian, the woman, plumper than most of her mother's friends, softer, more motherly, in quite the wrong dress—sat in separate chairs before the fire. The friend held possession of hers for quite a while. Marian never urged her to leave. So few of their well-provided guests came knocking any more, offered invitations even to lunch or tea. Nona was grateful until the woman hinted that none of them, *of us* (she democratically included herself) was clairvoyant. How can a wife ever tell what a husband does when off and free, at the office, the club, on the golf course, sailing? She meant how was anybody ever *sure* that Adam hadn't sold secrets.

Maybe came sourly out of her mouth and Marian abruptly stood and left the room.

Nona untangles a jumble of necklaces and lays them flat on velvet. "I'm going to grab a coffee."

Lorraine comes off the wall like a fighter out of the corner. "It's not your break."

"In a half hour."

"You can go then."

Nona brings her hands from behind her back where they have wandered, as if she and Lorraine are in a schoolroom instead of Flora's, as if they are children, Lorraine older and sharp. She speaks distinctly, showing her teeth, no longer prepared to listen politely to anybody's *maybe*: "I'm going *now*."

Lorraine grips indignation with the tenacity of a rat trap. She will extract *what happened* from Nona, but she can't jam an arm down Nona's throat and rip out a confession, so, shifting gears, like Marian's friend, she pretends kindness.

"You need to share instead of trying to be Super Woman holding it all in. I'm not just your boss, Nona. I care. In other circumstances we would have been best friends." Lorraine's nose grows longer than Pinocchio's and Nona's stomach turns over.

Lorraine hungers to be the one Nona shares all with, not from friendship or a humanitarian impulse but quite the opposite. Lorraine is the wicked queen offering a poisoned apple.

Nona understands that if, out of a lapse of consciousness, she told Lorraine any details, at some future date they'd come flying back at her like grenades with the pins pulled. But Nona won't give her one word beyond the necessary and this hardens the last molecule of Lorraine's heart. As the days slip by they are at war, and Nona wonders why Lorraine restrains herself from a long, shattering talk and giving her notice.

Sooner or later—perhaps she wants to have a face-to-face with the Laguna owners first—Lorraine will drive Nona out of Flora's.

I will survive, won't go, don't have to. . . .

Steel slowly forms inside Nona. She hunches against a knife thrust between her shoulder blades. But evasive action isn't enough. Her job at lovely Flora's has always been worm-ridden because of Lorraine, and now Lorraine will do her worst if Nona lets her.

Nona dreams of a whole field of Lorraines as high as corn and swaying in the wind, rubbing wickedness gleefully and calling out names. Nona wakes screaming and reaches for somebody, for Magic, who isn't there, and she weeps.

"Enough," she cries. "Enough!"

27

Mandy's Christmas break isn't a matter of a few short days but goes on and on like a shaggy dog story. It will be the fourth week in January before she returns to school. Cassie, who thought when Mandy left in September that she'd be shattered by loneliness, thinks now she will have a seizure if she doesn't put her daughter on the plane soon.

Each morning Cassie wakes hoping, her fingers crossed, but Mandy's mood doesn't swing from out of the glowering darkness and into the light. She is perpetually bad-tempered into the New Year. And not only does her dislike for Jake fail to diminish, it grows.

Watching Jake mow the lawn, Mandy rubs her thumbs in a superstitious gesture and comments, "He's scary."

"*Scary?* That's bizarre. Jake's nice. Ordinary." Neither adjective fits quite right. Cassie tries again: "He's wonderful."

"Nice, ordinary, wonderful. Ever see the movie *The Stepfather*, Mom?"

"Stop making fun of me!" Cassie answers with more emphasis than she thinks is called for but oh, how Mandy irritates her. Also, Cassie disconnects at even a hint that Jake is "wrong" somehow. *Wrong* has too many possibilities breeding like bacteria in it.

Unwanted, Fitz wanders into her thoughts and there's the *Insider* article rolling up like microfilm.

Jake's not Fitz and she's mad to flounder about full of suspicions. She is incited by her daughter, and her anger, as sticky as flypaper, traps common sense.

Of course Jake's not scary. He's quiet, laid-back. He walks an emotional trestle on arched feet and why not? Vietnam tattooed him with more than an American eagle.

Cassie reads up on the syndrome. Then PBS airs a special about veterans. She watches the long, painful hour, wondering if miles across town, Jake sits in the dark before his Panasonic while she's buried in bed under covers up to her neck.

Scary? Jake? No. Cassie's diagnosis is that he's battle-scarred still, that he's seen horrors too gruesome for life in the present tense to accommodate. He has secondary lesions of the psyche, and Cassie, as a physician accustomed to trauma, must be understanding. She feels emotionally clumsy but works to satisfy herself with this assessment—*easier with time, oh, yes, with loving*. But who does she mean, Jake or herself?

As for Mandy, Nona's right: She sours on any man not her father in her mother's bed. Tracy can get away with murder, with an advancing pregnancy that will probably swell her into a gorgeous madonna, while Mandy, if she could, would condemn Cassie to a state of perpetual chastity.

She's just a kid is Jake's analysis of Cassie's daughter, who, for all the attention he bestows on her, is no more substantial than a fly in his peripheral vision. *Let her live with her father for a while* is something else Jake says when Cassie complains. And *She should be moving out on her own pretty soon. Give or take a year.*

Chilled, Cassie makes them pâté on crackers (Ritz, Jake's preference) and argues. *I'll never let Doug have her,* and *She's only eighteen.*

Jake doesn't warm to kids. He has nothing of the fatherly about him. He's the lone shark swimming in a dark sea, a silent man with bad memories. Cassie hesitates even to ask: When did you see your own daughters last? Talk to them on the phone?

Time does not smooth out the edges. Cassie waits, turns over in bed to Jake, rises on a tide of lovemaking, and hopes. Jake, however, shrills in his sleep and wakes up periodically in a cold sweat that has a fetid odor to it.

He continues to keep Cassie on guard. She checks each word coming from her mouth with the scrupulousness of a research scientist, yet fumbles into saying the wrong thing.

Cassie concentrates, as if it were possible to magically pull gestures of tangible affection—other than during sex—out of Jake. Casual caresses, hugs and sudden kisses, can legitimize Cassie's feelings more in some ways than the breath-stopping encounters in bed. But even on the days when he's comfortable with their relationship, when he pads barefoot, cat quiet around her house, he keeps his hands in his jeans pockets and stays mute, won't speak up in loving confession. If the Viet Cong had ever captured him, Cassie thinks, his stoniness would have worn his torturers to the bone. Jake is probably waterproof, whip-resistant, as impervious to starvation, darkness, and light as he is to Cassie's meaningful touches, looks, and sighs. She can't coax or seduce expressions of affection, "love" words out of him, and feels ashamed for wanting him to say that he cares. What is a responsible woman, a physician, a specialist on whom others rely, bend to with hope and prayers in their voices, doing pussyfooting around a man who moves on the wind and leaves no footprints? She worries he will fly from her, as he almost did, and that he's no more trustworthy than an Alan, a Fitz. The thought of being alone again, once more single and looking, gives Cassie stomach cramps.

One night when she awakened at Jake's back, logy from dreaming, she kissed the ridge of his spine—lightly so as not to frighten him—and she whispered, as humbly as any woman in the caste of unsure females, "I want you to be happy." And that wasn't a lie. Even though he slept and couldn't hear her, she had to tell Jake the truth.

When Mandy retreats upstairs Cassie continues to watch Jake. He is mowing the lawn and it could be the first day she ever saw him. He hasn't changed, not one little bit, and is still given to his dark fits, to bouts of silence. Oh, Cassie thinks, stop complaining. They have had good times together. He plays her music, goes with her to the movies and out to dinner, and pleases her in bed. What more does she want? *What?* she whispers at the window when Jake and the lawn mower pass out of sight.

They finish a simple dinner, spaghetti carbonara and Caesar salad. They're alone, since Mandy's gone off to a friend's, though it's her last night before flying to Portland in the morning. Cassie has a D & C scheduled and can't take her to the airport. She suggests asking Doug, but surprisingly, it's Tracy that Mandy calls on.

"Mandy thinks having a baby is terrific," Cassie confides over coffee. "I don't like it."

Jake gives his usual shrug. "Stop worrying."

"I should just let her sprout, a weed or a dandelion? Stop worrying! Honestly, you haven't a clue."

Jake hunches and the thick brows blend over the high bridge of his nose. He scowls when he senses criticism.

Immediately Cassie apologizes. "Let's not argue. I hate to argue. Even with Doug I avoided fights." And was, she thinks with distaste, too much the peacemaker.

Jake's eyes are dark. There's no way to see inside him. He's not going to answer. He pours more coffee and puts his elbows on the table and Cassie blurts, "Why is there such little give in you?"

"According to you, everything's wrong with me."

"I never said that." How does she fall into such pits? At the clinic she speaks with patients, with the other doctors and nurses, after deliberating; she doesn't sail loose on the wind. But Jake gets her rattling along like a '41 Chevy. She has no restraint, no sense.

There is no espresso left in the pot and Jake gets up to brew more, maybe because he wants another cup or maybe to avoid further conversation. The latter, Cassie guesses, so is surprised when he says, "You know, between your kid, the clinic, those girlfriends, you've got no time for me, for just hanging out." In his jeans and work shirt with a wide leather belt, he is Mel Gibson, Kevin Costner, Tom Cruise, all the young movie stars Cassie would die to admit she finds attractive. Sitting in a darkened theater she retreats to girlhood. She becomes a captive of teenage dreaming. And because of that her conscience pricks her. What would Barbara say? Jena? Any number of militant patients hellbent on having a member of the movement for a physician?

Jake saunters to the table and Cassie enjoys each ripple of his slow swagger. I am, she thinks in dismay, on the same high wire as Nona, the same trapeze as April DeVito, and swinging through the air, in repentance ready to leap off into nowhere, she pushes ahead. "I have to give a lot of energy to Mandy. I want to. You're not in contact whatsoever with your daughters, so the pull of your own flesh is strange to you. You've let your girls blow away like puffballs. Maybe I am overly concerned, but what are you, Jake? A father done and gone. Why don't you get in touch? Drop them a letter, a postcard, if you're uncomfortable calling."

"Shut up about my kids," he says, plain and flat, the low serious growl of a Doberman or a shepherd that means business.

Cassie unhooks a foot from the rung of her chair in case she needs to move fast, for she thinks, appalled, he could hit me! He is capable of stretching his arm out and slapping my face. Maybe even punching me!

A thrill of alarm sizzles down her spine. The moment is suspended dangerously, hung between then and now. The girls buried under the house in Santa Monica had just such a moment, when control stretched thin as surgical wire. Of course Jake, even if he slaps her face, won't actually harm her. *Kill her* is what Cassie means, sickened that she's a woman sitting having coffee after a meal she cooked, opposite a man she loves, and fantasizing about his hurting her.

Jake breaks the spell and dissipates the smell of sulfur in the air. "It's late, time to be heading over to my place. Since it's Mandy's last night, you won't want me hanging around."

"That's sensitive of you," she says.

"Sarcasm, Cassie," he says, but sadly.

"No, stop!" She leaps up. "I meant it. It's sensitive, or you are, for realizing that Mandy might need private time with me. I appreciate your thinking of that." She bobs about the kitchen, overcome with a sudden hunger for him that she's ashamed to make plain.

He slams a closed fist down on the counter, rattling glasses. "Damn it, I'm not an ogre. You might think I'm a shithead leaving Texas, for not being Daddy Almighty—"

"Of course I don't think that! You're a wonderful man. I value you!" Take me to bed, she thinks. Just take me to bed and sink inside and let me have some feeling of belonging!

Jake crackles with annoyance. "Cassie, you're upset about Mandy and she's upset about Mom getting laid regular and at home—"

"That's an ugly way of putting it!" Cassie explodes.

He curls his upper lip, exposing a tooth. "How's 'keeping company with a man'?"

Cassie comes down quickly. "Better," she lies.

"Fine. Glad you're happy." He pulls on his jacket and Cassie hates for him to go, hates more her panic. One day he won't be here. (So what?) He'll leave. (So? So? Won't she be better off?)

It will do her in if he drives away, if he *dies*. It will, Cassie swears, as if in an argument with someone other than herself.

She wills her face to be flat and expressionless, a plane of no emotion, as Jake opens the back door through which he first entered her kitchen. A stream of light crochets in the mesh of the screen. A late-night caller backs out of the Levinsons' driveway. Tony home again? Tony staying?

Children and men, the two constants in a woman's life, the plumb weights off her heart, Cassie thinks.

"I'll call you tomorrow."

She can choose to say no. Options exist. She is neither bound by legal knots to Jake nor such a fool that she could live through his hitting her. Such fantasies! And what an easy side-shuffle for women like April. Cassie casts no stones. There, she thinks, gazing into Jake's eyes, smelling him like a wild animal as she slips into his arms, but for the grace of God . . .

"Okay," she says after his lips lift off hers, "call me tomorrow."

"Lighten up, Cassie."

"I try. I don't mean to think all the time, to worry."

His hand grazes her hair. He hesitates, not as eager to leave as she supposed. "What do you want, Cassie? I mean, of me?"

There are so many possible ways to answer, but Cassie chooses the simplest, which is unlike her. Jake might not be changing, but maybe she is. She says, easing out of his arms, "I don't know."

As it happens, it's more convenient for Tracy to pick up Mandy at the clinic and from there drive her to LAX. God forbid that Doug's pregnant wife should be burdened.

Self-satisfied, Mandy announces, "I'm trying to be friendly with Tracy. To have a *relationship* with her." She bends from the waist at the word and Cassie winces. "And she's putting herself out, Mom. In her condition."

Her condition! The grandmotherly expression leaves grit in Cassie's teeth.

"Maybe I can get you out before I have to be at St. John's."

"Don't bother, Mom. Honestly. You have your schedule. Tracy understands."

Tracy understands! Mandy implies that surgery is a wispy activity, bridge with the ladies, the local quilting society. Cassie inhales and then expels, "Whatever." *Whatever* is Mandy's word when she's out to madden her mother.

There's no reason for Tracy to be brought back to Cassie's private office, yet somehow she arrives, a frigate with her distended prow. Seeing the girl (Tracy disgustingly aglow with youth) Cassie has never disliked pregnancy more.

Pea in the pod, bun in the oven . . .

Tracy's hair splashes about her heart-shaped face in pre-Raphaelite curls. An inner light shines through the flawless skin. She is as tan as a Polynesian. Cassie almost forgets herself and launches into a lecture on the risks of skin cancer.

"Hi, Cassie, how's things?" she says as she sails into the office.

Cassie is already up and out of her chair. Damn wanting to stay to the very last minute with Mandy, who's eased her feet off the desk and in excruciating slow motion gathers her shoulder bag, books, down jacket, gloves, *Mademoiselle*, bag of homemade brownies and lemon cookies, all scattered about the office.

"Hello, Tracy."

"Ready, kiddo?" She smiles at Mandy.

"Two and a half seconds."

Cassie, who wishes her ex-husband's current wife out of her sight, flutters her hands in Mandy's direction and asks, "Can I help?"

Mandy seems deliberately draggy, as if she means to repack her purse, to root around for endless minutes, first for sunglasses, then "Where's my book?"

"Under the chair." Cassie points.

"What're you reading?" Tracy, emboldened, comes forward. She is uncommonly large and Cassie wonders if she's had an amnio, though she's under thirty. Twins? That will be too intolerable if Doug has twins with Tracy.

"John Cheever's short stories."

"Who's he?"

"For my American Lit class," Mandy replies without a hint of *oh, you dumbo*.

395

"I just read the latest Jackie Collins. Wow, is it great. *Très* sexy!" She giggles. "If I had my head on, I would've brought it for you. For the plane." She really does have teeth like gravestones, wide and blindingly white and occupying too much of her face. She has a horse's bite and if it weren't for one in the oven, for her pea in the pod, she'd be downright cheap. Later, around forty, she'll have stringbean arms and long chopstick legs with messy smudges of varicose veins. She promises, to Cassie's delight, not to wear well.

"Let me take a pit stop before we go, okay?" Mandy asks her mother, Tracy, as if either will say no.

"I'm going to have to dash for the hospital," Cassie objects, but Mandy's out the door, and Tracy, ignoring Cassie's stiffness, makes herself right at home.

"Listen, Cassie, as long as I'm here and we've got a sec, can I ask you a question?"

Cassie needs no crystal ball to reveal that Tracy's question won't be about the weather, that she'll solicit free advice, and—how *can* she! Can't the woman—girl!—understand that old used-up wives, whatever the circumstances, might not enjoy being so chummy?

Cassie's jaw aches but she gets out "Of course. What is it?"

Tracy spreads herself in the patient's chair, which she pulls closer to the desk. Cassie wavers between resuming her own chair and standing. The advantage of position is what she's after.

Tracy, however, has something on her mind that she can't get out fast enough, and Cassie has just touched the leather seat when Tracy confides, "I'm having, like, the worst dreams. Out of a slasher flick. Boy, they are just, like, unbelievable."

Dreams?

"Everybody dreams."

Tracy's legs shift to either side beneath the weight of her womb, and across from Cassie she is any pregnant woman with fear in her big eyes.

Cassie squints to see Tracy as a patient, not as a female impregnated by the same man who fathered her own child. To make the singular universal, the one into the many, Cassie, leaning on her desk blotter, almost closes her eyes to blur Tracy into indistinctness. Tracy, for her part, slides even nearer until only inches seem to separate them.

We're ridiculous, Cassie smarts, as if she's peering through the other end of a telescope trained on them both, wife number one and wife number two.

"Blood just all over, in puddles. Really gross," Tracy is saying, licking purple lips that don't quite fit together over those impossible teeth.

"Discuss it with your obstetrician if the dreams are really that upsetting," Cassie advises, knowing full well the fright quotient of Tracy's dreams. They ring the bell or—for surely Tracy can't be so idiotic—she wouldn't have brought them into this office. This is why, Cassie finally figures out, Tracy needed to pick Mandy up at Magdalene. And what about Mandy's hasty trip to the bathroom? Is her own daughter such a traitor that, per request, she's deliberately left her mother alone with her father's wife?

"I can't do that. He's one of these hotshot doctors. Like stuffed. A chest puffed up just waiting for the President or somebody to pin a medal on it. All very Big Daddy." She wiggles her upturned nose. "Doug says nothing but top of the line. Shit, it sounds like he's buying me a Mercedes."

"I don't think—" Cassie starts to protest that she's not the one for Tracy's confidences, that hearing any of this is as welcome as a broken clavicle, but Tracy is launched downriver. "He'll pat my head," she says, "and honk about pregnant fantasies and how I shouldn't worry. I just hate it when people tell me I'm an asshole for worrying. Having a baby might be normal but it's not normal for me. I've never had one before. Like it's not a rollerskate down the pier. Right?"

Unfortunately, Cassie knows precisely how Tracy feels. It matters not a whit that women have been giving birth since the beginning of time, dropping babies in caves, fields, at home with midwives, alone, in hospital delivery rooms, in cabs, on buses, planes, trains, along the freeway during rush hour. Having babies is as basic a fact of life as anyone can think of, but for the individual female it is always extraordinary, a once-in-a-lifetime event even if she has a dozen. Only a man would try to make pregnancy an ordinary occurrence, a nothing-to-set-your-hair-in-curls-about.

Cassie has no choice. She's a physician but, more, she's curious. "What are these dreams, besides bloody?" She finally caves in.

"It's really only one dream with different takes. Like the camera focuses differently each time but in the same scene. You know, things are rearranged."

Cassie recalls that Tracy had a brushing acquaintance with the movie business before Doug liberated her from the job market. The casting couch, Cassie tries to think nastily, but her longstanding antipathy to Tracy (on principle) is—to her disbelief—ebbing.

"See, I'm in this room with white walls and a white floor and a white ceiling," Tracy starts up, promising a version of an early Bergman. "Nothing's in color."

"Not everyone dreams in color. It's actually unusual."

"Whatever I dreamed in before I got pregnant, I'm black-and-white now," Tracy says.

"Go on." Her D & C is waiting over at St. John's and Mandy's departure time creeps up the clock. Cassie is tempted to tell Tracy to make an appointment, but that means having her in the office again, giving her a record—Tracy Morgan, Mrs. Douglas Morgan. Surely someone on the staff will recognize the name and at the least mention—*Hey, Cassie, what a coincidence!* No! Tracy's better off with her stuffed-shirt ob-gyn and out of Magdalene.

"I'm naked and on this hammocklike thing hanging from the ceiling, and slime's rolling up over my legs, onto my belly. Ugh, it's cold and it stinks."

"Slime? You mean a kind of liquid?"

"Yeah, well, but it's also a thing. Did you ever see *The Blob*?" Cassie shakes her head. "Anyway, it's sort of similar, but this is a *thing*, too, and it's got this itty-bitty head like in *Aliens* and it is ugly as the living dead. Yuck!" She shakes and loses the color in her cheeks. "It's got eyes too."

"Eyes?"

"And it's green—"

"In black-and-white?"

"I know it's green even if it's no-color. It *feels* green, and it's barf time except it is so scary, especially when it gets over my breasts and up to my throat—"

Tracy pales to milk-white, and sweat dampens the downy hairs crossing her brow. Cassie hurriedly moves from her chair. "Don't talk any more about it. It's just a dream, probably implying your fear of having a ba—"

Tracy is on a slide, unable to shut her mouth until she reaches the bottom, drained and wordless. "And then it's at my lips. Little wiggly yucky things slither into my mouth and some keep going up my nostrils. Oh, it tastes so sick, like dog-do!"

Tracy's eyes widen into dark moons hanging over her cheekbones. "Oh, I'm going to be sick!" With one hand she struggles to free herself from the grip of the chair, and with the other she tries to cover her mouth.

"Don't! Wait!" Cassie cries, grabbing for the metal wastebasket under the desk. But there's no time. Tracy doubles over and heaves a dark-pink vomit into Cassie's out basket.

"I know it's best."

"Best for whom? You? A trailer in New Mexico? A ghost town?"

Cassie sprawls untidily on the chaise in Eve's bedroom as Eve dresses. Her mood is as gray as the waning afternoon. It is Cassie's early day but not early enough to miss the last appointment, Mrs. Holland, a faithful patient since Cassie and Barbara and Jena first established Magdalene. Mrs. Holland, never Elizabeth. Mrs. Holland with violet eyes and lily-of-the-valley talcum powdering all her crevices and a stage II ovarian carcinoma. Though the five-year survival rate for mucinous cystadenocarcinoma runs around 60 percent, Mrs. Holland is frail. She has crossed into her seventies and is faltering. She is a brittle, birdlike creature and she has the look.

The look is something Cassie never speaks about with anyone. Other doctors will accuse her of witchcraft, of excess imagination, of an unprofessional attitude. Cassie fears their ridicule. As for civilians, even the best of friends can jerk back stung from an M.D. who believes death casts a gray shadow.

Mrs. Holland readying herself for the rigors of chemo wears just such a shroud. It blemishes her irises, and if it slips away, almost immediately it shifts back. Cassie knows that in the months to follow *the look* will intensify until Mrs. Holland wears all death's symptoms like adornments.

"Cass!"

Once more she is aptly named Cassandra and shamed. Precognition is nonsense, unscientific. There really is no *look*. Mrs. Holland has a fairly decent chance.

"Cassie, wake up. You're off touring gaga land."

"Just thinking about a patient." She must! Cassie thinks, calculating the odds once again.

"Don't tell me."

Since her hysterectomy Eve shies from bad news, from what can rip and tear. She rejects difficulties, plays at placidity, but Cassie still finds such softness suspicious. She can't define the precise change, tie it to an organic cause.

"Moving to nowhere, to resurrect a dirt street of broken-down buildings—"

Eve interrupts. "So, big deal, it's a major impossibility. We can try."

"Johnny can, but what about you?"

"Ah, Cass, first I was a hippie, smoking dope and living out of a knapsack, following Jordan like Ruth or Naomi, whichever biblical female trailed behind. Then I married my Abramson, twice my age, and after the bear, on a whim, William with his low budgets. And along the way real estate. Now it's Johnny and out to the desert. It's all definition and redefining."

"And you don't want Johnny to go without you," Cassie says shrewdly.

"So shoot me."

"Get away. I'm just selfishly unhappy about your going, that's all. So much of my life is caught up with you."

"Don't try to make me feel guilty, slinking off, away from friends, tossing aside, as darling Titus cautioned, my lucrative career."

"What do your sisters say? You're crazy, right?"

Eve laughs, "As if I care." She takes a white dress with red poppies off a hanger. "Here, should I wear this? Nona got it for me. Like?"

"Nona and her deals. No. Poppies make me think of drug dealers."

Eve returns the dress to the closet. "God, you are in a ditch. Maybe my black pants and shirt?"

"It's unfair for me to keep implying you're a nut case."

"I'll miss you too. At least you'll have Nona to pal around with. And you have Jake."

"Have Jake! As though I bolted him down on lettuce for lunch! Really! And it's not the same. It's nothing like our being friends.

Oh!" Cassie raises a fist to her eyes. "I am going to make an ass out of myself and cry."

Eve isn't so prepared for the end of this life and on to the romantic unknown next with Johnny that she can slough off Cassie's tears. She certainly feels bruised by the weepies now, though there are still weeks to be spent in town. At the last moment, as she climbs into the car after they hug with their arms tight and their perfumes commingling, when the heft of this friendship begins to slip, Eve expects to cry.

"I'll come back to L.A. on visits," she promises, thinking— hoping—that eventually the city will disquiet her by being both alien and familiar, for she isn't as nonchalant about leaving as she makes out to Cassie. It is proving harder to relinquish her job, the thrill of making deals, shepherding clients through escrow, being successful. Eve thought, even after the hysterectomy, and what she refers to as her little spasm of coming unhinged, that she still had ample emotional muscle not to be bothered by change. Not true. She wants to go with Johnny; to her surprise she's forged a commitment, and one that doesn't have the falsity of her marriage to William. But, God! she was just a hair away from getting Titus's office!

"And you'll fly down to New Mexico with Jake, don't forget." Eve continues making plans, in an attempt to buoy up her own flagging spirits as much as Cassie's.

"We'll get horses and ride some of the canyons. Come on, Cass, think of cookouts and sunsets!"

Cassie sniffs and the smile she manages is small and stingy. She dislikes feeling angry with Eve for being happy, but she is. "I just have a really hard time visualizing you in the simple life."

"Only simple for a while." Eve laughs. "I'm not taking a permanent ride back to nature. This is a business proposition, remember."

"Risky, if you ask me. But what do I know about business?" Cassie's tears have been discreetly blotted away with tissues. Tears have always sent the two women rushing into each other's arms, into instant consoling with touch and a drink or hot tea, but at this moment they are merely embarrassing.

The fabric of their friendship is fraying, and suddenly neither can think what to say. Eve launches into a story about her sister

JoAnne on a visit to Philly when Eve and Jordan shored up for a few weeks with Jordan's mother. "Sent to spy out the land for the enemy" was how Jordan put it, half-joking in his paranoia. Cassie remembers the story from years before but makes no attempt to divert Eve, who is moving about lighter and airier than at any time since Cassie's known her. It's no trouble to lie on the chaise and listen, to drift like a child before the lights are turned off. Certainly Cassie would rather semi-pay attention to an old story than think of Eve in New Mexico or of Mrs. Holland or Nona acting so fit and healthy, too much so in Cassie's estimation. Nona is a precancerous condition that needs vigilance.

Worst of all is the memory of Tracy thrashing about and heaving, weeping sweaty tears and wanting Cassie to console her. She meant for Cassie to explain her dreams, as if Cassie were a diviner of omens as well as a physician.

Are the dreams connected with Doug, and Tracy intuitively knows this? Is this why she seeks out Cassie's help?

Right now, though, Cassie tries to eject Tracy's greenish face from her thoughts, but Tracy persists in intruding. Go talk to your own doctor or *your husband*, but not to me!

So many strands. Such a jumble. How much neater is Eve's life now as Eve simplifies.

"And they got on like the proverbial house afire. Chatting up a storm about gardens, as if my sister was a dedicated horticulturist and had acres planted. But that's JoAnne," Eve says, still twenty-some years angry at her sister for hitting it off with Jordan's mother the afternoon she came for tea.

"When are you leaving?"

"Six weeks to two months. There's a lot to do out there—here also."

"Maybe we could have a going-away something for you in combination with a birthday party for Nona. It's her fortieth, remember."

"Four-O, the big banana." Eve taps the tip of her nose with a finger. "Why not? But don't you think we should call out the marines, hire the Philharmonic, paint the walls for her? Doesn't she need a lot of horns and drums right now?"

"It's hard. Maybe a big gala would be best, but if not, if a party makes her more depressed . . . Oh, Lord. I opt for safe."

"Don't you always," Eve snaps back, but smiling so Cassie can't take offense.

Eve's finally dressed and Cassie goes into the bathroom to pat cold water on her unnaturally warm cheeks. She calls through the open door. "You malign me. I have done the unexpected on occasion." Defending herself from being a drone and fearing she is one, Cassie adds, "I'm not so ordinary."

"Of course you're not, darling." Eve appears in the mirror. "You're special."

"Oh, special. We're all that."

28

The owners, Leonard and Howard, who haven't stopped by Flora's for weeks, are suddenly there two days in a row. The following noontime Howard arrives alone. Nona reads meaning in this. Events are tea leaves at the bottom of a cup. What, for instance, is he really saying when he comments that "Flora's a pleasant store. It feels right. Leonard calls it class, but there are other up-market stores that give you goose bumps, make you think you gotta wipe your feet before going in the door. That's not the modus we had in mind for Flora's. Women have a God-given right to be comfortable when they're parting with cash. Who needs to plunk down five hundred bucks and feel shit-o?"

He closes in on the counter, where the rim presses a ditch in his ample stomach. Not that he notices. He is riveted on Nona, who hears the steady drip drip of Lorraine's malice, pouring out lies, fanciful stories. Lorraine spits out the terrible gossip she read in the *Insider*. Now here comes Howard with drool on his lips. The heat of his mint-scented breath scorches desire in the air, and all Nona can do is smile. She is as honest, as lifelike in her response, as one of the mannequins, but her mouth moving turns Howard's large, loose ears pink.

He is Dumbo, sweet, blubbery, silly, inept at business. Leonard is the financial whiz, Howard the tagalong. But it is Howard who has family money, and it is Howard who signs the checks. Leonard never asks his opinion but when Howard volunteers the odd suggestion, Leonard inclines his head—like a little apple on a pipestem neck—and pays attention. On the other side of the counter Nona remembers all this while Howard ponders adding a small shoe corner. What does Nona think?

"I was just getting ready for lunch, Howard. Maybe we could discuss it then. If you want to go for a sandwich with me?" She lets the tip of her tongue poke like a furtive small animal between her teeth. Through all her vicissitudes, Nona has never behaved deviously, but she hasn't slept innocently either. She's observed and consequently knows all the gestures. She can narrow her eyes with the best of the *femmes fatales*, flutter her lashes, thrust out her bust at just the right angle. She can deep-breathe and bend for Howard to catch a long peek of her cleavage. Nona understands how to seduce a man for a night, a week. Her downfall is that she believes in both love and honesty and cannot switch movements with the ease of a figure skater. She doesn't glide off, a natural, upright, then swoop into breathtaking spins and turns. But Howard is too naïve to tell the true seductress from the amateur. He brightens in a blush as red as bougainvillea.

"I'd be happy to join you."

"Just let me grab my bag from the stockroom."

Howard is gallant. "Take your time," he says, and again Nona rewards him with a wet-lipped smile. She also brushes his sleeve with the back of her hand.

"You don't need me," Nona says when Lorraine catches her coming out of the toilet. Mae, an older saleswoman who works evenings and weekends, is in for Lorraine's accessories sale and she'll help if there's a rush over the early lunch hour.

"I can decide what I need," Lorraine sniffs. "Besides, I planned to take my break now. So you'll have to stay with Mae."

"Sure." Nona raises her brows and tries to look sympathetic. "Let me just tell Howard he has to wait for me until you come back. He won't mind hanging around."

"Why are you having lunch with Howard?" Lorraine is shrill. A nerve ticks in her cheek. As always she suspects treachery.

"Why?" Nona replies innocently. "Because he asked me."

Nona has Lorraine convinced that Howard issued the lunch invitation. More cleverly, by the time the waiter brings their chopped salads, she has Howard thinking how brilliant he is for suggesting they break bread together.

"I'm so pleased about having these few moments with you, Howard. I've been dying to talk to you for ages." Nona's eyelashes are spidery on her cheeks.

Howard preens. "Leonard and I are always there for advice, to hear any suggestions or, God forbid, complaints."

"That's sweet of you, Howard, and don't think I take having understanding bosses lightly. I *treasure* you and Leonard." She licks her lips. "You especially."

"Me? Why?" he asks breathlessly. No female, including his wife, whom he met in college, said *especially* to Howard before. He experiences the stomach-dropping thrill of a man on a loop-the-loop.

"Why you, Howard?" Nona laughs. "Because you're warm, kind. Not that Leonard isn't an extraordinary employer, but you"—her sigh tightens the silk over her breasts—"you're different." She's whispering and Howard is pulled like a stretched rubber band halfway across the wooden table. When Nona raises her glance she confronts her own miniaturized image in his pupils.

Howard is agog, his entrails ripped out and thrown to the floor. The hounds of lust and desire, of romance and adventure feast on his heart.

A plain man with zit scars in a picket fence along his jaw, Howard is creased with excess poundage and in no time at all he'll need a hair transplant. He waddles, and his hips tug the trousers of his expensive suit out of shape. But despite these negative factors he *is* warm and kind. Nona doesn't lie about this, even if in the fluorescent glare of the deli she views him as a commodity rather than a man.

Nona burnishes her compliments with more damp sighs and moist glances. Once or twice her fingers wander over his as she groans, "I don't want to be disloyal. Am I betraying Lorraine? Do you think it's wrong to take a dress from a supplier? Maybe I'm just being foolish and there's nothing unethical . . ." She trails off to lick her bottom lip, knowing *foolish* is the last thing Howard will say. "Of course I can't swear that Lorraine's giving Ricardo anything in exchange, any orders that she shouldn't. But you know we had that crepe de Chine blouse of his forever. Even half-price it was a dog with mange." She hesitates then confides, "It's cut badly."

Howard nods, his plump face solemn, as if he were an expert on merchandising, which he's not. Of all the investments in his portfolio, Flora's is the least successful, teetering most months on the thin line between red and black. In fact, Leonard advises deep-sixing Flora's, but Howard simply likes the store.

We can't hang on to a money loser, Leonard points out in accountant-ese.

"Of course, if things aren't managed properly . . ." Howard says, thinking out loud, drowning in the tide pools of Nona's eyes and not at all worried about being washed out to sea. *Can* Lorraine have been cooking the books? Making side deals?

"Ricardo is letting her keep the first dress, the one she won't wear because it's the wrong season. She didn't think he would at first but then he did and is giving her another one. Don't you think that's ultra-peculiar?"

"All for free?"

Nona tilts her chin like a child about to give an ambiguous answer. "I'm not sure, but that's what she implies."

"We can't be hasty. She might be getting a discount. Discounts arc rampant in this business," Howard says, reaching out bravely on his own and patting Nona's hand. He means to be avuncular but lingers.

"Oh, Howard, I want to believe the best of everybody!"

"Of course you do, a sweet person like you."

"Lorraine can just be bragging about getting two expensive dresses from Ricardo. And even if they are for nothing, that doesn't mean for absolutely sure that she's giving him orders she shouldn't. But those blouses! And she does have some skirts coming in that are a little flashy for Flora's. They're draped, with rhinestone brooches here." She stretches up so her hip bone rises to the table edge and as she does her breasts are as full and ripe as peaches. "And, Howard—" Nona bends forward, and with the fat man far out over his plate, their faces come within kissing distance. It wouldn't be much of a push for Howard's lips to settle on Nona's. "Howard," Nona whispers, "they're satin."

"Satin?" he asks in a conspiratorial hush.

"Satin's all wrong for Flora's. It's not our image."

"No, no satin," Howard agrees with alacrity, ready to cheer for nuclear war or mass murder, whatever Nona asks of him with her melting gaze and little pink tongue.

"I just knew in my bones that you'd understand." Nona's fingers are curled into Howard's sweaty palm.

He feels them sliding along his lifeline and gulps. "I'll talk to Leonard."

"I can't tell you how long." Cassie pauses. Staring through the doorway to the dining room arch and into the living room, she sees the couch and Tracy's carrot-color curls. "Yes, darling," she says into the telephone, the *darling* defiant and tight in her mouth, an odd word for Jake, who ignores it. "I know the Santa Monica Fourplex is only doing one night of the Three Stooges. Maybe we can still make it, then eat later." Listening, she sucks her teeth, stops, tries to loosen the taut tendons in her neck. Why won't he finish complaining? The sooner they hang up the sooner she can deal with Tracy and get moving. Jake's annoyance is as cold as dry ice, and no, he isn't angry, he says, but near enough in Cassie's estimation to make no difference. Not that he erupts into blows of temper (nor does he come close to hitting her, despite her fantasies); his retaliation is to withdraw turtlelike into his shell. A civilian version of friendly fire, Cassie thinks, as Jake says he'll eat alone, forgo the movie, watch TV, and see her on Saturday.

"I didn't invite her over here, you know," Cassie practically groans. All this over the Three Stooges, of all silly things!

"Send her home."

"You can't just kick out people like that." Your ex-husband's wife is an exception, Cassie thinks, but keeps quiet.

"I'll see you Saturday. I'm playing down in Inglewood, Goodwin's."

"Wonderful." Oh, God, another Saturday night at a seedy bar, nursing one glass of wine, since she drives herself, waiting for breaks and then for two A.M. when it's time to go home.

"Saturday."

That's too long. "I'll miss you," Cassie whispers into a dead phone.

Tracy is as polite as a convent girl when Cassie returns to the living room. "I hope I'm not upsetting anything," she apologizes. "Like, I should've called."

"It's okay, don't worry," Cassie lies, swinging her arms, waving the invisible magic wand she wishes she had to vanquish Tracy with.

What is she doing here?

"Doug's working late and I was just hanging around." She shrugs and her bony elbows jut out in wings.

"Working late." Cassie remembers from her own marriage to Doug his *working late,* who wears a dirndl maternity dress and sits before her on the rebellious couch.

"I was going for frozen yogurt. I got this craving, just like it says, but not for pickles, for frozen yogurt. Apricot with butterscotch sauce."

Cassie grimaces.

"A handful of chocolate sprinkles too."

Is she asking if I have some in the freezer? Cassie wonders, moving from the rocker—as uncomfortable with its motion as if she were the pregnant wife—to the stuffed chair nearer the couch. The fabrics on the two pieces of furniture strike Cassie as more combative than usual. She must, really must collect herself and do something to the room, since she will never learn to accommodate to the clash of stripes and floral print.

Tracy apparently notices no disharmony, but then she barely inspects the room. If Cassie found herself in the house of her husband's first wife she'd be dead-sure to memorize each detail, to soak up the atmosphere. She'd sniff the smell up her nostrils to sit back later and compare reality with imagination. But maybe Tracy was never curious about Doug's home when he lived with Cassie. What can his prior life mean to a leggy cheerleader pregnant with her first child? Living close to the beach and greedy for her old skinny figure?

"Well, how was the yogurt?" Cassie asks, crossing her legs. She throws her shoulders back and folds her hands in her lap, fidgeting for a relaxed position and unaware that the posture she assumes reminds Tracy of her high school principal. They'd both be more comfortable if she'd slouch, throw a leg over the chair's arm, loosen up. And why shouldn't she? It is, after all, her house. Half hers. The other half belongs to Doug, which means one fourth of it, of this very room, is Tracy's.

Cassie is jolted by the realization that she in part occupies Tracy's property and misses what Tracy says.

"I beg your pardon?"

"I said I never got to Penguin. Just driving this way . . ." There isn't, as far as Cassie recalls, any yogurt store, shop, stand, or parlor within miles. ". . . I thought I'd stop over and maybe we could talk." Shades of Nona, Cassie thinks. "You know so much about these things."

"By 'these things' I suppose you mean pregnancy, delivery, et cetera."

Tracy giggles. "Especially the et cetera."

Cassie, who deems none of this amusing, releases the smallest smile to be polite. Though why should she be polite, since Tracy isn't here by invitation?

"I got a perm yesterday. What do you think?" Tracy twists a curl around her fingers. "Pregnant women's hair goes straight."

Cassie cares not in the least if Tracy shaves her head. "It's very attractive," she says.

"Yeah, I thought so, but Doug says I look silly."

"It's your hair—wear it any way you want," Cassie replies, trying to recall if Doug ever mentioned *her* hair. She might as well have sprouted Rastafarian braids for all the notice she remembers him taking.

"Is that what you did with *him*?"

"I—" Cassie stops her tongue. "Honestly, there's no point in discussing Doug."

"Gee, I'm sorry. Don't be mad at me." Tracy draws the curl across her nose and pulls in her chicken shoulders with fright. Can this be the woman Doug threw over home and family for? This *child*? Faced with the original, all Cassie's anger at Tracy the unknown, Tracy the homewrecker, now seems stupid.

Still, a thin voice whines: What does Doug see in her?

Tracy has been holding her breath like a kid until the danger passes, until Cassie yields, resentful of losing in this childish game of wills. "I'm not mad at you," she says, not wanting to have to scoop Tracy off the floor. "Why should I be?" Because you're an idiot coming here grubbing professional advice.

"You think I'm dumb showing my face around you. No taste. Tacky Tracy."

"I never said—"

Tracy blows out her cheeks. "Oh, Doug's always babbling about what a lady you are, real finishing school—"

"*Me?*"

"And you wouldn't live in the same city with me if the facts were reversed." Tracy's expression reveals how unlikely that is in this lifetime.

"You're being hard on yourself. Obviously there's a reason for you—"

Tracy seems constitutionally unable to let Cassie finish a sentence. Nervousness excites her into continual speech and her hands into tugging and twisting each other. "Just thinking about being this way"—she pats her protruding stomach as if Cassie might miss what she implies—"inclines me to you, Cassie."

"What?"

"I feel real close."

Cassie shies. "Don't you have a mother?"

Tracy shifts on the couch. Her lower back throbs and the pressure on her bladder has her asking "Can I use the bathroom?"

Cassie groans. "Of course. It's the door on the left just as you come in." Tracy takes two, three steps, then glances over her shoulder like a worrying dog, imploring Cassie to go with her. "You can't miss it. The door's probably ajar. It usually is."

"Okay. I'll be fine."

How does Doug leave this girl when he goes to the office? She bleeds like a severed arm. Was she always so clinging, so afraid of her shadow? Cassie's surprised she managed the trip from the Marina to the Palisades. At night, no less.

"What about your mother? And I seem to remember a grandmother who came for Thanksgiving?" Cassie prods Tracy when she returns. She is in the kitchen brewing tea, throwing loose leaves in the china pot, a little chamomile, some mint.

"My mom lives in Hilton Head. South Carolina?"

"I've heard of it," Cassie replies. "But you don't sound Southern."

"Me? Nope." She daintily selects a lemon cookie from the tin Cassie offers her. "Oregon. Salem. Donna's down there because her husband's a golf pro."

"Not your father, I take it."

Tracy reddens and looks sheepishly down at the table. Except for her sloping belly she is a first grader waiting after the last bell for someone to take her home. "Daddy's been out of our lives forever. Donna says she barely remembers him, it's so many years. He's only unique because he knocked her up. After that she had her tubes tied. And I would've been aborted even though it wasn't legal in those days, never mind finding some quack to oblige. See, Donna had her period the first couple of months and by the time she cottoned to being pregnant it was way too late. She didn't show for ages either, not like me. I am a cow!" she wails unexpectedly, almost causing Cassie to drop the teacups.

Tracy's cries set the hanging brass lamp to swaying and Cassie restrains the impulse to put her arms around this girl whom she despises. Tracy the girlfriend, Miss Lovely who stole Cassie's husband. Tracy, the quake that split the fault line in Cassie's own marriage. *Why should I feel sorry for her?* Cassie wants to scream, even as she says, "You're not so enormous. In fact you're fine. Pregnant women are considered beautiful in many cultures."

"Not in Marina del Rey!" Tracy wails.

"You mean Doug."

"He's like my mother. One child is more than enough. It's the ecology. We shouldn't be overpopulating the planet. We're eating up the air and ruining the ocean. There's always yuck down on the beach. And what are we going to do about the trees? Our forests are deserts."

It's news to Cassie that Doug is such an environmentalist, since during their marriage he threw empty soda cans out the car window and was vocal on the pluses of nuclear energy.

One child. Cassie feels an unreasoning tremor of relief that Doug didn't want a baby with Tracy any more than he wanted a second with her.

"And you," Cassie, suddenly enlightened, says, "snuck one by him."

"Don't put it like that. I just asked him, when I was pretty sure I was, what he'd do *if*, and he said get rid of it. And I got scared. Women can die."

"Not today they don't," Cassie says, aware that Tracy resisted an abortion for different reasons. She asks, "Are you pro-life?"

"Sure I'm pro-life. Who'd hop on the bandwagon for death?"

"I mean are you anti-abortion?"

"Not if somebody wants one. Or has to. Getting raped and then having to have it would be gruesome. And I'm not in favor of bringing a veg into the world."

"Just no abortion for you?"

"Why can't I have a kid? You do!" Tracy hollers unexpectedly.

Her vehemence shocks Cassie, who yells back, "Don't blame me!" just as the kettle whistles. Relieved, she fusses with the ritual of pouring. She has eschewed the everyday mugs for the dinner party china. On a flowered plate she arranges the cookies and adds brownies she takes from the fridge. She uses lacy place mats and cloth napkins.

Tracy tries a brownie. "These are fantastic. Did you make them?" Cassie nods. "Doug never shuts up about what a sensational cook you are."

"I'm not so special. Anybody can do it. Just take the time and put in the energy."

"I'm okay. If I pay attention and don't start daydreaming I'll get a meal on the table, but I'm no Julia Child. Doug gave me her cookbook for Christmas and jeez, we are talking about major work."

"Julia Child is exceptional."

"So is Dr. Cassie Morgan."

Doug did enjoy her cooking, how effortlessly she produced meals. Among their friends she was lauded for being the most adept in the kitchen. Thinking back, Cassie recalls that Doug complimented her more on her *pot-au-feu* than her looks or her career.

"He thinks it's terrific how you do all your doctor stuff and run a house."

"He would mention that," Cassie says. And, she doesn't bother adding, do a whole *mea culpa* routine about not doing his share. Cassie, I'm sorry, I should've picked up the dry cleaning, gotten the meat from the butcher, brought the car in for servicing. Don't carry my burden. Had she ever accused him of that? She never thought so, but who could be sure, since she slept through most of their marriage?

What had Doug wanted?

"Has Doug been throwing my cooking up to you?" Cassie asks,

partly amused but still furious with her ex-husband. *This* coq au vin *isn't as good as my first wife's!* Oh, the poor child, who probably arrived at the altar thinking making hamburgers at home instead of bringing them in from McDonald's was a big deal.

Tracy grows skittish. "Doug's a wonderful husband. He's very understanding."

"That's a lie," Cassie blurts, not playing dead dog on this one. "Doug dances to his own tune and if you're out of step he pouts or yells or criticizes. But what he isn't is understanding."

Tracy aches to discuss their mutual spouse, *her* marriage, being pregnant and what's to come *after*, but feels obligated to launch some defense. She lists Doug's strong points, as if Cassie were a stranger met on a train and they're between stations. She eulogizes him with the zeal of an evangelist.

"A real prince among men," Cassie says sarcastically, but Tracy has no ear even for a broadside. At most she confesses, "He can be a little edgy when he gets home from the office. And it is true that he's not a morning person."

"He complains too."

Cassie, there's lint on my socks! Cassie, we're out of Gruyère, white wine, dandruff shampoo! Cassie, the faucet drips, the bedroom window leaks, the door squeaks, the coffee's cold, too hot, too weak, too strong. Cassie!

Is the Marina apartment large enough to accommodate the constant ricocheting of Doug's complaints? Tracy, having lost her grace and girlish figure, must have an awkward time dodging the barbs of Doug's surliness. During Cassie's pregnancy he sulked like a baby, and Mandy was *planned.* So how impossible is he now?

Is Tracy at Cassie's kitchen table because Doug has thrown her totally off balance? Because she hasn't a clue how to cope with the expectant father?

Her mother's apparently a dead loss, but "Granny's a love. She promised she'd fly out when it's time, but this trip just about did her in. Her arthritis is a horror show. Claws like the beast from the black lagoon." Tracy contorts her hands and the stiletto nails—probably stick-ons—seem tipped with blood.

"There are agencies. You can hire a nurse. Two. Three. If it's necessary a trained baby nurse will be with you around the clock."

"Some stranger. What does a stranger care? Like they'll do shit except for money. A nursemaid isn't family, somebody who knows me and old tubby here." She lattices her fingers over her womb.

Is this the modern, hang-loose, living-down-at-the-beach female Doug married for fun and games? His new lease on life is out of *Family Circle* rather than *Cosmopolitan*.

"Friends?"

"Course I've a quadrillion friends. I'm not a solo walk in space. Only, friends have their own shit to deal with, you know what I mean?"

Cassie thinks of Eve and Nona.

Tracy performs that funny little shrug of hers. "Besides, I don't know anyone who'll knit booties, God forbid an afghan." Cassie coughs into her napkin, desperate not to laugh at Tracy crinkling with indignation. "Everybody will make one quick stop on their way to West Beach or Rebecca's, do the ooh-and-ah routine, and then piss off. If babies went on sale at C.P. Shades, maybe they'd hang around for a while."

"More tea?" Cassie asks.

"Thank you," Tracy replies, pushing her cup and saucer across the table.

They are solemn with each other now.

"Have another brownie," Cassie suggests guiltily, aware that Tracy should be calorie-counting.

"Is it all right? I'm not too fat? Stuffed Shirt M.D. said I could gain thirty pounds and bingo, that was it. I passed twenty-five two months ago. Like it's supposed to be bad for the baby and he sniggered that I'll be la cow forever."

"How much weight have you gained?"

"I don't know," Tracy lies.

Cassie's practiced eye evaluates Tracy as over thirty, with two and a half months to go. "It's not the best idea to get too heavy." Tracy holds a brownie, undecided whether to eat it or put it back on the plate, waiting for Cassie to tell her what to do. How, Cassie wonders, has she gotten in this position? "Are you drinking milk?" she asks. Tracy winces. "You should be, for the calcium."

"I never liked milk when I was a kid."

Cassie is up and at the refrigerator. She pours Tracy a tall glass of milk. "Go on, have the brownie to get it down, but don't make sweets a habit."

Pleasure spreads over Tracy's face and Cassie notices a sprinkling of freckles on the bridge of her nose. "They just really are so good, I can't help myself," she says after a bite, after patting her mouth with the napkin.

Cassie murmurs, "Thank you," and watches Tracy primly eat her second brownie and drink her milk. She is reminded of herself as a child after school in a neighbor's kitchen. Well brought up, that's what you want people to say about you, her mother cautioned. And despite the wandering Donna, Tracy is well brought up.

As easily as she is Doug's wife, Tracy could be a friend, a sister, daughter, and the thought sends Cassie crashing her chair on the tile.

Tracy is startled. "Did I say something wrong?"

"You didn't say anything."

"It's real nervy of me pushing in on you. And you're so nice about it, listening to me and everything. Giving me a snack—" Cassie closes her eyes. Tracy hurries. "You get it, too, how I'm scared. How I want to have the baby and don't at the same time. How—" Tears spill in messy trails along her cheeks.

"Stop! Stop this very minute or I'll scream!" Cassie cries, near to screaming already. She waves a napkin at Tracy, horrified by the intimacy the girl is brewing up.

Tracy sobs, "I'm sorry!"

"Don't be. Just—" Oh, the wretched girl can't drive in this condition. "I'm going to phone Doug to come and get you."

"No!" she howls. "I'll be in shit city if he finds out I've been here!"

She's right. Doug's blood pressure has to soar if he pictures his wives sitting down companionably, gossiping—more or less—about his current marriage. Cassie needs no script to see that Doug acts sternly rather than hanging loose with Tracy. Now here she is floating out to sea, afraid and alone, minus a sensible soul to guide her.

"So what did you do?" Eve burns with curiosity. "Offer to be her doctor?"

"Can't. That's not ethical."

"I bet Cassie agreed to take care of the baby," Nona says. "She promised to help out and teach Tracy all about mothering. She'll be sort of a cross between a grandmother and mother number two. And if Tracy decides to take up discoing with a vengeance, she'll park the baby more or less temporarily/permanently in the spare bedroom."

Nona is cutting. The envy in her rises to the surface like boiling lava and Cassie physically pulls away, sucking in her breath, so as not to get burned. Nastiness is new with Nona, but it blooms flagrantly in the heat of her anger. Cassie has said to Eve: *I would have thought that being manager of Flora's counted for something, that she'd feel good, better, about things.* One goes on; life does.

"Let's not be extreme." Eve defends Cassie to Nona. "But I bet I get pictures in the mail. Baby at three months. Baby at six. And a running monologue over the phone about baby learning to walk and talk. Smart baby," Eve teases, "a dead cert for Harvard."

Cassie finds none of this funny. She fumes: "What do you think, that I've nothing to do but raise other people's children? That I can take time out and change diapers, et al.? Remember my practice?" Their kidding has teeth in it.

"You forgot to mention a lover," Eve reminds her. "Lovers are like gardens—they need tending to."

"How is Jake? He hasn't had equal time lately." Cassie listens for acid and ignores the question.

The restaurant chosen by Cassie for this two-pronged celebration is French and upscale, paneled in oak and discreetly lit, and the three women are at a blinding-white table by the back wall. Delphinium and orchids are as perfect as silk in the center. The silverware is heavy and the waiters, whose voices peak at the absence of men, are arrogant. Cassie second-guesses her choice now, but she wanted the best for this last evening together, a solid, meaningful memory to bond them.

Champagne pours into their glasses and Cassie lifts hers and toasts: "Nona, the youngest forty-year-old in Los Angeles."

"Hush!" Eve cries. "Don't say *that* number out loud."

"Oh, I've accommodated. Besides, I'm going to be permanently thirty-seven. That's realistic, don't you think?" What Eve and Cassie both think is that Nona has aged ten years since Christmas.

They go on to drink to Eve's new life and starting over.

"You make it sound as if I've gotten reincarnated. All I'm doing, kids, is moving."

"To a trailer in sagebrush land," Cassie says, still not reconciled.

The hovering waiter refills their glasses. They drink again but the champagne ceremony doesn't quite satisfy them. But what other wishes are there besides these obvious ones—long life, health, happiness? Eve accepts the sentiments as sincere, but she's heard these same words before and they strike an inauthentic bell.

Cassie's mind wanders—though she struggles to be in the here and now—after Tracy. She has a hunch that Tracy is anemic and wouldn't be against having a CBC done on her. Only she can't phone Tracy's obstetrician and suggest it. Maybe when she and Tracy have lunch tomorrow she can coach her in what to say. If Tracy is convincing, Dr. Stuffed Shirt should order tests.

"Cassie, you're miles off," Eve chides.

"What about Jake?" Nona won't give up on Cassie's love life.

Cassie protests, "I love him!"

The women burst out laughing, too loud for L'Abbé de St. Julien, where conversation is as hushed as prayer. The women at the surrounding tables all look Republican, society accomplices of Nancy Reagan; the men are perennially double-breasted. Only a stray whisper and the faint glassy tinkle of laughter glides across the antique carpeting.

"Bet you don't!" Eve challenges.

"Why do you say that? Just because I haven't been babbling about him? Why do we always have to talk *men*?"

"Silence is complicity," Nona says, with the sly openness of the innocent she no longer is. Eve busies herself with her napkin, as if she were in another country. Cassie's snippy retort at her kidding upsets her.

Already packed, the mover scheduled, storage space rented and paid for, her notice to the Booker Agency running out its last days, Eve is vanishing little by little. In most respects she's already gone—except for moments when she gets skittish and wants to stay the high-gloss real estate agent—and her old habit of calling truth to its face, of not ducking, of keeping Cassie and Nona on their toes, is packed in a carton. She won't say, therefore, *Whatever you are with Jake, it's no longer love*.

"You're so involved with Flora's. Ms. Minnie Mogul," Cassie is teasing Nona.

Nona is icy. "Howard hasn't absolutely confirmed the sale yet. And when he does it's still a matter of whether I can take on the store without incurring the national debt. It has to be worked out. Terms."

Nona in her executive suit, the Mark Cross briefcase on the floor by her chair, with a mouthful of terms from a business course she is auditing, arouses Eve into one last wicked turn. She smiles sweetly and asks, "And where is darling Howard performing all this laborious effort?"

Nona's look, if either woman could know it, is identical to Lorraine's. "Are you hinting that I'm sleeping with Howard?" Ice crackles in the air about the table.

Why are the changes Nona has gone through, still is, so heartbreaking? They've nudged her into growing up, protested that *surely, Nona, by forty!* And now here she is, having at last lost the final vestiges of innocence, shrewd and ungiving, dead-set against ever again trusting anyone.

"I just think one seizes opportunities. And Lorraine's leaving . . . Well, I don't see being a store manager forever. I said that to Howard and he understands."

She *is* sleeping with him, turning his head inside out, Eve thinks, but I bet she gave him blue balls before she let him into her bed. Of course by then he'd promised her the moon, Lorraine's job, the store itself on easy terms. How has he kept his partner from hollering unfair? Eve views the past few weeks as if Nona had filmed them. She admires Nona's finesse and makes no judgments. How can she? The past, like Abramson's ghost sneaking up to plant chilly kisses, has brought her to the border of humility. She casts no stones, not anymore, and going off with a man she needs loosens her grip on pretending.

"To the easy life." Nona makes another toast, drama in her voice.

"It's not at all easier, building a whole town out of scraps, putting together a deal that would stagger even Titus's best-heeled cronies when it's on paper. Hard work. Lots of elbow grease. Some challenge, hmmm?" Eve touches the cool glass to her forehead. "All that work!"

"You're going to make us weep over your calluses!" Nona says.

"It is hard work," Cassie says firmly, upset with both women because the evening goes in fits and starts and not as smoothly as she planned.

Eve smiles, "Dear one, thank God for you. Dr. Saint—"

"I'm no such thing!"

The food, *nouvelle* creations, decorator-lovely, arrives in a flourish. Three waiters fuss, their routine as elaborate and precise as a surgical procedure, Cassie thinks, a tightness in her chest. She's not the least hungry, though she will be later, and oh, if Jake were only the kind of man she could call at midnight. Come on over and let's get a pizza, extra cheese, pepperoni, sausage. Let's have beer. And don't laugh when I tell you about dinner.

What's there to laugh about? They're more like mourners than celebrators and if they don't watch their step, the evening will lie out in ruins on the cloth.

Already drenched regret and loneliness hang over their shiitake mushrooms and baby carrots *al dente,* muscovy duck breast, lamb riblets in raspberry sauce, braised scallops with cilantro, and each lift of a fork is labored.

Shadows cling in the recesses, underscore the brass sconces with their limpid light, settle on their napkined laps, ringed hands. For Cassie, Eve is essentially already gone, in jeans and a plaid shirt, scuffed boots, kicking up dust clouds and shielding her eyes from a merciless sun. And Nona . . . Nona's glow has been transformed into a brittle, diamond glint that sparks on the glasses and the silverware.

"Don't you like the lamb?" Eve asks.

Nona pushes the meat to the far side of her plate and cuts into the baby carrots. "Very static."

"Static?" Cassie asks.

"Goof, food's not static," Eve laughs.

"It is if I say it is," Nona replies, not in a pout, not with a giggle or a little girl's embarrassment, but sharp.

"What a witch you are! Happy forty!" Eve says. "Such a different female you're becoming." But she and Cassie know it's not Nona's birthday that has legislated this sea change. Maybe she was more granite underneath the sand than either of them supposed. "You'll have to come visit and get some nature."

"No, thanks! Nature!" Nona shivers. "Who needs all that dirt and rock?"

Eve rises in her chair and Cassie hastily interjects before the two friends can fight in earnest: "How's the apartment redecorating coming?"

"I've decided on ecru," says Nona.

On her way to the ladies' room Cassie passes a pay phone tucked into an alcove. Hidden from view she could safely call Jake. She wonders about asking him to come over later, to be there when she gets home. Brazenly she might suggest he warm the bed, but she won't.

She resists the phone and hurries into a stall where she sits, her face in her hands. How can she talk about Jake, face them, chin up, and confess that it's come to—

"Cassie, I think it's time we moved in together. My lease is up at the end of the month. What's the point in having two places?"

Cassie danced on the back porch, the few feet of wood being worn to the grain by her constant shuffle. His suggestion staggered her and she replied impulsively, "Oh, don't you think we should wait?"

She couldn't face him just then and looked over at the Levinsons', at Beth waving like a captive from her bathroom window.

"Wait for what?" He sounded hard, not like a man who was discussing moving in with a woman he cared about. It cost him a lot, this conversation. Cassie clenched her back teeth and felt even guiltier.

"Well, you and Mandy haven't ironed out your relationship yet. That's one thing," she said. Would he ask her what the other *things*—she hated to outright say *problems*—were? Oh, she hoped not. She wasn't prepared to draw up a list and dissect their time together.

Jake said, "Mandy's never going to call me Daddy and you know it."

"Why should she? You're not her father. But the two of you have to get along, that's all. And Mandy must accept you. She's my daughter, Jake. I love her." More than you, more than any man, Cassie didn't bother to add.

"Forget her accepting unless she absolutely has to. When we're living in the same house . . ." She'd never have believed Jake would be trying to talk her into this, and she would be shaking her head and mumbling about needing her *space*. Why, hadn't she loved him so much she broke into cold sweat at the thought of losing him? And now here she turned up her nose at a *commitment*!

Jake stood below on the grass. He had turned off the hose, and a long, wet stain streaked his denim shirt. His hair was pushed back off his forehead and he was tanned, healthy, so male and good-looking Cassie's knees went weak. But she didn't want to marry him or live with him or be responsible for or to anybody who caused her to dance over hot coals, and yet, as he listened to her archaic idiom—space, connected, authenticity anchored—Jake, who flinched but held steady under fire, she wondered if she was making a mistake.

He asked, when she ran down, "Is there some other guy?"

"Oh, how like a man. For a man there always has to be somebody else," Cassie cried. "I just don't see why we can't go on like we are. Why do we have to live in the same house except to save money?" *Which I have enough of*, she held back from adding, as she did from saying how obligated she felt to soothe him so often, to drain the coldness out of him with her warmth.

"We either move ahead or retreat."

"Jake, play me a song. Sing to me," she said, as if they weren't outside and he hadn't just finished tending her garden.

"Don't be difficult."

Replaying the conversation that she always dreaded to have with Jake but which, when it finally happened, wasn't nearly so bad, Cassie whispers in her hands: "I'm never difficult." She isn't, not like Doug or Jake or like Mandy, as she's so recently become. And, though she's slow as a dolt to realize it, she hates putting up with people (men, she means, because Mandy is surely only waltzing through a phase) who take catering to.

Still, she is close to tears and has been for days, since Jake asked her and she said no.

She was absolutely convinced one day he would simply go, but maybe she thought that because of Doug and his *another woman*. (Cassie is fighting tears, careful not to rub her eyes and ruin the liner and mascara, the deep-blue shadow, but Tracy as *another woman* makes her laugh out loud.)

Well, I can't be so upset if I'm sitting on the john giggling and worried about messing up my makeup so I'll look like a Picasso. The night after she understood that saying no to Jake was as good as slapping him with walking papers, that it meant he wasn't coming back, she lay in bed and stared at the curtains gently moving by the open window and pronounced an incontestable fact: Her life wasn't over. In fact, if she had a choice of keeping either Jake or Eve, she'd choose the latter without even thinking.

For in some ways, no, in many ways, she'll be lonelier without Eve. She won't replace Eve with another woman friend so easily, if at all. While Jake—from whom she gratefully learned she is neither dead nor so withered that she wants to live a loveless life—will always be a combination of good and troublesome memories until he fades, overlaid in her heart by somebody else. Oh yes, she thinks, blowing her nose and pulling herself together, no matter how stoically she endures she will leave a window of hope pushed wide open. Though she's not about to tell anyone, not Eve swirling away in the dust of her fantasies, or Nona so painfully icy and distant. Aware of how she too has been transformed in these past months, Cassie returns to the table wearing a broad smile that makes her jaw ache, and she crosses her fingers for her own future.

One white candle flickering its small flame on the chocolate truffle cake (crême fraiche on the side) quivers from an invisible spill of air.

Nona's lips compress in a delta of disapproval. Last year at a Melrose trattoria they tied balloons to her chair and aproned waiters sang happy birthday in Italian, but so much has happened since then. On the wave of the *Insider* article she's become quite the lady. She must be nearly like her mother, and high time, part of Eve believes, while the newer, softer part of Eve sorrows, *what a loss*. Nona's naïveté, the innocence that curled in silky tendrils of hair by her throat, had kept them all a little younger.

". . . a public spectacle."

"Apologies, darling, but it's because we love you."

Nona's lips part, or at least seem to in the uncertain light. Eve anticipates a declaration of Nona's own, or a disclaimer, perhaps a throwaway line, but the moment passes. They are, all three, no longer connected. They finish their cake in silence and drink espresso until only drops remain in the bottom of the cups. Cassie insists on paying the whole bill herself. Eve won't let her. "We're toasting Nona for crossing the Rubicon, remember?"

"And," Nona joins in, "wishing Eve bon voyage."

"We're equally committed," Eve continues.

Cassie listens to a further few minutes of argument. "Friends should agree to agree."

"It's *disagree*," Nona says, without tacking on her usual *Isn't it?*

"That, too," Cassie says. "But now, not a word. I'm taking you both for a nightcap. On me. Yes?"

She hates to let them go. Eve senses her unhappiness. Their cozy little threesome is breaking apart. Left to themselves, Cassie and Nona won't be as good friends. Not Nona as she is now. In a flash of precognition Eve sees Nona marrying chubby little Howard, trimming him down, taking him up the aisle. She promises herself she'll return for the occasion, that they'll party and get smashed on champagne.

"No more married men, unless we count Howard."

"That's really business."

"Or heartbreaks."

"Unhappy love affairs that put her into hysterics at three A.M."

"What about Dr. Rubin? Will his practice survive without her?"

"She'll have other physical ailments."

"If you say so, Doctor. But I think being happy—"

"Nona's no more happy now than she ever was!" Cassie cries.

"No, you're right, but she's not in sticky teenage misery either, which is an improvement."

At the round cookie-cutter-size table where their stockinged knees bump, they have turned toward the back of the club. They have watched Nona go to the ladies' room, seen how the men paint her with their lascivious glances, and now they observe her return.

The night is stealing away from them and as it does it has stiffened them so that they seem more and more wooden. Cassie thinks only memory will bind them now. She can almost swear that Nona won't drop around unannounced, sit and gossip with Mandy come spring break, that she won't be mothered and bullied. Neither she nor Nona will ever make the trip down to New Mexico.

"You know, it's silly. She's woken up, Sleeping Beauty off her slab with a vengeance, and we're acting as though she's terminal."

"What exaggeration!"

A man tall and so darkly handsome he's a cliché swings around on his bamboo stool by the bar and stops Nona with a hand to her upper arm. From the distance his fingers are spidery on her white sleeve. He will crawl up her throat and bite her just above the neckline of her blouse.

"Who's that?" Eve asks.

"Don't worry. Our new Nona is safely beyond strangers."

"Who has time to worry? These days I'm self-centered and preoccupied. Have to concentrate."

Nona arrives at the table cool and unruffled. The stranger swivels on his stool so he now faces in their direction.

Cassie asks, "Your admirer . . . ?"

"Just another pickup."

"Better than most," Eve says.

"Don't encourage her." Cassie drags a hand through her hair, worried that Nona will go off with yet another male none of them has any data on, that for all her transformation she will still take unacceptable risks at times.

"Why don't you stop worrying?" Nona says sharply. "You've made an art out of worrying. Me. Eve. Mandy. Doug's pregnant wife."

Cassie is stung. If Nona has ever criticized her she can't remember when or over what. She has to defend herself. "I'm not concerned about Tracy . . . or not so much. I only suspect *this* marriage won't last very long." And before either woman can accuse her of sour grapes, she explains: "Doug's no more ready to settle with Tracy than he was with me. Now that she's pregnant, and especially when the baby arrives, he'll huff around resenting every moment of family life. Doug's never been a man for hanging up pictures or taking out the garbage. And for God's sake, don't buy him slippers for Christmas."

"I wasn't planning on buying him a thing," Eve says. Out of the side of her mouth she observes to Nona: "Your recent conquest is drilling holes through you with those smoldering eyes. Is he an actor by any chance? He has that fiery TV look, as if he's eating his way into your living room."

"If you're so interested, go ask him," Nona says, goading Eve, aware how much she clings to Johnny. Having caught a man, Eve's wary, as she wasn't before, and won't so much as glance sideways at another male. Nona has a tight, scornful feeling toward such loyalty and though she pretends otherwise, she is pleased that Eve's dropping out of her life without her having to do anything about it. Their friendship has grown cheesy. Why did she ever admire Eve in the first place? And love—she won't think about love. Let Howard drone on about love.

The stranger raises his brows questioningly at her. Will she have a drink? is what he asked when she tried to pass and his hand stopped her. And go out later, take a ride, her apartment, his maybe? It's all a well-rehearsed play to Nona; she can mouth every one of the lines.

He lifts his glass.

Nona's eyelids flutter. She crosses her legs and her skirt rides up. One hand moves languidly down her thigh.

Cassie and Eve have their heads together and Eve is drawing invisible streets on the tablecloth. Here's Main and School and Devil Creek Road. Neither is watching Nona as her lips silently form the word *later*.

Whether she goes with the man, whether they sidle close together, touch, have sex, what does it matter? Why should she go with him? Or "Why not?" she says out loud.

Cassie's head comes up; Eve's glance follows. One or the other of them asks, "Why not *what*?"

RD2W